"I asked why you're here, Luke."

Rebecca moved clear of him, survival instincts finally coming to the fore.

Luke mirrored her stance, thinking it was such a simple question. Up until five minutes ago, he was sure he knew exactly why he was here—to see her, talk to her, and yes, convince himself that she was merely one of many women he'd known.

Trouble was, five minutes ago he hadn't seen her, hadn't touched her, hadn't looked into those liquid blue eyes of hers, the ones that were making his breathing a little unsteady.

Faster than ice dissolves when touched by a flame, his reasons vanished, and he told her honestly, "I came to see you."

"Why?" she asked, and instantly regretted the question. It didn't matter why—or did it?

"I came because—" his voice dropped to a husky timbre "—because I couldn't stay away any longer...."

Dear Reader,

When Susan Amarillas's novel *Snow Angel* was featured in our 1993 March Madness promotion for first-time authors, it was received with great enthusiasm. *Rendezvous* claimed, "If you like western stories, this one has everything...." Ever since then, Ms. Amarillas has been delighting readers with her western tales of love and laughter. This month, we are very pleased to bring you her newest book, *Scanlin's Law*, the story of a jaded U.S. Marshal and the woman who's waited eight years for him to return. We hope you enjoy it.

Also this month, gifted author Deborah Simmons returns to Medieval times with her new book, *Taming the Wolf*, the amusing tale of a baron who is determined to fulfill his duty and return an heiress to her legal guardian, until the young lady convinces him that to do so would put her in the gravest danger.

For those of you who like adventure with your romance, look for *Desert Rogue*, by the writing team of Erin Yorke. It's the story of an English socialite and the rough-hewn American soldier of fortune who rescues her. And from contemporary author Liz Ireland comes her debut historical, *Cecilia and the Stranger*. This month's WOMEN OF THE WEST selection is the charming tale of a schoolteacher who is not all he seems, and the rancher's daughter who is bent on finding out just who he really is.

Whatever your taste in historical reading, we hope you'll keep a lookout for all four titles, available wherever Harlequin Historicals are sold.

Sincerely,

Tracy Farrell

Senior Editor

Please address questions and book requests to:
Harlequin Reader Service
U.S.: 3010 Walden Ave., P.O. Box 1325, Buffalo, NY 14269
Canadian: P.O. Box 609, Fort Erie, Ont. L2A 5X3

SUSAN AMARILLAS

SCANLIN'S LAW

Harlequin Books

TORONTO • NEW YORK • LONDON
AMSTERDAM • PARIS • SYDNEY • HAMBURG
STOCKHOLM • ATHENS • TOKYO • MILAN
MADRID • WARSAW • BUDAPEST • AUCKLAND

ISBN 0-373-28883-2

SCANLIN'S LAW

Books by Susan Amarillas

Harlequin Historicals

Snow Angel #165
Silver and Steel #233
Scanlin's Law #283

SUSAN AMARILLAS

was born and raised in Maryland and moved to California when she married. She quickly discovered her love of the high desert country—she says it was as if she were "coming home." When she's not writing, she and her husband love to travel the back roads of the West, visiting ghost towns and little museums, and always coming home with an armload of books.

To Barbara Musumeci, a dearest friend who is far away but close to my heart. This one's for you. There's nary a horse in sight.

Chapter One

What the hell was he doing here?

Luke Scanlin swung down off his chestnut gelding and looped the reins through the smooth metal ring of the hitching post. Storm clouds, black and threatening, billowed overhead. Rain spattered against the side of his face. It caught on his eyelashes and plastered his hair to his neck. He shivered, more from reflex than from cold.

Three days. He had been in town three days. It had been raining when he finally stepped off the train from Cheyenne, and it was raining now. Aw, hell, he figured it was destined to rain forever.

Fifty feet away, the house, *her* house, stood like some medieval fortress. It was gray, and as intimidating as any castle. Three floors high, it was as impressive as the other Nob Hill mansions that lined both sides of California Street.

A wry smile played at the corners of his mouth. A princess needs a castle, he thought. But if she was a princess, then what was he? Certainly Luke Scanlin was nobody's idea of a prince.

That blasted rain increased, trickling off his drooping hat brim and running straight down his neck. "Damn," he muttered as he flipped up the collar of his mud-stained slicker. He was cold and wet and generally a mess, and still he stood there, staring up at the house.

His hand rested on the hitching post, two fingers on the cold iron, three fingers curled around the smooth leather reins. He ought to mount up and ride away, logic coaxed for about the hundredth time in the past hour. His muscles tensed, and he actually made a half turn, then stopped.

This was pathetic. Here he stood like some schoolboy, afraid to go in there and see *her.*

Well, *she* wasn't just anyone.

When he rode away that day eight years ago, he'd been so certain he was right.

The breeze carried the scent of salt water up from the bay, and the rain intensified, soaking the black wool of his trousers where they brushed against the tops of his mud-spattered black boots. Oak trees rustled in the breeze, sending the last of their golden leaves skittering along the street.

Beside him, the gelding nickered, his bridle rattling as he shook his head in protest at being out in the storm.

"Quiet, Scoundrel." Luke soothed the animal with a pat and stared up at the house once more.

Well, what's it going to be? You going to stand here all day?

He sighed. What was he going to say to her after all these years? Pure and simple, this was flat-out asking for trouble. *Leave well enough alone.*

But trouble was something Luke had never shied away from. A smile tugged at one corner of his mouth. In fact, he and trouble were old friends.

He started toward the house.

Rebecca Parker Tinsdale strode into the parlor of her home shortly past nine in the morning. The distant rumble of thunder accompanied her arrival. The storm-shrouded sunlight gave the white walls a grayish tinge, and the rich rococo-style mahogany furnishings only added to the dark and ominous feeling of the day. A pastoral painting by Constable hung over the fireplace, but the scene—a picnic on a bright summer day—seemed inappropriate, given the ominous dread that permeated the house.

She managed to keep her expression calm. Inside, fear was eating her alive. Her hands shook, and she buried them in the folds of her dark blue dress. The faille was smooth against her fingers.

In four carefully measured steps, Rebecca crossed the room to where Captain Amos Brody, chief of the San Francisco police, waited near the pale rose settee.

"Have you found Andrew?" She spoke slowly, struggling to hold the fear in check. Even as she asked, she could tell the answer by his grim expression.

If anything happened to Andrew... If he was hurt or...

Steady. Don't fall apart. Andrew needs you.

"Well, Mrs. Tinsdale..." Brody began, his rotund body straining at the double row of brass buttons that marched down the front of his dark blue uniform,

"I've had two men searching all night. They've looked everywhere, and I'm sorry to say there's no sign of the boy."

"Keep looking, Captain."

"Oh, you can rely on us," Brody returned in an indulgent tone. "I'll personally tell the men on the beat to keep an eye out."

Rebecca stiffened. She and Brody made no secret of their mutual dislike. That series of articles she'd been running in the *Daily Times* on police corruption was leading a path straight to Brody and half of his department. Still, he was in charge and, like it or not, she had to deal with him.

"Captain, I expect you to do more than keep an eye out. This isn't a lost kitten you can dismiss and hope it eventually finds its way home. This—" she emphasized the words, as though to drive them into his thick balding skull "—this is my *son*. And you *will* help me find him."

She saw him bristle—saw his Adam's apple work up and down in his throat.

They faced each other, the refined lady and the harsh man, each appraising the other. Rebecca had wealth, and she published a small newspaper. That gave her power. A mother's fear gave her determination. She knew Brody was the one who ultimately made the assignments, determined how and when and where things were done. It galled her to have to ask the man for help. If Brody chose to make only a halfhearted effort because of their feud, she might not know until it was too late for her—for her only child.

Outside, the rain spattered against the lace-curtained front window, drawing Rebecca's attention. Silvery streaks of water cascaded down the glass.

Andrew was out there somewhere, cold and afraid. He was only seven, so small, and so fragile since his illness last year. Terror, stark and real, swept through her, and she advanced on Brody. "Whatever it takes, Captain. Send more men, ten men, a hundred—"

"I'd like to do that, Mrs. Tinsdale, but I can't." Brody punctuated his statement with a nonchalant shrug that pushed her rapidly rising temper up another notch. "Finding one boy is small compared to the job of protecting this city. With less than two hundred men on the force, well, I have an obligation to *all* the citizens of this fair community," he finished, in a pious tone that would have made her laugh at any other time. "As it is, I've taken men from other areas to search, and—"

"I don't care about other areas." Condescending bastard, she thought as she paced away from him, her rage too great for her to remain still. She talked over her shoulder. "I don't care about other citizens." She turned back, her hands balled into tight fists, feeling the perspiration on her palms. "I don't care about anything or anyone but finding my son. I've been out there all night myself. Dammit, Captain, I expect you to do the same."

Brody nodded and held up his hand in a placating gesture that only aggravated her dangerously short temper.

"Mrs. Tinsdale, I know you're upset and all, but I've handled this sort of thing before and I know what I'm doing."

Rebecca closed on him, contemplating serious bodily injury. "Captain Brody, either you do your job or I'll ask the mayor to find someone who can." It was a hollow threat since the mayor was a strong supporter of Brody's, but she made it just the same.

"Now look here, lady," he sputtered. "I know you're upset, but don't tell me how to do my job. Before you start ordering me around, you might as well face facts. The boy's probably run off, is all. It's only been since last night." Maliciousness sparked in his blue eyes. "Sooner or later he'll get tired and hungry, then turn tail and head for home..." He paused thoughtfully. "Unless someone's taken him. Then, of course, it's another matter."

Her blood turned to ice. It was that thought that had circled in her mind all night, the way a wolf circles in the shadows of a camp. In a voice that was barely audible, she spoke the terrifying words. "Someone has taken my son?"

Brody gave a one-shoulder shrug, then picked up his cap, as though he were about to leave. "It's possible." He turned the dark blue hat absently in his pudgy hand. "I'll do the best I can, but you gotta remember this is a big city. It can be a mean city, too, and people, including children, disappear here all the time. Ships go in and out of this harbor with all kinds of cargo, if you get my meaning."

She did. God help her, she understood his meaning all too well. Her knees buckled, and she sank down in a chair. Brody was wrong. He *had* to be wrong. Andrew was lost. He'd gotten too far from home and become confused. Yes, that was it. That *had* to be it. To think otherwise... To think of some depraved person with her son, scaring him, hurting him, kil— No!

With sheer force of will, she refused to think that and, looking up, saw that Brody was still talking.

"—figure out who the boy is, what he's worth." She saw him glance around the elegant room, as if to confirm his appraisal. "Maybe they'll make a try for ransom, otherwise th—"

Brody broke off in midword, and she saw that his gaze was focused on the doorway behind her. Still seated, she turned.

An eerie silence fell as Rebecca and Brody stared at the powerful man standing two feet inside the parlor. He looked every inch the outlaw, dressed as he was in range clothes and a slicker. For a breathless moment, Rebecca thought Brody's prediction had come true.

The man was tall, with broad shoulders, and his dark countenance seemed in stark contrast to the refinements of a San Francisco drawing room.

She was about to demand his identity when her gaze flicked to his face and she looked straight into dark eyes, bottomless eyes, familiar eyes.

Her hand fluttered to her throat. "Oh, no..." The words were a thready whisper. She felt the blood drain from her face.

Speechless, Rebecca stared at him. Luke Scanlin. His mere presence emanated a power that surged through the room faster than lightning.

So he's finally here. The odd thought flashed in her mind.

"Hello, Princess," he said, in a husky tone that sent unwelcome and definitely unexpected shivers skittering up her spine.

What in God's name was Luke doing here? Not once in nearly eight years had she seen or heard from him, and now he strolled in here as though it were the most natural thing in the world.

Well, it wasn't the most natural thing, not in her world. Never mind those delicious shivers. He was firmly and irrevocably in her past.

Out of the corner of her eye she saw Brody take a menacing step in Luke's direction. "Mister, just who are you, and how did you get in here?" he demanded with an appraising stare. "Do you know something about this?"

"Name's Scanlin," Luke returned, with an impudent Texas drawl. He walked slowly into the room, his steps muffled by the thick flowered carpet. "I saw you through the window. When no one answered the door, I let myself in."

Luke never let a little thing like a closed door stop him from getting what he was after. What he was after right now was perched on the edge of a chair about five feet away.

Absently he sized the other man up and quickly dismissed him, keeping his gaze focused on the object of his visit.

Becky.

She was more beautiful than he remembered, and he remembered very, very well. A little thinner, perhaps, and obviously upset. He'd only caught the tail end of the conversation. "What's going on?"

"Scanlin?" Brody rubbed his chin thoughtfully and ignored the question. "You by any chance Luke Scanlin, the one who brought in Conklin?"

"Yeah, that's me."

"I've heard of you. Thought you were with the Rangers down around...San Antonio, wasn't it?"

"Amarillo," he replied. "I'm not with the Rangers anymore."

Luke closed on Rebecca, stopping in front of her. Dark smudges shadowed her blue eyes, and her skin was winter white. Her hair was the same, though, golden, and done up softly, tiny wisps framing the fine bones of her face. He'd remembered her hair down and loose around her shoulders, remembered it gliding like silk over his bare chest while he—

He gulped in a lungful of air and stilled the direction of his thoughts. Damn. He didn't know what he'd expected, but this wasn't it.

Rebecca stared at him as he dropped down on one knee in front of her. Absently she noted that his slicker left a smudge of dirt on the carpet.

"Becky? Princess? What's happened?" he asked, in a tender voice that was nearly her undoing. *Oh, Luke don't do this to me. Not now.*

All her defensive instincts were screaming that she should move, get up, walk away. She didn't. His face filled her line of vision.

He looked at her, his eyes as black as sable and just as soft, and her heart took on a funny little flutter. She had to stop herself from reaching out and brushing his cheek.

The years had been kind to him, she thought. He was as handsome as ever, maybe more so. His chiseled face was all high ridges and curved valleys, the sternness softened by the tiny lines around his eyes and mouth that showed he was a man who liked to smile. She remembered that smile, roguish and charming enough to melt granite. The other thing she remembered was that way he had of looking at her, lover-soft. The way he was looking at her now.

"Rebecca?" he said, his tone coaxing.

"Hello, Luke," she managed to say, surprised that her voice sounded so steady. "What . . . what are you doing here?"

Purposefully Luke plopped his rain-soaked hat beside him on the carpet and raked one hand through his hair. She looked so forlorn, like a lost kitten, and it was the most natural thing to want to wrap her in his embrace and protect her from whatever the hell was wrong. All things considered—things like his timing, and the fact that they weren't alone—he reluctantly decided on a more formal approach.

"My apologies for dropping by unannounced, but I—"

He fired a glance at the police officer, who was watching them with open interest, then back to Rebecca's worried face. Concern won out over formality, and he cut to the point.

"Somebody want to tell me what the devil is going on? I heard something about a boy being missing."

"That's correct," the policeman replied, in a tone tinged with an arrogance that rankled Luke. Arms folded across his chest, the man leaned one shoulder against the white marble mantel.

Luke reined in his infamously short temper and said, "And the boy is . . ."

"My son," Rebecca supplied, so softly he might not have heard if he hadn't been looking straight at her.

Holy sh—

Luke sank back on his heels, his slicker pouching out around his knees. Becky had a child, a son. All these years he'd never thought of her having a child. He'd known she had married. He'd also learned her husband had died last year. That was part of the reason he'd taken this assignment.

"Aw, hell, Becky, I'm sorry," he said, with real sincerity. And that need to protect prompted him to cover her hands with his, his thumb rubbing intimately over her knuckles. Her skin was ice-cold, and he felt her tremble. "Is the boy your only child?" he asked, as much from curiosity as from concern.

Rebecca's heart seemed to still in her chest, then took off like a frightened bird. A surprising reaction. She was not given to flights of fancy, and Luke Scanlin was definitely a fantasy—a young girl's fantasy. "Don't, Luke." She slipped her hands free and stood. "Yes, Andrew is my only child." She moved clear of him, survival instincts finally coming to the fore. "What are you doing here?"

He mirrored her stance, thinking it was such a simple question. Up until five minutes ago he'd been sure he knew exactly why he was here—to see her, talk to her and, yes, convince himself that she was merely one of many women he'd known.

Trouble was, five minutes ago he hadn't seen her, hadn't touched her, hadn't looked into those liquid blue eyes of hers, the ones that were making his breathing a little unsteady.

Faster than ice dissolves when touched by a flame, his reasons vanished, and he told her honestly, "I came to see you."

"Why?" she asked, and instantly regretted the question. It didn't matter why—or did it?

"I came because—" his voice dropped to a husky timbre "—because I couldn't stay away any longer."

His voice, his closeness, it was all too much, and she felt cornered. Moreover, she didn't like the feeling, not one bit. In fact, she resented Luke for making her feel this way. She feigned thoughtfulness as she took refuge behind the settee. "I have no time, Luke. My son's missing, and I have business with Captain Brody here. So another time, perhaps."

He recognized the dismissal. Oh, it was formal and polite, but it was a dismissal all the same. Luke wasn't buying. He was here and he was going to stay, though he still wasn't quite sure why. Missing children were hardly his line of work, not unless they held up a bank along the way. Maybe it was his lawman's curiosity. Maybe it was that the policeman annoyed the royal hell out of him. Maybe it was that he wanted to see her smile, once, for him. Whatever it was, he said simply, "I prefer now." He unfastened the buttons on his slicker and tossed it on the floor near his hat.

Brody spoke up. "Mrs. Tinsdale, would you like me to show him out?"

Luke straightened. A slow smile, one that didn't reach his eyes, pulled up one corner of his mouth. "Captain, you couldn't if you tried."

Brody shifted away from the mantel and took a threatening half step in Luke's direction. Luke did likewise. Who the hell did this son of a bitch think he was?

"Stop it!" Rebecca ordered hotly. "I won't have this in my house!"

Luke turned on her. Anger flashed in his black eyes. That short temper of his had shot up faster than a bullet, and he wasn't used to backing down. But this was her house, and—

"All right," Luke muttered, with a slight shake of his head to dispel the anger.

Brody, too, gave a curt nod and retreated to his place by the hearth.

Luke dropped down on the settee, making clear his intention to stay, in case there was still some doubt in someone's mind. "Okay, someone tell me what happened."

He was arrogant and self-involved as ever, Rebecca thought, her own temper moving up a notch. Looking at him sitting casually on her sofa, for the briefest moment she was tempted to recant and let Brody escort Luke out.

Who did she think she was kidding? Brody throw Luke out? Not hardly. Not without a scene. There was only one way to make him budge, and that was to give him what he wanted.

"My son disappeared yesterday," she told him flatly. *And it's all my fault.* She wasn't sure how, but she knew it must be. Her guilt added to her anguish.

"What time?" Luke leaned forward, resting his elbows on his knees.

Her mind wandered back to the terrible moment when she'd realized he was really gone. Disbelief had turned to shock, then fear. It was the fear that was twisting noose-tight in her stomach as the minutes slipped past. "What? Oh…" She began to pace again, her hem brushing the carpet as she walked. "Luke, I've already gone over this with Captain Brody." She nodded in Brody's direction, and he responded with a smug sort of nod.

"Well, tell me, then we'll all know," he said, his tone a mix of sarcasm and demand.

She was so astounded by his firm tone that she was more surprised than angry. And maybe that was the best thing. People made mistakes, said things better left unsaid, when they were angry. She needed all her wits about her when dealing with Luke.

She halted by the grand piano and looked out through the lace-curtained window. Rain sheeted on the glass, the lawn and the street beyond, casting blurred shadows, dark and menacing as the vivid fears she had for her son.

With sightless eyes, she continued to stare out as she spoke. "It was about four in the afternoon. I'd let him play in on the porch until dinner was ready. When I went to check on him, he was gone."

"Any sign of a struggle, of any...injury?"

She turned sharply. "What do you mean, injury?"

"Blood?"

"Dear God, no!"

"Could he have run off?" he countered quickly, not wanting to upset her more than necessary. "Maybe he's gone somewhere he isn't supposed to go? Boys have a way of doing that sort of thing. Maybe he's afraid to come home."

"No." She shook her head adamantly. "Andrew's not afraid of me. He knows, no matter what, I love him. Besides, I've checked with his friends, and no one has seen him. The only family we have is my mother-in-law, Ruth. She lives with us. She's out there now searching...like I should be, would be if—"

He held up a placating hand. "Just a couple more questions."

Luke stood and faced Brody directly. So the boy had been missing all night. He was beginning to get a bad feeling about this. Still, there was no sense jumping to conclusions. "All right, Captain, what have you done to find the child...Andrew?"

"Listen, Scanlin, this is none of your business," Brody flung back at him, obviously still smarting from the earlier challenge.

Luke didn't give a damn. "Becky's child is missing. I'm making it my business."

Brody slapped his cap on his head and made as if to leave.

Luke blocked his path.

"I asked you a question, mister, and I want an answer. What have you done to find this child?"

Brody took a couple of steps back and looked up at Luke. Rage colored his blue eyes. "Look, Scanlin, you don't have authority here, and I—" he thumbed his chest, near his badge "—don't answer to you. I'm handling this just fine."

"Sorry to disappoint you," Luke said, without an ounce of remorse in his voice, "but I do have authority here." With thumb and forefinger, he peeled back the edge of his gray wool vest to reveal a small silver badge. "U.S. marshal for this region, as of last Monday."

Brody puffed up like an overstuffed bullfrog. "So?" he sputtered. "This ain't a federal crime. This is local, and that means it's my jurisdiction."

"I wouldn't let a little thing like a technicality get in the way. Becky's in trouble. Her son's in trouble, and that's all the authority I need. This is personal." And it was, he realized with a start—very personal.

Brody's gaze flicked from Luke to Rebecca and back again. "Personal, huh? You and 'Becky' old friends?" he said smugly, in a way that implied something illicit. It implied something that could ruin a lady's reputation.

Luke grabbed a fistful of blue uniform and yanked the man up close, so close their faces were only inches apart. "I don't think I like your tone...Captain." He spit the words out harshly. "The lady and I *are* friends. You wanna make something more out of it?"

Brody covered Luke's hand with his own, trying to pry it loose. His pudgy fingers cut into Luke's knuckles. Luke responded by giving the man a shake. "Now either watch what you say, or you and I can step outside and discuss this more vigorously."

"Luke, for heaven's sake," Rebecca cut in. Luke ignored her this time. No way was he letting this bastard make a remark, start some gossip. He didn't know much about society, but he knew firsthand how hurtful gossip could be.

Brody's cheeks were mottled with red. His eyes literally bulged in his face. Through clenched teeth, Luke continued, "Well, what's it gonna be?" He saw Brody's gaze dart around the room, as though he were looking for help or an escape.

Luke's mouth pulled up in a crooked smile that held no warmth, a smile that said there was no escape.

Helplessly Brody bobbed his head up and down like a puppet on a string. "You and her—"

"Who?" Luke demanded.

"Mrs. Tinsdale! You and Mrs. Tinsdale are friends."

"Damned straight," Luke snarled. "If I hear anything to the contrary, you and I are gonna tangle, Brody." Luke released his hold so suddenly the man stumbled back a couple of steps before regaining either his balance or his composure. "Now, answer my question. What have you done to find the boy?"

This time Brody did answer, though to say it was curt would have been an understatement. Luke listened to Brody's half hearted excuse for a search plan. The man couldn't find his hat in a room full of spurs.

Good thing Luke had spent the past three days look-ing over the files in the office, the map of the city, po-lice rosters and the like. It was always his habit to familiarize himself with a town. Luke had never thought he'd need his knowledge so quickly, or for such an unhappy reason.

Without hesitation, he said, "Pull the patrolmen from the residential areas. Those are low-risk and can spare the men. Leave the business districts and the, ah...entertainment areas down by the docks at full staff. If there's any trouble, it'll be there first. Have the men here within an hour."

Brody smoothed his rumpled uniform over his belly. "Who the hell do you think you are, coming in here—"

"I think I'm the man who's gonna find that boy." If it wasn't too late, he thought but didn't say. Becky looked upset enough, without him adding to it, espe-cially if it wasn't necessary.

Brody made a derisive sound in the back of his throat. "The men won't like being pulled off duty to search for some kid who's probably holed up some-where, laughing his head off at all the excitement."

Rebecca spoke up. "Andrew would never—"

Luke cut across her words. "I don't want to hear your opinions, Brody. Do what I'm telling you, and do it now, dammit!"

Brody slapped his cap on his head and stormed to-ward the front door. "I'll see the mayor about this, Scanlin." He disappeared around the doorway.

"Yeah, well, tell him to wire President Hayes if he's got any complaints," Luke snarled. There were some advantages to being a U.S. marshal. Being a presiden-tial appointee was one of them.

Quickly he called out, "Right here, one hour—or I'll come looking for you."

The door slammed with glass-rattling force. With an anger he didn't mean to take out on Rebecca, Luke whirled and said, "I'll need a room."

"What?" she muttered. She was still trying to assimilate the fact that Luke was a U.S. marshal. Of all the places in this country that needed a marshal, why did he have to be here—now?

Suddenly his demand penetrated her thoughts. "What do you mean, you want a room? Don't marshals get offices and quarters?"

"Offices yes, quarters no—"

"Well, you *can't* stay here." she said, meaning more than in this house and more than this minute. She wanted him gone.

"Becky, my room is way the other side of town. The search area is here. I need to be close to the trouble."

He obviously wasn't going to go quietly. "Look, I appreciate you helping me with Captain Brody, and I appreciate you wanting to help with the search, but I hardly think you need to stay *here.*"

She started for the hallway. Luke followed, not bothering to bring along his hat and slicker.

She could be just as determined as he was. Lifting her coat from the mirrored hall tree, she pulled it on. The black wool was expensive and cashmere-soft against the side of her neck.

Luke positioned himself between her and the doorway. "Are you deliberately trying to make this difficult?"

"I'm not." It was already more difficult than anything should be. With both hands, she pulled her hood up to cover her hair. "Staying here isn't—"

"Do you want the boy—"

"Andrew."

"Andrew," he said with a nod. "Do you want him back or not?" He ran both hands through his hair, leaving furrows in the inky blackness.

"Of course, but—"

"I'm telling you, I need to be *here*. I need to coordinate with the police, and I can't do that if I'm running back and forth most of the time. Look, if it's so troublesome, I'll camp in the damned front yard. It wouldn't be the first time I've been cold and dirty."

She looked up then, saw the determination and the concern mirrored in his grim expression. Was there some plan to make her life as difficult as possible? She desperately needed help, had prayed for help, but not from Luke Scanlin. Anyone but Luke Scanlin.

Logic warred with fear—fear of herself and him and the sudden flare of pleasure she'd felt when he first walked in here. What kind of a woman was she to have even the barest trembling of desire when her son was missing?

Without thinking, she took a retreating step back. "Why are you doing this?"

"Because you need me."

"I don't need you," she countered emphatically.

"Well, you need someone, 'cause even I can see that Brody's not getting the job done. I do this for a living, and I'm damned good at it."

That she had no doubt about. It was the needing-him part that was grating on her already raw nerves. She needed Luke Scanlin like she needed to be trampled in a stampede, but it all came down to this: Brody was next to useless. Luke had managed to get more from the man in the past few minutes than she'd managed since last night. Andrew was out there, and if it would help her get her son back, she'd dance with the devil himself. Looking at Luke's hypnotic black eyes, she had a sinking feeling that the dance was about to begin.

"There's a guest room at the top of the stairs." She gestured with her head. "I'll have the maid show you."

"I can track down a guest room." He smiled, and this time he touched her shoulder, very lightly.

It was the second time he'd touched her. The second time those familiar shivers had skittered up her spine. No! She wouldn't give in to him. Not this time. Not ever again. Needing distance, she moved away. "Third door on the left." She fumbled with the ebony buttons on her coat. "The bed's made, and I'll have towels brought in when I return. The housekeeper's been sick. She'll be back tomorrow. My mother-in-law will be here tonight."

Luke smiled. It was a lopsided smile, filled with enough roguish charm to melt the coldest heart. If she stood here looking at that smile much longer, her knees were going to melt, that was for certain.

"I'll be back later." She was reaching for the shiny brass doorknob when his hand on her shoulder turned her to face him again. His dark brows were drawn together in a frown.

"Back? What do you mean, back? *Where* are you going?"

"Out." She made a show of tugging on her kidskin gloves while she slipped free of his touch. Darn those goose bumps.

Luke's expression drew down. "Out? Why, for heaven's sake? The police will be here in an hour, and then—"

"I'm going now." She turned the knob and pulled the door partially open. The rain dripped from the roof and made noisy *plick-plops* on the wooden planks of the porch. The sudden draft felt blessedly cold against the side of her face.

"Look," he started to say with a nod—a gesture Rebecca suspected was meant to pacify rather than to indicate agreement. He grasped the edge of the open door, holding it firmly, and looked at her in a way that was all too familiar, a way that brought better-forgotten memories rushing to the surface faster than lava in a volcano, and just as hot.

"This is crazy. We're gonna cover the same ground in an hour." He pushed on the door.

Rebecca held fast, as though this were a test of wills between them. Accepting help was one thing, surrender was another. This felt like giving in. "I'm going." She pulled, and he released his hold on the door.

She slipped out and pulled the heavy oak door closed behind her. She knew he was watching her through the clear etched glass. Until thirty minutes ago, she had thought she'd closed the door on Luke Scanlin just as easily. It seemed she was wrong.

Chapter Two

Rebecca took the front steps in five firm strides. She was angry, and it wasn't until the rain splattered against her cheeks that she realized she'd forgotten to take an umbrella. Clenched-jawed and angry, she kept going. She'd drown before she'd go back in there. She'd had enough of him for now. She'd had enough of him for good.

Raindrops clung to her eyelashes, and she swiped them away with the back of her gloved hand, then yanked her hood farther forward—not that it did much good. It was raining like hell. By the time she turned through the gate, her coat was soaked and the wet had penetrated through to her dress. Goose bumps were prickling across her shoulders, and a shiver was inching down her spine.

She made a sharp left turn that would have been the envy of any military cadet. Thunder rumbled, but failed to silence the steady *click-clack* of her heels on the concrete sidewalk. Her coat flopped open with each step, further drenching her dress. Nothing and no one was cooperating—not the police, not the weather, and not even the good Lord, it seemed. She cast her eyes upward. "How could you do this to me? Luke? You sent me Luke?"

With a sigh of resignation, she increased her pace, and promptly stepped in an ankle-deep puddle for her trouble.

"Thanks," she muttered, and kept going.

She passed the Johnson mansion, four colors of clapboard and geegaws in the latest style. *Circus tent* was the thought that flashed in her mind as she paused long enough to scan the yard and porch for the third time since Andrew had disappeared. The Hogans', next door, was more sedate—plain, white siding and blue trim, the usually pale green roof shingles now forest-dark from the rain.

A delivery wagon rumbled past, splashing her with more water. "Hey!" she hollered, but the driver kept going. So did she, scanning the yard yet again.

All the while, she kept thinking that Andrew was out here and Luke was back there. She wished it was the other way around. She wished Luke was gone—back to Texas or Wyoming or Timbuktu, anywhere but here. Part of her wanted to deny it, pretend it wasn't true, pretend that Luke Scanlin, the man who had changed her life forever, the one man who unknowingly had the power to ruin her life, wasn't sitting in her parlor.

She stopped still. He'd be there tonight. He'd be sleeping down the hall. He'd talk to Ruth. Oh, no! Oh, no, this wasn't going to happen. She wasn't going to take this kind of risk, not again.

When she got home, she was going to send him packing. That was all there was to it. She didn't have to explain or justify herself to him. In fact, the more she thought on it, the more she thought she didn't even *need* him.

Brody's going to find Andrew, right?

Sure. "I'll have the men keep an eye out," he had said. Yes, that would go a long way toward finding Andrew, she thought, her heart sinking as she faced reality.

Okay, so Brody was unreliable. Luke's take-charge attitude obviously was going to get the job done, she admitted—only to herself, and only because she was alone.

Since she was admitting things, she'd also admit she should have stayed at the house, should have waited for the search parties he was organizing. And yes, dammit, she was grateful for his help.

A smile tickled her lips. It had been something to see, watching Luke put that pompous Brody in his place. One side of her mouth actually curved upward in a sort of smile—not a real one, though. She wouldn't give Luke that much.

Water splashed and soaked up her stockings as she stepped off the curb and crossed the street. *What are you getting all worked up about?* she asked herself. *You can handle Luke Scanlin. You're not affected by him anymore, remember?*

Not affected by Luke Scanlin anymore? Yes, she remembered. That first year, she'd said it to herself more often than a nun would say the rosary.

She was entirely different from the way she had been at eighteen, a young girl whose head was full of adventure and romance. A young girl waiting for her knight in shining armor to whisk her away to his castle.

There were darned few knights in San Francisco, but a real Texas cowboy had come awfully close. She'd met Luke Scanlin at a party. He'd been a guest of Lucy Pemberton's brother, Tom. The rumor had quickly circulated that Luke was a war hero, on his way to join the Texas Rangers.

He had been tall, dark and handsome—*and* forbidden. At least by her mother, who had reminded her that he didn't have any social position, any name. In short, he wasn't *somebody*.

Luke hadn't seemed to know or care about such things, and that had made him all the more exciting. He'd been the stuff of Miss Pennybrook's romantic novels—the ones respectable young ladies were not supposed to read.

Never mind that she had been practically engaged to Nathan Tinsdale. Never mind that she had been expected to marry and settle down to a respectable life that had been all planned out for her since the day she was born.

Nathan had been older than she by nearly twenty years, a man who had chosen to forgo marriage in order to pursue business. He hadn't been nearly so appealing to a young girl as a cowboy who enticed her with word and touch until she surrendered to him.

Her hands shook, and it was from the memory, not the cold rain. She stopped still as feelings that were both deep and delicious washed over her. She remembered being in his arms. Her fingers brushed her lips as she remembered the sensation of his mouth on hers.

Excitement exploded in her like a shot. Despite the rain, her mouth was desert-dry. Her eyes fluttered closed.

Luke.

As quickly as the feelings had come, they were gone, replaced by guilt, gut-wrenching guilt. Dear God, what was the matter with her? How . . . how could she even think of anyone or anything else when her son, her baby, was missing?

She shook her head to clear away the cobwebs, send the ghosts back to their graves. What she and Luke had shared had been over a long time ago. Nathan was gone, but she had Andrew, and that was all she needed, would ever need.

It had been a fearful thing when she learned she was expecting. But somehow things had worked out, and from the first moment she set eyes on her baby, she'd thanked the good Lord for giving her this child. Andrew was a joy in her life, sometimes the only joy. Her world was built around him. Without him, there was a giant emptiness where her heart should be.

You'll find him. You'll get him back.

With a great sigh, she started walking again, startling a blackbird perched on a nearby picket fence. She watched as the bird took flight, and wished she could fly away from her troubles as easily.

Light gray clouds warred with darker ones, and it didn't take an expert to know this storm wouldn't be letting up anytime soon. She skirted a parked carriage whose shiny blue wheels were dulled by mud and crossed the street, turning left on Taylor.

She scanned the area, but she already knew Andrew wasn't there. She had covered this whole section twice yesterday. Still, she called out. "Andrew! Andrew, are you there?"

No answer.

She focused on the narrow houses that lined the street like ornately painted dollhouses. Straining to look between them, she clung to the faint glimmer of hope. Perhaps . . .

A mother's instinct told her that he wasn't here. He wasn't anywhere she'd searched already. Brody's admonition about Andrew being kidnapped circled in the shadows of her mind, and she held it off with the bright light of hope.

They needed a methodical search of the area, not some ragtag hit-or-miss stroll through the neighborhoods. And yes, Luke was right.

He'd been here less than an hour and already he was taking over. Luke had a way of taking over, she thought, remembering how it had been with them.

He'd taken over her life back then. She'd wanted to be with him every minute, and when she wasn't she'd been thinking about him, planning how to slip away to be with him. Then, two days after they made love, Luke Scanlin had gotten on his horse and ridden away. Just like that. A brief note saying he was off to Texas. He hadn't even come by in person to tell her.

Her heart lurched as she remember the devastation, the hurt. She'd feigned illness and locked herself in her room for a day. It had seemed that most of that time she spent crying, or cursing his name, or praying it was a mistake and he'd return for her.

A month later, she'd given up on that idea. She'd known the truth then, about Luke, about trusting him.

Well, she thought, her chin coming up a notch in a defiant gesture, she'd done a lot of growing up that month, and she'd made some difficult choices.

Thunder rumbled, and a single bolt of lightning slashed across the sky, seeming to dive into the bay.

It had rained the day she married Nathan. What a dear, sweet man he'd been. Even if theirs had not been a marriage of passion, it had been a good marriage. She'd cared for and respected Nathan. She was eternally grateful to him.

She could still remember how frightened she'd been when she told him...everything. He'd been so understanding, telling her that he was not so free of sin that he could judge her. At that moment, Rebecca had felt her life was beginning anew, and she'd been grateful to Nathan for giving her that chance.

They had spent their honeymoon in Europe, and it had been a wonderful time, spent visiting wondrous museums in England, dining at romantic sidewalk cafés in Paris, going to the opera in Italy. Then they'd returned to San Francisco, and she'd moved into the home he shared with his mother, Ruth. A warmth came over her at the thought of Ruth. She was the dearest person Rebecca had ever known. She'd welcomed Rebecca to the family with a love and affection that had never failed through all the years since.

Then a slick street, a steep hill, a horse that lost its footing, and Nathan's carriage had turned over, killing Nathan, the driver, and two pedestrians. It had been an awful, tragic time. This only a year after her father's death. When it seemed things couldn't get worse, her mother, too, had passed away, only six months later.

It had been more than she could bear. Confused, overwhelmed by it all, she'd withdrawn into herself, refusing to leave her room, refusing to see anyone, refusing to eat or sleep.

It had been Ruth who had stood by her, forced her to eat, sat with her while she slept, cared for Andrew when Rebecca wasn't up to the task. It had been Ruth who gave her hope and love and slowly brought her back and, yes, it had even been Ruth who insisted that Rebecca keep and run the small newspaper that was part of Nathan's estate.

Somehow Ruth had known that working would give Rebecca the focus, the purpose, she needed. With that purpose, she'd recovered, devoting her life to Andrew and Ruth and the paper.

They were her world, and they'd been there for her through it all, good and bad.

She owed Ruth her life, and the debt was more than she could ever repay.

She pushed a lock of water-soaked hair back from her face and stopped, staring hard at the dark silhouette of a woman standing near the corner on the opposite side of the street. Dressed in a black coat and holding an equally black umbrella, she was a dark form against the gray-black sky. Rebecca took another step and saw the woman sway, then clutch an oak tree for support.

"Ruth!" she yelled. Hitching up her skirt, Rebecca ran flat out to help. Jumping over the rivulet of water near the curb, she grabbed Ruth by both arms. "Are you all right?"

Ruth looked up. She was cold, soaked to the skin, and her whole body seemed to be shaking with the force of a small earthquake. It was the painful, frantic beating of her heart that was scaring the devil out of her. At seventy, a body had to expect such things, she supposed. At least that was what that quack Doc Tilson kept telling her. Trouble was, she kept forgetting that she was old. In her mind, she was still twenty, and she had a lot to live for, like her grandson and Rebecca.

So, gulping in a couple of deep breaths, she forced a shaky smile and said, "I'm fine. Just a little winded."

"Sure you are!" Rebecca obviously didn't believe her for a minute. "Stay here. I'm getting the buggy."

Rain trickled down from the oak tree, spattering on the walk.

"No." Ruth shook her head. "I'm fine, or I will be. I need a minute to catch my breath." She straightened to prove her point, and was rewarded with a sharp pain that started in the center of her chest and shot down her left arm, making her fingers tingle. She clenched her teeth, refusing to reveal the pain. Rebecca had enough to worry about.

"Come on," she said firmly, reaching out. "I'll just take your arm."

"No chance. I'm getting that buggy, then we're calling the doctor." She made a half turn to leave.

"I'm not helpless." Ruth started walking. Her steps were slow and measured, but she was determined to keep going. Rebecca had no choice but to snatch up the umbrella and fall in step with her.

"At least let me help you," she chided gently. "You're more hardheaded than . . . than . . ."

"A mule," Ruth put in with a smile that was forced. She took Rebecca's offered arm.

"Than a mule," Rebecca returned. Holding up the umbrella, she managed to give them both a little protection from the steady downpour. They stepped off the curb and crossed Taylor Street. "If anything happened to you, I—"

"Nothing's going to happen to me," Ruth told her, knowing what Rebecca was going through. She loved Rebecca like a daughter. Rebecca had been exactly the right one for Nathan. She'd been patient and kind and loving to Ruth's only son. Since Nathan had died, they'd been through a lot together. "Believe me. Nothing is going to happen to me. I'm too old and too cantankerous to die."

"You shouldn't be out here," Rebecca chided gently. Wet leaves, stirred by the breeze, clung to their shoes and the hems of their dresses. "You know the doctor said you should rest and—"

"Dr. Tilson's an old worrywart." She didn't have the strength to smile this time. "Besides, you can't think I'd sit at home when Andrew is—" pain clenched in her chest like a vise, and her step faltered, but she recovered and continued on "—out here lost." She gulped some air. That pain was increasing. Maybe she really had overdone it this time.

They turned onto California Street, and the house came blessedly into view.

Only half a block. Only half a block.

Ruth said the words over and over, counting the steps in her mind. Pretending she knew how many it was to the house made her feel better. All she needed was to sit down for a few minutes, maybe a cup of strong tea, and she'd be right as rain.

Poor choice of words, she thought, glancing up and getting a faceful of water for her trouble. Her dress was wet from the hem up and the shoulders down, the only dryness somewhere in the middle. She was cold clear through, and she clenched her teeth to keep them from chattering.

Rebecca paused. "Slow down, there's no hurry."

But there was. Ruth was afraid that if she stopped she might not get started again. All she wanted was to get home. Funny how home was the ultimate remedy.

And yet, with the house in sight, she was anxious. "Let's keep going. This rain is getting worse." She pressed on. One foot in front of the other. The pain was a constant now. "Tell . . . me about . . . Andrew," she managed, a little breathless.

"The police didn't find anything."

Ruth nodded her understanding. "We'll find him." She ground out the words firmly, needing to believe them as much as she needed Rebecca to believe them.

Rain cascaded off the tips of the umbrella in delicate rivulets. Rebecca covered Ruth's hand with her own in a reassuring gesture. They turned through the gate and up the walk. Ruth took the stairs slowly, one step, then the next, then the last. It hurt to breathe.

"I think . . . I'll lie down for a little while," Ruth said as Rebecca tossed the umbrella aside and started helping her with her coat. "If you'll help me up the stairs."

At the sound of the door, Luke glanced up from the large hand-drawn map he had spread across one end of the long, narrow dining room table. He wasn't alone. Three policemen had arrived about five minutes ago, with a less than friendly attitude, which he was ignoring. He'd also rounded up several of the neighbors, who were more than willing to help and had brought as many of their household staff with them as possible. All in all, there were nine of them.

Keeping an eye on the doorway, he said, "Now, gentlemen, what I want is a complete and thorough search of these areas." He pointed to the map, his fingers tracing the outline of an area approximately ten blocks square.

The policemen glared. "We covered that area," one of them snapped.

In a voice filled with concern, Luke said, "Did you cover it as though it was *your* son out there?"

The policemen all looked sheepish.

Luke turned to the others. "I want a complete search, under every porch, inside every stable loft, behind every outhouse. Look in chicken coops, doghouses and tree houses. Look anywhere big enough for a boy to hide. Remember, he could be hurt, could be unconscious and unable to call out. It's up to us to find him."

Everyone, including the policemen, nodded, and Luke felt confident that he'd get a thorough search this time.

They were finishing, and he kept expecting to see Rebecca appear in the doorway. He was still angry—well, annoyed, anyway—that she'd gone out, but he figured that now that she was back, she'd want in on this discussion. When she didn't come in, he said, "Excuse me a moment," and, edging sideways between the police and the mahogany table, he strode for the hallway, his footsteps muffled by the carpet.

One hand resting on the door frame, he paused to see Rebecca and another woman. Obviously someone she knew. The woman was short, barely over five feet, he guessed. Her black dress made her seem more so. Her white hair was pulled back in a knot at the base of her neck. She looked pale and shaky.

"Becky? Everything all right?"

Her head snapped around. "Luke, help me." She was struggling to help the woman out of her drenched coat. "Ruth isn't feeling well, and—"

"I'm—" Ruth swayed slightly, then collapsed like a rag doll.

"Ruth!" Rebecca screamed, making a grab for her.

Luke was there instantly and caught her. He lifted her limp body in his arms. At the sound of Rebecca's scream, the other men came thundering into the tiny hallway.

"What's happened?"

"What's wrong?"

Luke was already moving toward the steep staircase. "Where's her room?" he demanded.

"Top of the stairs, first door on the left." Rebecca hitched up her skirt to follow, but she hesitated long enough to address the neighbor standing closest. "Mr. Neville, please send someone for Dr. Tilson."

"Of course. Is Mrs. Tinsdale—"

"I'll let you know. Please hurry." She turned and took the stairs as fast as her confining skirt would let her.

Careering through the doorway, she skidded to a halt as Luke put Ruth's motionless body on the four-poster bed.

"I've sent for the doctor." She started unbuttoning the tiny buttons down the front of Ruth's high-necked dress. The foulard was wet and clingy, making the work difficult. "We've got to get her out of these wet things."

He was already slipping one of Ruth's shoes off. "Stockings?" he questioned.

She nodded and, lifting Ruth's skirt slightly, he pulled off her silk stockings, then helped Rebecca remove Ruth's dress and petticoats and corset. The woman was ill. This was no time to stand on formality. "What happened?"

"Bad heart." She pulled up the coverlet and glanced frantically at the door. "Where's that doctor?" It was a rhetorical question, born of desperation. She took

Ruth's hand in hers. "Ruth..." Rebecca rubbed her cold hand, trying to bring some warmth back. "Ruth? Can you hear me? Oh, Luke, she's like ice. If anything happens to her, too..." She rubbed her other hand. "She isn't moving." Her voice rose. Wild-eyed, she turned on him. "Why isn't she moving?" Terror welled up in her. "Oh, God! She isn't—"

Luke touched the woman's face, then checked for a pulse. "No, honey, she isn't dead."

Muscles relaxing, Rebecca swayed into him. "Thank God." He held her, and she leaned into him, feeling the warmth of his body, feeling the hard muscles, feeling secure. "She can't die," she murmured, and felt his fingers tighten on her shoulder.

"She'll be all right, honey," he said, with such confidence that she believed him.

She angled him a look, seeing the sincerity of his expression, and she was tempted to stay here in his partial embrace. It felt so good, too good. It would be too easy to give in to it.

She couldn't. She couldn't trust him, or herself, evidently. Dragging in a couple of lungfuls of air, she straightened slightly, and he released his hold, leaving her feeling strangely alone.

"Okay?" he asked softly.

She forced her chin up a notch, shoved the wet hair back from her face and said, "Thank you."

"Anytime," he said, and headed for the warming stove near the window. He made quick work of starting a fire.

Rebecca tucked the comforter more securely around Ruth and dragged a Windsor chair over to the bed.

"You oughta get out of those wet clothes yourself," Luke said as he closed the stove door with a bang.

"As soon as the doctor comes."

"You'll catch your— You'll catch a cold."

"Soon," she murmured, holding Ruth's hand. "Where the devil is that doctor?"

Luke crossed back to stand at the foot of the bed. "I take it this isn't a new problem."

"It's her heart. She's had trouble the last couple of years, but nothing like this." She craned toward the doorway. "Why doesn't she open her eyes?"

"Well, I'm no doctor, but I do believe that the Almighty has a way of taking care of things. As long as she's asleep, she's not moving around and she's not in pain."

Rebecca nodded her understanding. "This is awful. I feel so responsible. She hasn't slept since Andrew disappeared, and—"

"Neither have you I'll wager, and you *aren't* responsible for her, or for whatever has happened to Andrew," he said firmly.

She was only half listening, her gaze focused on Ruth. "I should never have let her go out there. I should have insisted."

"You take on a lot of responsibility. Seems to me the lady had something to say about things. You didn't push her out the door, you know."

She sighed. "I know you're right, but . . ."

The crackle and pop of the fire seemed to warm the room as much as the actual burning log. The sweet scent of pine saturated the damp air.

"Where's the extra blankets?" Luke broke the silence.

"Cedar chest."

Luke retrieved a heavy blue quilt and covered Ruth with it.

Rebecca kept staring at her mother-in-law, rubbing first one hand, then the other. "Ruth. You'll be fine." She said it like an order, or perhaps a prayer.

Luke watched from the foot of the four-poster bed, one hand wrapped around the smooth, cool mahogany. "This is your mother-in-law, right?"

Rebecca nodded. "It was too much for her." She turned to him with soulful eyes. "It's Andrew. She loves him so. He's her only grandson. They're very close—best friends, I guess."

Luke closed on her, rubbing her shoulder in a familiar way. "Don't give up on her."

"Never," she said firmly, glancing up at his down-turned face. "She's *my* best friend, too." Her voice cracked, and she swiped at the tear that suddenly slipped down her cheek. "I feel so helpless."

"I know, honey. Why don't you come over here and get warm, at least?" He gently led her the few steps to the stove.

The pale green drapes were pulled back, and she could see the storm continuing in all its fury outside. Lightning flashed across the morning sky, followed by a clap of thunder so loud it made her jump.

Her gaze swung back to Ruth, who didn't move. "Does it look like her color is coming back?" she asked cautiously.

"A little," he agreed.

She dragged in another deep breath, as though she hadn't breathed at all since they'd walked into the house.

The warmth of the stove reached her skin through the water-stained fabric of her dress. She instinctively turned and rubbed her hands together, letting the warmth inch up her arms. When she glanced up, he was staring at her.

Their gazes locked. His was dark and knowing, as though he could see inside her mind, as though he could touch her soul. Feeling awkward, she asked, "Why are you here, Luke?"

"I told you. I came to see you."

Absently she rubbed her hands together, this time refusing to look at him. "Why now?"

He seemed to consider her question, then said, "Truth?"

She stilled. "Truth."

"Because I had to know if the reality was as good as the dream."

"What dream?" She slanted him a look, not trusting herself to do more.

He crooked one finger under her chin and turned her face fully toward his. She looked into his eyes, eyes that were bottomless, soft, inviting. He brushed a wisp of hair back from her face, and her skin tingled from his touch. He was so close. Her control seemed to be slipping away.

His gaze rested on her lips. His voice was a husky whisper. "You, Princess. You haunt my dreams."

His words were explicit. Tiny sparks of electricity skittered across her skin, warm, exciting, stirring a familiar longing much too quickly.

Stop this—now! The words ricocheted in her brain, but her body refused to move, somehow refusing to give up the nearness of him. The air was ripe with sudden anticipation.

His mouth pulled up in a slow, lazy smile. "I've missed you."

Rebecca didn't move, held as she was by his hypnotic gaze. Her breathing got a little ragged. At least she thought she was breathing. She wasn't actually sure. He was too handsome, too charming, too dangerous. Oh, yes, he was very, very dangerous.

It was the danger that sparked her to say, "I haven't missed you."

If he took offense, he didn't show it. In fact, he seemed amused.

"Never play poker, honey. You can't bluff worth a darn."

The man was too arrogant for words. But she was about to try anyway, when there was a knock at the door. Almost in the same instant, a voice, a male voice, called, "Mrs. Tinsdale?"

Her chin came up a notch and, with a little smile of her own, she turned and called, "Yes, Doctor, in here." She went to meet him.

Luke introduced himself to the doctor and quickly left. She didn't even bother to glance up. If he thought she was at all bothered by him, well, he was wrong.

Never mind that she was distracted enough that she had to ask the doctor to repeat a couple of questions. What was wrong with her? Guilt twisted knife-sharp in her stomach. Ruth was lying in a sickbed, and here she was thinking about Luke.

No, she wasn't thinking about Luke. She was wishing he'd go to—well, to wherever it was marshals went to.

In the meantime, she had to get her mind back on the people who mattered.

Twenty minutes later, the doctor was ready to leave. He had prescribed bed rest, and laudanum for pain—which Ruth, who had awakened shortly after his arrival, adamantly refused to take.

"All right," she finally said, in a tone that reminded Rebecca of Andrew when he had to take a bath. It was good to see her awake and snapping at the doctor. It was good to have her back.

Feeling much relieved, she walked the doctor to the door.

"Now try to keep her in bed," he admonished quietly.

"I heard that," Ruth called, and they both smiled. "She's gonna be all right, Mrs. Tinsdale," the doctor said, with a reassuring grin and a pat on the shoulder. "She's gonna be fine."

"Thank you, Doctor." Rebecca grinned. "Do you mind letting yourself out?"

"Not at all. Not at all."

Still smiling, Rebecca turned to find Ruth sitting—not lying—in the bed. "Just what do you think you're doing?" She crossed the room, pausing long enough to get Ruth's nightdress from the closet.

"I'm getting up, of course."

"You'll do no such thing," Rebecca countered, with an emphatic shake of her index finger. "We're going to finish getting you undressed and then get you back into bed."

Ruth screwed up her face in protest, but she did put on the flannel nightdress. "What about finding Andrew?" She fumbled with the bone buttons, and Rebecca helped her.

"I've got help." She pulled back the covers and coaxed Ruth to lie down.

"What help? You mean Brody? Bah!" She fussed with her pillows until she was propped up.

"No, not Brody." Rebecca smoothed the covers. "Someone—"

"Can I come in?" a decidedly male voice said from behind her. She didn't have to turn to know Luke was there, in the doorway. She sucked in a breath and mustered her best formal pose. She needed all her composure when it came to Luke.

"Come in, Marshal Scanlin."

Rebecca was sitting in the Windsor chair and holding Ruth's hand. She was still wearing her navy dress, and Luke could see that she was drier now, though he figured that she was soaked to the skin underneath.

She should have changed, but she was stubborn to the end.

"Why, thank you, Becky." He used her familiar name, disregarding her formality. He saw the irritation flash in her eyes, and he had to fight the smile that tugged at his lips.

He stopped at the foot of the bed. "Ma'am," he said politely. "I'm glad to see you are feeling better. I saw the doc downstairs, and he said you were doing better, so I thought it would be okay for me to stop by."

For a long moment, Ruth didn't speak, didn't even move. She just stared at Luke. Feeling uncomfortable, he shifted his stance and raked one hand through his hair. "Ma'am, is something wrong?"

Ruth blinked, then blinked again. "No...Marshal, is it?"

"Yes, ma'am. Luke Scanlin. I'm the marshal for this region." He gave her his best smile.

"Have we met before, Marshal?" She kept on studying him. "You look like someone..." She shook her head, and Rebecca stilled.

Luke arched one brow in question. "Who?" He shoved one hand through his hair again.

Ruth's face drew up in a puzzled expression. "I..." Slowly her eyes widened. "So it's you..." Her gaze shot to Rebecca, then back to Luke. The color drained from her face.

Rebecca surged from her chair. "Ruth? Are you all right? Shall I send for the doctor?"

Luke made a half turn, as if to do just that.

"No." Ruth's voice cracked. "No," she repeated, holding up one hand. "I'm all right."

"Maybe I'd better go," Luke said.

"No, Marshall, stay," Ruth countered, more firmly. She adjusted her position on the propped-up pillows behind her back. Rebecca helped her.

"So it's me what, ma'am?" Luke asked.

"What? Oh, so, it's you who helped me to my room," Ruth answered quietly.

"Yes, ma'am."

"The marshal is new in town," Rebecca said, smoothing the covers before sitting down again.

"Well, that explains a great deal." Ruth's tone was thoughtful. "Under the circumstances, Marshal, I think you know me well enough to call me Ruth. 'Ma'am' sounds so old, and—"

"And old is twenty years older than you are...Ruth," he filled in, grinning.

"Marshal, I think I like you. I always did have a weakness for charmers."

"Not me. I'm telling the truth," he teased innocently.

Ruth laughed. "So this must be the help you said you had."

"Yes" was all Rebecca said.

"Well, Marshal, we are thankful for all the assistance we can get. Aren't we, Rebecca?"

"Grateful. Yes."

Luke came around to stand close to Rebecca. "I'm sorry we're meeting under these circumstances. I hope I can help find Becky's boy. Actually, one of the reasons I came up here was to tell you that the search parties have gone out and I'm going myself, right now." He touched her shoulder lightly in a familiar gesture. "They'll come back here as soon as they've covered their assigned areas."

Rebecca spared him a look that didn't last as long as a heartbeat. "Thank you."

He headed for the door.

Ruth's voice stopped him. "Marshal Scanlin."

"Yes." He didn't turn, only looked back over his left shoulder, one hand braced on the edge of the door frame.

Her expression and tone had turned serious. "It's very important that you find Andrew."

"Yes, ma'am. I know."

"I wonder if you do," Ruth said gently.

Chapter Three

The Barbary Coast was only a few short blocks from Nob Hill, but it might as well have been the other side of the earth. The Coast was several square blocks of the seediest, raunchiest real estate anywhere. It was the reason San Francisco was the most dangerous city in America.

Sin was for sale on the Barbary Coast. A man could name his pleasure and be certain to find it. He could lose his money in the gambling halls and saloons, lose his virtue in the brothels, or lose his life in the opium dens along Pacific Street. All in all, there were over five hundred concert saloons serving alcohol, and anything else, to the unsuspecting.

The good people of San Francisco gave the Barbary Coast a wide berth. The trouble was, so did the law. "Enter at your own risk," said some. "Let 'em kill each other, and good riddance," said others.

So it was only natural that when a man wanted something done that was, well, less than lawful, he'd come to the Barbary Coast.

That was exactly what Frank Handley had done last week, and tonight he was back, seated at a table near the back wall of Fat Daugherty's.

It wasn't much of a saloon, he thought, taking in the long, narrow room. The ornate mahogany bar took up all of one wall, and the mirror behind the bar had a couple of cracks as big as earthquake fissures. A bartender with a handlebar moustache and greasy hair was serving rotgut that the patrons didn't seem to mind consuming.

Cigarette smoke grayed the air, and the planked floor was sticky from too many spilled drinks and too much tobacco juice.

The place was doing a brisk business, though, he noted with a bit of surprise. Nearly two-thirds of the tables were taken, by groups of sailors—whalers, most likely—and wide-eyed farmers and cowboys in town to "see the elephant" before going home flat broke, if the cardsharps had their way. They usually did. Hell, Will and Finck were actually putting out a catalog of devices for the professional gambler who didn't mind using a little sleight of hand to ensure that he won. Yup, cheating was an industry, he thought, somewhat amused.

A man dressed in denim pants and a buckskin shirt edged past on his way to the bar, bumping into Frank with a thud, then glaring at Frank as though he were the one doing the bumping.

"Sorry," Frank muttered.

"Yeah," the man growled, and blessedly continued on his way.

Frank released the breath he'd been holding. He felt as out of place as a rabbit at a wolf convention. But he was here now, and he had business, so he leaned back in his chair and tried to look calm and composed.

The chair wobbled pretty much like Frank's confidence. One of the back legs was shorter than the others, so he leaned forward again, forearms on the edge of the table. His finely tailored gray suit was in sharp contrast to the stained and gouged surface of the square table.

He was waiting for the Riggs brothers, who were late. Where were they? All he wanted was to say his say and get the hell out of here. This was not his sort of place, after all. Frank had finer tastes. He preferred saloons like the one on Montgomery Street—slate billiard tables, gilt-framed paintings and glittering chandeliers.

If it weren't for his job, he wouldn't spend five seconds in a place like this.

Music started up from the out-of-tune piano. An argument broke out at the table next to him. A man shouting at another about fixed dice in a game of high-low-jack. The two lunged for each other, and Frank shrank back against the wall, praying he wouldn't get involved, or hurt.

The bartender scrambled over the bar, wielding an ax handle, and effectively and efficiently ended the dispute with a resounding blow across the shoulders of one man. Frank winced as the man sagged to the floor.

"I ain't puttin' up with no fightin' in here," he snarled, the saloon suddenly quiet. He waved the ax handle in the air to punctuate his order. Grabbing the unconscious man by the shirt collar, he dragged him toward the door. His boot heels left trails on the filthy floor. For the span of two heartbeats, no one moved. Then, as if nothing had happened, everyone went back to doing what they had been before.

Heart pounding, Frank slid back into his wobbly chair. If the Riggs brothers didn't show up soon, he was leaving. Instinctively he patted the envelope that was making a small bulge in his jacket pocket. Damn. He couldn't leave.

But, hell, he was a lawyer, not some street ruffian. Oh, sure, there were some who'd put his profession close to a criminal's, but they'd be wrong, emphatically wrong.

Lawyers were hired by someone to do a job that that same someone didn't want to do, or couldn't do themselves. And that was exactly what Frank was doing. Okay, so maybe it wasn't exactly legal, or ethical, but it paid well, very well, and no one got hurt. Frank had his code, too. It was simple. In business, everything was fair as long as no one got hurt—physically hurt, that is. Financially, well, that was another story.

Frank nodded to himself, pleased with his code of ethics. Across the saloon, a ruddy-faced man in a lopsided top hat kept pounding out music on the badly tuned piano. One of the saloon girls, dressed in nothing but white pantaloons, black stockings and a bright yellow corset, decided to sing along. The sound was reminiscent of fingernails on a chalkboard, and made his skin prickle and his ears ache.

He craned his neck, searching the room. God, where were they? He scanned the crowd again and flinched as the singer hit a particularly painful note that didn't exist on any known musical scale.

It was reflex that made him pour a glass of whiskey from the bottle he'd ordered when he came in. Good sense stopped him from drinking it. The liquid was the color of a polluted stream and smelled like the contents of a chamber pot. He grimaced.

He'd take Irish whiskey any day. Still, he toyed with the glass, hoping he looked at home. Where the hell were the Riggses? Five minutes. He'd give them five minutes, and boss or no boss, he'd—

"Evenin'," a male voice said, and Frank jumped at the sound, it was so close.

"We scare you?" Bill Riggs chuckled as he and his brother Jack circled around each side of him in a flanking maneuver. They dragged up chairs opposite him and sat down.

"You're late," Frank told them, feeling more than a little intimidated by the two hard-looking men.

"Sorry. I was—" Bill glanced at his brother, then back to Frank "—detained." He lounged back. "Upstairs."

Frank grimaced. "Take care of that stuff on your own time. Did you finish the job I hired you to do?"

"Sure." Bill smoothed the lapel of his rumpled brown suit. His white shirt was open at the neck and had no collar.

Jack leaned forward, his lean face grim, his blue eyes hard as winter. "You got the money?"

With a furtive glance at the nearest table, Frank discreetly slipped the envelope from his pocket and placed it squarely in front of him, his fingers resting lightly on the edges.

"This is half of the money. You get the rest *after* the exchange is made."

He pushed the envelope toward them. The white paper seemed to gleam against the dark pine table.

Bill pried the envelope partway open and ran his thumb across the stack of greenbacks before carefully slipping it in his jacket pocket. He looked up with a broken-toothed grin. "We're right pleased to do business with you, Mr. Handley." Elbows on the edge of the table, he looked at Frank Handley with a ferret-eyed gaze. "Just how'd you choose us for this job, anyway?"

Frank toyed with the full shot glass in front of him. Whiskey spilled over the top onto his fingers, making them sticky. "I needed someone who wasn't... squeamish about such things, and you boys—" he looked first at one, then at the other "—you have that reputation."

This time both men grinned, as though they'd just been congratulated for perfect attendance at Sunday school, instead of for being immoral thieves and worse.

"Nice to know a man's reputation is worth somethin' these days," Jack told him, then elbowed his grinning brother. "We're always lookin' for a little work... of one kind or another."

Yeah, Frank thought, he knew all about the brothers and their reputation. He'd asked around for someone who'd ask no questions and whose scruples declined in direct proportion to the amount of money paid. Everyone he'd talked with had mentioned the brothers, and they'd been right.

At the mention of kidnapping, they hadn't blinked an eye, just asked when and how much.

"So..." Jack reached across to help himself to the untouched glass of whiskey. Tossing back the brown liquid in one gulp, he wiped his mouth with the back of his hand. "What next? You want us to get rid of the kid? 'Cause that would be easier, and—"

"No!" Frank quickly glanced around to see if anyone else had heard his sudden outburst.

"No," he repeated, more softly, but just as firmly. He drew the line at murder. "No harm is to come to the boy. He'll be exchanged for the money tomorrow night."

"Why not tonight?"

"Because we want to give the mother a chance to worry a little. That way, she'll have to—" Frank broke off, then started again. "Just make the exchange tomorrow night. Nine o'clock, in the alley on Kearney, behind the So Different. I'll make arrangements for the ransom note to be delivered."

The brothers eyes him intently, and Frank could practically see them calculating, trying to figure how to make more out of this than he'd allowed for.

"And just how much money is the woman putting up for her brat?"

Frank frowned. "Don't get any ideas." His fingers trembled slightly, and he carefully hid them under the table. "Just do the job."

"Sure. Sure."

"I'll be across the street, at the Bella Union. Bring me the bag, and you'll be paid the balance owed you."

"Yeah. Yeah," said Bill, with a casual wave of his grimy hand. "We understand." He cleared his throat and winked at his brother. "Don't we understand, Jack?"

There was a smugness to his tone that made Frank's stomach clench nervously.

"Sure, Mr. Handley. We understand," Jack said.

The two men stood, almost in unison. "By the way, are you expectin' any trouble makin' the exchange?"

"Trouble?" Frank mirrored their stance, already eyeing the door. "What kind of trouble?"

Jack shrugged. "You know—law, for one, or them decidin' not to pay, that sort of thing."

Frank shook his head. "No, there should be no trouble. I'm certain she'll pay. She may come herself, or send a messenger. Either way, take the bag and turn over the boy, and no one is to get hurt."

"Okay. Okay. We've got it. Don't worry."

He started past Frank, then stopped when Frank said, "Don't mess this up. If you do, if you get caught somehow, you're on your own. If you tell anyone that I'm involved, I'll swear on a stack of Bibles that I've never seen you before in my life."

The two men didn't seem to take offense, and they certainly didn't seem concerned. "Don't you worry, Mr. Handley. We're not gonna get caught, and nothin's gonna go wrong."

Chapter Four

The sun was nothing but an orange glow in a gray sky when Luke got back to the house. That damnable rain had moved on about twenty minutes ago, and the clouds actually showed signs of breaking up.

He took his horse to the stable. It was white clapboard outside, dark stained pine inside. The place was fancier than half the hotels he'd stayed in, and this just for a horse.

"Well, boy," he said with a chuckle, "enjoy it, but don't get used to it."

Four stalls lined each side. The familiar scent of hay and the acrid scent of horses greeted him. A pair of chestnut carriage horses peered at him over the wooden stall gates. A couple of saddle horses also poked their heads out to check out the visitor.

A young stable hand of about fifteen hurried to meet him. "I'll put him away for you, sir," he said, his sandy hair falling across his left eye. He shoved it back.

"No thanks. I always take care of my horse." Spotting an empty stall, he asked, "This one okay?"

"Fine. Help yourself to whatever you want. Oats is there—" he pointed, "—and water's over there. I'll be in the back, working on some harness. You need anything, sing out."

"Will do."

With that, the boy turned and ambled away.

Luke stretched, trying to ease the tension out of tired muscles and joints. He shrugged off his slicker and tossed it over the gate.

It had been a hell of a day, and it wasn't over yet, he thought as he unsaddled his horse and hefted the saddle over the partition. The stirrup banged into the wood, and he actually checked to see if he'd scratched it.

"Hell of a place to keep a horse," he muttered.

Becky was waiting for him up at the house. He was stalling for time. He picked up a curry brush and set to work, but all the while he kept thinking about her.

It wasn't the first time. Now there was an understatement. Since the day he'd ridden out all those years ago, hardly a day, or night, had passed when he didn't think about her or dream about her or curse himself for leaving her. For a while there, he'd tried to convince himself she was just another woman, nothing more and nothing less than the others he had known.

It didn't work. Knowing other women didn't work. Nothing worked. It was always Becky.

Becky of the luminous want-to-drown-in-them eyes. Becky of the throaty voice that brushed his skin and his nerves like warm velvet. Vivid memories merged with lush fantasies, and all of them had to do with her naked in his arms.

He stopped dead, letting the sudden desire wash over him, enjoying the feeling.

Yeah, Scanlin, you've got it bad. There's a name for "it," you know.

Lust. That was it. Lust.

Sure, Scanlin. Sure.

His mouth pulled down in a frown. He went back to work, making long downward strokes with the brush. The horse shivered and sidestepped.

"Hold still, will ya?" Luke snapped, and ducked under the horse's neck to rub down the other side.

Being with Becky was getting more complicated by the minute. First off, he'd never figured on her having a child. Second, he'd never figured on her son being in trouble. And no way had he counted on the sudden intense feelings, the fierce need to comfort her, the drive to protect her, and the desire—oh, Lord, the desire that heated and swirled in him every time she got within ten feet of him.

He stilled, remembering her today. She'd been so proud, so controlled, this morning. Most women— hell, most men—would have fallen apart under the strain of a missing child.

She hadn't. She was strong, and he admired her strength. It was tough enough raising a child these days. Raising a child alone, a son, without a father to help her—that must be real tough.

The lady had courage.

But did she have enough courage to hear what he had to tell her?

He *could* tell her he hadn't found the boy, apologize, then turn it over to the local authorities again. He'd be out from under.

Scared, Scanlin? Gonna run out on her again?

Jaw clenched, he curled his hands into fists. He was here, and he was staying. She needed him. This was his chance to convince her. This was his chance to assuage some of his guilt.

You looking for absolution, Scanlin?

Perhaps.

Or perhaps forgiveness had nothing to do with why he was staying.

Thirty minutes later, he knew he couldn't stall any longer. He swung his worn saddlebags over his left shoulder. Slicker, bedroll and rifle clutched in his other hand, he headed for the house—and Becky.

His boots made watery puddles in the grass. The last of the rain dripped from the corners of the house. A blackbird, perched on the edge of the roof, watched his progress intently.

The evening air was as fresh and clean as it can be only after a rain, and it looked as though a fog bank was building over the bay. The street in front of the house was quiet, and as he rounded the corner he saw a light go on in the parlor.

Okay, Scanlin, what are you going to tell her?

Dragging in a couple of gulps of air, he reviewed the possibilities in his mind. Regrettably, there weren't many.

If kids wandered off, they were usually found within a couple of hours, playing somewhere they weren't supposed to be or with someone they weren't suppose to be with. Becky had said they'd checked. There was one more possibility. The boy could be dead—accidentally or not. That *would* explain why there'd been no trace of him.

That very unpleasant thought didn't sit well. Seeing a dead child—gunned down in a cross fire, killed in a Comanche raid—that was one thing he never got used to.

Besides, this was a city. Gunfights and Indian raids were pretty remote, especially in this neighborhood.

He glanced at the mansion. In his work, he knew people did things like this only for money or revenge. He discounted revenge. For the life of him, he couldn't imagine Rebecca doing anything so terrible that someone would want to take it out on her son.

His brows drew down thoughtfully. That left money. The lady certainly appeared to have more than enough of that, and there was always someone who figured he was entitled to a share—without doing any work for it, of course.

It was a hell of a thing to have to tell someone, someone special, that her only child had been kidnapped. He'd rather face down all four of the Daltons than have to do this.

Maybe someone else found him.

After two days? Sure. And maybe cows could fly.

He clenched his jaw so hard the pain radiated down his neck. Well, there was nothing for it but to go in there.

Inside the entryway, he hung his water-stained hat and damp slicker on the hall tree. Water puddled on the polished plank floor, and he would have cleaned it up, but where the hell would a person find a cleaning rag around this place? He tossed his saddlebags down with a thud—caused by his spare .45—and dropped his bedroll and rifle right beside them. He'd take them upstairs later.

The house was quiet, still and lifeless. Any fleeting hope that someone else had found the boy disappeared in the funereal silence.

He saw Rebecca step through the double doorway of the dining room. Her hair was down, all golden silk, tied back at her neck with a blue ribbon in a way that made her look young, that made him remember her that way.

She'd changed into dry clothes since he'd left. She was wearing a high-necked long-sleeved blouse that was pale blue, with enough starch to effectively hide the gentle swell of her breasts, and at least a hundred tiny buttons that would take a man an hour to get undone. Her skirt was straight and black, and it drew flat across her belly, provocatively outlining her hips in a way that Luke couldn't help appreciating.

She was head-turning beautiful, even in this tragic time.

She didn't speak, just stared at him with those haunting blue eyes of hers. The ones he'd seen every night in his dreams—only then they'd been filled with excitement and passion. Now they were filled with so much sadness he had to look away from the intensity of it.

He tried to say something, something encouraging, something promising. God, he wished he had come home with the boy. He saw her straighten, as though bracing for a blow, and he delivered it with the barest shake of his head.

For a full ten seconds, she stood there motionless, and he wondered if perhaps she needed him to tell her.

"I—" The words wouldn't come.

His hands drew up in a fist against the rage that filled him, that made his breathing a little harsh and his muscles tense. At that moment, he felt the loss as surely as if it were his child, and, without thinking, he crossed to her.

"Becky. Honey."

Rebecca jumped, not having realized he was so close. "I'm all right." It was a lie. Luke was her last hope, her certain hope. "All day, as the search parties returned . . . nothing. I kept thinking that you would—" She closed her eyes and turned away.

"I know," he said softly. "Becky, answer me one question. Is there anyone who would have something against you? Anyone who would want to hurt you?"

Her eyes flew open, sparked with astonishment. "No. No one."

"You're certain?"

She shook her head. "No one. Why?"

"Then, since the boy hasn't been found, all my experience is telling me that he's been kidnapped."

She didn't move. Deep down, she'd known all along that was the truth; she'd simply refused to acknowledge it until now. She rubbed her eyes against the tears that threatened. "Why?" she murmured, her voice thick with emotion. "Why is this happening?"

"I don't know, darlin'." His tone was soft and easy.

Fresh tears slipped down her cheeks. Dear God, hadn't she cried enough? Rage and fear mixed and mingled until she started to shake, and the tears continued.

"I can't—" Tears clogged her throat.

Wanting privacy, she started past Luke, but he blocked her way. He caught her face in his work-roughened hands and looked at her in that way that was uniquely Luke's, and much too familiar.

He had the softest eyes she'd ever seen, and a way of looking at her that made the world spin away. She could drown in those eyes and not care. She felt her defenses dissolving, releasing the pain and fear she'd stored there since Andrew's disappearance.

"Tell me what you're thinking." His voice caressed her like the summer sun. "You need someone. You're trying to carry the weight of the world on those slender shoulders of yours." His hands traced the line of her shoulders. Her skin warmed to his touch. "Everyone needs someone. I'm here for you." She didn't resist when he pulled her into the fold of his arms and kissed the top of her head, resting his cheek there. "Tell me your fear." He kissed the top of her head again. "It isn't half so bad when you put a little light to it."

That fear that had been circling in her mind grew fiercer, more intense. She slipped her arms around his narrow waist and pressed her cheek against the hard wall of his chest. He smelled like rain and leather. He felt like sanctuary.

Luke.

He was here, and she needed him.

"I—"

"Yes, honey?"

"I'm afraid Andrew is dead."

With the words came a great sob, and all the horror she'd held in check came rushing forth, threatening to carry her away if not for Luke's strong arms around her. Desperately she clung to him, her hands splayed against the soft cotton of his shirt, feeling the work-hardened muscles beneath.

"It's all right, honey. You go on and cry. You cry all you want."

And she did cry. Tears washed down her cheeks and stained the front of his shirt. She sobbed and cried, and he let her. Never once did he try to stop her.

"I'm here, honey. I won't let you go." He tightened his grip with one hand and rubbed her back with the other.

It felt so good to cry. It felt so good to be in his arms. When at last her crying slowed, she looked up at him.

"I shouldn't—"

He covered her lips with the tips of two fingers. "Shh. Don't." He leaned back and brushed the tears from her cheeks with his thumbs. "Of course you should. Aren't you allowed to have feelings? Aren't you allowed to break down sometimes?" He cupped her face in his hands. "Hold on to me."

And she did. Standing there in the entryway, she continued to cling to him, letting the strength of his touch and the slow, steady rhythm of his heart soothe her raw, aching nerves. All her earlier threats to send him packing were forgotten as she held on to him for dear life.

They stood like that for a moment or an eternity, she wasn't certain. It didn't matter. All she knew was that she felt safe and warm and protected. For the first time in two days, she felt good, and the fact that Luke Scanlin was the one who gave her that— Well, so be it.

He angled backward, and she craned her neck to look up at him.

"Luke, I can't..." She started to pull away. He tenderly tightened his hold and smiled down at her. There was a lazy lifting of his mouth, a gentleness in his eyes that made her sigh. She made a halfhearted attempt to return the smile, grateful for his comfort and his concern.

He surprised her when he reached up with the pad of one finger and traced her bottom lip, then pulled the ribbon from her hair, arranging it over her shoulders. A shiver of anticipation fluttered through her. Her heart rate moved up ever so slightly.

Their gazes met and held for the span of two heartbeats, and then his slid down to her lips and lingered. She opened her mouth to speak, but no words came forth. The world seemed strangely still, as though it were holding its breath in anticipation. She knew she wasn't breathing. How could she? All the oxygen in the room had disappeared. He was going to kiss her, she was certain of that. She was also certain that she was going to let him.

Slowly his smile faded. He was very aware of the woman in his arms—every curve, every flat plane seemed custom-made for him, only him. "Becky. Darling Becky." He dipped his head.

"Luke, don't," she ordered, and it stopped him for the span of one heartbeat. Hers.

His breath was warm on her cheek and lips, and she saw his eyes flutter closed an instant before his lips touched hers, lightly, lingering there only to lift away. It was a sensual invitation, one her body remembered even as her mind refused.

He waited to see if she'd object, if she'd move away. She didn't.

"It's been such a long time, Becky," he said, cupping her face lightly between his hands. "It's been much too long."

This time, when he lowered his head, he saw her lips part an instant before his mouth took hers in a demanding kiss that gave no quarter and accepted no retreat. She set off a hunger in him that plunged through his blood, heating, exciting. He leaned into her, wanting to feel her body against his, wanting to feel her, length to length.

His mouth slanted one way, then the other, and he felt her fingers digging into the fabric of his shirt and the flesh beneath.

He groaned deep down inside at the longing that was consuming him. He wanted her. He wanted her naked, and he wanted her now.

Rebecca was lost in a world of desire. She leaned into him, feeling his chest pressed hard against her breasts, her nipples pulled into tight, aching nubs. She twisted against him, trying to assuage the ache there. She felt his hand curving around the side of her neck, his thumb hooked under her chin as though to prevent her escape.

She didn't want to escape. She wanted exactly what he was offering. Longing, familiar as yesterday, unfurled within her, warm and pulsing, spiraling outward, touching every part of her, rekindling a fire she'd banked years ago.

It felt so good, so right, as though they'd never been apart. Her body awakened to his touch, nerves coming slowly to life with each passing moment, with each strong, steady beat of his heart and hers.

She made a small animal-like sound deep in her throat, and it was enough to send Luke's control spinning. His arm curved around her slender waist, his fingers digging into the boning of her corset. Damn, he hated corsets, hated all the cumbersome layers of clothes women wore.

She was like flame-warmed brandy, the kind that flowed smoothly down inside to set a man on fire, inch by delicious inch. And he was on fire. Lord help him. Rebecca was the spark that ignited his passion.

His body tensed with urgency, and his mind flashed on images of her naked in his arms, her wild mane of hair loose and falling around both of them, her soft breasts pressed against his bare chest, her long legs, bare and silky-soft to his touch, curved around his waist.

Urgency and primal need overcame judgment. His hand drifted lower, past her bustle, to the gentle curve of her bottom, and he groaned, wanting her more than he'd ever thought possible.

"Woman, you're setting me on fire. Do you know what you are doing to me?"

Maybe it was the momentary absence of his mouth on hers. Maybe it was the bluntness of his words. Whatever it was, warning bells went off in Rebecca's head, loud and clear.

Stop this! the faint voice of reason called, as though from a great distance. *Are you out of your mind?*

She pushed at his chest. It was like pushing on a stone wall, she thought, and panic fueled her sudden alarm. She tried again, tearing her mouth from his.

"No, Luke! Stop!"

Luke lifted his head. His eyes were glazed with passion, his breathing was ragged and unsteady, and it took a full five seconds for her order to register.

Disbelief replaced the passion in his eyes. "Becky, I didn't—"

"No." She shook her head adamantly, her loose hair spilling across her shoulders. "Whatever it is. No. No!" She shook her head again. Her breathing was unsteady and labored. No one had ever kissed her like that, no one except Luke.

She kept her hands braced on his chest while she fought to regain control and to shake off the delicious feelings that saturated every fiber of her being.

What was wrong with her? What kind of a woman was she? Her son was missing, and here she stood kissing Luke Scanlin, the one man in the whole world she'd loved and trusted, the one man who had betrayed her in ways she'd sworn never to reveal, never to forget.

This could not be happening. She refused to let it happen. "I am not the same schoolgirl you knew all those years ago."

"I can see that," he said, and ran his tongue along his bottom lip in a provocative gesture.

She took a purposeful step back. "Don't you *ever* do that again—" Her voice cracked, and anger sparked in her eyes. "You took advantage of me, Luke. It's not the first time." She hitched up her skirt and strode purposefully for the staircase. "You won't do it again. Not *ever* again."

With that, she turned her back and marched, military-straight, up the stairs.

Still breathing hard, Luke braced one hand on the smooth mahogany railing and watched her go.

He hadn't meant to kiss her, and he sure as hell hadn't meant to kiss her like that.

Like what? Like some cowhand who's been six months on the trail?

Heart racing, breathing shallow, he stood there for a moment. She was something, really something.

Spotting her hair ribbon on the floor, he picked it up. It slid across his palm and curled around his fingers. He could smell the scent of her rose perfume on the soft satin. He folded it carefully and tucked it in his shirt pocket.

Woman, I think you protest too much.

* * *

It was late. Nearly midnight, according to the clock on the wall of the guest room. He was stretched out on the bed.

Hell of a thing, a damned feather bed, he thought with a quirk of a smile. He'd heard about feather beds, but he'd never actually seen one, let alone slept on one.

He ran his hand lightly over the smooth white cotton covering. Feather beds were the best there were, like everything else in the room.

A lot different from the last place he'd slept before coming to San Francisco. That room over the Red Dog Saloon in Auburn had a rope-strung bed frame and a straw-filled mattress. The bureau had more gouges in it than a strip mine.

This bed was big. Big enough for two, and almost long enough for him to stretch his six-foot-two-inch frame out completely.

Abruptly he snatched up the two pillows and jammed them between his back and the walnut headboard. If he wasn't going to sleep, he might as well sit up. The bed creaked with the shifting of his weight.

Wearing just his black wool trousers, he crossed his bare feet at the ankle, his toes brushing against the smooth footboard.

Any other time, all he had to do was lay his head down and he was asleep. He never lost sleep worrying. Tonight was different. Tonight he couldn't get Rebecca and that kiss out his mind.

What the devil had he been thinking? Aw, hell, he hadn't been thinking. How could a man think when she was looking at him with those luminous blue eyes of hers?

It wasn't entirely his fault—the kiss. She could have stopped him. He'd expected her to. Instead, she'd kissed him back, and not some little tight-mouthed kiss. No, she kissed him as though she were coming apart in his arms, as though she'd been waiting for him, as though she were welcoming him home.

She had sent desire racing through him, faster than a prairie fire in July. All he'd known was that while she was in his arms, he wanted her, never wanted to let her go. Thoughts, images, lush and erotic, had flashed in his mind and sent his heart rate soaring. He'd wanted to give and take and please until they both went up in flames.

He dragged in a deep breath, and another. It didn't help. When had it gotten so hot in here? Swinging his legs over the side of the bed, he made to stand, but her hair ribbon, lying on the night table, caught his eye. He picked it up, letting the satin glide over his callused palm. Instantly he remembered pulling it from her hair, the cool smoothness of her hair entwined around his fingers.

No matter what she said, she'd liked that kiss, liked it as much as he did. He might not understand a lot of things, but he understood when a woman wanted him, and she did. She absolutely did.

But there were a few small obstacles; she'd made it clear she wasn't about to cooperate, and, of course, she was distraught over her son's disappearance. Then there was the little matter of their past history.

Okay, Scanlin. What are you going to do about it?

"How the hell do I know?" he muttered to the empty room.

She had money, position, power. He had the horse he rode, about five hundred dollars in the bank, and no more clothes than he could stuff in a couple of saddlebags. Not exactly the sort of man she was used to, he thought with a rueful glance around the tastefully furnished room. He squirmed; the damned feather bed was starting to make him uncomfortable.

He'd been a loner most of his life. Being with Becky, he was having thoughts about things like settling down, having a son. Yeah, a son. He'd like that. He'd like it even more if it was Becky's son. He'd be a good father, too, not like his old man.

He'd been fourteen when his mother died on that dirt-poor ranch they had down in Amarillo. A week later, his father had stopped coming home. Not that Luke had minded much, considering his old man had spent most of his time either drinking or beating on Luke. So Luke had waited two days, and when he asked in town, the bartender had said Luke's father had taken the afternoon stage for Lubbock with one of the girls from the Gilded Garter. He had never seen or heard from his father again.

Ain't fatherly love wonderful?

His muscles tensed abruptly, and he felt suddenly edgy. Standing, he crossed over to the white porcelain warming stove tucked neatly in the corner of the room, near the window. The carpet was green as grass and just as smooth against his bare feet.

There was already a fire going in the stove—the maid, he figured. There was a maid, an upstairs maid, he'd learned. There was also a cook, and a housekeeper, who was down with a cold, which was why no one had answered the door this morning.

He'd felt a little disconcerted at finding his bed turned down when he walked in tonight. It was all very

foreign, the thought of having people actually wait on
him, except maybe in a saloon.

He rubbed his bare arms against the chill, turning
his back for a little extra warming. He had to admit
this was a pleasant luxury. He'd spent a lot of time
cold and dirty, and there sure hadn't even been anyone to light a stove for him or turn down his bed.
Maybe that was why he'd barged in when he heard the
boy was missing. If that kid was out there—and he was
determinedly hanging on to that notion—then the little guy must be scared to death. Becky had said he was
only seven. Poor little guy.

Whoever had him had better be taking real good
care of the lad. Yeah, real good, he thought fiercely.
If they hurt him...well, Luke wouldn't take too kindly
to that.

He knew firsthand about being alone and so scared
that he cried himself to sleep, curled up in the back of
some stable.

That first year after his old man ran off, Luke had
scrambled for work. He'd swamped out saloons,
mucked stables and even dug outhouses, anything for
food and a place to sleep.

And scared—he'd never known a person could be
so scared. Then, one day, it had been as though he just
couldn't be scared anymore. Pride had welled up inside him. He might be digging outhouses, but he
wouldn't take the cursing or the snide remarks anymore.

He'd decided he was never going to be put down
again, by anyone. He gave an honest day's work for
an honest day's wage, and he expected to be treated
with respect, same as anyone else.

But respect, he'd quickly discovered, came faster when he could demand it—and a six-gun was a great equalizer. Luke was a natural with a gun, men said. Fast, others added.

As he got older, he'd done a little scouting for the army, but he hadn't liked all the rules. He'd done some bounty hunting later, and he'd been better at that—no rules and being on his own, he guessed.

He'd met Tom Pemberton in a saloon in Dallas. Tom had been having a little trouble with a gambler—apparently Tom had called the gambler a cheat, and the man had pulled a .32 out of his coat. Not liking gamblers much, and feeling sorry for the greenhorn who was about to have his head blown off, Luke had stepped in and laid his .45 upside the gambler's head.

Tom had been grateful and persuasive, and when he went back to California, Luke had gone along. He'd never seen San Francisco or the Pacific Ocean. He'd figured he would stick around a few weeks, then head on back to Texas to meet a friend who was joining up with the Texas Rangers. Luke had thought he might give it a try, too.

He hadn't known a man's world could be turned upside down in a month.

He'd met Rebecca at a party. They'd danced, and talked, and danced again. Tom had told Luke she was practically engaged. But Luke had been young—okay, arrogant—and he hadn't cared about rules, he admitted to himself now. She hadn't been married and that was all that had mattered. Apparently it was all that had mattered to her, also, because she had come out to meet him every day during the next week.

He'd never known anyone like her. She'd been so beautiful—not as beautiful as she was now, but beautiful. She had been smart, and funny, and so alive. Everything had been an adventure with her. The most ordinary things had been exciting when he was with her. All he had known was that he couldn't get enough of her, so it was no wonder that eventually he'd made love to her.

Seduced her, you mean, his conscience chided, none too gently.

Okay. Maybe. Anyhow, that was when everything had changed. Being with Rebecca hadn't been just having sex, satisfying a physical need. No, with Rebecca he'd wanted to please her more than himself, to give more than he took. Feelings so new, so intensely powerful, had rocked him to the very core of his being, and he'd panicked.

Yeah, Scanlin, you son of a bitch, you ran off in the middle of the night like a skulking dog.

But it seemed there was no peace and no escape from those feelings.

His eyes fluttered closed, and instantly the memory of their kiss flashed in his mind and ricocheted through his body like a shot.

It felt as though he'd been doing penance for the past seven years. Deep down, he'd figured he deserved every long, guilt-ridden, stupidity-cursing moment of it.

But along the way he must have done something right, because the Lord was giving him a second chance. A chance to free himself, he'd thought when he walked in here. Obviously he'd been wrong.

He glanced over at the well-worn Bible lying on the round walnut table near the bed. The cover was creased, and one corner was torn off. It was his mother's Bible. It was all he had of her. He'd taken solace in that book many a long, cold night by a campfire.

He chuckled and said aloud, "Never thought you'd get me to read it, did you, Ma?"

He could almost hear her laugh.

She'd had a nice laugh and a warm smile. The kind that made you want to laugh even if you didn't know why.

Rebecca had that kind of smile—not that she had anything to smile about these days.

He started pacing. A vision of Rebecca filled his mind...the biggest, bluest eyes he'd ever seen in a woman, and hair the color of sunshine.

Well, Scanlin, you gonna get it right this time?

Edward Pollard arrived shortly after eight that evening. It was really too late for a proper call, but he was confident that under these distressing circumstances allowances would be made.

He rang the bell twice and shifted anxiously from one foot to the other as he waited for the housekeeper to answer the door.

"Rebecca," he said, his eyes widening at the pleasant surprise, "where's Mrs. Wheeler?"

"Hello, Edward. She's down with a cold," she told him, stepping aside. Edward breezed past her. Oddly, her first thought wasn't that she was glad to see him, but that he was wearing another new suit, gray gabardine with a matching vest. Edward was always the very picture of the well-dressed gentleman. "I've just heard the terrible, terrible news about your son." He put his hat and gloves on the hall table. "I'm in shock. If only I'd been in town when this happened."

She allowed him to lightly kiss her cheek. "Thank you, Edward. I appreciate your concern."

"Is there any new information?"

"None," she said, preferring not to discuss speculations with him. She led the way into the parlor.

Edward was a frequent visitor, and so made himself at home. "You poor dear." He spoke as he walked to the liquor table by the hearth. "Let me get you something. Sherry, perhaps?"

"Yes, sherry," she agreed, thinking a drink was just what she needed after the day she'd had.

Rebecca's hand was surprisingly steady as she accepted the delicate crystal glass. She drank the thimbleful that Edward had poured her in one large swallow and handed him the glass. "Pour me another, please, Edward. Considerably more this time." She held up her thumb and forefinger to indicate how much.

He looked surprised, but he obliged, returning a moment later. "Now sip that slowly. We don't want it going to your head."

"Edward, liquor doesn't 'go to my head.'" She wasn't much of a drinker, but she never got that fuzzy feeling that people so often spoke of. Tonight, though, she thought she'd like to be fuzzy, or foggy, or anything else that would keep her from thinking of the man who was no doubt asleep in her guest room.

She leaned back against the fine rose silk of the settee, but she wasn't relaxed. They sat in companionable silence for a long moment, and she absently adjusted the folds of her black skirt, making creases with her fingers where there shouldn't be any.

Outside, the night was still. A few brave crickets made a halfhearted attempt at chirping. It was too late for them. Was it too late for her, as well?

Out of the corner of her eye she saw Edward take another swallow of her best bourbon. He had delicate hands, she thought, watching the way his fingers curled around the glass. And he had delicate features.

She vowed she wouldn't make comparisons and, ten seconds later, she did just that.

Edward was blond, neat, and always the height of fashion. He was polite and courteous to a fault. Luke was dark and handsome and provocative as sin. His hair was overly long, and his clothes were those of a cowboy, entirely out of place here. Yet when he walked into a room he had a commanding presence that made people turn and stare. She knew that first-hand.

She took another swallow of sherry to soothe her suddenly jumpy nerves.

Edward was everything a lady wanted in a man. Half the mothers in San Francisco were trying to tempt him with their daughters. Edward was considered quite a catch, and she understood that perfectly.

Oh, not that Rebecca thought of him that way, as a catch. She wasn't interested in anyone. She had her life all nice and neat, and she liked it just fine. As soon as Andrew was home, they—

She finished off the sherry in one long swallow, putting her glass on the side table with a delicate clink.

"How did it happen?" Edward's voice broke into her musings.

"I don't honestly know. He was playing on the porch, and then he was gone."

"I'm so sorry." His expression was serious, grave.

"Thank you, Edward. I appreciate your concern, and your coming here at this late hour."

"Anything for you, Rebecca." He faced her fully. "You know that, don't you?"

"You are a good friend, Edward."

She'd known Edward ever since she'd married Nathan. He had been an occasional investor with Nathan, and had always been their friend. Why, it was Edward who had held the first party for them after they returned from their honeymoon.

Oh, she knew that since Nathan's death Edward had wanted them to be more than friends. That was very apparent. He'd taken her to parties, the theater, anywhere she wanted to go, really.

She liked that. Edward was always the perfect gentleman. Unlike *someone* she could think of.

Unfortunately, thinking of that nameless someone made her fingers tremble and goose bumps skitter up her spine with a deliciously pleasant sensation. And the fact that it was so delicious annoyed her and, yes, frightened her a bit.

So she smiled, twisted in her seat and focused on her company. "I'm glad you're here," she told him, and was rewarded with a smile that had absolutely no effect on her pulse.

"Now, my dear, tell me everything that happened."

They had known each other long enough that he'd taken to using an affectionate term occasionally, in private only.

Rebecca related the entire story—her search for Andrew, how she'd sent for the police, their efforts. Then she said, "Captain Brody is a difficult man, and

I don't think he would have helped me much if Marshal Scanlin hadn't arrived.''

Edward paused, his drink halfway to his mouth. "Who?"

"Marshal Scanlin," she repeated nonchalantly, not bothering to mention that he was sleeping upstairs, in the room next to hers.

"I assume you mean a U.S. marshal?" Edward said casually, and sipped his drink.

She nodded.

"What's a marshal got to do with this? I mean, isn't this Captain Brody's jurisdiction?"

He took a large swallow of whiskey, draining the glass.

"True, but Edward, you know Brody. The man's hostile, argumentative and, well, perhaps worse."

"No, *my dear,*" he said in that patronizing tone that he used sometimes, the one that made the hair on the back of her neck prickle. "You've got Amos all wrong. He's been police captain quite a while, and he does a good job. He's just not very good with people, especially ladies, is all. I'm sure he's competent."

Rebecca stared at him in open surprise. "I know you and Brody are old friends, but surely you realize that we've been at odds for months. I've told you that there is every indication that he's taking bribes, looking the other way for gambling and...and women and who knows what else!" She made an impatient gesture.

"Rebecca, I don't know how you can say that." He shook his head adamantly. "You're treading on dangerous ground. It's a miracle you haven't been sued, or worse, with all these thinly veiled accusations in your paper. Fortunately, I've been able to persuade people that it's all harmless, and that you'll soon lose interest and move on."

"I will not move on, as you put it. Crime is up, and anyone with half a brain can figure out why. And I don't need you to defend me. I take care of myself."

"Of course you can, dearest. Of course you can. It's just that you're so obsessed with this Barbary Coast business. Surely there are more important matters to write about than who was in a fight in some saloon."

"Edward, how can you say that? This isn't the *Police Gazette* I'm running, this is a respected newspaper," she said proudly, "and it's my job to expose crime and corruption wherever I find it."

"What are you going to do, go down to the Barbary Coast and ask if anyone's been giving money to Captain Brody?" he retorted sharply.

"Maybe I will," she told him, ignoring his sarcasm.

"Rebecca!" His thin brows shot up. "I absolutely won't allow it! You can't possibly mean—"

"Oh, honestly, Edward. Don't be such a...a... banker. Don't carry on so." She wisely decided against being too pointed and telling him his worrying was beginning to annoy her greatly.

He toyed with the gold charm that sparkled on his watch chain. She was braced for another lecture when he surprised her. "Now, Rebecca, your determination to find a story is admirable, of course. And I'm certain you think you're doing good, but—"

He broke off and strolled to the piano, putting his empty glass down on the gleaming surface. "I'm sorry, my dear. This is neither the time nor the place to discuss this. I'm only upsetting you. Please forgive my thoughtlessness. Come. Walk me to the door."

As he picked up his hat, he said, "Is there anything I can do to help? Anything at all?"

"No, nothing. Thank you, Edward." She offered her hand, which he took. "Marshal Scanlin's helping, and the police, too. There's really nothing for you to do."

She was reaching to open the door when, without a word, Edward kissed her—and not on the cheek this time.

Surprise flashed in her eyes. "Edward, what's come over you?"

"I detest leaving you," he said, and squeezed her hand. "If we were married, dearest Rebecca, I'd be here for you all the time. You wouldn't have to go through this, or anything else, alone again."

"Edward, surely you can't expect me to think about marriage *now?*"

He pressed her hand against his heart in a gesture that was more dramatic than effective. "Why not? If we were married, I could hold you in my arms all through the night...."

"Edward! Please, remember yourself!" She pulled free of his grasp.

"You care for me, I know you do—"

"Yes, but—"

He tried to pull her to him again, and she braced both hands against his chest in denial, her fingers digging into smooth gabardine. "Edward, we've been friends for years."

"Liking each other is important, don't you think?"

"Well, yes, but... what about love?"

His blue eyes softened. "You know that I love you."

She sighed. "Yes, but I don't feel... I don't think—"

"You will come to love me, in time, I'm certain," he said. "We have the same interests, the same goals. It's so much more than most have, starting out."

"Edward," she said firmly, easily pulling free of his touch and stepping out of his reach. "I can't think now...not about this."

"All right, Rebecca. I understand." His tone contradicted his words. "It's just that seeing you reminds me how wonderful it could be. Think of what we could do together, with you at my side. The Tinsdale name linked with mine. I'm certain to be the next mayor." He shrugged and smiled. "All you have to say is yes."

Rebecca touched his arm affectionately, yet with regret, too. "You are the dearest man I know. You were my friend when Nathan died and I was so lost. Without you and Ruth, I couldn't have managed. And I do care for you, but not—"

"Let's put this conversation aside, and we'll take it up later, after Andrew is home and everything is back to normal," he interrupted. "You'll see. Andrew *will* be home safely, and we *will* be together."

With a light brush of his lips on her cheek, he left, closing the door with a gentle snap.

For a long moment, she stood there, staring at the smooth wood, wondering what the devil was wrong with her. Edward was dear. He was right when he said they were good together. And she was certain that Edward would follow his dream—perhaps even to the governor's mansion and beyond.

What woman in her right mind wouldn't dream of accompanying a man on such an exciting journey? She should be thrilled. Perhaps she should even love him. Trouble was, she didn't.

She started up the stairs, then stopped abruptly. "How long have you been standing there?"

Luke stood on the landing. He leaned forward, resting his forearms on the banister as if he owned the place, and her. He had an infuriatingly arrogant grin on his face. "So that's the competition."

He straightened. It was then that she realized he wasn't wearing a shirt. The man was half-naked, and heart-stoppingly gorgeous. It gave her heart a lurch. A warm blush popped out on her cheeks, like two rosebuds. She was staring right at his chest, and at the provocative curve of black hair that arched over each nipple, then plunged down his chest and disappeared into his waistband.

Her gaze flicked to his face. He had a wicked look in his eyes—hot enough to boil water.

Rebecca tore her gaze away, but stayed firmly rooted to the bottom stair. She wasn't going up there now. Not now! And she wasn't going to let him know that looking at him was turning her knees to oatmeal.

So, with as much firmness as she could muster, she said, "*You* don't have any competition."

His grin was immediate and devastating. "You're right about that, Princess. I don't, and thanks for the reassurance."

Her temper shot up. Before she could object, Luke turned sharply on his heel and strode down the hallway. Still smiling, he went to bed, and this time he knew he'd sleep.

Chapter Five

Rebecca didn't sleep well. In fact, she couldn't remember when she'd last slept. Oh, she was sure she had dozed once or twice—the nightmares were proof of that. Even now, if she closed her eyes, the terrifying dreams would return—Andrew frightened, cowering, crying for her, while she struggled in vain to get to him.

With a sudden intake of breath, she surged to her feet and left her bedroom. Heart pounding, she marched down the hallway. With each firm step, she willed her fears under control.

Stay calm. Andrew needs you. He'll be all right. Luke said so.

She stopped still, one hand steady against the smooth surface of the plastered wall near the closed door to his room. Abruptly she jerked her hand away.

His room. *His* promises. *His* plans.

What the devil was happening to her? Since when did Luke Scanlin matter so much to her? Since when did she need his word to make things right?

Since the moment he walked in here and looked at you with those devil black eyes of his.

No! You're not doing this to me. Not again.

Curling her hand into a fist, she prepared to knock on his door.

She stopped.

What was she going to say? Don't look at me in that way that makes my body pulse? Don't talk to me in that low, caressing way that soothes and excites me at the same time? Don't be so damnably tempting that for breathtaking moments I forget everything, including my son?

Guilt overcame fear, and she let her hand fall to her side, took an unsteady half step backward, then turned.

If he was right, and Andrew, her darling Andrew, had been kidnapped, then she was going to need him even more. She knew Brody wouldn't do more than "keep an eye out," which was as good as doing nothing at all. While she didn't trust Luke with her heart, in some strange way she trusted him to do the job he'd set out to do. After all, he was a U.S. marshal.

She was trapped. To send Luke away could put Andrew's life at risk. To let him stay could put all their lives at even greater risk.

One thing at a time, she told herself. Get Andrew back first, then deal with other...matters. She'd kept her secret from everyone, all this time. She would keep it forever. Feeling a little more confident, she went to check on Ruth.

"Are you awake?" she said softly as she peeked around the edge of the door.

"Come on in." Ruth was propped up in the bed and had a breakfast tray balanced on her lap. She fussed with the ruffle on her bright yellow nightdress, then twisted her gray hair up into a bun.

"You're looking better," Rebecca said as she crossed the room to stop at her mother-in-law's bedside. "There's a little color in your cheeks. I was awfully worried yesterday."

"I know, honey, and I am sorry." Ruth shifted to a more comfortable position in the bed.

"Any pain today?"

"None," she replied happily. "Did you get any sleep at all last night?"

"A little," Rebecca muttered, and sat on the edge of the bed, holding the tray to prevent spilling.

"Very little, would be my guess. Am I going to have to send for the doctor again?" Ruth's tone was loving. "We're a fine pair, aren't we?"

"Yes. I think we are." Rebecca smiled and covered Ruth's hand with her own, her fingers tightening in a way that expressed the love and reassurance she felt. "When Andrew's home, I'll sleep."

Ruth tossed back the coverlet and scooted toward the edge of the bed.

"Where do you think you're going?" Rebecca asked sternly.

"Lying around here isn't going to find Andrew, and I—"

"Oh, no, you don't." Rebecca yanked the covers free and gently nudged her back into bed. "There'll be no repeats of yesterday. Besides..." She made a show of smoothing the quilt. "Luke—Marshal Scanlin—thinks that Brody is right. That Andrew has been kidnapped."

Ruth stilled, surprise and fear reflected in her eyes. "What do you think?"

"I think . . . it's true," Rebecca returned in a barely heard whisper, and blinked hard against the tears that threatened.

Ruth squeezed Rebecca's hand. "You know, in some strange way I actually feel better knowing— thinking—that. I mean, if all someone wants is money, then they can have it. They can have it all. I just want my only grandson back."

"I know." Rebecca sighed inwardly. She, too, hoped that Luke and Brody were right, that it was a kidnapping, that all someone wanted was money. It was a strange, perverted kind of hope, but it was all she had, and she clung to it. Because if that was true, then it meant that Andrew wasn't dead. And Andrew couldn't be dead. The pain would be too much to survive.

Glancing up, she saw Ruth watching her, her mother-in-law's big brown eyes filled with concern. She forced a smile. "Why don't I take that tray down and let you get a little more sleep?"

"Rebecca, we'll get him back. At least you've got Marshal Scanlin."

Rebecca's eyes widened in surprise. "What do you mean, I've got Marshal Scanlin?" Feeling suddenly edgy, she released Ruth's hand and stood.

"Why, nothing, dear. I mean you've got someone you can count on to help you, to help us both."

"Help us . . . yes." She strolled over to the walnut dresser and fussed with the doily there.

"He seems a very passionate man . . . about his work, I mean."

"Passionate" was an understatement, Rebecca thought. It was heaven in his arms, she remembered with a sudden racing of her heart. She needed to keep her feet firmly anchored to the ground. With as much nonchalance as she could muster, she said, "I suppose so. This is the first time I've seen him in a long time."

"How long?"

"A little over seven years," she returned vaguely. "Why?"

"Oh, just wondering." Ruth gave a casual shrug. "I never knew any of your friends from before you married Nathan. Was the marshal a beau?"

"Certainly not!" Rebecca snapped quickly—maybe a little too quickly.

"I see." Ruth looked into the distance. "He's very handsome. There's something about his eyes... I can certainly see how a woman would be attracted to him."

"What woman?" Sudden apprehension inched up Rebecca's spine.

"Oh, any woman." Ruth's tone was innocent. "I mean, he's strong and dark, and much too charming. Oh, and exciting. After all, he earns his living in a dangerous profession. Almost like a knight, don't you think?"

"No, I most certainly don't think. He's selfish and arrogant, and he acts like he—" Like he has a right to make love to me, she almost said. A lush feeling moved through her, low and warm, making her knees tremble a bit.

Good Lord, he'd been here a day, and it was as if all the years had not intervened. Well, she wasn't going to give in to him. She wasn't going to let him shatter her life again.

Her chin came up in a determined gesture, and it was then that she realized that Ruth was staring at her with unconcealed surprise.

"Marshal Scanlin is only here to help find Andrew. Then he's leaving." Rebecca's tone was firm, as much for herself as for Ruth.

"I see," Ruth muttered again, in a way that was making Rebecca both anxious and annoyed. Her temper was short after her confrontation with Luke last night, and she wasn't looking forward to seeing him over the breakfast table this morning. She'd almost asked for a tray in her room, but that had felt too much like retreat, and that she refused to do.

Wanting to end this conversation, Rebecca crossed to the bed and picked up the tray. "I think I'll take this down and get a cup of coffee for myself." She was halfway to the door as she spoke. "Do you want anything else?"

"Why, no, dear. I think you've given me all I needed."

Rebecca arched one brow questioningly, but decided not to press the issue. "You just rest. I need you to get better. When Andrew comes home, I'll never be able to manage without you. That boy has enough energy for an entire company of cavalry."

Ruth chuckled. "That's true. Why do you think I taught him how to play checkers? It was the only way I could get him to sit still for a while."

They shared a smile, remembering the little boy they loved and the times they had shared.

"It'll be all right," Ruth added. "Andrew is coming home. I feel it."

Rebecca dragged in a steadying breath. "I keep telling myself that, but—"

"No buts."

"Okay," Rebecca agreed with a firm nod. "Now you get some more rest. And I need you and Andrew." Her voice was unsteady. "Don't you worry, Ruth. No one is going to take away your grandson."

With that, she headed for the kitchen.

There was a place set on the dining room table—crystal, silver, and sparkling white china. A dark blue napkin, folded in a triangle, accentuated the paleness of the blue linen tablecloth.

Rebecca paused near the mahogany sideboard. One place setting—obviously for her. Where was Luke?

She went into the kitchen.

"Good morning," Rebecca said to her housekeeper, Mrs. Wheeler, who was drying a plate near the sink. The smell of cooked ham and fresh-baked biscuits gave the large, square room a warm, comfortable feeling.

"Ma'am," the cook said by way of greeting. "Your egg will be ready in a minute."

"That's fine. Thank you, Emily."

Mrs. Wheeler promptly sneezed, then gently blew her nose in a lacy white handkerchief, which she kept tucked in the cuff of her stiff black uniform. Her slender cheeks were flushed a bright pink, and her pale blue eyes looked a little watery.

"Mrs. Wheeler, are you certain you're feeling all right?"

"Oh, yes..." She sniffed. "Fine."

It was Rebecca's habit not to stand on ceremony and, as she'd done every morning since she'd married Nathan, she went to the stove and helped herself to a steaming cup of coffee. More than any other room, she liked the kitchen. There was something homey, almost comforting, about the room. Since Nathan's death, sometimes she would slip down here late at night to make a cup of sassafras tea and reflect on her past, and her future—which didn't include a dark-eyed devil, no matter how handsome.

"Mrs. Tinsdale?"

The housekeeper's voice roused her from her thoughts. Snatching back her shaky emotions, she took a sip of coffee, smiled and said, "Sorry. What were you saying?"

"I was saying how sad I am . . ." She glanced at the cook, and back to Rebecca again. "How sad we *both* are to hear about Master Andrew."

"Thank you both."

"Is there anything we can do?"

Rebecca tried to sound optimistic. "No, nothing. The police are working on it, and Marshal Scanlin . . . By the way have you seen—"

"Oh, yes, the marshal," Mrs. Wheeler said, and grinned. A small breeze fluttered the bright yellow curtain at the window behind her. "He was here this morning."

"Really?" Rebecca kept her tone nonchalant as she strolled over to the kitchen table. She dragged out a ladder-back chair and perched sideways on its edge, coffee cup still in hand. "And do you know where the marshal is now?" she asked, as though she'd just asked when the milk would be delivered, revealing none of the excitement that he'd stirred in her when he kissed her.

Sunlight poured through the open window above the sink and glinted off the silver, laid out on the table, obviously ready for polishing.

Mrs. Wheeler sniffed, then coughed, then sniffed again. She dabbed at her red nose with her hanky. "He said he had to leave."

"Leave?" Abruptly Rebecca put the cup and saucer down on the scarred pine surface of the table. "Luke's gone?" she asked softly, not bothering with formality.

"Yes, ma'am," the housekeeper continued, edging sideways, away from the stove and the spattering butter. "He was here when I came down at six." She tucked an errant lock of graying hair back into her topknot. "I was surprised to see a man in the kitchen. He introduced himself, and he already had coffee going and was about to cook some eggs." She walked over to the table, her leather heels drumming on the flooring. "Seems like a nice man." She started to inspect the silver and continued talking. "You know, he offered to make eggs for me." She chuckled. "Can you imagine? Of course, I told him—"

"Where—" Rebecca's stomach clenched. Disappointment warred with desire. "Where has he gone? Did he say?"

"No, ma'am, he didn't say. Oh," she said, arching one brow, "I think he mentioned something about important business."

"Did he say when—if—he was coming back?"

"No, ma'am, I don't believe he did."

"I see," she mumbled, and reached for her coffee again in an attempt to be casual. All the while she felt like screaming. Damn the man. This was so typical of him—to breeze in here, try to seduce her and leave when she refused him.

She took too large a gulp of coffee, and burned her tongue.

Thank goodness she was smart enough to hold him off. And so what if he was gone? She didn't need him anymore. If he was right about Andrew being kidnapped—and she was more and more certain he was—then all she had to do was try to remain sane until the ransom note arrived. She'd pay the money and get her son back.

She sipped her coffee, more cautiously this time. No, she didn't need Luke. In fact, the less he was around, the better for everyone.

"Mrs. Tinsdale, your breakfast is ready." The cook's voice startled her, and she looked up.

"Why, thank you, Emily," she said, and stood and carried her cup toward the dining room doorway.

Luke paced back and forth in the governor's elegant suite in the Palace Hotel. His booted footsteps were muffled by the patterned carpet. He'd spent part of the morning at the police station, trying to find out if there had been any other kidnappings in the area in the past year or so.

The police were about as friendly as a pack of coyotes. Luke didn't mind much. He knew how to deal with varmints. So, after a few minutes of getting acquainted, which, in this case, meant pushing and threatening a little, he'd gotten the information he wanted.

There had been no kidnappings in the past year or so. They had no suspects. They had not heard any rumors, and they didn't know where to begin to look.

Disgusted, Luke had made a quick swing through the Barbary Coast, just to get the lay of the land. He was planning to go back later, maybe tonight, do a little looking, ask a few questions.

The governor was late. The only thing Luke hated more than damned meetings was damned meetings with politicians. Since he'd become a U.S. marshal, he'd had to learn to live with both.

He ran both hands through his hair in an agitated gesture, then paced the length of the room. Six long strides. The walls were painted a pale yellow, and the furniture was all dark wood and royal blue satin. There was a leather folder on the center table and some other files lay on the carved mahogany desk in the corner.

There was only one way in, a door, and there were three ways out, if you counted the two windows, which he did. *Always watch your back, and never get cornered.* Force of habit made him brush the worn handle of his .45, where it pouched out under his black wool jacket.

He paused by the desk. The surface was so highly polished, he could see himself in the dark wood. Some poor maid must have a hell of a time keeping this place up, he mused.

It didn't take an expert to see that the upholstered side chairs matched the settee and the tables. He squinted. What the heck were those carvings along the wood trim, anyway? He took a closer look. Little roses, or leaves, or both, he thought, running his hand lightly over the surface. The wood felt smooth and cold against his callused fingers.

He took another glance around and shook his head. Fancy. Real fancy. Must be the latest fashion. Of course, except for the names, Luke didn't know Chippendale from rococo, and he didn't really care. All he knew about style was that chairs were for sitting and tables were a place to prop your boots at the end of the day.

He chuckled. These spindly things were just like the ones at Becky's house. He could imagine himself propping these size-twelve boots of his on one of Rebecca's tables. Even if the thing didn't collapse under the weight, he was certain she'd give him hell anyway.

One corner of his mouth lifted in a smug sort of smile. He liked seeing her all riled up, seeing her guard slip away. That was the real Becky, the one she'd tried so hard to deny. Why? Last night she'd kissed him as though there were no tomorrow. It had left him breathless at the fierce wonder of it. She'd drugged his senses so fast, he'd nearly lost all control.

Desire stirred within him, and he shifted uncomfortably.

The click of the door opening brought him out of his musings. The governor walked into the room, closing the solid pine door firmly behind him. Tall and thin, wearing a well-tailored brown suit, he crossed the room, his hand already extended in greeting.

"You must be Marshal Scanlin," he said, smiling.

"Yes, sir," Luke returned, accepting the offered handshake.

"Please." The governor gestured toward the side chair, and Luke sat down.

"I'm not going to keep you long."

"All right."

The governor dropped down on the settee opposite Luke and flipped open a leather file on the table. Several newspaper clippings fluttered in the stirred air before settling randomly on the tabletop. "Have you seen these?"

"No." Luke tipped his head and quickly spotted the *Daily Times* banner above a headline that read Gambling runs rampant as officials refuse to act. With the tips of two fingers, he nudged the clippings aside, reading similar headlines on each.

"Looks like the *Times* is on a campaign to clean up the city." He straightened. "I can't fault them for that."

"Nor can I," the governor told him. "In fact, it's because of these articles that you're here."

Luke settled back in his chair, one booted foot resting on the opposite knee. "I'm listening."

"In recent months," the governor began, "I've become aware of an effort—a plan, shall we say—to form a new political machine in this state." The governor lounged back against the settee, his arm draped along its back. His suit pulled tight across his chest, and he unbuttoned his jacket.

"There's nothing new," Luke interjected, "or illegal about groups forming with their own political agenda.

"Ah—" the governor nodded in agreement "—but my sources tell me this one is different. This one is funded by the same men who control the crime in this city."

"There are those who'd say it wasn't the first time a politician had taken money from less than reputable sources," Luke said carefully. "Besides, politics aren't usually the concern of the U.S. marshal's office, unless there's a federal crime involved."

The governor's thin face drew up in thoughtful appraisal before he spoke. "As I told the president, this is a little different."

Luke didn't miss the less-than-subtle way the governor mentioned the president. It was no secret that Luke was here on direct orders from the president. "Go on."

Leaning forward, the governor continued. "What I'm talking about is not just a little questionable money being slipped into someone's campaign fund. This is an organized group based on corruption . . . at all levels . . . whose ultimate goal is to have their own men in the city government, perhaps eventually the state, too. You're here, Marshal Scanlin, because I needed someone from the outside. Someone I knew wasn't involved, wasn't on the take." He looked at Luke directly. "You come highly recommended. The president personally vouched for you."

"I appreciate his confidence."

The governor stood and paced to the window. "San Francisco—" he lifted the lace curtain and peered out through the glass as he spoke "—has become a center for crime. Gambling, prostitution, opium dens, sailors shanghaied off the streets in broad daylight. Why, there are even reports of men dealing in the white-slave trade. The crime is getting worse, and none of this can happen unless officials, highly placed officials, are willing to turn their heads."

Sitting straighter, Luke said, "Let me make sure I understand. You're saying there's a move by the criminal element of this city to take over the government through a system of bribes, and eventually put their own men in office?"

"Exactly." The governor let the curtain fall back into place as he turned to face Luke across the room. "This is serious. These people will stop at nothing, if the rumors I've been hearing in Sacramento the last few months are correct...and I believe they are."

Luke's brows drew down as he absorbed this news. Thoughtfully he said, "What about kidnapping?"

"What about it?"

"Did you know that Rebecca Tinsdale's son is missing?"

"When? Has there been a search? Maybe he's just run off." Concern was clear in the governor's voice and manner.

Luke took a long, deep breath and let it out slowly. "That's what I thought, but we've searched, and the boy's nowhere to be found. My hunch is, someone has him for ransom. You know, taking a child is easy, and the money's a sure thing, but now I'm wondering..." He shook his head.

"I'd say your hunch is right, considering that Mrs. Tinsdale owns the *Times*."

Luke's head came up with a start. "What?"

"Didn't you know? No, of course, you just got here. How would you know?"

The governor gestured toward the newspaper clippings. "Mrs. Tinsdale is the one who's been writing the articles on the corruption. It's her stories that have confirmed all the rumors and—" he gave an obviously grudging smile "—she's stirred up no end of controversy, I can tell you that."

"Dammit, why didn't she tell me?" Luke said, to himself as much as to the governor.

"You know Mrs. Tinsdale?" The governor arched one brow.

"Oh, yes," Luke snapped. "I know her. But obviously not as well as I thought."

"I want you to investigate this, Marshal." He pointed to the newspaper articles. "I want to have names and, most importantly, who's heading up this little scheme. Get me hard evidence, and I'll see to it that arrests are made, no matter who's involved."

"You mean like Captain Brody." Luke didn't bother to mince any words.

This time, the governor made a derisive sound in his throat, or a chuckle, Luke wasn't certain. "I gather this means you've met the illustrious chief of police?"

"We've crossed paths."

"Well, your suspicions are well-founded. I'm fairly certain Brody's involved, but the man's not smart enough to be putting something this well organized together. No, someone else is behind this, and that's who I want."

"The mayor, perhaps?"

"Maybe. I'm just not sure. In the meantime, you're new here. Your face isn't known, and the president tells me you are experienced in undercover work... a range war and some labor-union troubles, I believe, are the incidents he cited."

"Yeah." Luke nodded. "I've done a little undercover." He snatched up his hat and the leather folder before heading for the door. "I'll do my best, Governor."

"Get me names, Marshal. Hard evidence. I'll see to it arrests are made. If we can't arrest them, there are ways of exposing people and plans that will effectively stop their schemes dead in their tracks."

Luke nodded again and pulled open the door.

"Stay in touch," the governor added, with a final handshake. "I'll be leaving on Friday for the capital, so see me before then."

"Friday," Luke repeated, and strode from the room.

He skimmed over the articles on the carriage ride back to her house. The more he read, the angrier he got. The woman was stirring up trouble, and then she wondered what had happened to her son? No wonder even Brody figured it was a kidnapping. Hell, if the governor was right, Brody could be in on the whole thing.

He'd asked her point-blank if she had any enemies. "No," she'd said. Like hell. What did she think these were?

What on earth was wrong with her?

Damned if he knew, but he was going to find out. This whole thing had just gotten a lot more complicated, and a lot more dangerous.

Luke stormed into the house. He flung the leather folder down so hard on the hall table that it slid across the waxed surface and he had to make a grab for it to keep it from sliding off the other side.

Thirty seconds, and he was out of his jacket and had tossed down his hat.

Where the hell was everyone?

Most importantly, where was Rebecca? He was primed for battle, but it took two and so far he was the only one.

The house was still, and for a moment he had the uneasy feeling that something had happened in the time he'd been gone.

Had there been some news? Had the boy been found? Was he dead? It was a real possibility, and it was getting more real with every passing hour. No. He quickly discarded that notion. If the boy was back there'd be a celebration going on. If he was dead, well, there'd be the unmistakable sound of crying and the hushed tones of friends offering consolations.

If Luke had his way, it'd eventually be the former. And if she'd deigned to tell him about these damned articles and all the trouble they'd created, he might have had a better chance of getting the boy back.

He went upstairs. The door to Ruth's room was closed, and there was the barest hint of snoring, which confirmed that she was asleep.

All the other doors appeared closed, and he was about to go back downstairs when he noticed a ray of sunlight slicing across the carpet near the end of the hallway.

Striding in that direction, he found a door partially ajar and, pushing it open a little farther, he saw Rebecca seated at a small drop-front desk. Her back was toward him, and she appeared intent on some papers she had spread out in front of her. The room was small and square, and three walls were covered with floor-to-ceiling walnut bookcases. There were leather-bound volumes in neat lines, intermixed with scraggly stacks of papers. One good shake and they would slide to the floor. Her desk was between the two windows. Through the white lace curtains, he could see the front lawn and the street beyond.

So this was the lady's inner sanctum. The place where she worked. It wasn't what he'd expected, but then, there were a great many things he hadn't expected, it seemed.

With more harshness than he'd intended, he said, "Why the hell didn't you tell me you owned the *Times?*"

She jumped at the sound of his voice, surging to her feet and clutching her chest all at once. She wore a dark green dress with tiny white stripes. The neck was high and the skirt full, and Luke momentarily wondered why she was so intent on disguising her God-given attributes.

"You scared me," she said, a little breathless.

"Why didn't you tell me about the paper and about the articles?"

For the span of three heartbeats, Rebecca didn't move. She looked at him, filling her doorway like a dark specter, like the ghost who'd lived in the shadows of her life all these years.

Each time she saw him, it was as though she were seeing him for the first time. And each time she was overcome by the intensely masculine appeal of him. The way his white shirt pulled tight against the work-hardened muscles of his chest and shoulders, the provocative way his black wool trousers hugged his narrow hips and legs.

Their eyes met; his were focused fully on her, while hers drifted to his mouth, and she remembered the delicious passion of his kiss.

A shiver prickled down her spine, and she blinked against the sudden sensation. "I don't answer to you." She dropped down in her chair and pretended to go back to her work. "Besides, I thought you left."

"Why should I leave? I live here, remember?" He walked into the room, his boots making hollow thuds on the bare floor before he stepped on the square carpet in the center.

"You don't *live* here," she fired back as she struggled to ignore the suddenly vivid memories of being in his arms. "You're a guest—until Andrew is returned. That's all. And stop swearing at me!"

"I'll damned well swear if I want."

"Not at me, you won't. Get out and leave me alone. I'm busy."

"I know all about your work, sweetheart, and I'm staying."

"Do you want to test that?" She regarded him with casual disdain.

He arched one black brow in surprise, then said, "Okay, then, I'm staying until I get the boy back."

"Well, you weren't here this morning," she returned, shuffling the article she was working on until the pages were a scrambled mishmash. "If something had happened, you'd have been off doing whatever suited your fancy, I suppose."

He took another step in her direction, but she refused to be intimidated by him, not this time.

"I was not suiting my fancy, as you put it. I went by the police station, and then I had a meeting." He stood so close she could see the steady rise and fall of his chest. "It was important."

"More important than me?" The instant the words were out, she regretted them, regretted even more that after seven years, his leaving still affected her. He was too disturbing to her senses. Too dangerous to her plans. She squared her shoulders and steadied herself. "I *mean*—" she dragged out the last word "—your meeting was more important than *helping* me?"

His gaze sought hers, and as quick as that, his mood changed, softened. She could see it in his eyes. The man was more quixotic than anyone she'd ever known. Maybe that was why she was more intrigued than angry.

"Nothing—" he let the word linger between them before he finished "—is more important than you."

"Than *helping* me, you mean."

His mouth curved up in a lazy sort of smile that pushed her heart rate up about three levels.

"Whatever you say."

There was something in the huskiness of his tone that made her nervous, kind of skittish, like a sparrow eye to eye with the hawk. Feeling cornered and not liking the feeling, she skirted around him and strolled to the window. The wood made a scraping sound as she lifted the sash. The air was fresh and clean. The distinctive sound of a ship's bell carried up from the harbor.

"Now what were you asking when you barged in here... uninvited?" She never looked at him, only stared out the window as she struggled to maintain an aloofness she didn't feel. "I asked," Luke repeated in a much gentler tone, "why you didn't tell me you owned the *Times*."

She was quite breathtaking, Luke thought, watching the way the sunlight caught her upswept hair, the way her silhouette was outlined by the light. Yes, very, very beautiful. And he wanted her.

"I already told you that I don't answer to you. A great many things can change in nearly eight years. I can hardly tell you everything."

Luke dropped down in her swivel desk chair, making its gears squeak. He glanced at the papers on her desk. "Much as I'd like to know *everything*, let's stay with this, shall we?"

She spared him a look, seeing his hand resting lightly on the column she'd been working on, or at least trying to when she wasn't thinking about Andrew or Luke. "It's my next article on city corruption."

"I figured as much. Why?"

"Why what?"

He shook his head resolutely. "Why would you go stir up a mess like this? Why didn't you take it to the authorities? You had to know there'd be retaliation."

She turned sharply on her heel and walked to the desk. Her hands curved, white-knuckle tight, over the edge. "What do you mean, retaliation? There's no retaliation, and there weren't any authorities to take it to. None that I could trust, anyway. Besides, I put two years of my life into this paper. Do you think I'd give away a story this big? Circulation is up twenty percent."

"What's the big deal? Didn't you inherit the paper?"

"Of course," she returned, with a negligent wave of her hand. "But it was small, operating in the red, and about to close. Nathan had gotten it as part of a larger business deal. He was never interested in it, and just let it be. After he died, I decided to keep it, to see if I could make it into something."

"Why, for heaven's sake? You certainly don't need the money. Couldn't you have sold it?" He was astonished that she'd take on a job like this.

"I could have. As a matter of fact, I have an offer on my desk right now." She was thoughtful for a moment. "Why should I discuss this with you?"

"Why not? Is it a secret?"

"I have no secrets," she snapped, then abruptly walked over to the bookcase and scanned the shelves, apparently looking for something.

"Come on, Becky. I honestly want to know. Why would you want to run a newspaper?"

She glanced back, as though considering his question, then said softly, "Because it was mine. For the first time in my life, I had something that was all mine, with which to succeed or fail." She closed the book and returned it to the shelf. Surely you must understand the feeling of taking on a task, a seemingly insurmountable task, and succeeding."

"Well, sure. But I'm a man, and—"

Impatience flashed in her eyes. "And I'm every bit as smart and capable as you."

"No one said you weren't," he said sincerely, knowing it was true. He had great respect for any woman who could run a home and family singlehandedly, and add to that a complicated business like a newspaper... "But men don't have choices about these things. We're expected to..."

"To what?"

"I was going to say that men are expected to provide, to take care of our families."

"And I," she returned, speaking slowly, as if to make certain he understood, "I am taking care of myself and providing for my child."

"You mean you *have* to work?"

"I mean, I like it. No, I love it—every decision, every obstacle, every failure, every success. It doesn't matter. It's mine. Someday it will be Andrew's."

He didn't miss the possessiveness in her voice. And then he understood. It was her pride, her self-respect, that she'd built. He couldn't fault her for that. Wasn't that exactly what he'd spent his life doing?

"And I gather the paper is making an impact?" He already knew the answer, if the governor's reaction to her articles was any indication.

"Yes." She favored him with a smug smile. "And two months ago we moved into the black."

Luke knew pride was all well and good, but sometimes there was such a thing as discretion. "It seems that while you were building this newspaper, you managed to stir up no small amount of trouble."

Rebecca shook her head and sighed. "It's the primary function of a newspaper to inform the public. If there's trouble, then so be it."

He lounged back, the chair tipping and squeaking as he did. "From what I hear, these articles of yours have tongues wagging all the way to Sacramento. People are nervous."

"Good," she said adamantly. "That's exactly what I want."

"When criminals get nervous, they tend to take revenge. Dammit, Becky. I asked you if you had any enemies."

"I don't," she retorted. "I haven't done anything except point out the obvious—that there is no way the crime can flourish in this city without someone being paid off. The Barbary Coast is going twenty-four hours a day, and it's expanding. Someone is letting that happen. It's obvious who."

"You're dealing with—hell, you don't even know who you're dealing with."

"Of course I do. I suspect the mayor and Chief Brody, for starters. Probably some lower officials, clerks, policemen, and so forth."

"Suspect? Don't tell me you don't have any hard proof."

She blanched, but didn't back down. "Not yet. Nothing in writing."

Lord, she really was in over her head. "Has it occurred to you that someone might have taken your child, might have *harmed* your child, to get back at you for these stories? To stop you from finding hard proof?"

She paled, and a trembling hand fluttered to her throat. "No one would do such a thing! Only the lowest form of human life would do that!"

"Well, someone sure as hell did." He paced away from her. "Wake up, woman. These little articles of yours have rattled someone's cage, and they don't like it."

"If you're right—and I'm not saying you are—what would someone hope to gain?"

That was still a bit of a puzzle, but Luke figured things might clear up when the ransom note arrived. "I'm guessing they're letting you know they can get to you anytime they want. They can hurt you anytime. If they make a demand, you'd damn well better do it, is what they're telling you."

She stared at him for the longest moment, then slowly shook her head in denial. "No. I don't believe it. As much as I believe the mayor and the chief are involved in city corruption, I don't believe either one of them would do this, would take my child as part of some dastardly scheme to get even with me." She shook her head more emphatically.

"I'm telling you this paper is the cause of all your trouble."

"Not true. Why, only two years ago John Woodson's wife was dragged right out of her carriage in broad daylight. The perpetrators demanded money, and she was released, and neither she or her husband had anything to do with newspapers."

"I'm telling you you're wrong, sweetheart."

"I don't agree, and don't call me sweetheart. I'm not your sweetheart, or anyone else's."

"Really? That's gonna come as a big surprise to the joker who was trying to play kissy-face with you last night."

"How dare you mention such a thing!" Rebecca set her balled fists on her waist. "If you were any kind of a gentleman, you would have made your presence known or returned to your room until *Edward*—" she emphasized his name "—had left."

He chuckled. "Well, if I was any kind of a gentleman, I guess you'd be right. I must have missed school the day they were teaching drawing room manners."

"No, Luke, no one could accuse you of being anything but what you are—arrogant, presumptuous..." She faced him head-on. "As far as I'm concerned, you barged in here yesterday morning, started giving orders to everyone—including the chief of police—took over without asking or being asked, and eavesdropped on a private conversation with my guest." She paced back to the window. "I acknowledge your abilities as a lawman, and for that I am grateful, but as you can plainly see, we have nothing in common, and I do not have the time or inclination to reminisce about a brief...encounter that we are both better off forgetting about."

If he was insulted by her tirade, he showed no signs of it. In fact, she thought she heard him laugh, but she wouldn't give him the satisfaction of looking at him, so she couldn't be certain.

"Princess," she heard him say, "that was a fine speech. Trouble is, I don't see it quite that way. When I walked in here yesterday you were in trouble, and we both know it. Brody had you over a barrel, and there wasn't a thing you could do. You needed me then, and you need me now. If that's arrogant, then so be it. I did the right thing, whether you admit it or not."

"So you're always right."

"No, not always. Sometimes it takes me a while to admit a mistake." His voice took on a strange, husky quality that seemed to caress her already raw nerves. "Sometimes it takes years—eight years, to be exact."

Before she knew what he was about, he pulled her to him and kissed her, fully, intensely, possessively. About the time her knees liquefied, he tore his mouth from hers and in a fierce tone said, "You can't dismiss me. You can't dismiss the sparks that fly whenever we're together. You want me as much as I want you, whether you're willing to admit it or not. I'm a patient man. I can wait. I've waited eight years. I'll wait another eight, or eight hundred, but you're going to be mine, make no mistake about it."

Then, releasing her, he left the room.

Chapter Six

Rebecca quietly but oh-so-firmly closed the door. Her hand twisted around the brass knob as though she were wringing a chicken's neck. Lord knew she wanted to wring someone's neck.

She counted to a hundred. Her heart was still pounding like a Gatling gun. She clamped her jaw down so hard her teeth ached. She counted to a hundred again—this time in French—just for good measure.

She wanted to hit something or someone. Definitely someone—a specific someone, with the sable-soft eyes of the devil himself.

Damn the man. Damn his arrogance. In one fluid motion, she grabbed the white porcelain vase from the bookshelf and hurled it against the closed door. The distinct sound of breaking porcelain only momentarily eased her temper.

It was that momentary relief that sent her searching for something else to throw, something else to destroy the way he destroyed her carefully built defenses.

"Who do you think you are, Luke Scanlin?" She shook her fist in the air. "What kind of woman do you think I am?" she ranted to the empty room.

She kicked at her chair, sending it lurching across the room to slam into the wall with a hollow thud that made a sizable chink in the plaster.

She inspected the damage. "This is your fault, too!"

Everything was his fault. Every disaster, every heartache, every minute of lost sleep...it had all started the day Luke Scanlin walked into her life.

She stormed to the bookshelves, then back to her desk and back to the bookshelves again. The air stirred by her quick movements made the loose papers flutter in the breeze of her wake, like so many fingers shaking to rebuke her for her foolish actions. With narrow-eyed determination, she retaliated by flinging them off the shelf to float and tumble until they settled onto the floor.

She would show them. And she would show him. She would show everyone!

She hadn't needed him then, and she most certainly didn't need him now.

The man had a colossal nerve. How dare he think he could say he wanted her and she'd just swoon into his arms in gratitude!

You did swoon, her conscience reminded her.

"I was seduced," she countered through clenched teeth. "Then and now."

Call it anything you like, but he's right. You do want him.

She froze. The truth hit her like cold water on a hot day. She sagged down in her chair, her head lolling back against the smooth, cool plaster.

Like it or not, this was reality. Luke, the one man she'd thought she would never see again in her life, was here, and he'd made his desires very clear to her.

Oh, yes, very clear. Her pulse fluttered at the memory of his explicit words.

Dammit. She snatched back the thoughts, and the feelings. Well, the thoughts, at least. Having Luke rip through her life had nearly been her undoing once.

Her eyes fluttered closed, and in her mind she could see her mother's stern countenance as she admonished her to give up her flights of fancy, to stop romanticizing, to do her duty to herself and her family. None of which included a certain cowboy, no matter how handsome he was.

Yes, she thought ruefully, her mother had warned her, and she'd been so right. If only she'd listened. But all her life her mother had been the strict one, the demanding one, the disciplinarian, and, after a while, Rebecca had simply stopped listening.

Oh, it hadn't really been Mama's fault that she was so strict, so determined, so rigid. After all, she had been one of *the* Stanleys of Virginia—first family, and all that.

But the Stanleys had fallen on hard times, and what little was left had been finished by the war. Analise had been raised to be a spoiled belle, only with no money and no society left in the South, well, there had been no one to spoil her—except Papa. What little money he had, he spent on her.

So, they'd married. What a pair they had made— the underpaid college professor and the society belle. Mama was constantly after Papa to work harder, demand raises, demand promotions, and Papa, so engrossed in his books and his research he'd never even noticed that other, younger men were passing him by.

It was no wonder, then, that Mama had gotten more than a little desperate. One day she'd simply announced that she'd decided they were moving to California. There was gold in California. Not that she expected Papa to go prospecting. Heavens, no, that would be beneath them. No, she expected Papa to get a position in some nice school, and she expected Rebecca to attend one of those same nice schools, but for an entirely different reason.

You see, there was no society in California, at least not anything like in Virginia, where families had been on the same land for generations. No, in California, things were new, rules were . . . flexible, and the daughter of a schoolteacher and a disadvantaged Southern aristocrat had as much chance as anyone to marry up, to marry into society.

Yes, that was the life Analise Stanley Parker had aspired to. That was the life Rebecca had been trained for, educated for and told in no uncertain terms would be her destiny.

As far back as Rebecca could remember, she'd been taught the *important* things—how to arrange flowers, serve a formal tea or a formal dinner, play the piano and dance the latest dances. She'd been required to be well versed in the latest fashions, theater, gossip. Oh, yes, gossip was most important. One had to know who was in—and who was out—in this newly forming society. It wouldn't do to be seen associating with the wrong person, Mama would admonish her.

Rebecca lifted her head away from the wall and sat up straighter. What it had all boiled down to was how to fawn and simper over some man—the right man— until he offered for her.

It was planned, pretentious and preposterous. She had hated every minute of it, but she had loved her mother, so she had tried. But when she couldn't stand one more minute of fine embroidery, she would slip off to her father's study and its book-lined walls—just like these, she thought with a ghost of a smile.

Standing, she strolled over to the bookcases on the far wall. Sunlight filtered through the curtains and caught the smooth surface of each leather spine. Lightly, lovingly, she ran the tips of her fingers along the row. Her father's books. He'd left them to her when he died. It was all she had of him. That and a few faded tintypes.

Her hand paused on a volume of Plato's Dialogues. How Papa had loved to discuss philosophy. How she had loved her father, and now these books. Each one was like an old friend. Each one, a special memory of a time shared with her father.

Many had been the night they had stayed up well past midnight. Ensconced in his tiny study, they had explored the world through the pages of these books. They had shared views on education and women's rights and argued politics. He'd taught her all she knew about ethics and honor, about caring and loving.

Perhaps it was naive, but she had thought all men held the same high codes and principles. Perhaps that was why she had risked so much with Luke, or perhaps it was as simple as rebelling against a lifetime of rules and plans. Whatever it was, it was a mistake, she thought with stomach-clenching certainty.

A mistake that seemed certain to engulf her and drag her down, down the way a tidal wave engulfs an otherwise safe harbor.

Oh, in the endlessly long hours after Luke left, after she realized what had happened, the logical part of her mind had said that Luke hadn't made any promises. And it was true.

But certain things had been implied, even if they had remained unspoken. Hadn't they? A woman didn't give herself to a man unless she loved him. Luke had to have known that. He had to.

And if she believed that—and she did—then he had betrayed her at the most intimate level.

So now what? He was here. Right in the middle of her worst nightmare. She could send him packing, but she knew she needed him. Andrew needed him.

A cold chill raced down her spine at the thought.

Abruptly she stooped and started to gather the papers scattered across the floor. The white pages were smooth and cool against her fingers. She glanced up in time to see a hummingbird pause briefly near the open window, then dart away.

Rebecca wished she could leave her troubles behind as easily and as quickly.

But, like before, she had to face it through. Luke would not stay. She was certain of that. So all she had to do was keep him at a distance, and pray that Andrew was returned soon.

Once Luke realized that this time he couldn't get what he wanted, what she'd given so freely, so trustingly, before, he'd move on.

She gathered the last of the papers and tapped the stack lightly on the floor to even them in her hands.

She sat back on her haunches, her skirt flowing around her legs as she stared at the grouping of photographs on the top of her desk. One, in particular, in a small silver frame.

Luke Scanlin would never know of her heartbreak—or anything else. That was a vow she would not break.

Chapter Seven

Another man might have been angry. Another man might have taken her little speech to heart. Not this man. No, Luke was smiling as he stepped off the porch and headed for the stable. The sun was shining. Songbirds chirped in a nearby oak tree.

The lady was something. Her words said one thing, but her kisses, the way she melted into him every time he pulled her into his arms, told an entirely different story. He was right this time. She did want him. Lord knew he wanted her. It was only a matter of time.

Lady, there's no escape. You've met your match.

A smile lingered on his lips as he saddled his horse and rode out. He was headed for the Barbary Coast.

He was becoming more and more convinced that the kidnapping and the corruption were connected. How, he didn't know—yet. But he was going to find out. He was going to get that boy back. He was going to get the woman, too.

While you're at it, why don't you bring in the James gang. That seemed about as easy as the tasks he'd set for himself.

Twenty minutes and he was on "Terrific Pacific" Street. Gin mills, dance halls and bordellos greeted him.

It was late afternoon, and already the narrow streets were filled with milling people—men, mostly. The Coast was hardly a place for ladies—except certain kinds of ladies, he amended, spotting a woman dressed in nothing but pantalets, black stockings and a corset as she lounged near a saloon entrance across the street. His mouth curved upward in an appreciative smile. Hey, he was a man after all. He could look.

Get your mind on business, Scanlin. Time to do a little of that undercover work you've been recruited to do.

His hand rested naturally on the worn handle of his .45 as he pushed open the rickety doors of the Midway Plaisance and walked in. The place was large and square. It had been a long time since the floor had seen the business end of a mop. The scents of tobacco, whiskey and unwashed bodies made his nose crinkle. God, how many of these kinds of places had he been in the past few years? *Too many* came the reply.

A roulette wheel clattered an invitation, which he ignored. Nearby, a dark-haired man dressed in black dealt faro to a table of miners.

Luke shook his head. They had a better chance of striking the mother lode than they did of winning. Too bad they were too drunk to know it.

Edging between the tables, he headed for the mahogany bar that ran the length of one wall. It was scarred and worn, and the brass footrail hadn't been polished since the day it was delivered.

Wedging in between a cowboy and a sailor, he caught the eye of the greasy-haired bartender. "Whiskey."

The man quickly complied.

Luke tossed a two-fifty gold piece on the scarred surface. "Busy place," Luke commented absently to the man as he sipped the rotgut.

"First time?" the bartender commented. He spit in a glass, then wiped it clean with a bar towel that was as black as a witch's heart.

"Yeah." Luke thumbed his hat back and surveyed the room. "Couldn't come to town and not partake of a little...sin." He laughed, and the potbellied barkeep joined him.

"Well, if'n it's sin you're lookin' for, this here is the place, all right. You name it, we got it. If'n we don't, wait ten minutes—someone'll get it for you."

They laughed together. Luke helped himself to another drink. It burned like lit kerosene.

A bald-headed man was pounding out a melody on a piano so out of tune it made him want to grind his teeth. Luke guessed that was what the whiskey was for. A couple more of these, and he wouldn't even notice. Sure as hell looked like no one else minded.

The tables were crowded, and getting more so every minute. Cardsharps and working girls seemed to be appearing in proportion to the increase in the crowd. They must have a sixth sense about these things, he mused, turning to lean back, his elbows on the bar. He lingered for a few more minutes, long enough to get a feel of the place, before he decided to move on. There were a lot of saloons and brothels, not to mention opium dens. Those he planned to stay far away from.

He strolled casually down the sidewalk, pausing to glance in a window or two. He wandered down a couple of alleys, getting the lay of the land, so to speak.

After three more saloons and more rotgut than he wanted, he wandered into the Fat Daugherty's. It was pretty much like the others, a little squarer, a little fancier, in a run-down sort of way. There was still a bar along one wall. This one had a mirror behind it, adorned with a crack big enough to put your fingers in. On the wall opposite, there was a painting of a woman, generously endowed, and naked as the day she was born.

Located conspicuously under the painting was a roulette wheel, next to a table for dice. A bunch of slick operators were dealing cards at other tables scattered nearby.

Luke strolled over to the bar. He cringed, forced a smile and said, "Whiskey." A man should never switch horses in midstream, but next time he was going to ask for buttermilk!

A ferret-faced bartender served up the murky-looking liquid. "Thanks," Luke said casually, and plunked down a silver dollar.

He'd been making the rounds all afternoon. He wasn't exactly sure what he was looking for, but he'd know it when he saw it. How's that for vague? he thought.

But that was what police work was. He couldn't just walk up to someone and say, "Pardon me, do you know anyone who kidnaps children or bribes officials?"

No, he just hung around, chatting occasionally, drinking as little as possible and watching. In the past few hours, he'd seen more faces from wanted posters than he had in three years. Obviously he'd been wasting his time down in Texas. All the scum of the world was here.

Speaking of scum, there were a couple of men at a corner table that he'd been watching in the mirror for several minutes. They were dark, and unwashed, judging by their greasy hair, and they looked like they had slept in their clothes.

These two he didn't recognize. Yet something about them pricked his lawman's instincts. There was enough of a resemblance that he thought they might be related, but what had caught his attention was that, unlike everyone else in the place, they weren't gambling or cursing or playing cards. They had consumed an incredible amount of liquor, judging by the two empty whiskey bottles on the table and the one they were working their way through now.

Even with that, these two had their heads together like they were planning to rob the Central Pacific and they didn't want any one else to know. Now, he realized that this was a modern day Sodom, and the two could be discussing anything from drugs to whores, but still, they intrigued him.

And since he was in no hurry, he settled down at a table in the shadows at the end of the bar.

Shortly before dark, the bartender lit the gas lamps along the opposite wall, keeping the flame low enough to hide the faded pattern on the wallpaper. Why the devil would anyone put wallpaper in a saloon? Luke mused, taking another sip of his drink.

About that time, a woman with hair in a shade of red God never made sidled up to him. Having known a few whores in his day, Luke figured she was twenty-five going on forty.

"Hi, honey," she said, dragging out a chair to straddle, which left absolutely no question about her intentions. Not that he'd had any, anyway. She was wearing a dress that was above her knees and nearly below her nipples. She had enough rouge on her cheeks to make a rose jealous.

She was looking at him with what he guessed was her come-hither stare. "Buy a girl a drink, cowboy?"

Luke wasn't interested in whores. But he knew what kind of a life these women lived, and though he knew it was their choice, he also knew most women didn't *have* a lot of choices.

Become a whore or get married to some dirt farmer. The result wasn't much different. They still aged ten years in one and died way before they should. It was more sympathy than interest that made him say, "Sure." He signaled the bartender for another glass.

The woman leaned forward, pressing her breasts against the back of the chair in a blatant invitation, which Luke ignored. Okay, sort of ignored.

He sipped his drink. She downed hers in one swallow and wiggled her glass for another. He obliged.

Around them the crowd was getting thicker and noisier. Someone was yelling for another drink at the bar, and the bartender was threatening to cut off a vital part of his anatomy if he didn't shut up.

A sailor, too young to know what a razor was for, wandered over to fondle the girl.

"C'mon…" he managed to slur. He half fell across her shoulder, and she gingerly pushed him back.

"Not now," she told him sharply. "Can't you see I'm engaged?" She grinned at Luke.

The sailor stared, bleary-eyed, from the girl to Luke and back to the girl again. With an unsteady shrug, he wandered off in search of new sport.

"Business is good, I see," Luke said, half teasing.

"Not bad," she returned, emptying her glass again. "Could be better, though. If you get my drift," she added, her hand gliding up his thigh toward his crotch.

Smiling, Luke covered her hand with his, stopping her. "Thanks," he said softly, "but I'm not really interested. No offense."

"What's the matter, handsome?" she said, with a lilting tone to her voice. "If there's a problem with the..." Her hand inched closer to his crotch. He stopped her again. "Millie is just the one who can cure you."

Luke laughed. "Darlin', believe me, there's nothing wrong." Hell, every time he kissed Rebecca, he was painfully aware there was absolutely nothing wrong.

"How about you just keeping me company?" he asked, knowing that whores and bartenders knew everything that was going on. He also knew a whore's time was money, so he shoved a ten-dollar gold piece in her direction. "Just so your time's not wasted."

She looked genuinely surprised, and this time, when she smiled, he could tell she really meant it. She helped herself to another whiskey.

"So what brings you to town?" she said amid the din.

"Oh, nothing much. Just a cowboy up from Texas. Only been in town a couple of days, and thought I'd check things out."

She raked him with an appraising stare. "Honey, if you're what Texas cowboys look like, I think I might have to head south."

Luke chuckled at the flattery. "Thanks." He poured her another drink. "So tell me, is the Barbary Coast as bad as everyone says?"

She toyed with the drink. "Worse. You name it, it happens here. Shootings, gambling, opium, women..." She sliced a glance at him. "Boys, if that's your interest."

"Not mine," Luke assured her.

She seemed relieved.

"How's it all keep going on?" he inquired casually. "I mean, down in Texas, about the time things are getting to be fun, some upstanding citizen complains, next thing you know there's women's betterment leagues campaigning for temperance and such." He shook his head in disgust.

She laughed. It was a harsh, tinny sound. "Ain't it the truth? Everybody knows a man has to have a place to... let off a little steam. Too much... steam is bad, don't you think?" Her hand found his thigh again.

"Exactly."

Luke poured her another drink, then lounged back casually. "You know, I was riding around today. I noticed some mighty fine-looking houses not too far from here."

"Ain't that a sight? Them big mansions, not ten blocks from here." She shifted and fussed with a lock of hair that had come loose from her combs. Her arms were raised to give him an ample view of her full breasts, straining dangerously near the top of her dress. "Used to be Fern Hill, before them swells built up there. Lately folks have taken to calling it Nob Hill. Oughta be Snob Hill, if you ask me.''

If she moved another inch, Luke was certain, she was coming out of that dress. Not that he'd mind entirely. All things considered, he figured she wouldn't mind.

Business, remember.

Taking a big slug of rotgut, he winced and said, ''So don't they get pissed, looking down here and seeing all that's happening?'' He screwed his face up in a frown. ''Please, tell me there's no women's betterment league. I'd hate to see a fine place like this disappear.''

She laughed. ''Ain't no chance of that, honey.''

''Why?'' he asked nonchalantly, turning his empty glass in his fingers. ''If there's some secret, I'd sure like to know, so I can tell the boys what we're doing wrong…when I get home.'' He gave her his best smile, all dimples and charm.

The woman swilled her whiskey and leaned closer. In a conspiratorial tone, she said, ''You gotta know who to pay, is the secret.''

Luke's eyes widened in mock surprise. ''You mean like government fellas and such?''

In a hushed voice she said, ''Exactly. But don't ask me who, 'cause that I don't know. I only know a piece of everything I earn, everything the house makes, everything everybody makes, goes so we can keep in business.''

''Pretty slick,'' Luke said in a tone of admiration. ''I'll bet there's a lot of money goes through here in a week.''

She nodded again. ''But it's worth it. Everybody pays, and everybody's happy. Lord knows it's the first place I worked where I ain't worried about getting arrested all the time.''

He saw her glance around, as though checking the crowd for prospective clients. He didn't want to lose her. So he pressed the conversation to keep her interested.

"So how do they know who to pay? I mean, anyone could show up with his hand out."

She eyed him suspiciously. "Say, how come you wanna know so much?"

"Oh, just naturally curious, I guess." He gave a one-shoulder shrug. "Besides, like I said, when I get back to Texas I wanna explain this to a couple of boys I know who are running a saloon in Amarillo."

She seemed to consider this.

Damn. He'd pushed too hard, and now he'd lost her. What the hell was he thinking about?

She shifted in her chair. "I like you, honey," she told him, resting her chin on the curved back of the chair.

"Well, thanks. I like you, too." *Take it slower.*

Another waitress sashayed past, running her hand provocatively along Luke's shoulder as she did. He smiled.

"Yup," he mused out loud. "I think a man could get to like being in the saloon business."

The woman seated across from him chuckled. "Yeah, I hear it gets mighty cold down your way in the winter."

Luke nodded. "That's why a couple of us was thinking about doing something...different. You think we could make some money at it?"

"Sure, honey. If you do, send me a letter and I—"
She stopped abruptly, her gaze focused on someone or
something across the room.

Luke followed her line of sight and realized she was
looking straight at one of the two men he'd been
watching earlier.

"Someone you know?"

"Yeah," she said, in a quiet tone that seemed more
fearful than anything else. "My, ah...gentleman
friend. He doesn't like me spending too much time
with one man. Leastways not down here." She
snatched up the gold piece and dropped it in her
cleavage. "I gotta go." She lurched to her feet.

She hesitated long enough to say, "Thanks, cowboy. It's nice to talk to someone for a change without
being... Thanks."

Luke watched her make her way through the crowd.
When she reached the man, he grabbed her hard by
the wrist and pulled her down on her knees next to
him. Luke couldn't hear the words, but he could see
the fear in her face and the rage on the man's.

Whores weren't known to keep the best company,
he told himself. It wasn't any of his concern. Without
thinking, he polished off his drink and stood to leave.
He spared the girl one last glance. It was then that he
saw the man hit her.

Her scream was hardly noticed by those in the saloon. Luke noticed, though. Damn. He kept moving
toward the door, but then he saw the man drag her to
her feet and hit her again.

Son of a bitch. He didn't care if she was a whore—
he didn't stand for men brutalizing women. He'd seen
enough of that at home. Before he realized what he
was doing, Luke shouldered through the crowd.

"Hey!" he snarled. "Let go of the lady!"

The man cut him a glance. "Ain't no lady here." He gave an ugly sort of laugh and turned back to the woman, giving her a teeth-rattling shake as he did. "Next time I tell you to do something, maybe you'll remember." With that, he made to strike her again.

"Don't." Luke grabbed the man's wrist. "Not if you want to see morning."

All eyes suddenly focused on the two men. No one moved. The place was quiet as a church on Sunday.

The saloon girl gazed up at Luke. Blood pooled at the corner of her mouth. "It's... it's all right, mister. Really," she added tearfully.

Luke ignored her plea. "I'm not going to repeat myself." His voice was deadly cold.

The man continued to hold her, predator-tight. His free hand drifted conspicuously near the Colt tied to his wool-clad thigh.

"Back off, you two!" the bartender hollered. "I ain't havin' no trouble!"

"No trouble," the man repeated loudly, in a threatening tone.

"You son of a bitch," Luke said, in an equally threatening tone, "you're buying more trouble than you ever thought existed."

The saloon girl squirmed, trying to free herself. She clawed at the man's hand. "Please, honey, let me go."

"Shut up, Millie," the man returned, with a sharp shake to make his point.

Luke narrowed his gaze. "Well, it's up to you." Luke's tone was calm, more annoyed than worried.

That seemed to give the man pause. He looked around for his friends, as if needing reassurance that they were there to back him up.

Luke stood alone. His hand steady near his .45, he knew his only trouble would be the man in front of him, or the other one, who was trying to edge into the shadows.

"Stand still," he said flatly.

Startled, the man obeyed.

Finally the one holding on to the girl said, "Mister, just *who the hell are you?*"

"I'm the last man you're going to see if you don't let go of the woman—now!"

The man's eyes widened, and slowly he released his hold. The girl snapped free and ran toward the wall.

"A wise decision," he said. With his gaze still locked on the man, Luke said, "Lady, why don't you take a walk for a while, until things cool down or sober up?"

She made a beeline for the front doors.

"What's this to you?" the man asked, more puzzled than afraid now that he'd released the girl.

Luke grabbed a fistful of jacket and dragged the man halfway across the table. "I don't like bullies or cur dogs. You, you mangy son of a bitch, are both. Don't you ever let me see you hit a woman again."

Luke released his hold so abruptly the man sprawled on the table with a groan.

Luke backed away, then turned and went out the door.

He swung up in the saddle, and was about to turn away when a small voice stopped him. "Cowboy."

He turned to see the woman, her face already turning blue on one side. His hand curled into a fist, tightening on the rein enough to make the horse shy.

"You okay?" he asked, even though the answer was obvious.

She nodded.

He'd have liked to help her more, but he knew she'd probably go right back in there. There were a lot of things he didn't understand about women, and this was sure one of them.

With a cautious glance around, she came closer. Her hand resting lightly on his knee, she craned up to look at him. "Thanks. No one's ever done anything like that for me before. If I can ever repay—"

"You're welcome. Take care of yourself, Millie."

Her smile turned into a grimace, and she touched her cut lip. "Thanks, cowboy."

He touched two fingers to the brim of his hat, then reined over and rode for home.

Chapter Eight

Rebecca tried to convince Ruth to have dinner in her room. She was willing, even eager, to dine alone with her mother-in-law. It had nothing to do with avoiding a certain handsome marshal. No, she was merely trying to be thoughtful, considerate.

Unfortunately, Ruth had other ideas.

"Rebecca," she said, obviously surprised, "I appreciate what you're saying, but I've been cooped up in this room for two days, and it's about all I can stand. Besides," she continued as she pulled her wrapper from the wardrobe, "it wouldn't be polite to leave Marshal Scanlin alone."

"I'm certain the marshal wouldn't mind. I mean, he'd understand," Rebecca went on smoothly.

"Nope." Ruth was already slipping on her brown-and-white-striped wrapper. She did up the two dozen large bone buttons down the front and tied the sash. "I may not be up to wearing corsets, but I'm looking forward to getting out of this room." She adjusted the wrapper's high collar and long sleeves, then started for the door. "You coming?" It was a rhetorical question, and she disappeared out the door as she spoke.

With a sigh of resignation, Rebecca hurried out, and they entered the dining room together. The room was cast in early-evening shadows of blue and purple. On the sideboard candles flickered, reflected in the polished silver holders. Three places were perfectly set at the far end of the table, white china and fine crystal on blue linen.

But Rebecca wasn't appreciating the Wedgwood. No, her gaze went instantly to Luke. She hadn't seen him since that little scene this morning, which had been fine by her. She didn't have another vase to offer up to the god of bad temper.

Luke was by the window, seemingly unaware of their presence. His dark outline was perfectly silhouetted against the white lace curtains.

His forest green shirt was pulled tightly across his broad shoulders, and his denim trousers fit snugly down the length of his legs. She saw him run one hand through his hair, in a gesture of thoughtfulness, or perhaps annoyance—she wasn't certain which.

What was he thinking about? Was he thinking about the kiss they'd shared, about them being in each other's arms? Her pulse moved up a peg, and a delicious shiver prickled the flesh on the backs of her legs.

Stop it! she cried inwardly. *What difference does it make?*

None, she told herself, her chin coming up in a defiant gesture. Whatever Luke thought or wanted or expected didn't matter, not one whit. *She* was in charge. This was her house. Her life. And she was smart enough to never, ever, make the same mistake twice. He was not to be trusted. Besides, to let him get too close was to risk a great deal more than her heart.

"Good evening." Ruth's voice broke the silence, and Luke turned.

His smile was immediate, and devastating to her aching nerves. Discreetly, she dragged in a calming breath.

"Good evening to you, ladies," he said, helping Ruth with her chair. "Nice to see you up and around. I guess this means you're feeling better."

"I am." Ruth scooted her chair in and craned her neck to look around at him.

Rebecca eyed him suspiciously as he helped her with her chair. Where had he been all day? she wondered, then chided herself for wondering.

A shadow of beard grazed his chin, and his eyes were a little red. When she turned slightly, there was the distinctive aroma of...whiskey. Her eyes widened. Whiskey and... She crinkled her nose, testing. Whiskey and cheap perfume.

Why, that—

Anger stirred. Here she'd been fretting and fuming and worried about seeing him again, and all the while he'd been out getting drunk and who knew what else.

It was the "what else" that made her straighten, made her lips pull back into a thin line.

Her temper, the one she'd thought she'd banished, returned to a full boil. The man had the morals of an alley cat. Not that she cared. She most certainly did not care. It was outrage, not jealousy, that made her stomach clench. Obviously, when he said he wanted her, he'd meant immediately. When she didn't acquiesce, he'd gone out and found someone else to satisfy him.

Just like before. He would get what he wanted, then move on—or, in this case, move on when he didn't get what he wanted.

Well, there was a certain satisfaction in that, anyway, she added rather smugly.

If he noticed her staring, he didn't acknowledge it.

Ruth continued speaking. "Thank you for your concern, Marshal. And thank you for your able... assistance. Up the stairs, I mean. Rebecca told me it was you who gallantly came to my assistance."

"Why, ma'am—" he chuckled as he joined them at the table "—having a lovely lady in my arms is always a pleasure." His grin was roguish, full of boyish charm that, judging by the sudden pink blush on her cheeks, Ruth wasn't immune to.

Damn the man. He'd been here less than two days, and already he'd charmed every woman in the place. Well, not every woman. Not her. Not Rebecca Tinsdale. No. She was immune to his charms.

With a sharp snap, Rebecca opened her napkin and plopped it down on her skirt. The blue linen blended with the darker blue of her skirt. Let's get this over with, she thought sharply, and rang the dinner bell so hard it was a wonder the fine crystal didn't crack.

Right on cue, Mrs. Wheeler appeared with a platter of roast pork ringed with oven-browned potatoes that smelled every bit as good as it looked.

"I made extra," she said, with a little smile very much directed at Luke. "It's nice to have a man to cook for again."

"Mrs. Wheeler," Rebecca said flatly, more than a little disgusted, "you may finish serving."

"What?" Mrs. Wheeler looked a little flustered. "Oh, right away, ma'am." With a sniff and a cough that sounded more like a choking puppy, she hurried into the kitchen and promptly returned with a basket of biscuits and a bowl of green beans cooked with fat back.

The food smelled wonderful, but Rebecca didn't have an appetite. Wordlessly she passed the platter to Luke. Their fingers brushed, and for the barest of moments their gazes met and his lingered, amusement dancing in his dark eyes, as though he knew of that little scene in her office after he left.

"So, Marshal," Ruth began as she put her napkin on her lap and accepted the bowl Rebecca passed to her, "what news do you have about my grandson?" She passed the bowl without taking any green beans.

"Nothing yet." His expression was grim, serious. "I don't know if Becky has told you, but with certain new information—" he shot her an exasperated glance but didn't mention their little discussion "—I'm convinced that someone *has* taken the boy—kidnapped him." Softly, sincerely, he continued. "I'm sorry to be blunt, but there's no sense trying to hide the truth. If I'm right, and my gut tells me that I am, then all we can do is wait."

Ruth nodded, seemed to consider what he'd said. "There must be something more we can do."

Rebecca looked up hopefully.

Luke shook his head. "I suspect we'll be getting some sort of ransom demand. I've checked at the police station for similar crimes, men with histories of kidnapping or—" Child murder, he was about to say, but thought better of it. "Anyone who might seem a logical suspect."

"And?" Ruth asked.

Luke shook his head again, raking one hand through his hair as he did. "And nothing, I'm sorry to say. I spent the afternoon on the Barbary Coast, looking around." He didn't mention that he now believed that Rebecca was right about the corruption. "It's a waiting game."

"A game," Rebecca snapped, days of fear and anger over her son's disappearance merging with fear and anger over her unwanted attraction to Luke. The feelings were too intense, too great, to be contained, and she needed to lash out at someone. "Is that what this is to you? Some kind of game? We're going insane here, trying to get through the hours, scared that every passing minute means Andrew is—" Tears pooled in her eyes and slid down her cheeks. She swiped them back with the heels of her hands. "We're terrified, and you...*you* are out drinking and...and whoring." She surged to her feet and threw her napkin down on the table.

Luke mirrored her stance. "I was not out whor—"

"Don't deny it!" She raked him with a disdainful stare. "You can't deny it. Damn you, Luke." She swiped at her tears again. "Damn you for doing this...again."

Anger clenched and unclenched in her stomach until she thought she would scream if she'd didn't get out of there. Her gaze flicked to Ruth. "I'm sorry." Her voice cracked. "I can't—"

She strode from the room.

Luke watched her go, then turned an entreating stare on Ruth, who was watching him intently.

"I have not been out drinking and whor— Sorry. But I haven't." He dropped down in the chair, the wood creaking from the sudden weight. "Dammit," he muttered, more to himself than to Ruth. "I've been on the Barbary Coast trying to gather information. I found out that she's right. It looks like there are bribes being paid to officials. Now I just have to find out who and when and how much. I have a real strong feeling that the bribery and the articles in the paper and the kidnapping are connected."

Ruth leaned forward, her arms on the edge of the table. "Are you certain?" She tilted her head to one side. "How?"

But Luke was only half listening. Jaw clenched, he had his gaze fixed on the doorway. Dollars to doorknobs this was about that kiss, both those kisses. This was about her and him. But what the hell was she so angry about?

She liked the kisses. And just about the time things were getting intense, she'd haul off and pull away, like she was scared, or like she was hiding something, something she was afraid of revealing if her guard was down. But what?

He decided to find out.

"Marshal?" Ruth's voice stopped him halfway out of his chair. "How long have you and Rebecca known each other?"

The question came out of the blue, and he was momentarily taken aback. "What? Oh, I knew her... We knew..." A little too biblical, he thought, and started again. "We were friends, oh, going on eight years ago now, I guess."

"You know, Andrew has a birthday coming up in a couple of months." Her tone was completely nonchalant, and she reached for a biscuit as she spoke. "He'll be eight."

"Really? A December baby, huh?" He smiled. "I know you're worried sick about him, and I can't blame you a bit." His gaze flicked to the doorway again. "You know if there was something more to do, I'd do it."

"I know, Marshal," she told him sincerely. "And so does Rebecca. It's just that things have been difficult for her, especially since Nathan died."

"I'm sorry about your son's death, ma'am," he said softly, with great sincerity. "I know what it's like to lose someone you love."

"Do you, Marshal?"

"Yes, ma'am. My mother died when I was a boy."

"Then you do understand, Marshal. Maybe you can also understand what it's been like for Rebecca, her folks dying so close together, then Nathan—all within a couple of years."

Luke was startled. "I didn't know...about her folks, I mean. She never said."

"No, I don't suppose she would. She's like that—strong. Never asks for help. Never likes to admit she's in trouble."

Luke made a small chuckle. "Yeah, I have noticed that about her."

"I thought you might have. But don't give up on her. She needs you, whether she says so or not."

"Needs me?" Luke repeated cautiously, wishing it was true, wishing she did need him, and not just until Andrew was home again.

"Oh, yes. You have to help us get our boy back."

"Oh," he said, a little crestfallen. "Sure. I see."

"Do you, Marshal? I wondered," Ruth muttered.

"What, ma'am?" Luke cocked his head questioningly.

"Nothing. Maybe you should go and check on her, just in case."

Luke's head came up sharply. "You think?"

"Yes. Please."

He skirted around the table, his black wool trousers catching on the linen tablecloth, and he paused to put it back in place.

"Oh, Marshal..." Her voice stopped him at the doorway.

He glanced back.

"I'm glad you're here." She smiled, and he returned the gesture.

Luke headed for the parlor and found Rebecca seated at the piano. She wasn't playing, only sitting there running her fingers noiselessly over the yellowed ivory keys.

"Becky."

She looked up, jumped, really, as though she'd come back from some great distance, and he wondered briefly why she'd been so lost in thought.

He didn't like the tears on her cheeks, or the way her skin was funereally pale. Damn. Had he done that?

"Becky, honey, please don't cry. I didn't—"

He started toward her, wanting to explain, to soothe, to hold her and make it all better.

"No more, Luke." She shook her head and held up one hand. "No more."

He stopped near the settee, one hand curving over the smooth wood trim. "About today... what I said—"

"It doesn't matter."

"Of course it matters." At least it mattered to him, and he wanted it to matter to her. "Becky, I wasn't doing what you think I was doing. I was trying to get a lead on Andrew's kidnappers.''

"Of course you were," she said, in a tone that belied her words.

He ran his hands through his hair, leaving deep furrows in the inky blackness. "Dammit. Becky, I'm telling you the truth."

"Luke, you came in here smelling like a saloon..." She lightly tapped one piano key. The deep bass tone seemed to vibrate through the room. "You've been gone most of the day, for some meeting that was so important you had to go, but not so important that you remembered to tell me." She struck the next note. "Then you expect me to believe whatever you say?"

"Yes." His tone was adamant.

She craned her neck to look at him. "Why? Why should I believe you? I believed you once before, and look what happened."

"What?" He arched one brow in question and took another half step toward her. The air in the room seemed suddenly charged. "What are you talking about?"

"I'm talking about eight years ago." She closed the piano case with infinite slowness. "I'm talking about a young girl who believed that you loved her. I'm talking about a young girl who loved you enough to give you everything she had, and then you left."

Her words, her truth, hit him like a fence post in the chest. And just as though he'd been struck, he dragged in a lungful of air, then another, letting the words penetrate his mind as the oxygen did his body. "Oh, God, Becky. I didn't know. I *swear,* I didn't know." This time he did close on her, and, taking her shoulders in his hands, he lifted and turned her to face him. She refused to look at him, and that was the worst hurt of all.

She twisted away easily. "How could you not know? Did you think I was in the habit of having sex with every man I knew?"

"Becky, don't." His expression was grim. Of all the things he'd expected—accusations, threats, denial—he hadn't expected this, and he wasn't quite certain how to deal with it. Was this the reason she pulled away every time he got close?

He cursed himself for every kind of a selfish fool. She had loved him.

You had it all, Scanlin, and you walked away. Now it's too late.

The hell it was, came the resounding answer. If he'd had her love once, then he would win it again.

With all the tenderness and honesty he possessed, he said, "I was barely twenty. I'd been on my own since I was fourteen. I didn't know anything about love, about how it was between a man and a woman who cared for each other. All I'd ever known were whores, and—"

"And still do, I see." Sarcasm dripped from her voice, and his temper overcame his good sense.

He grabbed her by the shoulders and turned her to face him. "Look at me!"

She did, and the hurt and distrust in her eyes was like a living entity. It was enough to make him pull her into his embrace. "I'm sorry, honey. I'm sorry for a great many things," he said against the top of her head. Her hair was silky on his cheek, and the scent of her rose perfume tantalized his nostrils.

Gently he put her away from him, never releasing his hold completely. She was limp in his arms.

"I was not with another woman today. Not the way you mean. Yes, I was in a saloon. Actually I was in several. Yes, I talked to a woman. I did not, *did not*, make love to her."

For a full ten seconds, she studied him, and he held her gaze, refusing to look away, wanting her to know, to understand, the truth of his words.

Then, just when he thought perhaps she did, she looked away, and he felt his heart sink. "I believed you once. I can't, I won't, risk it again." She dropped down onto the piano stool, lifted the cover and began to play a sad, melodic tune. He didn't know its name, but the tone was clear. She was giving up on him. But he damned well wasn't giving up on her, or them.

"No, you don't, woman. You're going to believe me if I have to—"

The hollow thud of bare knuckles on wood caught their attention. Rebecca hurried to the front door, Luke close on her heels.

A young boy, not more than ten, stood there. His face was smudged, his dirty blond hair unkempt. His blue shirt was about two sizes too big, and his brown britches were riding a little high at the ankles.

"Yes?" Luke snarled. He wanted to finish his conversation with Rebecca. "What do you want?"

"I want the lady," the boy said firmly.

"What lady?"

"That one." He gestured with fingers that hadn't seen a washbowl in days.

Ruth joined them. "What's going on?"

"That's what we're trying to find out," Luke returned, exasperated.

The boy pulled a wadded-up piece of paper out of his pocket and offered it to Rebecca.

Her heart stilled, then took on a frantic beat. She knew this was it, this was what she'd been waiting for, praying for, yet she couldn't seem to take the note.

When she didn't, Luke did.

One eye on the boy, he scanned the note.

Bring ten thousand dollars at 9 tonight to the alley behind the So Different saloon, or the boy will be killed.

"Who gave you this, boy?" Luke demanded.

"A man down on Broadway. He gave me a silver dollar to fetch it up here to you."

"And I'll give you five more if you'll tell me the man's name." Luke fished in his pocket and snapped the greenback temptingly in front of the boy's face.

The boy's eyes widened. "Ain't nobody givin' names down there, mister."

"Have you ever seen him before?"

Even as Luke spoke, the boy was shaking his head and inching backward toward the open door. Luke caught him by one small shoulder. "Tell me what the man looked like."

The boy's brown eyes widened in fear, and he struggled to twist loose from Luke's grip. "Let me go, mister. I ain't done nothin'."

Luke held firm, but he did drop down on one knee to look the lad in the eye. "Look, a boy, a little younger than you, is in trouble. We're trying to help him. Do you understand?"

The boy stilled and nodded.

Cautiously Luke released his grip. "Please—tell us what the man looked like."

"Honest, mister. I'd help you if I could. The man come up to me and says to take the note here and he gives me the dollar." The boy produced the shiny coin, as if to validate his statement.

"But you must have seen him."

The boy shoved the coin back in his pocket. "He was tall...like you. I ain't never seen him before. Honest." He held up his hand in a pledge. "He was wearin' a hat and a black coat, kinda fancy-like. I couldn't see his face, 'cause it's dark out, and—" He took an instinctive step backward again.

"Okay." Luke fished in his pocket and produced a two-fifty gold piece, which he tossed the boy. "If you see the man again, come and tell me, and there's another one of these for your trouble."

The boy beamed. "Yes, sir, Mr.—"

"Marshal Scanlin."

"Marshal Scanlin," the boy happily repeated before he turned and ran off into the night.

Rebecca turned to Luke. "Is Andrew alive?" Her voice was a tremulous whisper.

"Yes," he said adamantly. He handed her the note and watched as she read and reread it. She kept staring at the crumpled yellow paper until finally he slipped it from her fingers.

To no one in particular, she said, "They want money, a lot of money, or they are going to...kill Andrew." Her voice broke. The world seemed to tilt on its axis. She dragged in some air and told herself in no uncertain terms that she was going to get him back.

Then reality hit her. "It's Saturday night. The banks are closed," she mumbled. She turned a terrified gaze on Ruth, who was looking as pale as winter snow. Rebecca continued, "I don't have that kind of cash in the house." Or anywhere else, she suddenly realized.

"Where am I going to get the money?"

Chapter Nine

She needed money, and she had three hours to get it.

"What about the bank?" Luke prompted.

"The bank is closed." She paced away toward the bottom of the stairs and back.

"They'd open for you," Luke suggested. He wished like hell *he* had the money. He didn't. He had about forty bucks in his pocket, and another fifty in his saddlebags. Hardly a drop in the bucket.

"Open the bank," she repeated numbly.

"Yes. Of course. I mean, they do that kind of thing for—" for rich people, he meant to say, but couldn't.

"There isn't that much cash." She turned to him, her eyes wide as a frightened doe's. "Everything is tied up in stocks, bonds, annuities, mortgages. Why would they wait until the banks were closed, until I didn't have a chance to borrow—" Her expression lit up. "Borrow," she repeated. "Yes, that's it!" Grabbing her coat, she charged for the door.

Luke was so startled, it took him a couple of seconds to react. When he did, he snatched his hat and jacket from the mirrored hall tree and raced after her. "Where are you going?" he demanded, keeping pace with her as she went to the stable.

She ignored him, ordering the stable boy to hitch the buggy.

Luke circled around in front of her. "Where are you going?"

"Edward." She paced back and forth like a caged tigress, straw crunching under her shoes and clinging to her hem. "Edward can give me the money." Then, to the stable boy, she said, "Hurry, John. Hurry."

"You mean that pompous—" He ground his jaw shut to keep from finishing the statement. She was in trouble, and now was not the time to evaluate her . . . friend. It stuck in his gut like a lump of dried mush, this helpless feeling. Needing to keep busy, he helped the stable boy finish the hitching.

As he snapped the last ring, she was already climbing up onto the black leather seat.

"I'm coming with you," Luke said in a no-nonsense tone, and swung up beside her as the stable boy ran and opened the double doors.

She gave him the briefest of looks, as though to say, "Are you sure?" or "Thanks"—he wasn't certain which. He only knew that there was no way in hell he was letting her go alone.

With a sharp snap, he slapped the leather reins on the horse's rump, and they lurched out of the stable.

"Which way?" he shouted as they cleared the gate.

"Left!" She grabbed the edge of the seat as they made the turn at breakneck speed. The horse's hooves beat a tattoo on the pavement as they careened through residential neighborhoods. Rebecca shouted directions at every turn, praying that Edward was at home and not out at some meeting or social fund-raiser for his upcoming campaign.

They turned on Jackson, then Leavenworth, the oak trees whizzing past like silent sentinels. The only light was from the moon and the lights that shone in the windows of houses.

"There!" She pointed. "The pale blue one near the corner!"

Luke reined up sharply, the horse skidding so hard he nearly sat down in the harness.

She was out of the buggy and up the sidewalk before he could help her.

Luke stayed in the buggy. He might have driven her here, but he didn't have to watch. He hated that she had to do this, hated it even more that she was going to another man for help.

Rebecca pounded on the door, her heart in frantic rhythm with her urgent knocking.

"Edward! Come on. Come on." She shifted from one foot to the other, the wood planks creaking and giving with each motion. Why didn't they answer the door? This was taking too long, and—

The door swung open. She pushed past a uniformed butler with gray hair and a gaping expression. "Ma'am?"

"Edward," she demanded, already handing the butler her coat. "Mr. Pollard. Where is he?"

"Ma'am, I—"

Edward stepped out of the dining room, a dinner napkin in his hand. His white shirt was in stark contrast to his midnight blue suit. "Rebecca, what a pleasant surprise!" He dabbed at his mouth. "Won't you join me for—"

"Edward, thank goodness you're home!" Heart pounding in her chest, she rushed toward him. Her hair came down from her pins, and she blew it back. "You've got to help me." Her tone was desperate.

"Certainly." His fine blond brows drew down in concern. "Rebecca. What's happened?"

She allowed him to wrap her in the curve of his arm and escort her into the parlor. She could feel the warmth of his hand through the fabric of her blouse. Oddly, his touch was not comforting, and she stepped free and circled around a burgundy settee.

The room was dungeon-dark, paneled as it was in walnut. Not at all to her taste. The furniture was equally dark, burgundy brocade. Matching crystal gas lamps on either side of the mantel provided the only illumination. The drapes were open, as were the French doors.

Night air and the first traces of fog wafted into the room, like mist in a graveyard. She snatched back the direction of her thoughts.

"Edward, please. I need money. A great deal of money. I need it now!"

"Is it Andrew?"

"Oh, Edward..." Gut-wrenching fear consumed her until she thought she would surely collapse from the pain. "I've received a ransom note."

"Oh, no." He sank down on the settee.

"They want ten thousand dollars. *Tonight*."

He visibly stilled. "Do you have that much cash?"

"No." She paced to the double doors. The camel-back mantel clock tick-tocked, losing pace with her increasing urgency, and she turned back to Edward.

"You know I'll help you any way I can." He stood and went purposefully to his desk. "I have some cash here, and I could write a check—" As he produced the dark blue checkbook, he looked up in sudden realization. "That won't help, will it?"

"No." She shook her head again. "They want *cash*, or they are going to kill Andrew." She clenched and unclenched her fists until her hands ached. "Please, Edward. You've got to go to the bank and get the money."

Their gazes met, but then he looked away. Eyes downcast, he lowered himself into his chair. "You know I'd do anything for you, but—"

She raced to the desk. "It's a loan, Edward. You know I'm good for it."

"Rebecca..." he began already shaking his head. "That's a great deal of money. The bank is closed until Monday."

"Yes, I know that," she snapped, impatiently wondering if he was being deliberately dense. "I wouldn't be here otherwise. You are a vice president of the bank. Surely you can—"

"But that's just it. I don't own it. The board of directors would have to make such a decision, and they're...well..." Frowning he absently fingered some papers there. "I don't know if they can be reached." Even in this dim light, he refused to meet her eyes. "I know Mr. Wilson left town yesterday for his daughter's wedding in Los Angeles, and I think Mr. Rubens was planning to accompany him. Without them..." He made a helpless gesture.

"Edward, please." She braced her hands on opposite sides of the desk. "This is my son."

"I know. I know." He reached in his desk and produced a small metal box, flipping open the lid to reveal cash. "I'll give you all that I have on hand— about eight hundred dollars."

"Not enough." She slammed her hand on the smooth walnut surface of his desk for emphasis.

"I'd help you if I could, you know that. I mean—"

"I've got to have that money!" she raged.

"Isn't there some other way? Something you could sell, perhaps?"

"Sell? What would I sell at this time of night? My house? My jewels? My— Of course!" She turned on her heel and rushed from the room. Snatching her coat from the hall tree, she didn't bother to put it on as she practically ran up the walk toward Luke.

It struck her then that she was somehow glad he was there waiting for her, strong and tall and steady. It felt reassuring to see him there.

Luke saw her bolt out of the house and tear down the steps. Moonlight filtered through the oak trees, casting the ground in moving shadows, and he strained to see her expression. That damned bastard had better have given her the money, or else he—

One close look at her face, and he knew the answer.

"What happened?" he asked, his voice deadly quiet.

"Edward can't give me the money without the board of directors' approval, and they're unavailable." She struggled into her coat and shoved her disheveled hair back from her face.

"Why, that son of a bitch…" He started toward the house. He'd get that money for her, one way or another. "I'll tell him about approval," he snarled. She stopped him with a touch.

"No, Luke, there isn't time."

He helped her into the buggy. He'd remember this night and that bastard, and sooner or later their paths would cross again.

He swung up on the buggy seat. "Don't worry, honey. I'll figure out something. Hell, just say the word and I'll rob that damned bank for you."

"This is no time for jokes. I—"

"I'm not joking. I've never been more serious. You need money, and I'll get it for you." His expression was as hard as granite. "Whatever it takes to get the boy back."

"I believe you're serious," she said into the sudden quiet.

"Damn straight. Hell, I'm half outlaw anyway. Gotta be, in my line of work."

She believed him. Believed he'd rob a bank for her if she asked him. Not because she asked him, because he was determined to help her and Andrew, with no thought for himself.

In that instant, everything changed. Fears faded and were replaced with a new emotion, familiar yet vague. But there was no time to examine it more closely now.

She touched him on the arm, feeling the soft cotton of his shirt and the hard tendons of the work-toughened muscles beneath. "Thank you for your offer," she said softly, sincerely. "It's not necessary. Just get me home."

"All right." Luke slammed back into the seat, slapped the reins hard on the horse's rump, and they took off. The wheels made a high-pitched whine that was the melody to the pounding staccato of the horse's hooves as they retraced their path.

All the while, the clock was running out. "Okay, how about this?" he said, making the turn onto Pine

Street. "I'll go to the meeting place. I'll pretend to have the money. Then, when they hand over the boy, I'll—"

"No! I'm not taking any chances. I can get the money."

"How?"

They pulled into the stable, and Rebecca jumped down the instant the buggy stopped. The horse pawed the straw-covered floor, seeming to sense the tension. "Leave him," she instructed the stable boy and, hitching up her skirt, she ran full out for the house. Luke followed.

He caught up to her in her office. She was rummaging through papers.

"What are you doing?"

She didn't even look up. Papers scattered like leaves until she found the one she was looking for. She held it high like a trophy. "This." She waved the paper. "It's an offer to buy the paper. I've had it for several weeks. It's exactly enough money, and they said the offer was good indefinitely."

Luke eyed the proposal suspiciously. "How's that help?"

"Because they offered cash. Some eastern group who want to branch out. See?" She waved the papers under his nose, her finger tapping the pages. "If they want it, they can have it, but they've got to give me the money *tonight*."

She scrawled her name on the document in the required places. "Let's go." She breezed past him, and he fell in step behind her.

"Where to?"

"The lawyer's office."

Ruth was halfway up the stairs when they started down. "Did you see Edward? Did you—" She turned as Rebecca and Luke charged past.

"No," Rebecca called over her shoulder as she headed for the door.

"No?" Ruth shouted from her place on the stairs. "What do you mean, no?"

Rebecca stopped long enough to give Ruth the barest details. "Edward can't help without the board of directors' approval."

"What are we going to do? I've got some cash upstairs. Maybe they'll take less, or—"

"I'm selling the paper." She waved the documents in verification of her statement.

"No, Rebecca, you can't! That paper is every—"

"It's nothing if I lose Andrew. We're on our way to the lawyer's house. They offered cash, and if he's got it, then we're set."

"And if not?"

Rebecca stood very still. For a full ten seconds, she didn't speak, didn't move. Then she said simply, "He must."

With Luke at her side, they drove out of the yard.

She gave instructions, and Luke followed them. Occasionally he stole a quick glance in her direction. Her delicate face was bathed in moonlight. Her chin was set, rigid, actually, and she kept her eyes focused straight ahead.

He could only begin to imagine what was going on in her mind. Perhaps the realization that she could have her son back in a few hours if, and only if, she could raise the money.

Damn, he wished he could do this for her. He wished he'd found the boy days ago, but it was a big city, and looking for one small boy was like looking for the proverbial needle in a haystack.

It galled him that he was so helpless in this, that he could only drive her around and wait while she begged for help, for money. A fierce protectiveness welled up in him—not that it did much good.

There wasn't anything he could do except stand by and wait, and waiting was not something he did well. No, Luke Scanlin was not known for his patience, nor was he known for his willingness to forgive and forget. He wouldn't forget this night, or that bastard, Edward, who wouldn't help her.

There were only two things that mattered in her life, and now she'd have to sell one to save the other.

This goddamned lawyer better have the money.

Fifteen minutes later, they pulled up at the lawyer's home—white clapboard with dark green gingerbread trim.

This time, when she bolted from the buggy, Luke jumped down and went along. This time, they were getting the money. There'd be no taking advantage of her—not now. It was the least he could do.

Ten long steps up the front walk to the wooden porch. A hideous little gargoyle stood guard outside the door. Luke knocked on the door. He could see lights on through the stained-glass panels.

The door swung wide. A portly man of about forty, with thinning brown hair, answered the knock.

"Mrs. Tinsdale. What a pleasant surprise. I wasn't expecting you. Please come in." Smiling, he stepped aside.

"Mr. Handley." Rebecca walked past him into the small, square entryway. "I apologize for the late hour but I've come to see you about that offer to buy the *Times*."

He shot Luke a questioning glance. "I don't believe we've met, sir. Frank Handley." He offered his hand.

"Luke Scanlin. U.S. marshal for this region." Luke wasn't one for titles, but under the circumstances, he thought this was a good time to use his. Just to let the man know there'd be no deceptions—not tonight, not with Becky.

His handshake stopped in midmotion, and his gaze flew to Luke's face. "Marshal? Did you say marshal?"

"That's right. Is there a problem?"

"What? Oh, no." He released Luke's hand abruptly. "I was just startled, is all. Maybe I should ask you the same thing?"

"Everything's fine . . . so far," Luke returned politely, but didn't bother to smile.

"Good. Well, please, since this is business, let's go into the office."

He led the way down the narrow, carpeted hall beside the stairs, to a room near the back of the house. The gas wall sconces were barely a flicker, and he turned them up, the gas flame hissing in response.

The office was barely ten by ten, just enough room for a small mahogany desk, one matching file cabinet and two Windsor chairs.

"Have a seat, won't you?"

Rebecca took the chair by the warming stove.

"I'll stand," Luke said at the lawyer's questioning glance.

"Suit yourself."

"I always do."

Luke folded his arms across his chest and leaned one shoulder against the smooth doorframe, effectively blocking the doorway.

The lawyer hardly hesitated. He was good, Luke thought with grudging admiration, and he should know. He'd seen enough of them over the years, what with trials and all.

Rebecca broke in. "Mr. Handley, about the sale."

Frank Handley circled around his desk and sat down, his swivel chair squeaking as he twisted.

"I've brought the papers, signed." She balanced them on her lap. "You had said cash. Is that right?"

"Yes, that's right."

"Here. Now," Luke clarified from his place in the doorway.

"Yes. I have the cash in the safe."

Rebecca straightened, and Luke could see her sigh. There was even the barest hint of a smile. "Fine. Then we have a deal."

She stood and offered him the papers, which he accepted. He glanced at the signature, then went to a safe hidden behind a painting—so obvious an idiot could have spotted it.

Thirty seconds, and the small door swung open with a squeak. He produced a tan envelope bulging with cash, which he handed to Rebecca.

"You're welcome to count it, if you like."

She clutched the envelope to her as though her life depended on it. In a way, it did. It *would* save her life, for God knew that if she lost Andrew, her life wouldn't be worth living.

"No, that's all right, Mr. Handley. I trust you."

She started for the door. Luke blocked her path. They exchanged a glance. His gaze quickly flicked to the lawyer, the one who was Cheshire-cat pleased with himself. Something about the man bothered Luke. Maybe it was that there had been no haggling, no discussing, no questions. Maybe it was that the money had just been sitting there waiting, as though they'd known she'd sell.

Oh, hell, it was more likely that his suspicious nature was getting the better of him. After all, the offer had been made weeks ago, and, she hadn't turned them down, so why shouldn't the money be sitting here waiting?

Still, his male pride, pride that was all tied up in knots because he couldn't reach in his pocket and produce the needed money, made him say, "You sure about this?" His tone was executioner-quiet.

"I am."

He saw tears pool in her eyes, and that helpless feeling inside him quickly turned to rage.

He let her pass, though it felt more as if he were letting her go. Somehow he was going to make this up to her. Somehow he was going to make her see that even though he didn't have thousands in the bank, he was still the one she needed.

The ride back to the house was somber. She had the money, but the cost he knew had been terribly high. The paper was her heart. Andrew was her soul.

"I'm sorry this is happening, Becky."

She nodded, clutching the envelope to her breasts. "I have the money, that's all that matters. Andrew is all that matters."

The horse's hooves click-clacking on the street and the hum of the buggy wheels irritated her already throbbing nerves. Houses, lights blazing, passed like soldiers in review, while oak trees stood shadowy sentry duty. There was no breeze, just the light gray misting of the incoming fog.

"You know, I can't help wondering why that lawyer had the money on hand, instead of in a bank." Luke shifted the reins to one hand.

"The offer said cash," Rebecca explained. "It was supposed to be an incentive. No lengthy paperwork, no financing."

"But cash? I mean, most people, when they say cash, they mean in a bank, write a check, that kind of cash."

"I don't know, and I don't care. All I know is, I've got *exactly* the amount of money I need. What time is it?"

He fished his watch out of his pocket and clicked open the cover, twisting it to catch enough moonlight to read it. "Eight. We've got an hour."

He let her off in front of the house, and watched her hurry up the walk before he drove the buggy around to the stable.

"Put it away," he told the boy. He saddled his horse and led him around to the front. There was at least one thing he could do. He could deliver the ransom. Walking into dark alleys was something he was all too familiar with. If someone was going to get hurt, it wasn't going to be her.

The entryway was empty when he walked in. He went upstairs and found Ruth with Rebecca, in her bedroom.

The room was large, square, and conspicuously feminine. All soft shades of blue and green. There was lace at the windows and lace trim on the bed coverings. The furniture was cherry, polished to a gleaming shine. It looked just the way he would have imagined Becky's room.

"You okay?" he asked, knowing she was far from it, but needing to say something, needing to let her know he was there for her.

"Yes." Her back was to him. She was rummaging in her wardrobe cabinet. "I'll be ready in a few minutes."

"Ready?" He arched one brow suspiciously. "Ready for what?"

Her head snapped around. "Why, to go, of course." She pulled out a black riding skirt and a dark print blouse.

"Just where is it you think you're going? I'm taking the money."

"I thought you'd say that."

"So?"

"I'm going with you." She dropped down in a chair and hitched her skirt to her knees, then started undoing the buttons on her shoes as if he weren't standing ten feet away, gaping at her stocking-clad ankle.

His mouth dropped open. He snapped it shut. The woman was more brazen, more stubborn, than most men.

He shot a help-me glance at Ruth, who shrugged helplessly.

Okay, then, he'd handle this himself. Taking a firm step into the room, feet braced, he gave her his sternest look. The one that had made Johnny Jenks think twice, then decide surrender was better than dying. "I—" he emphasized the singular word "—am making the delivery. *You* are not coming along."

That fierce look of his failed miserably. The woman didn't even hesitate. "Yes." She tossed her shoes aside and pulled her blouse free of her waistband, shooting him an impatient look. "I am."

"No," he countered, as though he were talking to a headstrong child. "You aren't. You don't know what we're dealing with here. I do this for a living, remember?"

With cold determination in her eyes, she advanced on him. He held his ground, though he'd seen kinder looks in the eyes of warring Comanches.

Ruth spoke up from her place near the foot of the bed. "I tried to tell her it was too dangerous."

"Thank you," he said, in a smug confirmation that didn't slow Rebecca's advance one iota.

"Now, you listen to me." She jabbed the tips of two fingers in his chest, and he flinched in surprise. "I'm going. That's *my* son. It's *my* money, and—"

"I know it's *your* money, dammit. I just drove you all over town to get it," he snapped, still smarting from the frustration and the blow to his pride.

"Either you take me, or I go alone. But make no mistake, Scanlin—I'm going. Now..." She jabbed him again, and this time he retreated a half step. Comanches could take lessons from her. "You coming with me or not?"

"Dammit, Becky, you can't—"

"Yes or no, Scanlin. Those are the only words I want to hear."

"This is wrong. It's dangerous as hell."

"Yes or no."

He didn't doubt for one second that she was bullheaded enough to do exactly what she said. Trouble was, she'd probably get herself, and maybe that boy, killed in the process.

Every instinct he had was screaming that this was a big, big mistake.

He was cornered.

"All right!"

"What?" she countered, with a smugness that rankled his dangerously short temper.

"Yes, I'm coming with you."

"Fine." She turned away, already beginning to unbutton her blouse. "Now get out of here so I can change."

Ten minutes later, Luke was still fuming.

He paced the length of the entryway. He'd had a Missouri mule once with a gentler disposition than her. He clenched his jaw so hard, pain inched down his neck and up behind his eyes.

Yeah. Okay. He knew she was worried about the boy. So was he. He knew she'd been frantic. He would be, also, if it were his son.

He kept pacing, his boots making hollow thuds on the polished planks.

Yeah, he also understood that sitting around doing nothing, waiting, wasn't his style—or hers, obviously.

But this was dangerous, more dangerous than she could begin to understand, and he didn't have time to explain the fine points of the outlaw mentality. How they were about as trustworthy and honorable as rabid wolves. Make that hungry, rabid wolves.

He should have been in that alley an hour ago. He should have gotten there first so that there would be no chance of a trap, no chance of being surprised. As it was, with all this running around trying to get the ransom, they'd make the deadline with only minutes to spare. That triggered a warning bell in his mind. He didn't have time to think about it now, but later, after everyone was home, then . . . He nodded thoughtfully to himself.

For about the tenth time in as many minutes, he checked his .45, the one he had tied low on his right thigh. He hefted the gun, testing the cylinder, the weight and feel, as though he were shaking hands with an old friend. Yeah, he mused, slipping the weapon smoothly into the worn holster, sometimes this was his only friend. Tonight he also had a .32 in a shoulder holster under his jacket. Just in case.

He paced away again, this time to stand in the open doorway. The sky was filled with stars, like diamonds on a jeweler's black velvet cloth. The moon was half-full, the other half faintly visible, like a shadow. It was hard to believe that something so terrible was happening on such a beautiful night. It was a night for lovers, just enough chill in the air for a man to put his arm around his girl under the pretense of keeping her warm.

Yeah, a night for lovers. Too bad he and Becky weren't going out somewhere, maybe to a restaurant or a theater. He'd like that.

Instead, he was taking her into an alley on the Barbary Coast. If it weren't so awful, it would be appropriately funny. They were about as opposite as the Barbary Coast and Nob Hill, he mused, not for the first time.

He sucked in a slow breath to calm his nerves. His heart pounded heavily in his chest, and his fingers curled and uncurled in a nervous gesture. Yes, he was nervous. The famous Luke Scanlin was downright scared.

He'd faced outlaws and Indians, robbers and range wars, but this was different. All those other times, nothing had mattered. He'd had nothing to lose but his life, which he'd always figured wasn't worth much anyway. He'd had no family who'd miss him or mourn. Hell, he'd barely had enough money to get himself buried, whenever that necessity arose.

He leaned one shoulder against the doorjamb and settled his battered old Stetson a little lower on his forehead.

All evening he'd hardly been able to keep his thoughts on the business at hand. His mind had been on that revelation of hers. She'd said she had loved him. All those years ago, Rebecca had loved him.

He shook his head in disbelief. He could have had it all. This could have been his.

He made a derisive sound in the back of his throat. Not this, he thought, glancing over his shoulder at the mansion spread out behind him. But he could have had Rebecca. Maybe they would have had a child, a son.

Becky's child. That thought settled gently in his mind. He'd like that—like that a lot.

He wanted her. He had realized after that first kiss that he had always wanted her, had come back to claim her. But was it too late?

Abruptly he lifted away from the doorframe. He had work to do, a child to bring home, and a woman—his woman—to protect.

His arm brushed against the gun securely tucked in the shoulder holster under his jacket. He adjusted it to a more comfortable position.

A glance at the clock on the mantel in the parlor showed it was twenty to nine. He'd already been to the stables and had another horse saddled for her. He stopped pacing at the bottom of the stairs.

"Becky—"

He broke off when he spotted her on the top step. She was dressed in a black split skirt that brushed the tops of her riding boots. The ebony buttons down the front were unfastened, revealing the split in the skirt. She wore another of those high-necked blouses, this one in a navy blue print. Her hair was down, tied back with a ribbon.

She looked a little pale, dark smudges obvious under her eyes. Her usually sensuous mouth was drawn into a thin line. She was tired, and more than a little afraid, he knew, and he remembered her tremulous voice when she'd admitted that weakness to him.

He wanted to pull her into his arms, to hold her, to tell her that he would bring her son home. She could trust him. She could believe in him. Sadly, he knew now that he'd destroyed her trust once before. But times had changed, and so had he. He was going to regain her trust, and then her love.

First, he was going to get that boy back.

Ruth was hot on Rebecca's heels. "Now be careful. Don't take any chances." She shook her finger in admonition.

"I won't." Rebecca pulled on her black kid gloves.

Ruth was still talking as they joined Luke near the door.

He picked up the shotgun he had propped beside the mirrored hall tree.

"Get Andrew and get the blazes out of there."

"I will," Rebecca said.

She raked Luke with an appraising stare that focused mostly on the arsenal he had with him. "Is that necessary?"

"Yes, and *this* isn't up for discussion."

She shook her head and gave Ruth a quick kiss on the cheek.

"Rebecca," Ruth said as they started out the door, "bring our boy back. I—" She broke off and swiped briskly at the tears in her eyes. "When you see him, tell him I love him."

They hugged again. Then, abruptly, Rebecca pulled back. "I know, Ruth. I'll tell him. No one is going to take your grandson away from you." She turned and went out the front door.

Luke followed and motioned toward the waiting horses. "More manageable, less conspicuous," he said at her questioning glance.

"All right."

He gave her a leg up.

"Sidesaddles." He said it like a curse, then swung up onto his horse. The gelding pawed and pranced sideways, seeming to sense the tensions of his rider.

The night was oddly still and empty. No traffic, no pedestrians. A quiet residential neighborhood.

On the Barbary Coast, however, it was the shank of the evening, and things were just heating up, so to speak.

Rebecca stared in obvious amazement at the gaudy buildings that lined both sides of Pacific Street. Men gathered on street corners to drink openly, leer, and make comments that were lewd enough to make her blush.

Half-naked women leaned out of second-story windows, yoo-hooing to Luke and any other man who'd give them notice. In the bay beyond, two dozen ships, sails rolled and tied, bobbed in the harbor, while moonlight glistened on the moving water, making it look silver-bright.

The distinct smell of salt water and cheap whiskey irritated her nostrils. Somewhere close, there was an alley where she'd hand over money and ride home with her son.

She tried to focus on the street ahead, though she watched Luke out of the corner of her eye. He looked dark and powerful and more like an outlaw than a marshal. She saw a muscle flex in his jaw and knew he was tense, nervous about this exchange.

But she was confident. Yes, she understood there was the potential for danger. After all, those involved were ruthless enough to take her child. Still, they had asked for money, which she'd brought. They wanted the money, and she wanted her child.

It'll be fine. She said the words over and over in her mind, like a litany. Needing to hold on to the thought and the promise.

"We're almost there," Luke's voice startled her, and she jumped, instinctively tightening her grip on the reins. The horse sidestepped in response, and she steadied the mare with a pat.

A drunk staggered into their path and, frightened, she reined in sharply. The cowboy wandered away, seemingly not even realizing they were there.

It was with a shaky smile of relief that she cut a glance in Luke's direction. But he wasn't looking at her. His expression was cold, harder than granite, and his hand rested conspicuously on his gun.

Just as quickly, she saw him relax, saw his hand move down to rest lightly on his wool-clad thigh.

"Here." He gestured with his head, never looking at her.

Luke nudged his horse in front of her, and both horses stopped at the gnarled hitching rail in front of the So Different gambling hall. Men milled around on the boardwalk, and the sound of distinctly feminine laughter carried outside over the sound of a reed organ.

Tying his horse, he came around to help Rebecca. His hands closed around her waist, and he felt the stiff bone stays of her corset beneath her blouse. As he lifted her down, her hands naturally rested on the tops of his shoulders, and he could feel the tightening of her fingers for that instant she was suspended in the air.

Instinctively their gazes sought each other. Black eyes locked with royal blue as she slid down the front of him. It was a simple motion, not uncommon, yet for them it was highly provocative, and each of them tensed with sudden awareness.

Lost in the sensation, the closeness, Luke hesitated, his hands tightening perceptibly at the longing that surged through him.

As though she sensed his awareness, her lips parted, the words she'd meant to say unspoken as she lost herself in the depths of his bottomless black eyes. Her breath came in shallow gulps, and she thought she saw his head dip when—

"Hey, lady!"

That quickly, the spell was broken, and Luke released her, stepping back. Rebecca fussed with straightening her blouse.

"Hey, lady!" a young sailor carefully enunciated from his place near the batwing saloon doors. His face mottled red, his blond hair sticking out in haphazard directions, he staggered toward them, catching himself on the porch post with an elbow. "You wanna dwink?" He waved a half-full bottle of Kendall's whiskey in her direction.

Luke was making a show of tying up the horses. Not because they needed to be tied, but because he was trying to get his breathing back to something close to normal. So he only spared the man a quick appraisal. "Drunk and working on being disorderly," he told Rebecca, then told the sailor, "No, she doesn't."

Rebecca didn't feel quite as confident as Luke about dealing with an inebriated man and, though he did seem frightfully young and was unarmed, she edged a little closer to Luke.

Luke wasn't worried about the sailor as much as what was waiting for them in that alley about twenty feet away. "He's just feeling his oats."

Luke took the money from the saddlebags, where he'd put it earlier. It was hard to believe that ten thousand dollars could make such a small package. Men worked their whole lives for this much money, and here it was all tied up in a nice little parcel.

"Let's go. The alley is over here." He remembered the locale from his trip earlier today, and was glad now that he'd done a little scouting around, even if it had cost him yet another argument with Becky.

Giving the sailor a wide berth, he escorted Rebecca onto the walkway. But the sailor was evidently determined not to take no for an answer. He cut across their path, waving the bottle under Rebecca's nose this time.

"Come on, 'oney," he slurred, taking a long swallow of the caramel-colored liquid, a small trickle dribbling down his chin. He grinned, then wiped the top of the bottle on his blue woolen sleeve with an unsteady flourish.

"''ave a taste." He shoved the bottle in her direction, his hand slamming into her breast.

"No!" she screamed, more disgusted than fearful.

Faster than she could blink, Luke grabbed two fistfuls of the man's shirt and, in one motion, slammed him up against the wall. The bottle crashed to the ground, the glass breaking with a sharp clink and the remaining liquid running between the cracks in the walkway.

That was when she realized Luke's gun was jammed tight under the sailor's chin. Good Lord, she hadn't even seen him draw. The look on his face was hangman-cold, and sent an icy shiver up her spine.

"''ey," the sailor mumbled, trying to move and seeming confused about why he couldn't.

When the man touched Becky, rage had exploded red-hot in Luke's brain, and he took it out on this unwary victim.

"The lady is with me." Luke shook the man, whose reddened eyes widened in surprise. "Don't touch her. No one touches her."

The sailor's head bobbed up and down like a rag doll's.

"Luke," Rebecca begged, pulling uselessly on his arm, "don't hurt him. He didn't mean anything. He just scared me."

Luke's eyes were sharp with fury. "Don't you think I know he scared you?" He shook the man again. "Did he hurt you?" He slammed the squirming sailor against the wall with a head-banging thud that made him groan.

A crowd had gathered. Miners, cowboys, saloon girls, all staring at her, at them. Embarrassment replaced fear in Rebecca.

Someone offered three-to-one odds on the "cowboy"—Luke, she supposed. Oh, God, this was awful.

"Luke." She tugged on his elbow, harder this time. "I'm fine."

Brows knitted in anger, he glared at the sailor, then back to her again. He studied her through narrowed eyes, seemingly unaware of the crowd. Then, without a word and in one motion, he released the sailor, turned, took her by the arm and escorted her away, as though he hadn't nearly killed the man.

A chill ran down her spine as she stepped out to keep pace with him. Her boot heels scraped on the uneven boardwalk.

"Luke, you almost killed him."

"If he hurt you—if anyone hurt you—I *would* kill them." This close she could see that his breathing was rapid and his eyes were hard as obsidian, and she knew, without a doubt, that he meant every word he said.

Luke Scanlin was a man capable of great tenderness, and now she knew he was a man capable of equally great rage. A man capable of making his own law. Scanlin's law.

That frightened her more than anything, for what would he do if he knew the whole truth?

Taking a step, freeing herself from his grasp, she forced herself to be calm, as calm as possible when everything and everyone she cared about was at stake.

When he halted, she said, "Is this the alley?"

"Yes." He eyed her sternly. "I wish you'd change your mind and let me do this. It's not too late to—"

She shook her head. "I'm going."

He thumbed back his hat. "Okay." Luke glanced around. Satisfied that no one was paying them any mind, he said, "I want you to do everything I say." He pulled her out of the way of a group of cowboys who were strolling by.

"Agreed," she said firmly, determined to get on with this, determined not to let the terror that was fast pushing her heart rate to something equal to a stampede, get the best of her.

"Stay close and stay behind me. Do you understand?"

She nodded.

"If there's any trouble—" he bent to look her straight in the eye "—any trouble," he repeated, as though to force the words into her mind, "then I want you to run like hell. Don't worry about me. Don't worry about Andrew. Just run. Do you understand me?"

"Trouble? What kind of trouble?" She shook her head in denial. "I've done as they demanded. They'll be satisfied to take the money and leave, won't they?"

"I don't know." He glanced toward the alley, which resembled the opening of some monster's mouth in a yawn. "I'm going to do my best to get him back, but you've got to know that anyone who would take a child isn't... well... It's not like we're dealing with honorable men here."

Her stomach drew in tight. She didn't like the direction of his thoughts. "But they said—"

He cut in, obviously annoyed. "I know what they said. I'm telling you to let me handle this. Do everything I say, when I say—and not before—and maybe we'll all get out of this alive."

"This has to work." Rebecca's voice cracked. "I have to get Andrew back. He's so small, and he'll be so afraid without me."

This time Luke didn't hesitate to pull her into his comforting embrace, and he was pleased when she let him. He felt her body tremble, and he rubbed his hand up and down her back in what he hoped was a soothing gesture. Then, putting her away from him slightly, he gave her a little smile. "It'll probably go fine. I tend to worry too much," he lied, smoothly trying to calm her, and praying that she'd remember his instructions.

She looked so forlorn, so vulnerable, that he couldn't help brushing her cheek with his knuckles. He lightly kissed her forehead, some small part of him thinking it might be for the last time. "You ready?"

She nodded and said a silent prayer. *Please, God, help us save Andrew.*

"Remember what I said." It was an order, gently given.

They stepped off the walk and turned into the alley.

Chapter Ten

Rebecca squinted, trying to make her eyes focus in the sudden darkness. Shapes and shadows mingled and merged, making all indiscernible. The only light was the moon, partially obscured by the rooftops.

Anxiety sent her heart pounding in her chest, so loud she was certain Luke could hear it. Her breath came in shallow gulps.

Andrew was out there somewhere. Desperately she scanned the long, narrow confines of the alley, searching for the familiar silhouette of a small boy—her boy. Wishing, hoping, that she'd see him, hold him in her arms again as she silently pledged to ask his forgiveness for somehow failing to keep him safe, and promised that she'd never ever let go of him again.

But she didn't see Andrew, or anyone else, and dread coiled inside, snaking up her spine. Instinctively her hand sought Luke's, touching his back, feeling the smooth cotton of his shirt. He seemed to know what she needed, and he reached back without a word, his work-roughened fingers closing around hers in a blessedly reassuring gesture.

Behind his back, Luke transferred her hand to his other one, freeing his gun hand. He was prepared for trouble.

He moved ahead slowly, each step carefully measured, testing the trash-littered ground before putting his weight fully on his foot.

They were out there somewhere. Waiting. He could feel it, prickling over his skin like electricity before a storm. One sound, one misplaced step, could reveal his position—and Rebecca's.

No matter what happened, he'd protect her—with his life, if necessary. Muscles tensed along the tops of his shoulders and down his back. His eyes strained to peer into the shifting shadows created by the buildings and the debris stacked along the raw wood walls. He listened for every sound. Eight years of survival had taught him well. He hoped like hell it was enough.

The alley was still. This guy, whoever he was, had known exactly which one to choose. The muffled sound of a piano carried through the plank walls of the Boar's Head.

Rebecca stumbled slightly, and he tightened his grip on her hand. She responded in kind, as a way of letting him know that she was all right. He felt her close, felt the heels of his boots brush against the hem of her skirt. That was fine. The closer the better. Less chance of someone singling her out.

One step. Then another. Then another. He walked Indian-soft on the hard-packed earth, feeling it slippery beneath his feet, though from what he didn't want to know. The smell was stale whiskey and rotting garbage and the acrid scent of an outhouse.

Just the kind of place vermin like this would choose. He stayed shoulder-rubbing close to the wall, inching along. His free hand slid on the raw wood. Splinters caught and plowed into his finger tips.

He ignored them. Every fiber of his being was focused on the job, the task at hand. His heart pounded erratically in his chest. It was a new sensation for him. Lord knew this wasn't the first time he'd walked into some trap or ambush. Somewhere along the way he'd made peace with the inevitable realization that one of these times he wouldn't make it out. What did it matter?

But this time it mattered a great deal, because *this* time he wasn't alone.

Without turning, he laced his fingers through Rebecca's.

Rebecca was glad for the tightening of Luke's hand on hers. She was glad he was here. No matter what had happened before, she was very glad he was here now. For reasons she didn't fully understand, she trusted him to get Andrew back, to get them both safely out of here and home.

Something small and fast brushed across Rebecca's feet. "Oh!"

"Rats," Luke whispered through clenched teeth.

She gulped down a sudden rise of bile and steeled herself to continue.

Another small, cautious step, and then another. It was like walking on eggshells, she felt the need to be so quiet, so cautious.

Where was Andrew? Why didn't they show themselves? They hadn't changed their minds, had they? No!

"Luke, I—"

"Shh..."

Luke stopped abruptly, making her come up short. Her hand slammed into his back, and she felt the muscles wire-tight there. He nudged her behind him, trapping her against the rough wood surface of the saloon wall.

"What?" she whispered, pushing lightly on the hard plane of his back. Heart racing furiously, she peered around his shoulder into the blue-black darkness.

Luke didn't answer.

"Is it Andrew?" she said softly, remembering his admonition to be careful and do as he said.

He didn't answer her, didn't even glance her way. She could see that he was staring hard into the blackness near a stack of wooden crates. Packing straw spilled over the top and onto the dirt.

When Luke finally spoke, his voice was so hard, so cold, it didn't seem to come from him at all.

"You gonna stand in those shadows all night, or are you coming out?"

Her heart pounding like a runaway locomotive, she lifted herself on tiptoe and tried to peer around him again. This time he purposely inched in front of her, blocking her view. She sank back, annoyed. "Let me see."

He didn't.

For a full ten seconds, nothing moved. Just when she was about to ask him who he was talking to, a scratchy male voice that seemed to come from nowhere and everywhere said, "Hey, mister, you got the money?"

"Depends on who's asking." Luke sounded as though he were negotiating a deal for a two-dollar saddle instead of paying a ransom.

How could he be so calm? Rebecca wondered briefly. This time she did inch free of him. "It's Andrew, isn't it? Can you see him? Move so I can see him!" She pushed at Luke. She might as well have been pushing on a slab of granite, for all the good it did her.

About that time, Luke pulled his hand free of hers. She felt his elbow brush against her ribs as his hand moved closer to the gun tied to his thigh.

Her earlier joy was instantly replaced by alarm. "Please, Luke, tell me—is it Andrew?" she begged him, desperate to see her son.

Fear tied a knot in her stomach as large as a hangman's noose. "Luke, give him the money." She shoved the small cloth bag into his hand.

He didn't move, didn't acknowledge that he'd felt the bag in his hand.

That was when she heard the scratchy voice again. The man was still unseen, at least by her. "Who you got with you, mister?"

"Where's the boy?" Luke said flatly, ignoring the question.

"Like I said. Money first."

A shadow moved in the darkness and slowly emerged enough that Luke could make out the distinct outline of a man. One man.

His first thought was for Becky and her safety, and, for a second, he cursed himself for allowing himself to be bullied into bringing her. But there was no time for self-recriminations now.

He shifted, bracing his feet, making certain that Becky was behind him and hoping she remembered his instructions to run if things went wrong.

"Gimme the money," the man said harshly.

"Boy first," Luke replied. Son of a bitch, there was no kid, and the odds were the boy was already dead, he thought with heart-sinking sadness. But if there was even one chance in a million, he'd play out the hand.

"You do what I'm tellin' you or we'll kill that kid," the man threatened. "Now gimme the goddamn money."

The odds had just gotten a little better. Maybe they really did have the boy as insurance and were planning to do away with him later. "How do I know you've got the boy? How do I know you're the ones?"

He felt Rebecca's fingers curl and dig into the muscles of his upper arm, and knew what she was thinking. It was the same thing he was thinking. This would tell it all.

"Little kid, about eight, black hair, black eyes, wearing brown pants and a white shirt."

"Yes," Rebecca said, softly enough that only Luke heard. He also heard the terror in her voice.

"So where is he?" Luke pressed, convinced now that the boy was alive. And there was no way he was turning over the money without the boy.

"The kid's safe. That's all you have to know."

"When do we get to see him?"

"After we get the money, dammit."

Luke felt Rebecca's hand on his back. "Luke, give him the money." She slid out from behind him before he realized what she was doing.

"Here," she announced, waving the parcel in front of her. "Here's the money."

"Becky!" Luke grabbed her arm and jerked her hard against the wall. The packet fell to the ground at his feet. "Stay put," he growled, in a fierce voice that made her hesitate long enough for him to say, "Okay, mister. You want the money, here it is." With the toe of his boot, he nudged it forward into a small spot of yellow moonlight.

"Luke," Rebecca said, and squirmed behind him, making it difficult for him to concentrate. "Where's Andrew?" She squirmed again. "Did he take the money? Where's Andrew?"

Luke spared her a glance. "Wait," he growled quietly.

"But—"

Out of the corner of his eye, Luke saw the man inch forward, like a rat going for the bait. Come on, he silently coaxed. Come on. If he could get this guy, then he could make him talk.

The man, clad in dark clothes, crept into the light. Recognition hit Luke about five seconds before the man looked up.

"You," the man snarled, staring at Luke with ferret eyes.

"Small world," Luke answered. "You still beating up women?" Dread was moving fast through him, tensing his muscles, turning his blood to ice. This was the same man he'd had the run-in with at the saloon. He should have known any man who'd beat a woman wouldn't be above stealing a child. Trouble was, this kind wouldn't mind killing one, either.

"Mister, you know a man could get hisself killed, poking around where he ain't got no concern."

"Now, you know, I agree, except I do have a concern here. I want that boy. It's that simple. Turn him over and you can have the money... all ten thousand—"

The man's head came up with a start at the mention of the amount. It was almost as though he hadn't known how much was there, which was odd, unless . . . unless someone else had sent the note. A boss perhaps?

The man inched farther into the light and, bending, reached for the money.

"Don't," Luke said, and edged his hand closer to his gun. The unmistakable click of a gun's hammer being pulled back stopped him cold. Another man, one Luke also recognized from before, stepped out of the shadows. Damn. He should have known.

The first man picked up the money and regarded Luke smugly. "I sure do appreciate you comin' all the way down here to bring us this—" he tossed the packet in the air once and caught it "—money."

The kidnapper drew his gun as his cohort joined him.

This was going from bad to worse. Luke knew exactly what was about to happen, and he wasn't going to let it. They were both silhouetted by the light, and Luke was at least partially concealed in the shadows. He figured he could get one for sure, and maybe the other. Anyway, he'd keep them busy long enough for Becky to get away.

In a hushed tone, he said, "When I tell you, make a run for it." Discreetly he moved his hand toward the .32 concealed under his jacket.

"No!" she shouted, and bolted out in front of him. "Where's my son?"

Panicked, Luke grabbed for her. "Becky, no!"

"My son!" Becky shouted, and lunged at the two men. It was all the distraction Luke needed. In one motion, he shoved Becky hard away from him, drew his gun and fired twice.

He heard her groan as she slammed into a stack of wooden crates. He'd ask her forgiveness later. Right now, he was trying to keep them both alive.

One man doubled over and crumpled to the ground, dead in a pool of his own blood. The other man took off, firing as he ran. Luke dodged for cover. "Stay down!" he ordered Becky as he scrambled to his feet.

"Luke!" Becky's scream echoed through the alley.

"Stay down!" he ordered again. Gun drawn, he ran flat out after the other man. Down the alley, he saw the man duck into the back door of a saloon. If the boy was alive, he wouldn't be for long—not if that guy got to him first.

Luke hated leaving Becky in the alley, but he didn't have any choice. He kept going, and momentum propelled him into the closed door with a force that rattled his teeth. He hammered on the door with his fist. The knob turned when he tried it, but the door refused to open.

"Son of a bitch! Open the damned door!"

Heart racing, he hurled his shoulder into the door. Once. The wood creaked. The vibration ricocheted through him with bone-jarring force. Twice. The distinct sound of wood tearing spurred him on.

"Dammit, come on! Give!" he ordered the solid door, slamming into the pine with all his strength.

The wood shattered and split. Half stumbling, he fell through the door into a small, cramped storeroom.

He was scrambling to his feet when he heard Rebecca calling his name. Seconds later, she grabbed his arm. Her skin was deathly pale in the dim light of the storeroom, her eyes were bright with terror, and her clothes were covered with dirt. "I'm coming with you," she said, clutching the money in her left hand.

"No," he snapped, in a tone that brooked no argument. "This time we do it my way." In one quick motion, he concealed her in an alcove of boxes. He shoved the gun from his shoulder holster into her hand. "Don't move. Do you understand me? Don't move from this spot. If anyone tries anything, comes near you, kill 'em."

She stared blankly at the gun in her hand. "I can't. I—"

He shook her—hard. "Do it." A little softer, he said, "Stay put, and trust me."

Luke didn't have time to argue with her. That bastard had a head start, and it only took a second to pull a trigger. Luke spun on his heel and disappeared out the other door.

Rebecca stood in the cramped storage room, surrounded by crates labeled Whiskey and Beer. She stared down at the gun Luke had shoved in her hand, feeling the smooth wood of the handle against her palm and the cold metal against her finger, where it curled naturally around the trigger.

It had all gone so wrong. How? How had it happened? Luke had been right—all along he'd been right about tonight. If he hadn't been here, they would surely have killed her and taken the money.

Fury beyond anything she'd ever known consumed her. These men had taken her son. One was dead, lying in a pool of blood with all the other garbage. She felt no sympathy for him, no remorse. Her grip tightened on the gun. Amazing how something so small could take a life, she thought.

She glanced up at the closed door. How long had Luke been gone?

The sounds of voices mixed with piano music, each drowning out the other until there was nothing but an unpleasant din. She paced to the door and back, the gun in one hand, the money in the other. She'd been willing to comply with their request, to give them all she had for her son.

Now it was as if a clock were running in her head, the minutes ticking past with every beat of her heart. Time was running out. If Luke didn't find Andrew... If Andrew was already dead...

She glanced down at the gun in her hand. For the first time in her life, she understood blood lust, the desire to kill another human being.

The saloon was packed tighter than a stockyard feeder lot, and smelled about the same, from the unwashed bodies and unwashed clothes. Men stood four deep at the bar, and every table in the place was full.

Luke made his way around the room, his gaze searching every whiskered, red-eyed face.

All right, where are you?

The roulette wheel was going full out, and the click-click of the little ball grated on his nerves. A gray-haired man was dealing faro at a table near the bar.

A scantily clad woman was dealing blackjack, and winning easily, since the men seemed more interested in her endowments than in her hole card.

Luke scanned the room again. Maybe the man wasn't even in here. Now that gave him pause. Maybe he'd just ducked through here and headed out the double doors. Damn, if that was true, then he'd never find him.

Tobacco smoke was thick as fog, and the smell of cheap rotgut made his stomach turn. He kept one eye on the staircase that led upstairs. There were rooms up there, the girls' rooms, but they offered a place to hide or a place from which to take aim. This guy wouldn't hesitate to shoot into a crowd if he thought it would help him.

Luke kept moving, scanning faces, drunken faces, puffy faces. Searching. Searching. Moving in the direction of the stairs.

When he got close to the bar, he grabbed the narrow-faced bartender by the front of his stained white shirt and dragged him up close. "You see a man come in here, maybe bleeding?"

The man shook his head frantically.

"Listen, you, I want that man." Luke shook him hard. Everyone gave them a wide berth, and no one tried to interfere. "Where is he?"

"I—" The barkeeper swallowed hard, his brown eyes bulging in his head. "I ain't seen no one."

Furious, Luke let go. Damn.

Time was running out. The frantic pounding of his heart told him he'd lost that scum, and most likely the boy.

How could he have been so stupid? He should never have let this happen. What kind of a lawman was he? He should have known. Ah, hell, he did know better than to walk into an alley like that—and with Becky. He should have locked her in her room and done the job he'd spent the last eight years of his life perfecting. The one time she counted on him, he failed. *No, make that two times, Scanlin.*

"Hello, sweetie," a saloon girl purred.

"Not interested," he said shortly, and kept working his way through the crowd. He was headed for the stairs.

Six doors faced the balcony and the saloon beyond. One was as good as another. Gun drawn, he turned the brass knob and shoved the door open with a bang.

A half-naked whore looked up, startled. "What the—" she muttered. The naked man she was draped on top of looked embarrassed.

He yanked the door closed.

Two steps, and he twisted open the knob on the next door. Empty.

Moving fast, he tried the next door. Locked. Not for long. One good kick, and the door flew open, banging into the wall and nearly slamming shut again.

A woman screamed. Luke took in the scene in the blink of an eye, then flattened himself against the wall beside the partially opened door.

"Give it up," Luke ordered. "This is the U.S. marshal."

Gun drawn, he pulled back the hammer. He sucked in a deep breath, like a man about to dive underwater. With steely determination, he hurled himself around the doorway.

The kidnapper was slumped on the end of the bed. Bloodstained and pale, he was packing bandages against his wounded side. "Hold it right there, you son of a bitch!" Luke yelled.

As though by magic, a gun appeared in the kidnapper's hand. He fired three, four shots. The woman screamed again.

A bullet whizzed past Luke's head like a saw blade and buried itself in the plaster wall. Luke dived for the bed, his shoulder bouncing off the iron footrail, and slammed into the floor with a thud that made him see stars.

It was all the time the man needed to jump through the open window. Momentarily dazed, Luke staggered to his feet and raced to the window to peer out into the darkness. The man was gone. He had escaped down the back staircase.

Angrier than he'd ever have thought possible, Luke turned back to see the woman he'd helped earlier, pale and shaking, hugging the wall for all she was worth.

She didn't move, didn't give any sign she even knew he was there. "Millie! Where'd he go?"

When she didn't respond, he grabbed her shoulders and began to shake her.

"Millie. Come on. Where'd he go?" She thrashed her head, her red hair falling down to cover half her face.

"You know what he's been up to, don't you? Don't you?"

She gave a shaky, dazed sort of nod.

"He's gonna kill that child if I don't get to him first."

Luke knew the instant that recognition dawned in her eyes. "He . . . can't." She swallowed hard, as if gulping down the horrible realization.

"He can, and he will. That boy is a witness."

Panic pounded in his blood and his brain. Like a drowning man, he made one last desperate attempt to survive. "In the name of God, Millie, if you know where that boy is, tell me!"

Chapter Eleven

"He's here."

If she'd announced she was about to join a convent, he couldn't have been any more surprised or disbelieving. "Here? What do you mean, here?"

He scanned the room in one swift motion. Ten by ten, a rumpled, bloodstained bed, a scarred table and a broken kerosene lamp, a well-used camelback trunk behind the door.

"What do you—"

Millie opened the trunk. A wardrobe of gaudy dresses burst out. It was as if she'd opened a can of worms.

"Boy," she said softly, "you all right?"

Nothing happened. Nothing moved.

Then a small voice said, "Yes." A second later, an equally small face, dirty and tear-stained, peeked out from the mix of faded satin and frayed lace.

Rebecca paced the confines of the storeroom. Four steps to the broken door, and four steps to the one Luke had disappeared through.

Luke was out there somewhere, and so, God help her, was her son. Where was he? Why hadn't he come back? Had he found Andrew? Was he in time?

Not knowing was driving her insane. What ever happened, she had to know. So she stuffed the money into the inside pocket of her skirt. Concealing the gun in the folds of the black velvet riding skirt, she reached for the door and went out into the saloon.

"Andrew?" Luke said in cautious disbelief.

"Yes, sir" came the polite reply. He didn't move out of the trunk.

A Christmas-morning grin slashed across Luke's face. Good Lord, there must really be such things as guardian angels, because someone was sure watching over this boy.

Anger was forgotten, and fear was replaced by elation. "Andrew, are you all right?" Luke dropped down on the bare planks, hard against one knee. He snapped his gun back into the holster. "Are you hurt?"

"No, sir."

Luke let out the breath he'd been holding. "You can come out now." The boy was a welcome sight after all the grim visions that had fluttered through Luke's mind the past twenty-four hours.

Staring into the child's sable black eyes, eyes that were wide with uncertainty, Luke felt his heart melt. The kid was all right. The feeling of relief wrapped around him like a warm blanket in winter.

Thank you, he said silently, with a quick glance upward.

"Who are you?" the boy inquired, his voice shaky. Luke saw his chin quiver, and smiled when he also saw that the boy was struggling not to cry.

"I'm a friend of your mother."

At the mention of his mother, a grin flashed across the boy's face. All charm and dimples, Luke thought. He'd be one to get his way with that smile.

"Will you come here to me, Andrew?" He knew the boy was frightened, and he didn't want to snatch him up and scare him further. But he had to strain not to, because Becky was down there, and he couldn't wait to see her, to see the look on her face when he walked in with this miracle in his arms.

"Where's my mother?" the boy inquired, shifting in the trunk, pushing a red satin dress to one side.

"She's downstairs. I'll take you to her."

The boy seemed to consider this. Then, slowly, he climbed out of the trunk. While he did, Luke glanced up at Millie.

"How?" he asked directly.

She gave a small shrug. "Jack brung him back the other day. He locked him in the toolshed behind the old stables." She patted Andrew's head affectionately. "I took him food, and we talked. I felt *real* bad. I mean, taking a boy from his folks ain't right. I tried to tell Jack to take him home, but he wouldn't hear none of it." She touched her bruised face and forced a little smile. "You know how Jack is. I brung him up here tonight figuring maybe I could sneak him back to his mama.

"But why didn't you tell me today, when I was here?"

"Why should I?" Her expression was puzzled. "I don't know you from Adam. Still don't for that matter, but you helped me out today, and I think you're all right.'' Her hand rested lightly on Andrew's shoulder, and he leaned against her leg. It was obvious that if Millie hadn't intervened, the boy would have died, if not from a bullet, then from not being found. Kids died quick without food or water.

"Lady, you saved his life and, in a way, mine." He knew he wouldn't have cared much about living if he'd had to face Becky with the horrible alternative. His grip tightened on the small boy in his arms. "Just so you know, I'm the U.S. marshal for this district. Luke Scanlin." He produced his badge as proof. "I owe you, Millie."

Millie smiled, her eyes crinkling. "I knew you was too good to be an *ordinary* cowboy."

"Pretty ordinary," he told her. "You might wanna consider leaving town for a while, all things considered."

"I was thinking along them same lines myself. Texas seems to be on my mind a whole bunch of late." She winked.

Luke chuckled and shook his head. "You and Texas will get along fine."

He turned his attention to the boy, who was watching him intently from four feet away. "Andrew, what say you and I go find your mother?"

"Yes!" Andrew squealed, with all the joyful enthusiasm of a seven-year-old. And Luke understood perfectly. He was feeling pretty joyful himself.

Luke scooped the boy up in his arms. "It's a little crowded downstairs right now, so I think it's better if I carry you."

Luke looked at the boy in his arms. His black eyes were bright with excitement, his black hair was short and rumpled, and his face was the same heart shape as Rebecca's.

The strangest sensation came over Luke, like nothing he'd known before. It was a feeling akin to the possessiveness he felt for Rebecca, yet different. He narrowed his eyes and studied the boy. There was something... He shook his head. Probably relief at finding the boy, he mused. He smiled again.

"Sir," Andrew inquired, looping his small arms around Luke's neck, "are you really a marshal?"

"I am. No one is going to hurt you now, Andrew, and I'm going to make sure no one scares you or tries to hurt you again."

Luke saw the boy's chin quiver again, saw him swallow fast, and knew he was trying to keep from crying. It was one of those things boys seemed to know at birth. Never cry. No matter what, never cry. But if ever a boy had a right to, it was this one.

Luke felt like crying a little himself, he was so happy. So he pressed the boy's face to his shoulder in a gesture of understanding and an offer of privacy. His little body shook, and a small damp spot soaked through the cotton of Luke's shirt. But nary a sound came out of the boy's mouth to reveal this breach of male resolve.

Something instinctive made Luke kiss the top of the boy's head and cradle his hand against the back of his neck, feeling the smoothness of his coal black hair above his little shirt collar.

"Come on, cowboy. We're going home." And he was. He was going to get Becky, and the three of them were going to do just that.

Chapter Twelve

She'd never been in a saloon before. Gas lamps blazed bright against dirt-smudged mirrors. Too many tables were crowded into the square room.

"Hiya, honey," a drunk slurred. His breath was strong enough to knock down a mule.

This time, Rebecca didn't panic, didn't scream. With a cold look, she elbowed past him and pushed deeper into the crowd. Luke had come this way, though where he was now was anyone's guess. All she knew was that her son was somewhere out here—maybe in the saloon, maybe not—and she couldn't just stand here and wait.

She edged between the tables, but nonetheless, dressed in her riding shirt, she stood out from the other women present, who seemed to have forgotten to put their dresses over their pantalets and corsets. Any other time, she might have been offended, but tonight, after what she'd been through already, nothing could faze her.

The talking, shouting, piano playing, all blended together in an ear-deafening roar. Briefly she thought, *So this is what men call enjoyment.*

She didn't see Luke anywhere. She decided to work her way toward the front door. If she didn't see Luke in here, then she'd head outside, and if he wasn't there, then she'd go from saloon to saloon, if that was what it took.

She kept scanning the crowd, looking for Luke's familiar frame, looking for his dark head, his broad shoulders.

She was ten feet from the double doors when she happened to glance behind her. That was when she saw them.

Against a backdrop of peeling paint and bawdy saloon misfits, Luke was holding Andrew in his arms, as though it were the most natural thing in the world.

"Oh, God." Her heart stopped beating in her chest. She was certain she wasn't even breathing. The sight of them together would be forever imprinted on her brain.

As though he knew she was there, he looked straight at her, and she saw him smile. That was all—he just smiled. His eyes sparkled with joy and tenderness and understanding.

And there was the briefest hesitation on her part, at seeing them together, seeing Andrew's small arms clinging to Luke's neck. With a mother's desperation, she rushed in their direction, pushing, shoving, clawing her way between men who were totally unaware of the scene around them.

All she cared about was that Andrew was alive and safe. Everything else would take its course. Andrew was all that mattered to her, and she was heartbreakingly frantic to hold him again.

"Mama! Mama!" Andrew yelled at the top of his lungs. His small voice was so out of place in this den of iniquity that everyone present turned to stare.

The piano player stopped playing, the room became strangely quiet, and men, suddenly aware, parted to let Rebecca through. Their gazes moved from the beautiful woman to the dangerous-looking man standing on the stairs.

Luke's gaze had followed her through the crowd. And as she reached for her son, he gave her a smile. Its effect was devastating, and suggestive enough to make her falter for the barest second.

"Madame," Luke said with great formality, his eyes sparked with happiness, "I give you your son." With that, he let the boy slip into her waiting arms as she handed him the gun she'd been holding.

Tears streamed unchecked down her cheeks, and she hugged her son tightly, her fingers wrapped around his rib cage and legs. A cry of relief broke from her lips. "Andrew! Thank God, Andrew!"

Andrew is all right. She hugged him and kissed him and hugged him some more, and the joyful words resounded in her head and heart.

Holding him in her arms, she knew this wasn't a dream. It was real. They had done it. No, told herself, Luke—Luke had done this wonderful deed.

Risking his own life, Luke had given her back her son. Joy greater than any she'd ever known bubbled in her laugh and shone in her eyes as she cast her gaze up to meet his.

With her son cradled in her arms, she said simply, "I don't... Oh, Luke, thank you."

"You're welcome," he returned, in a voice soft with emotion.

It was then that she realized a crowd had gathered around them, staring openly.

Luke moved in closer. Without even asking, he hoisted Andrew into his arms. "Come on," he ordered gently with a firm hand on Rebecca's elbow. "Let's get out of here."

He pushed through the crowd and out the double doors onto the sidewalk. It was instinct that made him glance around; there was, after all, a kidnapper still at large. The quicker he got them out of here and home, the better he'd feel.

"I think it would be easier if Andrew rode with me, considering sidesaddles and all."

Reluctantly she agreed, not because she didn't trust Luke, but because she hated to let go of Andrew even for a second.

"Up you go, cowboy," Luke said as he swung Andrew up on his gelding's back. "Hang on to the horn," he told him. Going around, he gave Rebecca a leg up, then paused, his hand resting dangerously near her thigh. "Becky?"

She looked down into his upturned face. "Are you all right? I mean, did I hurt you... earlier, when I pushed you? I didn't mean to—"

Without thinking, she brushed his cheek with the tips of her fingers, feeling the warmth of his skin against hers, the prickle of whiskers. "I'm all right."

She saw his eyes flutter closed. His hand covered hers, and he turned his face into her palm, lingering there, reveling in her touch. When he looked up again, his eyes brimmed with tenderness and a knowing passion that held her a willing prisoner. His touch, his closeness, made long-denied feelings warm and stir.

As though sensing the electric tension, her horse stamped and shifted, breaking the spell. They exchanged timid smiles.

"All right, then," he said loudly, swinging up on his horse and settling Andrew securely in front of him. "Let's go home."

As they rode, those words haunted Luke. *Go home,* he'd said. Too bad it wasn't true. Too bad it wasn't his home, his wife, his son.

A sadness replaced his joy as he watched Rebecca, beaming at Andrew and telling him how much she'd missed him and how much his grandmother was missing him, too.

He felt very much the outsider.

Perhaps that was why, when they stopped at the house and Luke hoisted Andrew down, then helped Rebecca, he didn't follow them inside.

But Rebecca stopped walking and turned back to him. "Aren't you coming in?"

He glanced toward the porch, smiling when he saw Andrew catapult himself into Ruth's waiting arms. Luke's sadness got a touch deeper.

"Naw," he said quietly. "You go on and enjoy your reunion."

Absently he toyed with the reins of the two horses, slapping the ends against his palm.

"You have to come in. Ruth will want to thank you, and—"

"Thanks aren't necessary. Just doing my job."

Rebecca stepped up directly in front of him. "It was more than your job." She touched his chest lightly with the palm of her hand, and he sucked in a steadying breath. "You...you aren't leaving? Tonight, I mean? Are you?"

"I thought in the morning, if it's okay with you?"

He could feel her hand, warm and delicate over the area of his heart, and he didn't move, didn't want to.

"I wish you'd come in." Her voice was as warm and tempting as whiskey. "We'll be up half the night, I'm sure, and—"

He nodded, taking off his hat and hooking it over the saddle horn. "I'm going to the police station to take care of…unfinished business." Like a body in an alley and a kidnapper who was still on the loose.

He'd been so scared, for her, for the boy, for them, and now it was over. Though he was glad, really glad, there was a sense of finality, of ending, that he hadn't quite expected.

He had no more reason to stay, no more reason to see her, except that he didn't think he could be anywhere within a million miles of her and not see her, not touch her.

"I'm happy for you, Princess," he began, uncertain what he was trying to say.

She smiled—it was a slow, lush smile—and her hand, the one that was on his chest, glided provocatively up to curve over his shoulder. Then she did something he was totally unprepared for. She lifted up on her toes and kissed him. Not a big kiss, but not some little cousin-type kiss, either.

"Thank you," she said on a throaty whisper, which brushed across his nerves like a summer wind.

As though in slow motion, Rebecca stepped back, her gaze never leaving his. She let her hand drop to her side, and was unprepared for the sense of loss that came when she did.

The moment was tense with anticipation. The cool night air did little to soothe her heated flesh. He made a motion as though to reach for her. Instantly, her body flared to life, and she became more aware of the effort it took to breathe.

"Princess," he murmured, his voice husky. His face was bathed in moonlight. His strong features held a sensuality that was nearly irresistible. Nearly.

The voice of reason was annoying but insistent. *He's not for you.* There was more at stake here than her heart, a great deal more, now that Andrew was back.

With more strength than she'd thought she had left, she took a faltering step backward. "I can never repay what you have done this evening," she said honestly, wanting him to know that no matter what else, she understood the risks he'd taken and was sincerely grateful.

He was silent for so long she thought he wouldn't answer, but, as she turned toward the house, he said, "I'd do anything for you, Princess."

On the front stairs, one foot resting on the step above, she hesitated and, without turning, glanced back over her shoulder. He was there, watching, a violet shadow against a black-velvet sky.

Dressed as he was in range clothes, he was a man in contrast to this time and place. He was everything she disdained in a man, rough, violent, and yet he exuded an intensity that was as riveting and compelling as the lure of Satan himself.

Without a word, without a touch, he stirred the promise of pleasure that she'd long ago assured herself she'd overcome. Determinedly she went into the house, closing the door quietly on the man and his enticing invitation. She stood there, unmoving, for a long minute, while pulse points throbbed and heated the sensuous centers of her body.

What was this ability he had to stir the flame of desire so easily in her?

"Oh, Luke," she murmured, very, very softly. "What have you done to me?"

Rebecca spent the next hour telling Ruth all that had happened. They plied Andrew with a lifetime's supply of cold milk and oven-fresh cookies—it seemed Ruth had needed something to do while she waited for their return. Rebecca, sensing that Andrew was still upset from his ordeal, was more than happy to give in to him.

Seated at the kitchen table, Andrew reached for his fourth molasses cookie, and Ruth, in a conspiratorial way, dragged the plate more fully within his reach.

Rebecca poured another cup of coffee and briefly related the events of the ransom delivery and Andrew's subsequent rescue. She mentioned that she had retained the money, which she would put in the safe later. She carefully did not mention that she—that they—had almost died in that disgusting alley. She was adamant, though, in telling her that Luke had risked his life and had saved them both. To which Andrew enthusiastically agreed.

Ruth listened to Rebecca's narration, but she was more intent on her expression, the way her eyes lit up whenever she mentioned the marshal's name, the way her cheeks flushed. And when Rebecca was finished, Ruth said, "Marshal Scanlin is a good man. I hope he comes to visit often."

"Me, too," Andrew piped up, his mouth full of cookie, which he promptly washed down with a cheek-bulging gulp of milk that left a snow-white mustache on his upper lip.

Rebecca laughed—really laughed. It was the first time she'd laughed in days. It felt good, and she knew Luke had done that for her, too, for without Andrew there could be no happiness in her life.

The next two hours were spent talking, playing four games of checkers, which Andrew won, and eating more cookies. Somewhere around midnight, an exhausted Andrew climbed onto Rebecca's lap and promptly fell asleep, snuggled against her shoulder.

It didn't take much to put him to bed. He roused when she washed his face and hands and slid his nightshirt on—the one with the blue stripes not the solid green one. He climbed in his bed and was asleep instantly.

"I think I'll do the same," Ruth said from her place near the partially opened window. The night fog seeped in, falling over the windowsill in a gray mist that pooled on the floor before disappearing in the warmer inside air.

"Close that window, will you?" Rebecca asked, and Ruth obliged.

"Good night," Ruth said, stifling a yawn. "He looks fine, doesn't he?" She smiled and lingered beside Rebecca.

"Yes. He doesn't appear to be hurt. I checked when I changed his clothes."

"That's good."

"I'm trying not to remind him of it too much. If he wants to talk about it, fine, but now that I have him home and he's unhurt, well, I don't see any reason to keep reliving it, do you?"

"None. Let's try to get on with our lives, and, as you said, be here for him if he needs us. Lots of love and keeping him close for a while is probably all we can do." She gave Rebecca's shoulder an affectionate squeeze.

Rebecca patted her hand in reply. "Thanks." She fussed with smoothing the linen sheets. "I think I'll just sit here awhile."

Ruth nodded, a few wisps of hair coming loose from the bun at the back of her neck. "I'll see you in the morning. Maybe we can all sleep in."

Rebecca chuckled and glanced at her sleeping son. "I wouldn't count on it."

Ruth grinned. "Good night, dear, and thanks for all you did. I'm so thankful that you're all right and Andrew is back. We owe the marshal a great deal, don't we?"

"Yes," Rebecca said softly. "I owe him more than you know."

With a confirming nod, Ruth went to her room.

Rebecca moved to the rocker. Loosening her collar and removing her boots, she lounged back in the chair to watch her son sleep. She smiled at the little sound he made on each expelled breath, more like humming than snoring.

A pain in her back was the first indication that she'd fallen asleep in the chair. A quick glance reassured her that Andrew was, in fact, sleeping peacefully in his bed.

Flexing her shoulders and back, she stretched, yawned and stood, only to flex again. Bed, she thought, and, leaving the door to his room partially open, she headed for her room.

Luke was alone in his room—correction, Rebecca's guest room. Yeah, that was him, a guest. He'd be leaving at first light. No sense prolonging the inevitable.

He thought about packing. Why bother? Packing for him was getting dressed and throwing a couple of shirts in his saddlebags. That took a whopping two minutes. Goodness knew, he was in no hurry to get back to his rooms over on Washington. Oh, they were nice enough, better than most, but they were just rooms.

Sitting on the edge of the bed, he stripped out of his shirt and kicked off his boots. The warming stove was working overtime, competing with the chill from the half-open window. The night air was damp and heavy. Goose bumps prickled the bare flesh of his back.

Everyone must be asleep by now. A smile teased his lips. That little guy was probably out like a light.

If Luke lived to be a hundred and ten, he'd always remember the look on the kid's face as he emerged from that trunk, his ebony eyes wide with surprise and fear, his black hair all tousled.

A strange feeling moved through him, a lightness in his chest. It was a new feeling, yet not unpleasant, and he narrowed his eyes in puzzlement. That was the second time he'd felt that way. The first had been when he saw the boy for the first time.

He shrugged off the feeling and strolled over to the window. Pulling back the curtain, he peered out into the night, watching the stars twinkle and blink in the cloudless sky.

Shoulder against the window frame, he let his eyes drift closed and his mind wander. As always, his thoughts went to Becky. Tonight, in that alley, she'd been courageous and determined. He'd been damned proud of her. She was one to cross the river with, as the drovers said. Then, later, there by the front walk, when she hauled off and kissed him, he'd just stood there, 'cause he was afraid he'd drag her into his arms and kiss her back and never stop. Yeah, he'd like that, kissing Becky and touching her, feeling her exposed flesh slid against his as they—

His eyes snapped open, and he shifted uncomfortably at the sudden swelling in his loins.

Abruptly he straightened, letting the curtain fall back into place. It was a good thing he was leaving tomorrow, he told himself firmly as he crossed the room. Yeah, a real good thing, because she'd made it clear that she had no more feelings for him. That kiss tonight had been merely a thank-you, nothing more.

He grimaced at the truth, his hand unconsciously curling into a fist. "Ouch."

Glancing down, he saw a half-dozen splinters embedded in the fingertips of his right hand. Souvenirs, he thought wryly.

Fishing in his saddlebag, he found his small sewing kit. Sliding a needle free of its paper holder, he sank down on the bed near the side table and turned up the lamp.

"Ouch," he muttered again, digging at the offending sliver.

The first splinter poked its head up enough for him to grab it with his teeth and spit it out. A drop of blood glistened ruby red on his fingertip, and he wiped it on his pant leg.

Next.

"Ouch," he muttered again, a little more intensely this time. Working with his left hand was about as awkward as trying to pick up eggs with a snow shovel.

"May I help?" a softly feminine voice said, and he knew without looking that it was Rebecca. There was no other voice that caressed his senses quite so easily.

His heart lurched, then took on a slow, heavy rhythm. Turning his head, he let his gaze travel across the carpeted floor to where she stood in the partially opened doorway.

Her black riding skirt was badly wrinkled and its hem caked with dirt, and her usually stiff-fronted blouse was opened at the collar and her sleeves were rolled up. Her cheeks were flushed and her hair was tousled, loose tendrils curving provocatively around her face. She looked like a woman who'd just roused from sleep, or just made love. His heart slammed against his ribs.

Erotic images flashed unbidden in his mind, those same images he'd banished not ten minutes ago. His throat convulsed and, for a full five seconds, he stared at her, willing the images and the sudden hot reflexes of his body to still.

He wasn't having much success.

"Please, come in," he finally returned, when he was certain his voice would work.

Rebecca didn't move. About the same instant she spoke, she'd realized he was sitting there half-naked. She saw his tight, corded muscles flex and stretch as he moved slightly. She should look away. She should *go* away.

She stared right at his chest, at the black hair that arched over each nipple, then plunged down his chest to disappear into his waistband. It was uniquely male, and provocative beyond reason.

Her gaze flicked to his face, chiseled and heart-stoppingly handsome, with a wicked look in devil-black eyes.

She should never have come to his room. But she had seen his light on, and she'd wanted to thank him, that was all, she told herself—not quite as convincingly as she would have wished.

Caught up as she was in the nearness of him, the voice of reason was faint, but it was insistent, screaming *Run for your life.*

She didn't. Closing the door, she crossed to him and sat down beside him on the bed, sinking a little into the feather mattress. It was madness, this attraction to him. Insanity, to give in to the sudden surge of longing. But then he smiled at her in that knowing way of his, and the first tremors of desire stirred deep inside, warm and inviting. She could no more leave than she could stop breathing.

Not trusting her voice, she simply took his hand in hers. He had nice hands, she thought, long, graceful fingers. She remembered those same fingers touching her, brushing seductively across her cheek, caressing her neck. In another time, those hands had stroked her body, heating her flesh . . .

"Is the boy asleep," he asked, startling her.

She swallowed hard. "Yes."

"Is he all right? I mean *really* all right?"

"Thanks to you."

He lifted his hand free of hers to cup her chin, and he looked at her with eyes as black as midnight fire. "You scared the hell out of me, running out in front of me like that." It was the kindest of rebukes.

"I'm sorry. I didn't mean to."

"I know," he told her with a half smile. "I'm sorry, too. Sorry you had to go through that, and especially sorry you had to see me . . . kill a man."

She heard the sudden sadness in his voice, saw the regret in his eyes. It surprised her, this remorse. He'd seemed so calm that she'd thought he was unaffected. She could see now that she'd been wrong, and the need to console him made her say, "You had no choice. He would have killed us both if you hadn't—" Her voice broke as the reality tore at her insides.

"Shh, honey. It's all right." He kissed her cheek, ever so lightly, and brushed the hair back from her face.

It felt nice, his kiss, the way his lips caressed her skin. Tears pooled in the corners of her eyes. The fears she'd controlled all evening would no longer be denied. "I thought they were leaving," she told him through a muffled sob.

"I know." His gaze never left hers as he lifted her hand and kissed her palm. It was a provocative gesture that soothed and excited her at the same time.

"When . . . when they didn't bring Andrew, I thought he was—"

He stopped her words with the touch of two fingers to her lips. "Don't." His eyes brimmed with tenderness and passion.

"What about tomorrow, and the next day, and the next? What about sending him off to school, or out to play? Can I be with him every minute, every second? I want to keep him locked safely in his room until he's twenty-five, maybe longer."

Luke chuckled. "Princess, I wish life were that easy." He kissed her palm again, leaving her flesh warm and moist, making her heart rate increase by half.

"All you can do is take precautions, warn him to be careful, and then—then you have to let him go. You have to trust."

For reasons both obvious and vague, she trusted Luke. At least for tonight, this moment in time, she trusted him completely. Knowing that, feeling that, she leaned her head into the curve of his shoulder, taking solace from the warm smoothness of his bare skin against her cheek. His strong arm wrapped around her shoulder, pulling her tight against him.

It was wrong, she thought in the dim recesses of her mind. Wrong to be here with him. Wrong to touch him and be touched. Wrong to linger. He was dangerous, more dangerous than even he knew, and yet she could not deprive herself of his comforting strength.

She stayed that way for several seconds, letting his steady heartbeat drum away the fears and rage of the past few days, and perhaps even longer.

"A year from now—" she felt his breath caress the edge of her ear, tiny shivers of delight raced down her neck "—this will seem like a bad dream. As though it never happened. You will have forgotten all about it . . . and me."

There was note of sadness in his husky voice that touched her heart, and, without thinking, she said, "You're not an easy man to forget."

She felt, more than heard, him chuckle. "Why, thank you, Princess." He kissed the top of her head in a familiar way that made her crane her neck and press her face into the side of his neck. He smelled like leather and musk and felt like salvation to a lost soul.

She let her eyes drift closed, lost in the enticing nearness of him and the soothing effect his touch had on her exhausted nerves. At last, she looked up. He was watching her with a slow, easy smile that she understood all too well.

"Becky," he whispered, his fingers tightening perceptibly on her shoulder. She was so beautiful, so close. If only she'd stop looking at him with those luminous blue eyes of hers, he might, *might,* have a chance of not kissing her.

Being here, with her in his arms, was too intimate, too seductive. The door was closed, the night was still, and a parade of erotic fantasies was flashing in his mind, hotter than a lightning strike.

He hated what she'd been through, hated that he hadn't been able to do more for her. He wanted her to know this. "I'll always be here for you, Becky. You know that, don't you?"

Rebecca was lost in the depths of his soft, knowing gaze. Her heart fluttered in her chest like the wings of a frightened butterfly, yet she was not frightened. No, she had never felt as alive as she did right now. Nerves that had been frayed with exhaustion now pulsed with anticipation. A forgotten longing stirred deep within her, heating, swirling, reaching out to enfold every part of her.

She knew he was going to kiss her. She could see it in the passion that sparked in the depths of his eyes. So it was no surprise when his hand moved around to cradle the back of her neck.

The world stilled, as though poised in expectation. There was no sound except the uneven pounding of her heart.

Her eyes fluttered closed an instant before his lips touched hers. It was the barest of kisses, a tasting, a testing. He lifted his head. His gaze traveled over her face and searched her eyes, as though he were seeking an answer to an unspoken question.

Her lips parted, perhaps in reply, perhaps in surrender—she'd never know, because he covered her mouth again, fully this time, completely. It was not a gentle kiss, it was harsh and fierce, as though he were claiming what was rightfully his.

She should have been outraged. She should have denied his claim. But her body flared to life like a skyrocket, white-hot and riveting.

There was nothing but the lush sensation of his mouth on hers. His arms drifted down to her waist, pulling her tighter against him. Her hands glided up his arms and slid around his neck, her fingers dug into the firm flesh of his back, and she clung to him, giving herself up to the rapidly increasing desire.

At the first touch of her lips on his, desire exploded in Luke like a gunshot. Everywhere their bodies touched was on fire. He was acutely aware of her fingers curling, nail-sharp, into the top of his shoulder. Tendrils of her hair caressed his face, like a temptress's touch, which heated his blood. He turned toward her. His fingers dug into the fabric of her blouse, feeling the stiff bones of her corset. God, how he hated corsets and clothes and anything else that kept him from having her. And he did want her. He wanted her so much that, with expert ease, he pulled her blouse from her waistband. Swiftly his hand moved toward the row of buttons that held the blouse closed.

Is this it, Scanlin? You gonna seduce her? You gonna take advantage? Her earlier accusation came back to haunt him.

With steely determination, he tore his mouth from hers. Every muscle in his body screamed in protest. He still held her in his arms, unable to release her completely.

He looked at her, her eyes dilated, her cheeks flushed, her sensual lips parted in a provocative way that was making this magnanimous gesture of his damned difficult, maybe impossible.

On a husky whisper, raw with emotion, he said, "You take my breath away."

The logic that had guided Rebecca's life was strong. *Stop this! Stop this now!* Swallowing hard, she cleared her throat. "I should go," she said, but her muscles refused to work.

Uncertainty flashed in his eyes, but then his mouth curved up in a tantalizing smile that sent her pulse rate higher than a kite on a summer wind. "I like seeing you like this," he said. He tucked a loose strand of hair behind her ear, his finger sensually tracing the rim before gliding, feather-light, along her jaw.

Delicious shivers prickled down her neck. Her eyes drifted closed as she reveled in the sensation of his touch and the heat that was building in the core of her. "Like what?" she murmured, only half-aware of what she was saying.

"Like this," he repeated in a hushed tone, touching her open collar. He let his hand linger there while his fingers slid inside to brush the sensitive, swelling mound of her breast.

Her breath caught on a rapid intake of air and, though her heart was pounding a frantic rhythm, her body went absolutely still, poised, waiting for him.

He didn't disappoint her. Through the cotton of her blouse, he brushed his thumb over the peak of her breast. Once. Only once.

Her nipples pulled up into marble-hard peaks, and delicious heat radiated outward to coil tightly in the junction of her legs.

Luke's voice was rich, and lover-soft. "I was thinking about you before you came in."

"Were you?"

"Oh, yes." He cupped one side of her face with his hand. "You do that to me, you know. Make me think about you...make me want you."

She looked alarmed, as though he'd just revealed some great secret. Perhaps he had. His passionate gaze never wavered as he reached around her and removed the remaining pins from her hair. His fingers combed through the tumbling silken threads. "I always think of you with your hair down...like this...like the last time." That quickly the memory, lush and primitive, of her naked and wild assailed his senses. The sudden swelling between his legs was strong and potent.

He hovered close, overtaking her with the sheer male power of him. His thumb teased her bottom lip, but he didn't move. It was as though he were waiting for something, she thought, perhaps giving her a chance to change her mind, to flee this madness.

She didn't want to flee. God help her, she wanted this. She wanted him.

Sensing her surrender, Luke gracefully dipped his head toward hers. "Rebecca..." was all he said an instant before his lips brushed hers. Desire, long denied, surged to the surface with electric clarity.

"Luke, please . . ." she managed to say, though uncertain what she was asking for.

His breath mingled with hers. "I want you, Becky." His voice was quiet, yet tinged with urgency.

With the pads of two fingers, he turned her face up to his. "If you stay here, I'm going to make love to you. You must stop me now, or . . ."

His hand dropped away but his gaze sought hers and held her as surely as if he were touching her. He waited, willing her to know, to understand, that he was giving her this chance. Prepared to let her go, he wondered if a man could die of wanting a woman.

She smiled then; it was the barest curving of her lips, but all the encouragement he needed.

With infinite slowness, as though still uncertain he'd read her correctly, he lowered his head. When she made no effort to stop him, he covered her mouth with his.

The sensation of Luke's lips on hers was startling in its intensity. His lips, warm, gentle and exploring, offered her an invitation to carnal delights. He cupped her face between his hands, the tips of his fingers threading into her hair.

With each beat of her heart, his kiss deepened, becoming more and more demanding. For Rebecca, there was no thought of resistance. There was no thought at all. She reached up to meet him, opening to him, welcoming him.

His tongue grazed her bottom lip, tracing its curve, teasing the corners of her mouth in a way that sent waves of desire pulsing through her. When his tongue demanded entrance, she eagerly obliged, feeling him lave at the tender flesh inside her lower lip.

A rhythm as old as time pulsed low in her body, and she let her tongue glide into his mouth, feeling his groan. He tensed, and, taking her firmly by the shoulders, he turned her fully toward him and pulled her against the hard plane of his bare chest.

Desire, raw and savage, exploded within her. She clung to him, her hands curving over his broad shoulders, her fingers clawing at his flesh.

Luke kissed her lips, her cheeks, her brows. He blazed a fiery path of moist kisses along her jaw, pausing to nip and lick the sensitive flesh behind her ear. Pleasure shot through him when she moaned in response.

His mouth caressed her throat and, greedily, she arched back to give him better access. His breath fanned her moistened skin, inciting her desire to greater heights, as though she'd been waiting for him all these years. Perhaps she had.

Luke knew the instant she gave in to him. The instant her muscles relaxed, the instant her body swayed toward him. He heard her moan. It was the barest of sounds, but enough to send his heart racing faster.

Sitting side by side was awkward, so he stood, pulling her up to him, desperate to feel her full length against his.

Deftly he managed to unbutton her blouse and slip it from her shoulders. His mouth quirked up in an appreciative smile. She was wearing black. Black corset. Black camisole. It was fine lace, and sheer as gauze, and he could see the crest of her hardened nipples straining at the translucent material.

"You are a temptress," he murmured against her lips.

His mouth blazed a moist path down her throat, his teeth nipping at her flesh, then kissing away any hurt.

She shivered, trembled, and felt the coil of heat beginning to swirl and spiral inside her.

"I don't mind being tempted," he added, his hands already reaching for the straps of her camisole. He slid them down, returning to tug the fine material low enough to free her firm, ripe breasts above the stiff corset edge.

The cool air was like ice to her heated flesh, which made her skin prickle, her nipples pull even tighter.

"Oh, Luke...what...are you..."

"Exactly what I said. I'm making love to you," he told her, his voice raw with emotion. Slowly, he drew the tip of her nipple into the wet, warm interior of his mouth. With tongue and teeth, he teased and enticed, until Rebecca was certain she would die of the enchantment.

He paused to move to the other breast. "Don't stop," she pleaded. Her hands threaded hard into his hair as she held him to her.

"Don't worry, honey. I have no intention of stopping."

She was dimly aware of his hands around her waist, of him lifting her and settling her on his lap. Her riding skirt bunched up around her knees and covered his wool-clad thighs.

Having her seated in front of him gave Luke better access to her mouth, her shoulders and her delicious breasts. Those dusty-rose peaks begged to be kissed.

His hands splayed over her back, he held her to him, taking his fill of her. As his tongue licked and curled around each nipple, he heard her groaning in pleasure.

His blood turned to fire as he felt her move on his lap, felt her press and squirm against his throbbing manhood, straining against the wool of his trousers.

Blindly he fumbled with the laces of her corset, cursing the double knots until they came loose. His fingers actually shook as he worked the laces free, one after the other.

She never moved, never tried to stop him. Slowly, so slowly, he pulled the laces through the eyelets. As the corset loosened, her breasts eased down, looking fuller, rounder and more even more enticing, if that was possible.

When he reached for her constricting waistband, he said, "Stand up."

Passion-driven, she complied. Her knees wobbled a bit, and he hooked his arm around her for support.

His fingers moved to her waistband, unfastening the buttons and pushing the skirt down to pool around her stocking-clad ankles.

Blood pounded in his ears and neck as he looked at her, in her camisole and pantalets. She was all long legs and bright eyes, and the insistent throbbing of his arousal made him wonder if he could wait much longer.

With urgent hands, he cupped the contours of her buttocks and hauled her to him, wanting to feel the length of her against the length of him. She was lush and luscious and she was inflaming his desire faster than a storm moving over the wild Texas prairie.

She molded herself to him. All heated flesh and soft, throaty purring. He groaned as he captured her

mouth once more, feeling his desire cresting and
knowing he had to have her soon.

He pulled the tie on her pantalets and felt it ease
down between them.

Rebecca felt his fingers intimately touching her like
fire on her skin. The flimsy material of her camisole
pulled erotically against her hard, cresting nipples, her
flesh aching for his touch, his mouth.

He found the edge of the camisole and began to lift
it, shirtlike, over her head. The thin lace caught on the
fullness of her breasts. But Luke was not daunted. He
wanted her naked. Taking her lush breasts in his hand,
he lifted them and slid the material over her nipples
with his other hand. He tossed it aside.

She stood naked before him, dressed only in her
stockings, the smooth black silk a lush contrast to her
paler skin.

Reverently, as if in prayer, he knelt before her. With
exquisite slowness, his hands encircled her thigh. She
gasped. Her body weak from the sensation, she
clutched at his shoulders. His touch a heated caress,
he rolled the silk languidly down her shapely leg.
Lifting her foot, he slid the stocking off, brushing a
finger across the length of her sensitive insole, making her shudder. He guided her foot to the carpet.

Thinking she could stand no more, she swayed, her
nails digging into his flesh as he lifted her other foot
and repeated the sensual gesture.

Her legs shaky, her muscles turned the consistency
of sweet, sun-warmed honey. She swayed again. He
caught her in his powerful embrace and settled her
gently on the bed, apricot flesh against stark white
cotton. She was an erotic vision. It would be a dream

come true for him as soon as he was deep within her. He shed his trousers and joined her on the bed.

Rebecca felt his weight for an instant before he shifted upward, supporting his upper body on his elbows. The feather bed bunched up around them, shutting out everything in the room but the two of them.

Stop this now! Rebecca's voice of reason called, as though from a great distance.

But her body was consumed by desire, and the voice was silenced by the demands of her body.

Luke's mouth devoured hers. Breathing was nearly impossible. Surely she didn't need to breathe. All she needed, all she wanted, was to feel. And she did. Her body was alive with feelings so raw, so intense, so powerful, that there was no room for thought.

The mat of hair on his chest prickled the sensitized flesh of her breasts and nipples and ribs. Everywhere he touched, she was on fire.

She clutched at his shoulders, feeling the fine sheen of perspiration against her fingers. She exulted in him, every touch, every movement, stoking the flame of desire to new intensity.

Fearlessly, driven by a force more powerful than any she'd ever known, she began to move beneath him, her body too inflamed to remain still.

Her hand played down his back, touching, tracing, the corded muscles pulled wire-tight as he levered above her.

"Luke..." She clawed at him. "Luke, please..."

"I will, darlin'. I will."

There was no more thought, no more hesitation. His mouth found her nipples once more, rougher now, and he took his pleasure in hearing her moan, feeling her buck and writhe beneath him.

His hand wedged between them, seeking the juncture of her legs. Wanting to touch her, to stoke the fire of passion, to make her ready for him.

"Open your legs," he ordered, his voice gentle yet demanding.

She hesitated.

But his fingers stroked her body from hip to breasts and back again in a rhythmic way, his hand always pausing to caress her aching nipples, to make her moan and strain toward him, and make the tight core of longing between her legs throb and pulse ever stronger.

He nuzzled her jaw and licked the inside of her ear. This time, when she felt his hand slip between her legs, she eagerly opened them to accept his touch.

Luke's fingers glided expertly to the center of her, feeling the slick moistness gathered there. Levered on one elbow, his leg firmly between hers, he slid two fingers into the folds of her womanhood.

Instantly she bucked and grabbed for his wrist, but he stroked her again, and she groaned in pleasure, her hand dropping back to her side, her legs opening wider.

Lightly he ran his fingers over the sweet wetness of her, watching the play of emotions on her face, watching passion draw her mouth down.

"Is it better there?" he whispered next to her ear. "Or...there?"

She whimpered her answer.

"Ah," he murmured, and stroked the spot, deeper and more fully. "There."

"Oh, yes," she told him through clenched teeth. "There. Please. There."

She bucked and twisted and clutched handfuls of the bedding as he teased her relentlessly, his own passion increasing with every touch.

She moved against his hand, pressing hard against his skilled fingers. He knew the release her body was seeking. His arousal was hard and pulsing and pressed hard against her hip as his own body begged for release.

He felt her movements increase, and knew she was close. He needed to be inside her when she reached her orgasm, needed to feel her convulse around him.

In one motion, he slid his hand free and moved between her legs.

His throbbing erection was poised at the entrance to her heated core, the wetness clinging to his aching tip. She moved then, straining up toward him, her hands at his hips, pulling him to her.

He thrust into her, feeling her sticky wetness surround him as he glided fully into her. He withdrew and thrust again, testing, coaxing, wanting her to match him in need and pleasure.

She was wild beneath him, arching her back to take more of him inside her. Her hardened nipples brushed against the plane of his chest, her hands roamed his back from shoulder to buttocks and back again.

With each touch, each movement, the flame inside him grew until it was like a prairie fire, hot and impossible to stop.

His mouth took hers roughly, twisting, slanting, demanding, and she met him, biting at his lip, sucking at his invading tongue.

Too many days, and far too many nights, had fueled his desire. He could wait no longer.

His thrusts became bold, full, reaching for the depths of her. Again and again he pounded into her, and she rose up to meet him each time.

Her breathing was ragged. His was nearly nonexistent. She took all he offered, and demanded more. She touched and kissed and nipped at his shoulder. She was feverish and wild, and he felt the first tiny tremors of her orgasm. He knew it would be only seconds. He withdrew fully and plunged into her with a slow, deliberate thrust that made her cry out her pleasure.

He covered her mouth with a silencing kiss, letting himself give in to the desire that threatened to carry him over the brink of all control.

He felt her orgasm a second before he poured himself into her.

The world around them dissolved. There was only the two of them and this bliss, this rapture they found in each other's arms.

Chapter Thirteen

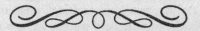

The first rays of sunlight were cutting through the partially opened window when Luke awoke. There was a fog-laced dampness in the air that felt soft and good against his bare torso, the part that wasn't covered by the quilt.

He stretched, flexing the muscles in his shoulders and back, and rolled over onto his side. His head cushioned on the down pillow, he caressed the empty place next to him. She was gone. She'd slipped silently from the bed as the morning doves cooed their wake-up call. He'd roused from his blissful sleep in time to see her closing the door.

They didn't need to speak. They'd said it all last night. With touch and taste and words whispered in flame-hot passion, they'd said and done it all.

Well, maybe not all, he thought with a smile that didn't come close to expressing his feelings. There were no words for this bliss, this contentment. He felt good, really good. He felt alive and right, as if he could conquer the world single-handed. He sure as hell was willing to try.

That smile turned into an all-out grin, and he chuckled to himself. He was in love. No ifs, ands or buts about it. Luke Scanlin was head over heels a goner. He didn't mind at all. Nope. He liked the notion. Liked it a lot.

He turned, putting his head on her pillow. The barest trace of her rose scent lingered there, stirring lush, heated memories of their wild lovemaking last night. His heart eased down into a slow, steady rhythm, and he let the feeling, new and exciting, wash over him. Love. From the minute he'd walked in here two days ago, from the second he'd kissed her that night in the entryway, this had been inevitable. It was as sure and certain as his next breath—no, more so, he decided with a gentle smile. He could stop breathing more easily than he could stop loving her.

Luke pushed down the covers—the cotton was soft and smooth against his fingers—and swung his bare legs over the side of the bed, his body making the shifting feather bed sink. The house was quiet. It was barely sunup, and way too early for the family to be up and around. They'd be sleeping in, he figured, and Lord knew they deserved it. No one had had a minute's sleep since this kidnapping mess started.

Sunlight caught his eye. He squinted, then rubbed the sleep from his face. He stood, relishing the way the cool air made goose bumps prickle over his body. He figured he'd get dressed and head on down to the kitchen, maybe get some coffee and wait for her.

He ambled over to the blue porcelain washbasin on the stand near the window and splashed some cold water on his face.

"Argh," he muttered as the water trickled down his neck, and he grabbed for the white linen towel. Another ten minutes and he was shaved and his hair was brushed. He fished his best shirt out of the bureau, frowning at the wrinkles in the white cotton. Someday he had to learn how to fold things.

He tried hand-pressing it. The hand-pressing—cowboy for laying it on the bed and pushing it flat with his hand—wasn't working any better now than it had any of the other times he'd made this same futile effort. Aw, hell, he thought, snatching up the shirt and putting it on anyway. He wanted to look good, special. Frowning, he pushed at the wrinkles where the shirt draped down his chest. He was behaving like some schoolboy on his first date.

He chuckled. They were long past the courting stage. Ah, yes, he thought with a sudden warming in his blood. He stilled the direction of his thoughts and made to button his shirt. Good Lord, his hands were actually trembling. He held his hand up. This was what she'd done to him. He'd faced the entire Johnson gang, all four of them, with steadier hands than these.

He really did have it bad. Ah, he thought, pulling on his black wool trousers and stuffing his shirt into the waistband, he didn't mind being all hot and bothered, because after last night, he knew she was, too.

Yeah, she had come to him. He had given her a chance to leave, and she'd stayed. He'd told her in explicit detail what he was going to do to her, to every inch of her, if she stayed, and she had. Wild and wet and passionate beyond anything he ever imagined, she'd stayed with him until the early morning. They'd made love and dozed in each other's arms, only to wake and make love again. She was insatiable, and he was exhausted, but blissfully content. He dragged in a long, slow breath and released it just as slowly.

Nothing could be any better than this. Okay, well, one thing. Waking up leisurely with her curled and naked in his arms.

With a confident smile, he headed for the kitchen.

Lost in thought, Rebecca sat in the window seat in her bedroom, watching pink and yellow streaks of sunlight chase away the night. The cooing of mourning doves caught her attention, and she pushed back the lace curtain to look out more easily.

The world looked perfectly normal, the way it did every morning. Except it wasn't normal. Nothing was as it had been. Nothing would ever be the same again.

Fear fluttered through her, and she drew up her legs, her chin resting lightly on her knees. Her silk dressing gown fell away, and she tucked it securely around her body. Beneath it, she was still naked from a night of lovemaking.

Two hours. Two hours she'd been sitting here. At least she thought it was two hours. The time, like the night spent with Luke, was a blur in her mind.

She remembered quite clearly seeing the light on in his room, remembered going in with the intention of thanking him for saving her son. That was the polite, reasonable thing to do, wasn't it?

He'd looked so helpless there, trying to pull those splinters from his fingers. More like a little boy than the harsh, cold man who had accompanied her into that alley. Maybe it was his helplessness that had gotten past her wall of defenses. Maybe it was simply exhaustion from the days and nights of worrying. Whatever it was, it had seemed that one moment she was sitting on the edge of the bed, helping him with the splinters that laced the tips of his fingers, and then ... then she was in his arms. He was kissing her with a passion that inflamed her senses; holding her with a strength she was powerless to overcome; touching her with an intimacy that ignited an all-consuming desire.

Oh, God, how could this have happened? Heat and guilt and shame washed over her like a tidal wave, leaving her breathless and frightened. This *could not* have happened. It was too awful, too terrifying, even to contemplate. A shaking started inside, the subtle beginnings of an earthquake. Her muscles cramped.

Rebecca Tinsdale did not—repeat, did not—give herself wantonly to men, and certainly not to this man ... never to this man.

Her arms encircled her knees, pulling them tighter against her, and her head lolled back against the smooth, cool plaster wall, trapping her hair tightly behind her. Annoyed, she shifted and pulled it over one shoulder.

As she glanced down at her hair where it covered one breast, she remembered Luke arranging her hair in just such a way, his knuckles brushing enticingly over her breast, and her nipples puckering into hard, aching nubs.

She swallowed hard against the sudden memories.

This was awful, and getting worse by the second. It had seemed so innocent when she went to his room. A simple conversation, nothing more, had been intended. An expression of thanks, and a goodbye—most importantly, a goodbye. How could it have gotten so out of control? How could *she* have gotten so out of control?

All she had to do was close her eyes, and the images of them together flashed hot and erotic in her mind, making her pulse quicken. Like a series of mind-searing photographs, they flashed one after another; naked and writhing under him, her legs wrapped around his waist, his mouth sucking on her nipples, while she moaned and pleaded and demanded more.

Heat seared her mind and body. Her breathing got a little more intense, a little more unsteady. Oh, this was worse than she'd thought.

In all the years of her marriage to Nathan, their times together had been nothing, *nothing,* like this. There had been quick kisses, an occasional coupling under the covers in the dark. Over the years she'd convinced herself that that was married life, that her memories of lovemaking with Luke were merely exaggerated daydreams.

Now...oh, now she knew, with a heart-pounding certainty, that they were real—wonderfully, deliciously, luxuriously real. Last night he had done things, said things, made her feel things that, in her most vivid dreams, she'd never imagined. How could she? How could she possibly know that a man and woman could give and take and please each other in ways such as that?

It was wrong. It had to be wrong. Everything about it was wrong, and yet...yet it felt so right. She'd never felt so alive in her life.

That earthquake inside was racing toward her soul, threatening to destroy her in the process.

How would she face her family, her friends? They would know what a wanton she had been. Surely no one could do the things she'd done with this man and survive intact.

Abruptly she stood and paced toward the closet, pausing to gauge her reflection in the mirror. Could it be? She looked exactly the same. There was no scarlet brand, no mark to indicate what she'd done. Perhaps it would be all right. She would simply go on as before, she thought with a confident tilt of her chin.

The terror inside her began to subside—for about thirty seconds, until she realized that this was not over. She would have to see him, at least, this morning. Maybe not. Maybe she'd take her breakfast in her room and hope that he would be gone by the time she went downstairs.

She sighed at the absurdity of that idea. She was going to have to face him sooner or later. The question was, what was she going to say?

Ah, so now we're down to it, Rebecca. How do you feel? What do you want?

How did she feel? She felt glorious. What did she want? She wanted him to leave, to go away and never, ever come back, because he was too tempting, too dangerous, and she had responsibilities to others that had to supersede all her personal feelings, no matter how heavenly.

She frowned. Logic and guilt merged in her mind, and her joy was replaced by hostility. It galled her, how willingly she had surrendered to him, despite all her fine words and pledges.

Well, all was most certainly not lost, not yet—and she intended to keep it that way. There would be no repeat of eight years ago.

She was not the naive girl of eighteen he had seduced and left shattered and disillusioned. No, dammit! She was a woman now, assured and in control of her life and her emotions, she told herself fiercely.

After all, she had made the choice to stay with him last night. She conveniently ignored her guilt-ridden thoughts of moments ago.

Feeling more confident, she strode for the wardrobe cabinet. She yanked open the door and grabbed a blouse, forest green, and a skirt, straight and black, to suit her ever-darkening mood.

She shrugged out of her dressing gown and washed up in the basin next to the wardrobe, scrubbing her face and arms hard, wishing she could wash him out of her mind as easily.

She put on her undergarments and reached for the corset she'd worn the night before. As she picked it up, the laces slipped to the floor, and she snatched them up. She started the arduous task of threading the laces through the dozen or so sets of eyelets, her resentment building.

A shiver passed through her as she remembered his expert fingers loosening the laces with exquisite slowness, freeing her breasts and body to his masterful touch, his mouth teasing the valley between her breasts.

Her eyes slammed shut against the sensual images.

"No," she said out loud to the empty bedroom. "No," she repeated more firmly, her hands curling into fists.

Would it always be like this? Whenever she saw him, would she remember every touch as though it were happening again?

With every speck of will she had, she would resist the temptation of Luke Scanlin, and all that he stirred within her. Not just for herself, but for the others, and for the secrets she guarded. Oh, yes, for those secrets most of all.

What was done was done. The past could not be changed, but the present could.

She would face Luke straight on, the same way she'd faced most things in her life. She would handle this calmly, firmly, and with dispatch. Now that she'd given herself to him, there was nothing to keep him here...once again, she thought with a tinge of sadness, he would go. She was certain. Only this time it was the best thing—the only thing for all their sakes.

The distinctive aroma of fresh-brewed coffee greeted Rebecca as she pushed through the kitchen door. It was too early for the staff to be up, she was thinking, when she heard, "Good morning, darlin'."

Luke. His tone was cheerful. He was perched on the edge of the kitchen table, acting like he owned the place. "I made coffee." He gestured with his cup. "Want some?" He wore a white shirt and black wool trousers, and his hair was damp and finger-combed back from his face. It ought to be illegal for a man to be that handsome this early.

For the span of two heartbeats, all she could do was look at him.

His smile was warmer than sunshine, and his eyes were soft and familiar; his expression was like an unspoken invitation. She fought the impulse to walk to him, to touch him, to ask him to take her in his arms again.

Her gaze flicked to his hand, curved around the white porcelain cup, and she remembered that same hand curved over the sensitive flesh of her breast. She was flooded with memories, and she couldn't speak or tear her gaze away.

Erotic thoughts, flashes of their naked bodies writhing and moving together, the moaning sounds of pleasure, the pleading demands, all seemed to engulf her in an instant. Swift and crystal-clear, they heated her body with anticipation and flushed her cheeks with shame.

It was the shame and fear that she hung on to like a lifeline, in a desperate attempt to strengthen her crumbling resolve.

Pulling herself up to her full height, she faced him squarely. "I expected you to be gone this morning."

He stilled, his coffee cup stopped in midmotion. His eyes widened in open surprise, and she saw him straighten slightly. He raked her with an assessing stare. It took every bit of willpower she had to stand there and not flinch. She was braced for an argument.

Evidently he wasn't. "Not exactly the greeting I was expecting. Most people are at least civil to their lover the next morning." He put his cup down and advanced toward her. "Have you forgotten already? Maybe you like to be kissed first thing in the morning? You have to tell me these things."

He was dark and powerful, and his intentions would have been clear even to a cloistered nun. She was not as immune to him as she had thought. As she watched him close in on her, her throat went dry and, God help her, she actually felt her body sway toward him, as though reaching for the enchantment that logic demanded she refuse.

Teeth-gnashing willpower kept her anchored to the spot. It didn't keep him from touching her, though. If only he wouldn't touch her. If only he weren't so heart-stoppingly handsome.

Though it felt like a retreat, self-preservation made her take a firm step backward. "Don't touch me!"

Alarm was obvious in her voice, and it gave him pause. His hand dropped away. "What?" His tone was incredulous.

"I said, don't touch me."

Luke stare at her intently. "That's not what you said last night."

She spun away and walked to the cupboard near the sink. Reaching up, she helped herself to a coffee cup. "I don't know what you're talking about," she said, pleased her voice sounded so casual, so calm. She didn't turn around to face him.

"I'm talking about us making love last night—until just a few hours ago, actually," he added, his tone firm.

Discreetly she gripped the edge of the counter, needing support. "We... I... Last night was a mistake." She straightened and turned to face him, though her hands still sought the support of the counter.

"I don't think so."

"Well, I do. Furthermore, I will not discuss it, now or ever again. It will *not* happen again. And if you bring it up or mention it to me or anyone, I will continue to deny it."

Here in the middle of this kitchen, on a bright October day, her announcement could not have surprised him more than if he'd been struck by lightning.

Was this some kind of a joke? It was a joke—right? Okay, her expression was grim, but she had to be joking.

His mind was working overtime. What the hell was going on? Could she have been that wild, that willing, and not care anything for him? Could he have been that wrong?

Not moving, he sought her gaze. That was when he knew. She was serious. He could see it in the hard glint of her eyes, as clearly as he'd seen the unbridled passion in them last night. It wasn't anger or even shame. No, what he saw there was fear, stark and raw. He knew it, had seen it in men's eyes before they made a deadly miscalculation.

But there was no miscalculation here, no reason to flee. Was there? Their lovemaking had been beautiful, passionate, endless.

His head came up with a start. Was that it? Was she afraid of the passion he'd ignited in her, afraid of her wild abandon?

Being with her, making love to her, had been more than he'd remembered, more than he'd imagined. What they had shared was soul-searing in its power. But her eyes held only fear and regret. It was perhaps the regret, most of all, that ate at him.

His desire faded under her cold stare. What had been blissfully beautiful dissolved, transformed into something quite different, something dark and ugly and cold.

An hour ago, he would have bet his life on her, on them—he'd been that certain. When she walked in here ten minutes ago, he'd been ready to reveal his feelings, tell her he loved her, tell her she'd given him all he ever wanted from this life.

Instead, here she stood, telling him that she wished last night had never happened. It hurt.

Though his expression was hard, Rebecca saw the emotions cloud his eyes. He raked both hands through his hair, his mouth pulled down in a hard line.

"Let me see if I have this right. You're telling me that what happened— Sorry," he said sarcastically, "that *nothing* happened. Is that it, sweetheart?" His face was stiff. A muscle played back and forth in his cheek. "If it wasn't you who left bloody claw marks on my back, then who the hell was it? Tell me, and I'll thank her for a mighty fine fu—"

"Go to hell, you arrogant bastard!" she snarled at him.

His eyes narrowed and his face went stone-hard. Rebecca inched backward, suddenly afraid, knowing firsthand the fury he was capable of.

But he never moved. In a voice that was tinged with barely controlled rage, he said, "I don't care what you say or what you do or how you lie, it won't change things. We *did* make love, and dammit, it was good, really good." His voice softened. "You enjoyed every breathless minute of it as much as I did. You can lie to yourself and you can lie to me, but I'm in your blood, sweetheart, and God help me, you're in mine."

Rebecca cringed, hating herself for hurting him, hating him for being right. She had enjoyed it, but the risk was too great. If her secrets were revealed, lives would be in jeopardy. There was no way she could explain without revealing the very thing she was guarding so fiercely. If she stayed with him, let him stay with her, it was only a matter of time until he guessed. No, she had to end this, had to send him away. It was her only choice, her only hope.

"It's over. Please leave."

"You're dismissing me? What's the matter... I'm not good enough for you, Princess? Afraid of what people would think if you were consorting with a common cowboy, instead of some high-class banker?"

"That has nothing to do with it, and you know it."

He shrugged. "It appears I don't know anything, sweetheart," he offered smoothly, glancing around the room with a disdainful look before focusing on her again. "Except you, of course. I know *you* quite well."

Heat flushed her cheeks, and she drew in a sharp breath, the air fueling the rage inside her. "Please accept my sincere thanks for your assistance in returning my son," she replied, her words cold and flat. "If any remuneration is required, I'll have the bank send you a check."

"Payment is not mine to accept," he said, with equally cold politeness. He started for the door, his boots drumming on the polished plank floor. "It was you who came to my room, remember, so if anyone is due payment . . ."

He tossed a gold piece on the counter. It landed with a piercing clink. He walked out of the room. For a long moment, she stood there, trembling with rage.

Damn the man. She grabbed hold of the counter edge, her fingers white-knuckle tight. She clenched her jaw so hard pain shot down her neck, then ricocheted up to give her a pounding headache. She wanted to shoot him. How dare he say such a thing to her—no matter what they'd shared, what she'd done, how she'd hurt him!

She rubbed at her temples, hard enough to make the headache worse instead of better. How she could have been attracted to him for even one instant was beyond her. She dragged in a couple of cleansing breaths, trying to still the anger that his remarks had evoked. She never wanted to see him again, she never wanted to hear his husky voice or see his sable-soft eyes or feel his provocative touch.

She dispelled the image of him by pounding her small fist on the smooth pine of the countertop. Yes, she thought with satisfaction, she'd made her feelings perfectly clear.

Luke Scanlin was gone from her life for good.

Chapter Fourteen

He was there before breakfast the next morning. Rebecca stood in the shadows inside the back door.

Every single member of her household, including all the servants, was in the backyard. They were laughing and shouting and throwing a ball in ways that made no sense to her.

"Here. Throw it to me, Luke," Andrew shouted. His small foot was braced on a five-pound sack of cornmeal that was leaking badly, apparently from being kicked.

"Run, Jack," Mrs. Wheeler called to the stable boy, who was racing between the other sacks of cornmeal and headed right at Andrew.

Luke tossed the leather-covered sphere to Andrew, and it sailed right past him. He took off after it while Jack slammed into the sack Andrew had just vacated.

There was more shouting and cheering, and Andrew was hollering something about the game not being over. Everyone was laughing and having a good time.

Mrs. Wheeler picked up a large stick and rested it on her shoulder, seemingly heedless of the dirt mark it left on her navy blue uniform. The usually perfect bun at the nape of her neck was loose and half-down.

Her cheeks flushed as she took a couple of swings with the stick. ''Okay, Marshal, pitch it,'' she said with a fierce determination that was undermined by her ear-to-ear grin.

It was at that exact moment that Rebecca stepped out into the sunlight of the porch.

''What the devil's going on?'' she demanded more harshly than she'd intended.

Everyone turned to see her standing there. In a glance, Luke took her in. Her black skirt, curve-hugging tight in front, with yards of fine muslin gathered over the bustle in back. Another of those high-necked blouses, this one in royal blue, tucked securely into her narrow waist. Her hair was done up in a style that was prim and proper, accenting her neck, all smooth and warm and soft. Beautiful as always, he thought with a sudden flash of familiar desire that he mildly resented.

''Mama!'' Andrew exclaimed, his high voice breaking into Luke's thoughts. ''Look! Luke's here! Isn't that great? He's teaching us to play baseball!''

''Great, dear,'' she muttered as she took in the scene in a heartbeat. Every face was bathed in a radiant smile that bespoke relief from the anguish and fear that had stalked them. Songbirds, finches and doves, sang merrily from the oak trees that bordered the yard. Even the sky was bright and clear and blue—not all that common in San Francisco.

It was good to see Andrew so happy, so excited—a miracle actually, considering the ordeal he'd been through. Now here he was, playing in a childish reverie. That was terrific. Trouble was, it was Luke who had brought the color back to his cheeks and the spark of excitement to his eyes. Why did it have to be Luke? Hot resentment flooded through her. *He can't be here. He can't!* her consciousness screamed in denial. This wasn't supposed to be happening. She'd thought she'd seen the last of him. Hadn't she made her feelings clear? With a sigh, she realized that now was not the time or the place to confront him.

Whatever his reason for being here, it was obvious that Andrew was thrilled. The two had taken an instant liking to each other. If there had been any doubt in her mind, Andrew had dispelled that yesterday. From the moment he got up and found Luke gone, he'd done nothing but talk about him. Luke was brave. Luke was strong. Luke was a marshal who'd saved him from the bad men. Luke. Luke. Luke! Until finally, in a fit of temper, she'd said, "He's gone and he won't be back, and I don't wish to discuss him any further."

Ruth had looked startled at the vehemence in her tone. Andrew had looked genuinely hurt. Rebecca had been instantly contrite. After all, it wasn't Andrew's fault that she was in this state of emotional turmoil. It was Luke's.

No wonder, then, that she was furious to see him. *Besides,* her rapidly elevating temper coaxed, *just look at the man.* He was dressed in faded denim, which molded provocatively to his legs like it was put on wet, and his midnight blue shirt was loose and opened at the collar. He wasn't even wearing a tie—not that he ever had, but it would be nice to see him conform, once in a while, she thought ruefully. His hair was too long, his hat was too old, and his black jacket barely concealed the gun he had tied to his right thigh.

Gun. The word and the reality slammed together in her mind. Good Lord, he was wearing a gun! Yes, she'd seen him wear one before, but not with her child so close. Not while he was in *her* backyard, playing with *her* son.

"Good morning," Luke called, with a smile that was warmer than sunshine. He waved, as though yesterday hadn't happened. "We were beginning to think you were never getting up."

"Oh, Mama likes to sleep late on Sundays," Andrew supplied, rushing up to stand next to Luke and cling to his hand.

Rebecca bristled. "Why are you here?" she demanded bluntly. "I mean, it's early." She stepped farther out onto the porch, squinting in the harsh sunlight. "We usually don't *receive*—" she emphasized the word "—until late afternoon."

If he noticed her rebuke, he gave no indication of it. Luke's hand rested affectionately on Andrew's shoulder in a way that made her uneasy. "Is it early? I didn't realize," he drawled smoothly. "I didn't know. I haven't been to bed yet."

I'll just bet, she fumed inwardly, remembering his affection for cheap perfume and cheaper whiskey. "Come on, Andrew." She motioned to him with her hand. "We have to go in now." She made a half turn, certain he would comply. To her great surprise, he didn't.

Andrew's eyes widened in puzzlement. "Aw, Ma, I don't—" His gaze immediately flicked to Ruth, who turned a questioning stare on Rebecca, as if to say, "Why?"

Rebecca ignored the unspoken question. She didn't want to say, *Because Luke Scanlin is here and he heats my blood and makes me want him.* Her pulse fluttered unsteadily.

"Andrew!" Rebecca repeated in a no-nonsense tone.

Andrew merely inched closer to Luke. Luke's hand moved more fully around the boy's shoulder in a gesture of noncompliance, which fueled that quickly rising temper of hers. Andrew pushed protectively against Luke's denim-clad hip, his back nestled against the holstered gun.

Alarm made her shout, "Andrew! Get away from him, right now!"

Luke's black eyes glowed with an anger that his expression did not betray. He cocked his head slightly to one side in thoughtful consideration. "Why?" His tone was calm, and there seemed to be a slight nodding of heads, affirming that the same question was on everyone's mind.

"The gun! He's—" She pointed.

"What?" Startled, he glanced down, relieved to see the weapon still securely hooked in his holster. His gaze flicked sharply back to her. "He's safe," he told her, folding his arms across his chest in what felt like a challenge. "He'll always be safe with me. Won't you, cowboy?" he added affectionately.

"Yup." A beaming Andrew craned his neck to look up at Luke's face. Even from this distance, Rebecca could see the adoration on her son's face, adoration that had always been reserved for her alone. Until Luke. Tears glistened in her eyes. He'd obviously won over her entire staff, and Ruth, and now even Andrew. Damn the man. Was there no limit to his charm? Was no one immune?

She was, she told herself firmly and, as though needing to prove it, she stepped down off the porch and took a step, one step, in his direction. "Guns, Marshal, are dangerous, and I prefer *not* to take chances."

"So I've noticed." His words were innocent, but charged with a smoldering intent that sent a shiver down her spine. "You needn't worry, Becky. I wear a gun for protection, mine and other people's." Moving his gun hand, he ruffled Andrew's hair playfully.

The implication of his words was lost on Andrew, but she understood. Oh, yes, she understood, with gut-twisting reality. He was here for Andrew, to protect Andrew. One of the men who had taken her child was still out there. Andrew was a witness. No matter what had happened between them, Luke had not forgotten that her son could still be in danger.

And here she'd been thinking only of herself, assuming that he was here because of her, when all the time he'd come to protect Andrew. Oh, God, how could she have been so foolish? She felt about two inches high. She wanted to apologize. She wanted to thank him. Pride wouldn't let her do either.

"Andrew, I think all this activity is too much for you," she said in a more subdued tone. "I don't want you to get overtired." She turned to her mother-in-law. "Ruth, do you think *you* are up to all this?" It was a gentle rebuke.

"Lord, yes," Ruth replied with a negligent wave of her hand. "You think I'd miss a chance to play base-ball with my only grandson?" She winked broadly at Andrew. "Besides, I'm not doing anything. I'm the... the..." She shot Luke a questioning look.

"Umpire."

"Ah, yes," Ruth repeated with a smile. "I'm the umpire." She thumbed her chest.

"Oh, really?" Rebecca replied absently. "That's very nice, but why don't we all go in and—"

"Nooo, Mama," Andrew whined. "The game's not over."

Luke ruffled Andrew's hair again, making him grin and laugh before he raked it back with his stubby fingers.

"Why don't you join us? You like games, don't you?" Luke added, in a deep, husky tone that made Rebecca take a faltering step backward. With a pat on Andrew's shoulder, he said, "Go get your mother."

"Oh, yes, Mama." Andrew raced across the grassy yard to fetch her. Tugging firmly on her hand, his voice shrill with excitement, he said, "You can do it, Mama. Don't be afraid. Luke will teach you. Won't you, Luke?"

He was already pulling her reluctantly toward the place where Ruth and Mrs. Wheeler were standing, about ten feet from Luke.

"Of course," Luke said. "It would be my pleasure to teach you...everything I know." The words were innocent, the tone was not. Nor were the erotic images that flashed, hot and luscious, in her mind.

Was he deliberately trying to...to... *What? Inflame your senses?* If he was, then he was doing a really fine job of it—not that she'd tell him so, of course. Mostly what she felt was trapped and, judging by the smug way he was regarding her, he knew exactly what he was doing. Moreover, he was enjoying every minute of it.

So the trap tightened, as if she were a rabbit in a snare. The more she struggled the tighter it got.

Her trap was emotional, not physical. Luke was a danger to her safe, orderly life, to her peace of mind, to her secrets, yet he was protection for her son. At least for Andrew's physical safety. The rest . . .

She wanted him far away from her, but close to her son. How could she have one without the other? How would she survive his constant nearness?

There had to be a way. There had to be a middle ground, but right this minute she didn't have the vaguest idea what that would be. For sanity's sake, her only hope was that the police found the kidnapper soon.

In the meantime, Luke was here, and she had to grin and bear it. There was no point in arguing. Sending him away would mean putting Andrew at risk. This was his job, after all, and, grudgingly, she decided to let him do it.

"All right," she said cautiously. "I'll play along . . . for a while." She meant more than the game.

Relief flashed in Luke's eyes. A smile threatened the corners of his mouth, but he restrained himself. So, she understood his meaning, and more than just the part about protecting Andrew. He was here for that, certainly. He liked the little guy—liked him a lot. She wouldn't send him away now. It was a start, anyway. Shifting his weight to one leg, he watched while the others surrounded Rebecca and tried to explain the game to her.

He'd like to explain a few things, too, but they had nothing to do with baseball. No, he had indoor sports in mind, very private indoor sports. Standing away from the others, he let his mind wander while he half listened. Ruth and Andrew were both talking at once, each telling Rebecca the rules of the game.

"Luke will throw the ball..." Andrew was explaining.

Luke smiled at the boy's enthusiasm. He sure could have used some of his energy yesterday. Goodness knew he'd needed something, and that bottle of whiskey he bought had only given him a headache. And it hadn't been cheap, either. It had been good single-malt whiskey from Kentucky. He'd sat in his room all night, drinking and reflecting about her and about that scene in the kitchen.

The more he'd thought about it, the angrier he'd gotten. At one point, he'd actually made up his mind to say the hell with the whole thing. It was a little vague what the whole thing was, but it was certainly anything that had to do with that woman. Yeah, even through a whiskey haze, he'd been sure of that.

But giving up didn't sit well with him. He was a man who was used to getting what he wanted. He wanted Rebecca. Trouble was, the lady didn't seem inclined to cooperate. So he'd forced himself to sit there, and the whiskey haze had made sure he did just that. At first he'd been angry, angrier than he'd ever been. Half a bottle of whiskey had dulled the anger to a manageable level.

"Then you hit the ball..." he heard Ruth saying. He was watching Rebecca, and the hurt he'd felt yesterday curled cold inside him. If she'd reached in and wrenched his heart out of his living chest, it couldn't have hurt more. He'd been so euphoric, so elated, so certain and so damned wrong. Luke had thought he knew women. At least, he'd thought he knew this woman. Evidently, he hadn't.

Looking at her now, he figured he should have known what the outcome would be. She was a lady, a woman with a position in San Francisco society, and he was a cowboy—sure a U.S. marshal, but mostly a common cowboy.

Well, dammit, this cowboy loved her. And no matter what she said, she cared for him. No woman could give herself so completely to a man and not care for him. Could she? He was damned if he knew, but he was gonna find out.

"...run really fast," he heard Ruth say. The sound of her voice jolted him out of his musings. He looked up in time to see her pointing to the bags of cornmeal.

Rebecca was nodding, her sensuous mouth drawn down in determined concentration. He knew that look, had seen it often enough. The anger he'd shrugged off circled near the edges of his mind. Abruptly he straightened, not willing to give it credence. "Okay, let's get going." He cleared his throat and tossed the ball lightly a couple of times. "The championship of the backyard is about to be decided."

Andrew returned to his place against the fence. He paced back and forth, his small face drawn in a frown that made Luke chuckle.

Ruth turned to Rebecca. "Now, I don't want to pressure you—" amusement danced in her eyes "—but the honor of women everywhere is at stake here, so if you don't hit the ball, we'll never hear the end of it." She shook her head in mock despair.

A grinning Mrs. Wheeler nodded in agreement.

"Fine." Rebecca hefted the stick to her shoulder. "Let's get this over with."

"Come on, Luke!" Andrew shouted through cupped hands. "Mama can't hit!"

"Really?" He smirked. "Glad to hear it."

"Hit it, Mrs. Tinsdale," the housekeeper called encouragingly.

Rebecca braced her feet in the soft grass. She focused on Luke, saw him pull back and release the ball. It whizzed past her head faster than a crazed hummingbird.

"Hey," she muttered, her gaze darting to Jack, who'd caught the ball and tossed it back to Luke. "Try that again, mister." Her competitive spirit rose to the surface. She wasn't about to let him win.

Again the leather sphere sailed past. She swung and missed. The action took some of the wind out of her and made a lock of hair come loose from her comb and bob up and down over her left eye. She blew it back.

"Strike two," Ruth said, apologetically.

"One more and we got 'em!" Andrew called jubilantly from his place near the back fence.

Rebecca didn't understand the rules exactly, but she knew one more wasn't good, so when she saw Luke prepare to throw, she braced her feet and...

"Swing!" Ruth yelled, obviously forgetting her impartiality.

Rebecca swung with all her might. The stick and the ball collided hard enough to make her teeth rattle. The ball flew past Luke's head and dropped inside the fence, about twenty feet from where a startled Andrew was racing to retrieve it.

"Run!" Ruth and Mrs. Wheeler shouted simultaneously. "Run and touch the sacks with your foot!"

Dazed, Rebecca hitched her skirt up above her knees and took off as if she were being chased by hornets.

"Get the ball," Luke called to Andrew.

"Keep going!" Ruth hollered, jumping up and down as if she had wagon springs on the soles of her shoes. "Run faster!"

Andrew scooped up the ball and threw it, but it fell far short of its destination, so he had to rush forward and repeat the process.

"Throw the ball, Andrew!" Luke shouted, laughing, as he ran toward home base.

Rebecca touched the second sack, then the third, and saw Mrs. Wheeler waving her on to the starting point.

Halfway to Ruth, she saw Luke step between her and the coveted home base.

"Here!" Luke shouted, arms held high, while he effectively blocked her path.

"Faster, Rebecca! Run!" Ruth shrieked, hopping up and down.

Rebecca put her head down and charged for home. A pain stitched her side. Her breath was short. She kept going, determined to win. She was moving so fast, she couldn't have stopped if she wanted to. Full force, she slammed into what felt like a brick wall. It was Luke's chest.

Together, they went down. Luke cushioned her fall, and Rebecca sprawled full length on top of him. His legs tangled with her skirts. His arms wrapped around her waist. When she looked down, he was laughing, really laughing. Tears glistened in his eyes, he was laughing so hard, and soon so was she.

The group converged on the spot, yelling and shouting, but mostly laughing.

"She's safe! We won!"

"She's out! We won!"

Luke sobered, and with genuine concern said, "Are you all right?"

"Fine," she replied, embarrassingly aware of their position, though no one else seemed the least concerned.

She squirmed to get up, but his grip around her waist tightened enough to give her a moment's pause. Then, in one motion, he rolled them over and stood, pulling Rebecca up with him. The group surrounded Luke and Rebecca, everyone arguing about who was the winner.

Brushing himself off, Luke said, "It was a nice try, Becky, but you were out by a mile."

"She was safe, Luke, and you know it," Ruth countered.

"Absolutely!" affirmed Mrs. Wheeler.

"Positively not!" Jack, the stable boy, put in, then looked startled that he'd been so outspoken with his employer.

"Safe!" Luke groaned in a playful tone. "How could she be safe? Didn't you see me catch that ball?" He was brushing dirt off his sleeve.

"Yeah," Andrew chimed in, taking Luke's side. "Didn't you see?"

Ruth and Mrs. Wheeler both gave Luke rather smug looks that said the decision was made. Both women hugged Rebecca. "You were wonderful."

Luke raked both hands through his hair, then settled his hat on his head. "Okay. I give up. You win."

"Naturally," Ruth said, amusement sparking in her eyes.

"Well," Luke added, "if I've got to lose, this was a rather pleasant way to do it. I'll have to remember the benefits of having ladies play." There was a wicked gleam in his eyes that made Mrs. Wheeler chuckle and Rebecca blush.

"Come on, Luke," Andrew argued, "you can't let 'em win like that. She was out, and—"

Luke swung Andrew up on his shoulders. "It's okay, cowboy. A man's got to be a good loser... sometimes. You've got to choose your fights, and then, when it's really important...never give up." He looked at Rebecca, the double meaning of his words obvious. Feeling awkward, she broke eye contact first.

With a knowing smile, Luke started for the house, Andrew balanced on his shoulders.

"Lemonade! Can we have lemonade?" Andrew called out to Mrs. Wheeler.

"Coming right up," the housekeeper agreed, and hurried to oblige.

"Wait for me," Ruth called after her. "You never put in enough sugar."

"Sure I do."

The two were still discussing how much sugar was enough as they disappeared inside.

Rebecca stood in the center of the yard. The breeze off the bay gently rustled the hem of her skirt against her ankles. Lord, look at me, she thought with irritation. There were grass stains on the front of her muslin skirt, and there was dirt, brown dirt, on her elbows and front. She looked like she'd been in a brawl and come out the loser.

That stray lock of hair bobbed in front of her face again, annoying her. She blew it back. It plopped down again with a vengeance.

She should be angry. She should be really angry, she told herself as she made a futile effort to brush away those grass stains. Instead, she chuckled. Then she laughed. She was a mess, but she'd had a good time. It had been fun, she realized. For all the dirt and stains, she'd had a really good time. Running around the yard like a kid. What would the fine ladies of San Francisco society say if they had seen her? Probably have apoplexy. She chuckled again, and, still brushing at her sleeve, headed for the house.

Shoving back that errant lock of hair back, she secured it with a comb. She spotted Luke near the porch, Andrew still balanced effortlessly on his broad shoulders.

It was a sight that brought her up short. The two men in her life; one who was everything she cared about, the other who had the power to destroy it. There they were, chatting together, clearly unaware of the torment this scene caused her.

They were engrossed in conversation, Andrew nodding solemnly at whatever Luke was saying. They were so natural together, so easy, as if they'd known each other forever. In a way, they had.

She hurried in their direction, fear outweighing all other emotions. Luke gave her a mischievous grin that sent tiny sparks skittering across her skin.

"Lemonade!" Mrs. Wheeler called from the porch with a wave. Luke plopped his hat on Andrew's head and gave him an affectionate swat on his bottom. Giggling, Andrew took off at a run.

"Come on, Luke," the boy called over his shoulder, the hat down around his ears.

Luke waved, but didn't follow. He waited for Rebecca. She stopped directly in front of him. His expression was unreadable and, for a second, she tensed, worried about what he would say to her.

The breeze ruffled his hair. He combed it back with his fingers. His eyes assessed her boldly. "It was a lonely night."

She had been prepared for any of a dozen different remarks. She had not been prepared for that simple statement. Nor was she prepared for the sudden tingling in the pit of her stomach.

Unsteady, she tried to change the conversation. "That was nice." She gestured with her head toward the playing area behind her. "I liked that."

"That's two things I now know you enjoy." His voice was soft, and disturbing to her already sensitive nerves. She felt a blush warm her, then travel up her neck. "Is the game a new one?"

His smile was immediate, and rich as sun-warmed honey. "Ah, no, Princess, it's as old as time."

Her stomach did that funny flip-flop again. "I was talking about baseball." She glowered, refusing to respond to his seductive charm.

"I wasn't." His words were blunt. His tone was lush.

"Hey, you two," Ruth called from the porch, blessedly breaking the spell he was weaving much too easily around her. "Lemonade's ready. Come on. We've got ice melting in here." With a wave, she went back inside.

Luke took a measured half step in Rebecca's direction. Towering over her, he said softly, "We've got ice melting out here, too." He pretended to brush a lock of hair back from her cheek.

She shivered in response, then stiffened, steeling herself against his sensual caress.

"Don't."

"Don't what? Don't touch you? Don't want you? Don't care?"

"Yes."

"I can't do that."

"You have no choice."

"Neither do you."

She shook her head emphatically. "That's where you're wrong. There are always choices, and I—"

"Rebecca, dearest," a male voice called. Startled, they both looked up, to see Edward striding across the yard toward them.

Chapter Fifteen

Instantly the mood changed.

"What the hell?" Luke muttered.

Rebecca, desperate for any interruption, skirted around Luke and greeted Edward warmly.

Luke watched the two of them. They were both all smiles. It didn't make a bit of sense. How the hell could she do that, greet him like that, after the way he'd wormed his way out of helping her? Now, if she'd asked him to shoot the man on the spot, that would have made sense.

It's none of your business, he warned himself.

The hell it isn't, he thought with a rush of possessiveness that made his hands curl into fists. He had to resist the urge to strike the man.

"Rebecca." Edward's brows drew down as he appraised her appearance critically. "What on earth has happened?"

"We were playing."

His gaze shot to Luke, then back to Rebecca. "Playing?" he repeated cautiously.

Rebecca understood his meaning, and resentment flared. He had no right to question her. But Luke was watching them too intently and, feeling that Edward was the safer of the two, she forced a smile and said, "Baseball, Edward. We were playing baseball with Andrew and Ruth."

"Oh, I see," he confirmed, in a way that said he didn't see at all. And that rankled her even more.

Edward straightened, adjusting the sleeves of his perfectly tailored blue suit.

"Morning, Ed," Luke said, with a nod but no trace of a smile. "A bit early for calling, isn't it? I mean, Becky and I haven't even had breakfast yet."

Edward's brows drew down. "Sir, I believe you have the advantage." His tone was polite, and if he was surprised, he hid it well. The man was too smooth, too slick, and Luke took an instant dislike to him.

"Name's Scanlin," Luke said, not bothering to offer his hand. "And yes—" he glanced over at Rebecca, then back to Edward "—I believe I do have the advantage."

Edward's gaze turned razor-sharp. "Just what—"

Rebecca stepped between them, her color high. Anger sparked in her eyes.

"Edward..." she said warmly, her hand resting lightly on his sleeve. She offered her cheek for a kiss, then cut Luke a quick glance to make sure he noticed. He did.

"Marshal, I believe you said you were leaving."

Luke didn't move.

There was an awkward silence before Edward said, "Ah, Marshal, Rebecca was telling me last night over dinner—" he let the implication sink in "—that you were instrumental in the return of Andrew."

"Yes, that's correct. And I understand that you were not."

Edward's head came up with a snap. His eyes sharp with unconcealed anger, he took a half step in Luke's direction. Luke held his ground.

"Wait, you two." Rebecca demanded. "I won't have any trouble here." She flashed them each an angry look. "Luke, maybe you'd better go."

She saw him stiffen, saw a muscle flex in his cheek, and she thought for a moment he would refuse. Thankfully, he didn't.

Without a word, he strode for the porch and disappeared inside.

Rebecca let out the breath she'd been holding. Forcing a smile she didn't feel, she slipped her arm through Edward's, and they strolled toward the big oak near the back fence. She didn't think now was a good time to go into the house, because Luke might decide to linger awhile.

"Rebecca, is that man still staying here? You told me he left yesterday."

"He did," she answered, not liking this cross-examination. "He came back this morning."

"To stay?" His tone was sharp.

"Of course not. I told you he was here to see Andrew. We were playing baseball." She angled him a look. "I made a home run."

"Is that so?"

The significance was plainly lost on Edward. Even so, a little feigned enthusiasm would have been appreciated.

She sighed. "Why are you here, Edward?"

"What? Oh, I'm sorry to call so early, but I wanted to come by before you made any plans. The governor is in town, and I was hoping you would come for luncheon. You know how much he likes you."

She stopped. "Edward, I can't possibly. I mean, Andrew—"

"Of course, we'll take the boy, too, if you like, though I suspect it would be quite boring for him—political talk and all."

There was something in the way he always referred to Andrew as "the boy" that was unpleasant. She pushed the feeling aside.

"Edward, surely you can understand that under the circumstances I can't possibly go to luncheon today."

He looked genuinely puzzled. "Why, dearest? Andrew is home safe. Surely you can spare a few hours for something important to me."

Two days ago she'd begged him to help her save her son, and he'd failed her miserably. Now he was here asking her to put aside her plans and her feelings to do something as trivial as going to luncheon?

Anger nuzzled the edges of her mind. She'd thought she'd gotten past this. They'd had dinner last night, and Edward had explained his situation, offered his apologies and pleaded for her forgiveness until finally she acquiesced.

Yet now she was unable to restrain herself from making comparisons. Luke hadn't hesitated, hadn't pleaded rules and restrictions and fear of recriminations. He'd gone with her, stayed with her, put his life on the line, all for her.

Suddenly Edward came up lacking. But they had been friends, good friends, for a long time. It was difficult not to at least *try* to be understanding.

Again, Rebecca forced a smile she didn't feel. "I would like to help, Edward. But I won't leave Andrew. Not now."

"You aren't worried something will happen, are you?" He touched her arm. "I'm absolutely certain there will be no more trouble."

"I'm not so certain. Marshal Scanlin has reminded me that there is another kidnapper at large. Besides, Andrew is still frightened. You must understand."

"But, dearest, Ruth is here, and the servants..."

"I'm not leaving Andrew."

"But, Rebecca, to give up an opportunity to meet with the governor... His support could make all the difference to my campaign in the upcoming city election."

So that was it, Rebecca thought with a mix of disappointment and frustration. Edward saw Andrew's safe return much as he would any business deal. Transaction complete. Next.

"I'm sorry, Edward. I'm not interested in the governor or...anyone else at the moment. I nearly lost my son, and through a miracle—" a dark-eyed cowboy of a miracle, she thought but didn't say "—I have him back. As I told you last night, since I no longer have the paper, I intend to spend more time with my son."

"Rebecca, dearest, of course you want to be with your son." His tone was contrite. "I was being a rude and selfish bore. Please forgive me."

"Of course, Edward," she replied, out of courtesy, not sincerity.

He looked doubtful but didn't press the point. "I am sorry about the paper, but you'll find that you won't miss it." He brightened. "I intend to count on you heavily for your guidance and support in the upcoming campaign. Why, I'll venture to say that we'll be so busy you won't have any time for regrets."

"We'll see," Rebecca murmured, and started for the house. Edward fell in alongside her.

"Rebecca."

"Yes."

"About the marshal..."

"What about him?"

"You are certain he's no longer staying here?"

"I told you so, didn't I?" she snapped.

"Yes. Yes. It's just that people will talk, and—"

"I really don't care what *people* think, Edward. It's none of their business."

"Now, dearest, don't get upset. I know you've been under quite a strain, and you haven't been thinking as clearly as you normally would."

"I am thinking quite clearly, thank you very much. I'll have anyone I like stay here or not, and I don't give a da—"

"Rebecca!"

She sighed. "For heaven's sake, Edward. My son was kidnapped, Ruth was ill... The man is an old friend, and a professional lawman. He was the one who risked his life to get Andrew back."

Edward looked serious. "I never meant to imply anything wrong. It's just that Andrew is home now, and the man is still here."

"He's not here. How many times do I have to say it?"

"Yes, dear. I'm only looking out for your own good."

There was that paternal tone again and, right on cue, her temper edged up. She knew he was right. She had run the risk of gossip having a stranger—a single, handsome, unmarried stranger—stay with her. Having him there had been an even greater risk, one that the good people of San Francisco would never suspect.

They climbed the three porch steps and went into the back entryway and down the hall to the front of the house. She avoided the kitchen, fearing that Luke was there. She didn't want another scene.

"It's very thoughtful of you to worry about me and my reputation, Edward." She couldn't keep a tinge of sarcasm out of her voice. "Please don't. I scandalized this town when I kept the paper, and they managed to get over it. I think everyone will get over this, too."

"This isn't a matter for joking, Rebecca."

"What makes you think I am?" She pulled open the front door. "Now, you'll have to excuse me. I want to spend the rest of the day with my son."

"I'll give the governor your regrets."

"Please do." She closed the door softly behind him and headed for the kitchen.

"What do you mean they aren't here?" She addressed Ruth, who was finishing a glass of lemonade, the ice cubes clinking against the side of the crystal.

Ruth peered at her over the rim of the glass. "Well, a policeman came, saying they needed more information on the kidnapping. The marshal said he'd take Andrew and bring him back."

"And you just let them go?"

"Well, yes. I mean, Andrew is safe with the marshal." Her brows drew down. "He said they'd be back in a couple of hours."

"How could you do that without asking me?"

"What was there to ask? The marshal needed Andrew to help relate the whole story to the police."

"But Andrew—"

"Was more than happy to go along. I saw you were with Edward, and I thought you might be talking business or some such, and I didn't want to disturb you. If it had been anyone but the marshal, of course, I would have said no, but under the circumstances, Andrew can't be with anyone better."

"Or anyone worse," Rebecca muttered.

Chapter Sixteen

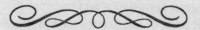

Luke kept Andrew wedged securely in front of him as they rode double. They were headed for police headquarters, on California Street. Saddle leather creaked as Andrew shifted and squirmed in the saddle.

"We coulda won, you know, Luke," Andrew pronounced, twisting his small body to look back at Luke.

"Next time, partner," Luke countered. He adjusted his hat lower against the midmorning sun. "There's always next time."

Andrew's face screwed up in serious consideration, and Luke chuckled. He hadn't realized that kids took things so seriously. Of course, his experience with children was virtually nonexistent, so this was a learn-as-you-go proposition.

"You wanna hold the reins?" he asked.

"Can I?" Andrew craned around, his black eyes sparkling with anticipation, then bounced up and down.

"Sure. Sit very still." Luke threaded the reins through Andrew's fingers. The thick leather was so wide he could barely hold them. Luke knew the gelding had a soft mouth, and so he cautioned, "Now don't pull back, okay? You don't want to hurt him."

"I'll be real careful" came the solemn reply.

Luke kept his hands resting lightly on his thighs, letting the boy get the feel of the horse. "Do you know how to ride?" he asked after a minute or so.

"Well, no. My papa was gonna teach me, but he went to heaven before he could."

Luke felt a tug of sadness for the boy, knowing what it was like growing up without a father. "What about your mother?"

"She said she's gonna . . . soon. Real soon."

"You think she'd mind if I gave you a lesson?"

"Oh, no, sir." The eagerness in his voice was unmistakable.

So Luke spent the next couple of minutes explaining the fine points of riding in the Western fashion. He didn't know the first thing about those tiny little saddles the dudes seemed to prefer. As they continued, he realized he was enjoying this—a great deal. There was something about being with Andrew that felt, well, familiar, which was silly. They'd only just met. Still, it was a feeling he'd had from the first. It was a nice feeling, and he gave in to it.

He showed Andrew how to neck-rein as they turned onto Stockton Street. He'd decided to take the long way around. Carriages rolled past them, their wheels humming harshly against the hard street.

The horse was well trained, and moved along at a steady pace. "Now give him a pat," Luke told Andrew. The boy did, and the horse shivered in response, making them both laugh.

Down the street they rode, past the small shops—a tailor's, a butcher's, and a hat shop with a flashy red hat in the window that Luke instantly thought would look perfect on Rebecca.

He frowned. He should have asked her before—well, at least told her they were leaving. But dammit, it galled him the way she'd just forgiven that weasel and welcomed him into her home again. Damned if he was going back out there and interrupt their intimate little chat.

How could she do that? he wondered with jaw-clenching anger. How could she stand there and talk to the pasty-faced little weasel? Hell, she treated that bastard better than she treated him, and he, *he,* was the one who'd stood by her. What the devil was wrong with her?

He steeled himself against the sudden rage and got his mind back on immediate business. He had to get this child to the police station and see what they could do about motivating the officers to get up off their duffs long enough to find that other kidnapper.

Turning onto Sacramento, they made their way past an odd mix of houses and stores, and cut up Kearney so that Andrew could see the fire station. The doors were open and the firemen were outside, washing the fire wagon. Its bright red paint glistened in the sun. A dalmatian barked happily at a freight wagon that lumbered past.

"What's her name?"

"Whose? The dog?"

"No. Your horse."

"Oh." He chuckled. "*His* name is Scoundrel."

"What's a . . . a . . . scoundrel?"

"It's something you don't want to be, cowboy. Believe me."

"Are you?"

"Depends on who you ask, I guess." Now, Becky might have a real strong opinion on that one, he mused.

Andrew was busy tugging on the reins, making the horse chew on the bit, shaking his head and making his bridle rattle.

"Here, let me help you." Luke gently reached around to guide his hands, easing the reins. "Remember, this is a living, breathing animal, sort of like you and me. You have to treat him kindly, not like a toy."

Andrew nodded his head, banging into Luke's chest with the movement.

"Okay, now you try," Luke told him.

Andrew did, and his eyes were wide when the horse obeyed each command. "Look, Luke, I did it! He likes me, I think."

"Sure he likes you." And so did he, Luke realized. The boy was smart and eager, and all he needed was someone to show him. Luke thought he wouldn't mind being that someone. As they rode, the boy cradled in the curve of his arm, an easy feeling curled, warm and comfortable, in Luke's heart.

It was a real surprise. A man could get to like this real quick.

Of course, Andrew was a special kid. Luke had known that right off. The way he'd hung on, refusing to cry, while all hell was breaking loose around him. A hell of a special kid. Becky had done a good job with him. Must have been tough, what with her husband dying and all. Good thing she had Ruth. Anyone with eyes could see she thought the sun rose and set in this boy. And it was just as obvious that the boy felt the same way. Lucky kid. Things might have gone a little easier for Luke when he was a kid if there'd been a grandmother to care for him.

You did all right anyway, Scanlin.

Yeah, but it had been tough, damned tough. Nothing that he'd wish on anyone else.

Hey, where'd all this melancholy come from all of a sudden? he asked himself. *Get back to work.*

He spotted the city hall and, lifting the reins from Andrew's fingers, stopped the horse.

Luke slid down and then helped Andrew dismount.

"Where are we goin'?" Andrew asked cautiously.

Luke dropped down on one knee and took Andrew's shoulders in his large hands, feeling sun-warmed cotton smooth against his touch. He pushed back Andrew's breeze-tousled hair.

"Now, we're going in here, because we have to make a report of everything that happened to you."

Andrew went pale. He didn't move.

Two uniformed policemen strolled past and went inside.

"Andrew?" He lifted the boy's chin with his thumb. "It's all right. There's no one in there who's going to hurt you. They need to know if the men said anything to you, told you anything that might help the police find the bad men and put him in jail. Do you understand?"

Andrew nodded, but his expression was grim. "I don't wanna talk about it. Can't we go home?" He made a half turn, and Luke turned him around.

He rubbed the boy's shoulders, feeling them tremble beneath his hands. Poor kid, he was scared to death, and with good reason. The kid put up a brave front, though. This morning at the house, no one would ever have known anything had happened.

"Andrew, you're not alone," he said, very softly. "I know you were scared when those men took you. I know you were even more scared when no one came for you."

Andrew nodded again. His chin quivered, and he stared hard at the toe of his shoe. "It's all right to be scared. I'm scared a lot of times."

Andrew lifted his head cautiously, and Luke saw the tears glistening in his black eyes. "You are?"

"Sure." He gave a little smile.

"But you're a marshal, and you have a gun..."

"Guns don't always help. Sometimes the things that scare you the most are things you can't fight with a gun. Things like being alone in the dark."

"Are you afraid of the dark?"

"In a way," he said, thinking that the dark he was afraid of was the empty place in his heart.

"Will you trust me, Andrew? Will you believe I wouldn't let you do anything that would hurt you?"

A tear pooled in the corner of Andrew's eye and trickled down the side of his nose. Luke pulled off his neckerchief and swiped at the tear. Then he looped the neckerchief around Andrew's neck and made a show of placing it just so.

Andrew studied the knot as if he were considering the fate of the nation. Then, slowly, he looked into Luke's face again and said, "Okay."

Standing, Luke took the boy by the hand and led him inside. The police were on the first floor. A series of offices surrounded an open central area with a large front desk, which was manned by an enormous sergeant. Dust motes floated in the sunlight pouring through the large window behind the desk.

"Scanlin," Luke said, by way of introduction. "Here to see Captain Brody."

He squeezed Andrew's hand in reassurance.

Brody's office was large, square and surprisingly neat. File cabinets and bookshelves lined one wall.

Brody greeted them from behind his desk and, though he didn't offer Luke a handshake, he was particularly kind to Andrew, letting him sit in his swivel chair while he perched on the corner of the desk, asking questions.

It took the better part of an hour to fill out the necessary forms, make notes and answer questions. Luke hovered like a lion over a cub while Brody and one of his assistants asked questions of Andrew—descriptions of the men, where he was kept, if he'd heard the men say anything about where they were going.

Andrew bravely told everything he knew. Occasionally his chin would quiver and his gaze seek Luke out. Luke would answer with a smile or a wink of encouragement, and that seemed to be enough. Brave kid, Luke thought with admiration.

When they finished, Luke spoke to Brody out of Andrew's hearing.

"Did you find the body?"

"Yeah, we found it. Bartender in the saloon said he was Jack Riggs. He had a brother named Bill. It was probably him that got away."

"Well, if you know who you're looking for, then you shouldn't have any trouble finding him."

Brody made a derisive sound in the back of his throat. "Come on, Scanlin. You know it's not that easy."

"Yeah," he reluctantly agreed.

"Besides, who says he hasn't ridden outa here by now?"

"Not in the condition he's in. I'm sure I winged him. How bad, I don't know, though."

"We'll keep checking. In the meantime, the boy's back and Mrs. Tinsdale should *finally* be happy."

Luke bristled, remembering Brody's earlier snide remark about Becky and knowing now about the articles on police corruption. "Yeah, she's happy, no thanks to you." He turned sharply, took Andrew by the hand and walked out.

"You were very brave," Luke said, lifting Andrew up onto Scoundrel's back. The boy was still pale and quiet, and it gnawed at Luke to see the little fellow so unhappy. Since he was the one who'd brought the boy down here, put him through this, he felt, well, responsible.

"You know, Andrew, I was just thinking about ice cream." He feigned a frown. "I don't suppose you like ice cream . . . do you?"

"Ice cream. Sure I do. Strawberry!"

"Strawberry? Really?" He grinned. "Why that's my favorite, too." Gathering the reins, he swung up behind Andrew, settling him comfortably on the tops of his legs. He handed him the reins, helping him a little. "What do you say we go find us some ice cream?"

"Yes!" He bounced up and down in excitement.

With a shift of his weight and a nudge of his spur, the horse turned left and headed down Kearney Street. It seemed that what wasn't a bank or a hotel was a market or a bakery. They passed the post office, the customhouse, several cigar stores and a couple of harness makers.

San Francisco was a thriving metropolis, that was for sure. And you'd think in such a city there'd be at least one ice cream parlor.

He stopped to ask a merchant who was sweeping the walk in front of his restaurant.

"Clayton's, over on Montgomery. It's a family place. They don't serve no liquor, just ices and sweets."

"Thanks." Luke touched two fingers to the brim of his hat. Out of the corner of his eye, he saw Andrew do likewise in a way that made him feel pleased.

Fifteen minutes later, they were seated in one of the swankier places in town. Not exactly your run-of-the-mill ice cream parlor, Luke thought, taking in the cut-crystal chandeliers, antique mirrors and European paintings.

"Two dishes of strawberry ice cream," Luke told the uniformed waiter, who returned a few minutes later with two heaping dishes of a fluffy pink confection.

Andrew made quick work of his, spilling a little on his shirt and leaving a little more on his chin. Luke ordered another round. A boy could never get enough ice cream.

"Tell me, Andrew, what do you like to do for fun?" Luke said in between bites.

"Well, sometimes Grandma and me play checkers. I like that. Grandma's not very good," he said, shaking his head sadly, "so I win most times, but she's fun. She tells me stories, too."

Luke nodded, and took another spoonful of ice cream. "Do you like school?"

Andrew seemed to consider this for a moment. "Sometimes. I like arithmetic and reading. I don't like spelling." He shoveled in another mouthful. "Too many letters. Numbers are easier, 'cause there are only ten and I can remember those."

"Ah," Luke returned with great seriousness, while struggling not to laugh. "What do you like to read?"

"In school they make us read McGuffy's reader." He screwed up his face. "It's about dogs and cats and people just walking around and stuff like that. But Grandma Ruth helps me read the good books."

"Good books?" Luke was intrigued.

Andrew took another bit of rapidly melting ice cream and ignored his napkin to wipe his mouth on his sleeve. "The ones about Deadwood Dick and Jesse James."

"Ah," Luke said knowingly, "you mean the dime novels, the adventure stories."

"Oh, yes, they're fun. Did you read the one about the Comanche raiders? I liked that one the best so far, I think. About a hundred Indians stole some horses and killed the rancher, and one Texas ranger had to go get 'em back and there was a big fight and the ranger killed all the Indians and took back the horses to the rancher's wife and she was real glad." He said it all in one breath.

"My goodness, Andrew, are you sure there were a hundred Indians and only one ranger? I mean, I was a ranger, and we—"

"You were a ranger!" Andrew shouted, making everyone in the shop turn and stare.

Luke grinned. "Well, yeah, before I was a marshal I was a ranger."

"A ranger..." Andrew repeated, in a reverent tone that actually made Luke blush. He couldn't remember the last time that had happened.

"Well, it's not all like they write in the books. Mostly you're alone all the time, and it can be dangerous."

Andrew's small mouth drew down in a frown. "I know. I told Mama once I was gonna be a ranger, and she got all funny and sad like and said she didn't want me to go away. Was your mama sad when you went away?"

"My mother died when I was a few years older than you."

"Oh," Andrew returned, his voice suddenly small. "My father died, too."

For a moment they were both silent, the man and the boy, so much alike in so many ways.

The sound of music carried in through the open windows, and it was getting louder, as though the music were moving closer. People around them began to crane their necks or stand, trying to see out the glass windows that bordered the street.

Luke twisted in his chair, the cane creaking as he shifted his weight. That's when he saw the wagon go past. It was big and enclosed and painted in bright, garish colors, red and yellow and green.

"What the—" He went to the door. Andrew dogged his steps.

People crowded around the windows, peering out. Luke stepped out onto the sidewalk as a second wagon rolled past.

"A circus," he said, grinning at a white-faced clown doing a handstand. He glanced back to see Andrew hanging back near the doorway.

"Come on, cowboy. Look. It's a circus." He held out one hand, and Andrew rushed forward, slipping a hand into his.

The music was louder now, a pump organ with pipes sticking up through the roof of one of the wagon. The noise was ear-piercingly loud.

More clowns romped and skipped past, distributing hand bills that announced that the Dubin Circus had arrived in San Francisco and would be setting up in Golden Gate Park.

Glancing down, Luke thought he would forever remember the wide-eyed wonder on this child's face. It was obviously a first for him.

It didn't look like much of a circus to Luke. It seemed a little old, a little worn, not at all like the one he'd seen in St. Louis one year. But seeing it with Andrew made it look fresh and new and exciting.

The red wagons lumbered past, stacked high with rolls of brightly striped canvas and long poles bobbing up and down while they extended beyond the wagon beds. A woman dressed in pink tights was riding bareback on a white horse.

She stopped long enough to say, "Circus tomorrow, handsome."

Luke smiled. "Thanks."

"Bring your son!" she added as the white horse pranced and pawed the ground. "He's gonna be a looker like his father." She winked and nudged the horse, who pranced away.

"He's not—"

She was out of hearing distance. What the devil made her think they were related? He glanced down to see that Andrew was mesmerized by the spectacle. There was a clown, and a trained bear that rolled and tumbled down the street. There was a rather scrawny-looking mountain lion in a cage that snarled and lunged at the iron bars. Andrew jumped and squeezed Luke's hand. Luke squeezed back.

He was about to suggest that they head for home when he spotted the elephant. What the devil they were doing with an elephant was anyone's guess, but they had one.

When the elephant lumbered past his trunk moved, snakelike, in Andrew's direction, brushing across the boy's chest—in search of food, no doubt. Finding none, it quickly retreated.

"Did you see?" Andrew asked, a little breathless. "The elephant touched me...here," he explained, running his hand lightly over his chest, now smudged with dirt, as well as strawberry ice cream.

"I did see."

"I never saw an elephant before, except in a picture book at school. Do they really eat through their nose?"

Luke chuckled. "It's called a trunk, and no, they use it like a hand and pick things up, then put them in their mouths."

"An elephant ... And the pretty lady. Did you see the lady all dressed in pink? I never saw Mama dressed like that."

Luke laughed. "No, I don't suppose you ever will." *Though I wouldn't mind,* he thought.

The boy was so excited, and Luke was enjoying being with him. It was impulse that made him say, "Do you want to go watch while they set up?"

"Oh, could we?" It was a plea, not a question.

"Sure, let's go."

The word of Andrew's rescue and of the shooting spread quickly through San Francisco's social elite.

People began calling shortly after noon. Neighbors, friends, business associates, all with congratulations on Andrew's safe return, many wanting to meet the man who had saved Rebecca's son.

She tried to focus on serving tea, offering sandwiches and cakes and making conversation. Yes, she was very grateful for the marshal's help. Yes, Andrew was unhurt. No, she didn't miss the paper. It seemed she answered the same questions over and over, until she finally had a pounding headache.

The last of the guests lingered interminably long. Rebecca was seriously considering making up some excuse about an appointment or some such thing in an effort to induce them to leave. The words were forming on her lips when Andrew, looking more like a ragamuffin than the well-dressed young man who'd left here this morning, barreled through the double doors and skidded to a halt in front of her.

Any concern she had had about Andrew being at the police station disappeared. There was not the slightest indication that anything traumatic had been suffered. In fact, he looked inordinately happy, she thought grudgingly.

"Hi, Mama. We had ice cream, and we went—"

"So I see." She touched the pink smudge on the front of his shirt. "Is that where you've been...all this time?"

"Oh, no, we—"

She cut across his words. "We have company, dear. You can tell me later."

Luke strolled in, looking tall and dark and head-turning handsome, just like always. And, just like always, those same darned goose bumps scampered up her legs.

Evidently Mrs. Hillebrand and her teenage daughter were not unaffected. They stared openmouthed at Luke, and Rebecca was tempted to caution Ariel not to drool in polite society.

She made introductions.

"Mrs. Hillebrand and Ariel, may I present Marshal Scanlin?" Her voice was flat, and she kept her anger barely under control. They'd been gone for hours and hours without a word, and now Luke strolled in here calm as you please, without any apologies, any explanations.

"Ladies," he said, tossing his hat down on the pale silk side chair. He acted as though he were coming home, which he wasn't, she thought petulantly. He took each woman's hand in turn. His smile was radiant, boyish and charming. "I'm always pleased to meet two such lovely ladies."

Mrs. Hillebrand blushed. Ariel giggled. Rebecca seethed.

Devilment sparked in Luke's eyes as he settled comfortably on the settee. Andrew squirmed into the vee of his legs, and Luke pulled him fully onto his lap.

"Marshal," Mrs. Hillebrand began, "everyone is talking about what a hero you are."

"Not at all," he said as Andrew lounged back against Luke's chest.

"Of course you are. I'm certain Mrs. Tinsdale agrees. Don't you?"

"Oh, yes," she said, tight-lipped.

"Just doing my job." His chin was resting on Andrew's dark, tousled hair in a pose that would have seemed casual to most, but made her pulse race. She curled her hands around the arms of the chair, as if the smooth wood could steady her nerves.

Mrs. Hillebrand was still talking. "My goodness, facing desperadoes all alone like that, saving Andrew from the clutches of those awful people. Why, it's wonderful!" Her chubby face lit up in a smile.

"Yes, wonderful," Ariel agreed with a sigh.

"There's even talk that you should run for mayor."

Luke grinned and chuckled. "I'm not a politician, ma'am. But thanks."

Mrs. Hillebrand reached for her tea, the cup rattling in the saucer as she lifted it from the serving tray. "Well, Marshal, we've had politicians, and my husband, for one, says it's time for someone else, someone who's not a politico to run this city."

Rebecca couldn't believe her ears. Good Lord, people were talking about running him for office. What office? Police chief? Mayor? King? It wasn't that she didn't think he could do a good job. She did. He was honest and dedicated, to give the devil his due—so to speak. But was there no end to this? Why couldn't he leave? Go back to his marshal's job? Better yet, go somewhere else and be marshal?

"It's very flattering," she heard him saying politely, with a smile that was making young Ariel blush again. "Please thank your husband for me, and—" his smile widened "—thank you ladies, too." In one motion, he stood, lifting a giggling Andrew with him. "I think it's time to get Andrew cleaned up." He peered at the boy tucked under his arm like a sack of potatoes. "What do you say, cowboy? Time to wash up for dinner?"

"Okay, Luke."

Luke put him down, and he ran to Rebecca and gave her a big hug. "Oh, Mama, I had the best time ever. Luke showed me how to ride his horse, and then we had ice cream, and then we went to watch the circus men put the tent up, and—''

"All right, Andrew." Rebecca silenced him with a gentle look. "Later, remember?"

"Oh. Sorry," he muttered, more to his shoes than to anyone in particular.

Mrs. Hillebrand stood, as did Ariel. "Well, we have to be going. Very nice to meet you, Marshal. I'm sure we'll see you again. I understand you're staying with Mrs. Tinsdale."

She said it so casually that if a person wasn't paying close attention, he might not realize the importance of what she was asking. It was provocative, to say the least.

Normally, Rebecca took this kind of question in stride; it was part of life, especially in San Francisco. Tonight, however, all things considered, she was aching for a fight, and if these two busybodies wanted one, they'd come to the right place.

"I really don't think—"

"May I?" Luke cut in smoothly. "Mrs. Tinsdale was kind enough to let me *use* a room as my headquarters while we searched. I have my own quarters, at the Halifax on Washington Street. Perhaps you know it?"

Mrs. Hillebrand never faltered. "Why, yes, I believe I do."

"Well, if you ladies will excuse me?"

"Of course."

His back to the others, he winked at Rebecca. Then, grinning, he said, "All right, Andrew, race you to the stairs."

Andrew took off as if he'd been shot out of a cannon, and Luke followed at a more respectable pace.

Rebecca escorted the ladies to the door.

After closing the door, she turned and sank back against it. She stood like that for several minutes. Luke had come to her defense, she realized. She was startled by the act, and by the fact that he'd done so with such grace that the ladies hadn't even hesitated to believe him.

Her earlier feelings of fear and anxiety quieted. If he didn't suspect anything by now, surely he never would. But her heart still fluttered frantically in her chest, and she thought that it was as much the instant attraction she felt each and every time she looked at him as it was her fear that he would discover her secret. He lingered in her mind, inflaming her senses. She allowed herself to acknowledge the feelings, though she refused to surrender to them, just as she refused to surrender to the man.

Mrs. Wheeler roused her from her musings. "Dinner will be ready in twenty minutes, Mrs. Tinsdale. Shall I wake Mrs. Tinsdale?"

"No, that's all right, I'm going up anyway. I'll call her." She started up the stairs.

Luke was washing the last of the soap from Andrew's face with a yellow washcloth. Andrew, with the smoothest bit of pleading ever seen outside a courtroom, had convinced Luke that a complete bath wasn't necessary. In one of those man-to-man things, Luke had agreed—but only after swearing Andrew to secrecy.

Stretching, Luke dragged the towel from the rack beside the bed and tossed it to Andrew.

"Okay, where do you keep your clean shirts?"

"There," Andrew said, and pointed. "Top drawer." Andrew was busy finger-combing his damp hair. It looked more smashed than combed, Luke thought, chuckling. Two persistent cowlicks were giving him fits. "I hate to tell you, but we're gonna have to comb it, cowboy."

"Aw, Luke. It's good enough." Andrew smashed at a particularly ornery cowlick, licked his fingers and tried again.

"No sense doing that," Luke explained. "I know. I've tried. Why do you think I keep mine long?" He ran his hand through his hair to illustrate the point.

Andrew's chin came up in determination. "Then I'll grow mine, too."

"Ah, well, we'll see what your mother has to say about that."

Luke was grinning as he walked the three steps to the walnut dresser, his boots cushioned by the royal blue carpet. The top of the dresser was covered with a white lace doily. He glanced at the collection of tin soldiers lined up military-straight on one side, and the two silver frames with photographs on the other side.

"Did you say top drawer?"

"Uh-huh."

The drawer slid out with a scraping sound to reveal a half-dozen or so shirts, all starched, ironed, folded and arranged neatly in two stacks. Since Luke was doing the choosing, he chose his favorite color—blue, like Becky's eyes.

Seemed everything he did made him think of her.

As he thought of Becky, his eyes naturally flicked to the photographs. Nudging the drawer closed with his hip, he picked one up for a closer look. The silver frame was cool and smooth against his fingers.

The faces staring back at him were smiling, happy. A much younger Andrew, about two, Luke guessed. Cute face... He looked like someone...

His eyes narrowed as he stared at the fuzzy photograph. He angled it slightly, catching the fading light through the lace curtain covering the window. A thought stirred in the back of his mind, a feeling that he couldn't quite get ahold of. He decided to stop trying. These things had a way of coming along in their own good time.

He let his eyes wander to Rebecca. She was wearing a dress—dark, full skirt, high neck, of course. She was smiling. Her hand was resting lightly on the sleeve of the man beside her.

"This your father?"

"Yes."

Luke glanced over to make sure he hadn't upset the boy. It appeared he hadn't, so Luke moved a little closer to the window and pushed back the curtain with one hand to get more light.

He'd never seen Rebecca's husband, and he was curious. What kind of a man would she marry? He had his answer. He was tall like Luke, but that was where any resemblance ended. Where Luke was dark, he was fair. Where Luke was cowboy, he was society gentleman.

He had a nice face, though, kind, Luke decided grudgingly. He could see the family resemblance to Ruth—same eyes, same mouth. His gaze flickered to Andrew, who was still working on the cowlick.

Andrew looked like... who? Rebecca, he guessed. He sure didn't look like his father.

He glanced at the photograph again, for an instant imagining himself there, imagining what it would be like to have a family, a son.

Suddenly a sadness washed over him. Regrets and mistakes came to mind, making him feel the loss intensely. He tensed and put the photograph down with a clunk. He had enough trouble dealing with the present; there was no sense dredging up the past.

"How's this one?" He held up the shirt.

"Good. Mama likes that one. Blue is her favorite color."

"What's yours?" Luke asked, unfastening the small buttons and helping Andrew slip it on.

"I like red...and green," Andrew said, firmly glancing up from the last of his buttoning.

"Red, huh? You mean like the fire wagons?"

"Oh, yes. I like the fire wagons. Mama got me a toy one last year for my birthday. Wanna see it?"

"Sure."

Wearing only his shirt, Andrew charged out of the room. Luke could hear his bare feet thudding on the plank flooring. A door slammed. Andrew barreled into the room, hefting a fire wagon with a double team of snowy white horses attached to the wagon's tongue.

Luke held up the toy for a careful inspection. "That's a beauty. Looks like the one we saw today, doesn't it?"

"I know. It's my favorite toy. I got it for my birthday last year. You can play with it sometimes, too, though, if you want."

"Why, thanks, cowboy. Next time I get some free time, I'll take you up on that, okay?"

"Okay."

Luke helped him with his trousers, then socks and shoes. He reached for the comb. "What are you getting this year... for your birthday?"

"Ouch," he groaned when the comb caught in a tangle.

"Sorry." Luke started again.

"I don't know what I'm getting this year?" He brightened. "Maybe I'll ask for a pony, now that I know how to ride and all."

"Well, you might need a little more practice."

"Would you help me?"

"Sure," Luke agreed, happy to spend time with the boy. That niggling thought got closer to the surface of his mind. There was something he'd forgotten... or something...

He shrugged. "Say, when is your birthday? Do you know?"

"Sure I do." Andrew seemed indignant. "It's December tenth."

"December. That's right. I remember your grandmother telling me. Do you mind having your birthday so near Christmas?"

"Naw. Mama always makes a big party. It's like having Christmas two times."

Luke was still chuckling when he dropped down on one knee to help Andrew tuck his shirt into the waist of his brown wool trousers. Andrew's stared up at him, black eyes staring back at equally black eyes. A strange feeling moved through Luke, a sudden lightness that made his breathing shallow. A thought flashed crystal-clear in his mind. All the air rushed out of his lungs.

He did some fast arithmetic. He'd left Rebecca in March—seven years and nine months. Dear God, could it be true?

He searched the boy's face as though he were photographing it, as though he were seeing him for the first time. In a way, he was. "Are you certain, Andrew? You aren't guessing?" There was an urgency to his voice.

"No," Andrew said, somewhat indignantly. "I know my birthday and my address, and I can write them down. You wanna see?"

"No." Luke brushed the hair back from the boy's face. Without standing, he took Andrew by the shoulders and turned him to face the mirror. Almost shoulder to shoulder, the two looked into the glass. The reflection that stared back sent an icy chill down Luke's spine.

"Luke, we've got the same color eyes. Isn't that great? We've even got the same cowlick. Look! See, mine's here and yours is . . ."

"Here," Luke said very softly. Suspicion became reality, soul-shattering reality. Luke sank back on his heels, his hands still resting on Andrew's . . . on his son's shoulders. Oh, Lord, he had a son. A son. The word turned into a soft, gentle feeling that wrapped itself forever around his heart.

He glanced away long enough to look at the photograph on the bureau. The fair-haired couple and the child, a boy with raven black hair and equally black eyes, just like the eyes that looked back at him every time he looked in the mirror.

His fingers tightened slightly, possessively, on Andrew's small shoulders, and tears welled up in his eyes and slid unchecked down his cheeks.

Luke knew Rebecca was there even before he looked to the doorway. "Why didn't you tell me?" His voice was soft with emotions too new to name, and he thought at this moment that no man could be happier than he was. The woman he loved had given him a son. He didn't care about the rest, about having to find out himself, about the lost years. He was overjoyed to know. He would forgive her the rest.

Rebecca's voice was very calm when she spoke. "Andrew, why don't you go on down to dinner? Grandma is there already, and she'll be lonely. Tell her we'll be along shortly."

Andrew slipped free of Luke's light touch. "Okay." "See you later, Luke."

"See you later, son," he couldn't resist saying, testing the word and the feeling.

Andrew didn't understand the double meaning of Luke's remark, but Rebecca did. She saw the tears on his cheeks. It tugged at her heart, her guilt and regret and anger. There was one more feeling that overwhelmed the others—the sense of duty. She had a duty to the people she loved, Andrew and Ruth. She owed them security and love and protection. She would protect them, even at her own expense. Rebecca stepped into the room and closed the door softly, leaning back against it, effectively blocking it, as though she could keep the secret locked up as easily.

Luke stood and started for her, wanting to take her in his arms, to hold her and tell her that he forgave her for keeping the secret.

She stopped him with an upraised hand. "Just what is it you think you know?"

"I know that Andrew is my son."

"I say he's not."

Luke hesitated. He walked to the photograph and held it up for her. The dark-haired boy and the fair-haired couple. No, Andrew had Luke's eyes and hair and coloring. The imprint of his features was true and unmistakable. He glanced back at Rebecca. "Like hell he isn't. I should have seen it from the first. He's my son."

"Try and prove it."

The silence in the room was overpowering in its intensity. It took a full thirty seconds for the reality of her words to penetrate his brain.

In a voice that was hard and cold and ripe with menace, he said, "Goddamn you, Rebecca. All this time, and you never told me. You took what we shared and turned it into something dark and immoral. You hate me so much that you would keep my son from me."

"I thought you were too busy chasing fame and excitement. Once you got me in the hay, you used me and left." She said it plainly; it only took a few words to explain a mountain of anger and distrust.

"Sure I left, I—"

"Don't give me that story about being young, because I'm not buying it."

"I don't *have* to explain my life to you. If you'll remember, sweetheart, no one forced you into the hay with me. You went willingly...both times." With that, he leveled the mountain.

"Yes, Luke, I did." Her voice was ripe with sarcasm and regret. "I absolve you of all responsibility. There. Are you happy? It's not your fault. None of it. You can leave with a clear conscience."

"I've tried to explain to you."

"A little late, isn't it?" She advanced on him this time. "About a lifetime too late."

"You got married." He said it like an accusation.

"Yes." Her tone was defiant. "I got married. Thank goodness Nathan was *willing* to marry me, knowing I was pregnant with another man's child."

"You could have written, wired. I would have come back."

"Oh, certainly. A letter addressed to Luke Scanlin, Somewhere, Texas. Yes, that would have been a perfect choice. In the meantime, I could have gotten bigger and bigger, disgraced my family, risked my son's name, all in the faint hope that the man who thought so little of me as to take my virginity and then ride off would want to come back and get married."

"Dammit to hell, Rebecca. If I'd known, I'd never have left. I'm not that much of a—"

"*Bastard,* I think, is the word you're looking for."

He started for the door. "It didn't have to be like this."

She blocked his way. "What are you going to do? Tell him? Are you going to go down there and shatter his life? If one word of this gets out, the scandal will be unrecoverable. Andrew's name will be forever ruined in this town."

"Then we'll go to another town."

"This is my home, and Andrew's, and Ruth's. Have you forgotten that Ruth thinks Andrew is her grandson, her *only* grandson? They love each other dearly. Are you going to take that away from them, too?"

"Damn you!" he said finally, feeling trapped. "He's my son and I want him."

"He's *my* son, and you can't have him."

"Watch me."

He stormed from the room. Rebecca raced after him. She caught up with him at the bottom of the stairs. He stood in the doorway of the dining room and, for a frantic moment, she thought he was about to say the words that would change her life and lives of those she loved forever.

"Luke," she entreated. "You can't."

He looked at her with eyes as hard as granite, then turned on his heel and slammed out the front door.

Ruth turned to Rebecca. "What's come over him?"

Chapter Seventeen

He needed a drink, and he needed it now. If ever a man deserved to get drunk, this, he fumed, slamming out the front door, was the time. He headed for his horse, tied at the hitching post.

He snatched up the reins and the gelding shied and shook his head.

"No one cares what you think," Luke snapped, swinging up without bothering with the stirrups. Yeah, a drink. A hell of a lot of drinks. After all, a man was entitled to celebrate when he became a father—even if it was eight years too late, he thought bitterly.

He reined over so hard the gelding reared and shook his head in defiance. Luke held on easily, and instead of softening his touch, he yanked harder, spurred the horse in the sides and took off down the street.

Ten seconds, and he reined up as hard as before. The horse skidded and pranced and pawed the ground. What the hell was he doing, racing through the city streets like this?

What's wrong with you, Scanlin. You wanta hurt someone?

The answer was a resounding yes. He wanted to hurt someone the way he'd been hurt. That, however, was impossible. The kind of hurt he was feeling went deep, to the very core of him.

She'd lied to him. The woman he had come back to, the woman he knew he loved, the woman...*that* woman...had lied to him.

All through the nightmare of the kidnapping, she'd never said a word. All the time that had been *his* son out there. The child might have died, and he would never have known. When had she been planning to tell him—when they lowered the coffin into the ground? Had she been planning on telling him at all?

He knew the answer. His hand curled tight around the reins, and the leather cut into his fingers. Muscles tensed along the tops of his shoulders and down his spine. He urged the horse into a lope as he headed for the waterfront. That was a good place to get drunk and get into a fight. Right now, that was exactly what he wanted.

He turned onto Pacific Street. The sun was already down. The street was crowded. A patchwork quilt of miners, sailors and businessmen mingled on the sidewalk as they made their way along. They were looking for entertainment, for fun.

Fun was the last thing on his mind. He was sulking, brooding, and a man needed a dark place to do that. So he passed up the fancier places, the Palace and the Golden Lady.

He spotted the Purple Crescent at the end of the street. It was all peeling paint and raw wood. The glass windows hadn't seen a soap-filled sponge since they'd been put up. The lettering announcing beer at twenty-five cents was so faded as to be more smudge than paint.

He tied up at the gnarled hitching post and pushed through the batwing doors. A couple dozen tables cluttered the dirt-caked floor. The scent of burning tobacco and unwashed bodies overpowered the brisk saltiness of the night air. There was a painting of a voluptuous woman, buck naked, hanging over the bar.

The place was crowded. Most of the men were standing around the faro table or over at the roulette wheel. Luke shouldered his way through to the bar.

"Bottle" was all he said to the bartender. He tossed some coins on the scarred surface of the bar. "Let me know when that's gone."

The barman nodded, gathered the coins with one hand and set down the bottle and a glass with his other hand.

Luke took both, then moved toward an empty table near the back staircase. It was as close to a dark hole as he could get.

It was habit that made him sit with his back to the wall. Out of the corner of his eye, he could watch the comings and goings on the staircase. There seemed to be a lot of those—grinning men with scantily dressed women.

Just his kind of place, he mused, tossing back a drink and feeling the rotgut burn a path to his stomach. Yeah, this was the kind of place he was used to. It was the kind of place Rebecca had accused him of taking full advantage of.

Well, dammit, he hadn't before, but he was here now and—he tossed back another drink—maybe he'd just go on up those stairs. Might as well, since she'd accused him of the act.

She'd accused him of a lot of things tonight, of using her, of not caring, of leaving her. Well, she was wrong! He tossed back another drink. The alcohol was beginning to work—he felt the first signs, muscles uncoiling, a fuzziness in his brain.

Lifting his hat, he raked one hand through his hair and settled it back in place.

"Hello, cowboy," a female voice said from close by.

His gaze traveled up the trim navy skirt, past the pale yellow blouse opened at the neck, to a familiar face.

"Millie?" He took in the traveling costume and the washed face. She looked like a kid—all blue eyes and freckles, except for that red hair, of course, that was a dead giveaway.

"Yeah." She grinned and made an awkward attempt at a curtsy. "It's me."

He managed a trace of a smile. "I hardly recognized you in your...out of your working..." He dragged out a chair. "What are you doing here? This isn't your place."

"I come by to collect some money from Sally—" she motioned with her head toward the upstairs "—before I catch the night train for Salt Lake. What about you? What are you doing here?" She settled in, her elbows on the gouged surface of the table.

"I'm on my way to getting drunk," he said flatly, and poured another drink. "You want one?"

"Sure." She signaled the bartender, who brought another glass. She helped herself to the liquor. "Is the boy all right?" She sipped at the drink.

"Yeah, the boy is fine. He's more than fine." He glanced at her. "He's great."

"I'm glad." She smiled a broken-toothed grin. "I'm real sorry for what happened. Is there any news of Jack?"

"None that I know of. The police are supposed to be looking. My guess is, he left town."

She nodded. "I hope so. Anyways, I ain't taking no chances. I'm heading out, like you suggested."

"Good."

Millie emptied her glass and poured another.

"So if everything's okay, how come you're here—" she hefted the half-empty bottle "—soon to be drunk?" She glanced around and, quietly, for his ears only, said, "This ain't a good place for marshals, especially if they're a little fuzzy...if you get my drift."

"I'm not fuzzy, as you put it. Though God knows I'd like to be."

"How come?"

"How come, she asks," he muttered to no one in particular. "Well, Millie," he said with great ceremony, "it seems I'm celebrating."

"Celebrating?"

"Yeah." He filled her glass to the brim. "Today, I became a father." He toasted her with his drink before he emptied the glass.

Her blue eyes flashed in surprise. "What?"

"Yeah. It's something, isn't it? Turns out the boy, Andrew, is my son."

Millie let out a low whistle. "And you didn't know?"

"Hell, no, I didn't know," he snapped. "That damned woman never told me. All these years I had a son, a child, and I didn't know."

"Oh, my." Millie seemed to be considering this for a long moment. She turned her half-full glass slowly between her fingers. Looking at the glass, she said, "So how come you didn't know?"

"I told you, his mother didn't tell me." He shifted in the rickety chair, and the wood creaked in protest.

"It's usually pretty obvious when a woman's pregnant. Kinda hard not to notice." She still didn't look at him.

"Dammit, Millie, I wasn't here. I was in Texas. All she had to do was write me, and I woulda come back. I woulda married her, for chrissakes. She knew that."

Millie sank back in her wooden chair. One hand holding the drink, the other in her lap. She raked him with an appraising stare that was tinged with enough surprise and contempt as to make him shift uncomfortably.

"What the hell's wrong with you?" Luke didn't like being the object of her scrutiny.

"I figured, from the kid and all, his mama is some society lady, right?"

"Society," Luke repeated with disdain.

"So you're tellin' me you got some society lady pregnant, then you rode off and left her like she was..." She straightened. "Nobody."

"No," he retorted. "It wasn't like that."

Millie arched one brow questioningly.

"It wasn't like that," Luke repeated, more vehemently. "All she had to do was tell me. I woulda come back. I woulda married her, if that's what she wanted."

"Aren't you the hero?" Millie tossed back her drink. The noise of the saloon filled their silence. The constant click-click of the roulette wheel grated on

Luke's nerves. He reached for the quarter-full bottle, wondering why the whiskey wasn't helping to blot out the anger.

He signaled for another bottle, and the bartender obliged.

"That ain't gonna help a guilty conscience, you know," Millie said as he pulled the cork and tossed it aside.

"What guilty conscience? I'm not the one who did anything wrong here. She's the one who didn't tell me, remember?"

"Sounds to me like you're the one who left, *remember?*" she flung back at him.

"Say, what's this to you, anyway? Why are you taking her side in this?"

"I ain't taking her side. I don't even know her. But if I was some rich society lady and I let some cowboy get me in a family way and then he rode off and left me, I'd be plenty scared. I know I wouldn't have too many choices."

"Choices? Sure she had choices. She coulda told me."

"Did she know where you where?"

"How many times have I gotta tell you, I was in Texas?"

"Ah…" She nodded. "Texas, according to all you boys, is mighty big. Did she know where you was?"

It was a full ten seconds before he answered. "No."

Millie gave a knowing nod. "She musta loved you a lot, to take a chance like she done."

"Loved me! Now there's a laugh." He rocked his chair back on two legs, his head resting against the smooth plaster of the wall. "She loved me so much she didn't tell me I had a son for nearly eight years. If I hadn't guessed I never would have known.''

''What else would you figure would make her risk everything to have your baby? She sure as hell didn't have to.''

Luke went very still. He slowly lowered the chair to the floor. In a voice that was so soft she had to lean in to hear him over the noise, he said, ''What do you mean, she didn't have to?''

Still leaning in, Millie replied, ''There are ways to take care of... unwanted babies.'' She sat back, her face grim. ''Believe me, I know.'' The was a hint of sadness in her voice.

The truth of her words hit him like cold water on a hot day. Rebecca hadn't had to have the child. He knew that, had heard about treatments, elixirs, even certain women who knew how to end an unwanted, embarrassing pregnancy.

''She didn't, did she?'' he muttered. ''But—''

''No buts about it. She took a hell of a chance. I mean, I've heard them rich folks don't take kindly to this sorta thing. Daughters get sent away, or—what do they call it? Oh, yeah, disowned, for rolling in the hay with the wrong man.''

''Yeah,'' Luke put in. ''I'm the wrong man, all right.''

''It doesn't appear so. She had your baby, didn't she?''

The words tumbled around in his brain like thunder.

She didn't have to...

Could have ended...

Took a risk...

Must have loved you...

Slowly, reality dawned on Luke. She had spent the past eight years guarding this secret. She had protected their child from scandal and harm.

She'd been afraid, of everyone, and especially of him. He'd been the one who could guess, he'd been the one who, with one word, could destroy her life and Andrew's.

So she'd guarded her secret, protected the child, right down to, and including, lying. He should have seen, should have realized.

But like an arrogant bastard, he'd accused her, threatened her, when what he should have done was take her in his arms and hold her until she stopped being afraid.

When he looked up, Millie was watching him closely. "Thanks, Millie." He reached over and covered her hand with his in a gesture of sincere gratitude.

"What are you gonna do?"

Luke stood. "First, I'm going to put you safely on that train. Then I'm gonna go claim what's mine."

Two men met in the elegant private room of Barry and Patten's saloon. Downstairs, the crowd was heavy, busy with the business of sin. It was easy for the men to slip in and out without anyone giving them the least bit of notice.

The room was perched on the balcony overlooking the stage, where, in thirty or so minutes, the latest songbird from New York would be entrancing the customers.

The burgundy drapes were drawn against prying eyes, and the two men seated themselves at the linen-covered table. One candle flickered in the glass globe in the center. A gas wall sconce glowed dimly, giving the room an almost romantic feel, and Frank Handley thought that more than once this room had probably been used for an illicit meeting.

He pulled out a chair—red satin and gilt trim. Elegant, with a touch of the wicked.

"We'll have whiskey," Frank told the uniformed waiter. "Make sure it's Irish."

His boss sat opposite him. His slender face was hidden in the shadows, but Frank didn't have to see his face to know he was displeased.

The music of the reed organ carried upstairs. An energetic version of "Camptown Races," if he wasn't mistaken. Silently he hummed along in his head.

The waiter returned with the whiskey, served in cut-crystal glasses imported from Ireland.

"Anything else, gentlemen?" he asked with a slight bow.

"Nothing," Frank returned, already reaching for the bottle. "See that we aren't disturbed."

The waiter nodded, gave another small bow and left.

The bottle clinked against the glasses as Frank poured the drinks. He shoved one toward the other man, the glass leaving a track in the white linen cloth.

"All right, Frank," the man said softly, holding his glass up to study the contents against the flickering candle on the table. "What the hell happened?"

"I don't know." Frank took a sip of the liquor, needing to feel the calming effects of alcohol on his nerves.

"I pay you to take care of things. You were supposed to have it all set. Nothing was supposed to go wrong. Now we have a dead kidnapper, and another one running loose somewhere—'' he took another swallow of whiskey ''—and I'm out ten thousand dollars, I might add.''

''I had it all set.'' Frank knew this wasn't a man to cross. ''All they had to do was turn over the kid. I'd pay them off and send them out of town for a while. How was I suppose to know they'd get greedy?''

''All right, Frank,'' the other man said softly. ''I'll make it work, though I wish to hell I had that money. I need it for...'' He lifted his eyes negligently. ''I need it. At least the newspaper is mine. She doesn't know, does she?''

''No.'' Frank smiled. ''She doesn't suspect a thing. She thinks it's an eastern syndicate.''

''Good. Let's keep it that way. It's only a matter of time until she comes to me.'' He lounged back, and a smile tugged at one corner of his mouth. ''In the meantime, I want you to put the word out, discreetly—'' he sliced a glance in Frank's direction ''—that Jack Riggs has money, and if anyone finds him and wants to take the money away, well, you would be grateful.''

''They'll kill him for that kind of money,'' Frank said on a sudden intake of breath.

The other man gave a one-shoulder shrug. ''Just put the word out. The wolves will hunt him down if he's in town, and what they do then, well, it's out of our control.''

A chill snaked up Frank's spine at the cold way the man could order someone's death. ''But murder—''

''Not murder,'' the other man snarled. Then, more gently, ''I told you, it's out of our hands. Besides, if they'd followed orders, no one would have been hurt, now would they?''

Frank shook his head.

"So, there, you see. It's not our doing. They brought it on themselves. If Jack is arrested and talks, it's you he'll name, Frank, and if anyone looked really hard, they might find the connection between you and me. I'm only looking out for your best interests."

"I understand." Frank drained his glass.

The man chuckled. "Don't look so worried, Frank. It'll be all right. I'll take care of you."

The man stood, tossed some money on the table and left.

Frank lingered awhile over his whiskey. He'd never bargained on murder.

Chapter Eighteen

Luke didn't go to Rebecca's that night. He didn't go the next morning. Oh, he wanted to. He just didn't know what to say. And even if he had he doubted she'd give him more than two seconds before she slammed the damned door in his face. Let's face it, they hadn't parted the best of friends. That was a polite way of saying they'd argued. Okay, they'd fought. Hell, they always fought, except when they were making love.

If fighting with her was hell, then having her in his arms was heaven, pure and simple. Holding her was magic, like holding a flame in the palm of his hand — too hot to hold and too exciting to release. It was a fire he was more than happy to be consumed by.

He dragged in a deep breath and held on to it, letting the oxygen fuel the fire that flared inside him. His eyes slammed shut. Dear God, how he wanted her.

But she didn't want him. At least she'd made it clear that she was determined *not* to want him. Now that was an entirely different matter, he thought, intrigued by the notion. He didn't believe her, didn't care what she wanted. He wanted her and his son, and he damned well was going to have them.

She, on the other hand, was convinced that to love him was to expose Andrew to scandal and to deprive Ruth of her only grandson—who, unfortunately, wasn't her grandson, at least not by blood.

He didn't want to hurt anyone, but, dammit, there had to be a way.

So he sat here in his office, feet propped on the corner of his desk, trying to come up with a plan. Trouble was, he didn't have a plan, not even a remote glimmer of a plan.

With unfocused eyes, he stared at the white plaster wall opposite his desk. He kept thinking, turning the problem over and over in his mind.

Sunlight poured through the dirty windows, and he idly watched the dust motes floating in the air. His gaze flicked from one white plaster wall to the other, and he felt confined. He hated offices, hated being cooped up inside. This place was the size of a jail cell, with barely enough room for his desk, a couple of chairs, and a well-used filing cabinet on the back wall, under a faded picture of George Washington.

Why the hell did every government office he'd ever been in have a picture of George Washington? he suddenly wondered, distracted. You'd think there hadn't been another president since.

Dammit, this was getting him nowhere. Sitting up, he let his feet slam to the floor. He toyed with the mail, a month's worth, piled high on his desk. A couple of wanted posters, an official notice of a change in reporting procedures, something that looked suspiciously like an invitation, and a note from the governor.

He slit the white envelope with his pocket knife. The note said the governor had had a change of plans. He was leaving for Los Angeles and would be back next week to attend a social event. He'd want a report then on Luke's progress.

Luke tossed the note down, letting it flutter to a stop on top of the other papers scattered over the smooth walnut surface. He was a lawman, not a paper pusher, he thought irritably. Yeah, that meant he was short on organization and long on action.

Ha! You couldn't prove either, looking at him now.

Well, don't just sit there. Do something.

Yeah, get moving. He always thought better when he was moving, working. *Like maybe a little of the work you were hired to do.*

There was that investigation into city corruption he was suppose to be conducting for the governor, among other things. With a mumbled curse, he set about organizing the office. He took to the files first, straightening, sorting, putting the damned things in alphabetical order. It was menial work that required little brainpower, so he was able to keep trying to come up with a plan to win Rebecca.

He spent the next couple of hours sorting through the reports and such that had mounted up between his predecessor's leaving and Luke's arrival. He made up letters to a half-dozen prospective deputies. He'd never win any awards for penmanship, he thought, glancing at the scrawled names and addresses.

He cleaned out the desk drawers, made lists of things he needed to do and cleared off the top of his desk. By midafternoon, he was finished, and he still didn't have a plan.

He spotted that invitation-looking envelope and thumbed it open. Yup, an invitation, all right. Seemed there was a meeting today at—he glanced at the school clock ticking loudly on the wall over the file cabinet—two o'clock. He was already ten minutes late, *if* he was going to go. A group of business leaders, wanting to talk about the future of the city that they had such a large investment in.

He wasn't much interested in meetings. Right now, he wasn't much interested in anything but Rebecca and his son. A lightness moved through his chest at the thought, making his breathing a little ragged.

It was an incredible feeling to know he had a son. He wasn't a man much given to flights of fancy, but this—this was so incredible he wanted to cry, he wanted to shout every time he thought about it, which was about every other minute.

He reviewed the situation one more time. His goal was very clear. He wanted Rebecca and he wanted his son. They were a package deal, and he absolutely didn't want it any other way.

He walked the two long steps to the window, leaned his shoulder on the smooth wood frame and looked out, only absently aware of Hansen's delivery wagon lumbering up the street toward the corner of Third.

He was thinking. If he tried to take the boy, she'd fight him. He couldn't blame her. What mother would give up her son? Certainly not Rebecca, he realized with more than a little admiration and gratitude.

He ticked off the options. Confrontation, demands, threats? She'd only dig in harder. No, he thought, tapping the invitation on the edge of his hand again. He had to move slowly, carefully. He couldn't afford to make a mistake. A man only got so many chances, and he was well beyond his limit.

Luke glanced down at the invitation he held in his hand and cut a confirming glance at the clock. Two-twenty. Ah, hell, he'd go to the meeting. Maybe by the time it was finished he'd have an idea.

In the past two years, Rebecca Tinsdale had become a power, a force to be reckoned with, in San Francisco politics. With her newspaper, she had been able to shape public awareness and thereby public opinion on candidates and issues, at a time when the other papers in town seemed content to cover national news and ignore the local controversies.

Whether they liked it or not, business leaders and politicians had sought her out, asked for her endorsement or given her little bits of information, in the hope of discrediting their competition.

Rebecca had long since recognized what was happening. While she welcomed these visits, these requests, these bits of gossip, she had always made her own decisions, based on fact and fairness.

It was that trait, perhaps, most of all, that had gained her the respect of so many of San Francisco's community leaders. It was, she suspected, why she'd been invited to this little gathering today, though exactly what the issue was, she wasn't certain.

She was certain that they knew of her son's kidnapping and of his safe return. San Francisco wasn't so big that news didn't travel fast in the right circles.

With Edward at her side, she walked into the grand dining room of the Hotel du Commerce. The men she was there to meet were conspicuously seated around a table for six near a potted palm in a corner.

The rich green carpet cushioned her steps as she and Edward followed the maître d' between tables adorned with white linen and fine silver. She paused twice to speak to people she knew, to accept their good wishes.

The warm afternoon sunlight filtered through the delicate Irish lace curtains that covered the four front windows, opened to coax a breeze. There was none. The room was warm, and she was grateful their table was in a shadowed corner of the room.

"Gentlemen," she said, taking in the three men with one greeting. Edward helped her take off her jacket.

The men stood, almost in unison.

"Mrs. Tinsdale."

"Rebecca."

They were all dark suits and celluloid collars. Except for their ages, they were very much alike, right down to the fashionably short, slicked-down hair.

She allowed Edward to help with her chair.

She sat next to John Riding, with Edward on her left. They chatted amiably while the uniformed waiter took their beverage order, then left, returning shortly with a pot of tea for Rebecca and coffee for the men.

"We'll wait awhile before ordering lunch," Henry Franklin told the waiter, glancing toward the open doorway.

"Expecting someone else?" Rebecca asked as she poured her tea, the rich burgundy liquid filling the translucent white china.

"I had hoped so," Henry muttered.

John Riding spoke up. "Mrs. Tinsdale, we were so sorry to hear about your boy, and relieved when we heard he'd been returned safely."

John was younger than the others. He had inherited money, then and very astutely doubled it. He owned the opera house, and several of the larger stores in town.

"Thank you," Rebecca returned, glancing into his dark brown eyes. She liked John and his wife, and considered them friends.

"It must have been a terrifying experience," Henry Franklin commented. Along with his partner, Logan McCloud, Henry owned the largest fleet in the harbor and controlled most of the city's shipping. He was older than the others, his dark hair already showing signs of gray near his chubby face. His much younger wife had given birth to their first child only a few months ago.

"How is Mrs. Franklin?" Rebecca asked politely. "And the baby?"

"Oh, fine. Fine," he replied with a schoolboy's grin. "Thank you for remembering. And thank you for the lovely gift."

"Of course. Please tell Mrs. Franklin I'll call sometime next week, if she's receiving."

"I'll tell her. I know she'll be glad to—"

Merl Gates cleared his throat, obviously impatient with all this idle chitchat. Rebecca suppressed a small smile. Despite his gruffness, she liked Merl. He was direct to the point of being abrasive, but he was upfront and honest and never reneged on any pledge or promise. "The word around is that the new marshal pulled off a tricky bit of rescuing."

"That's correct," Rebecca returned flatly, not wishing to discuss Luke Scanlin in any way, shape or form. Just the thought of the man, of the power he held over her, made her palms sweat.

"Heard tell there was a shoot-out. One man dead and the other got away. That right?"

"Yes," she said softly, remembering the terror of that night alone in the blackness, with only Luke to help her, to save her. If he hadn't pushed her clear, she might have been killed. If he hadn't risked his life to follow that despicable man, she might never have seen Andrew again.

No wonder her hand shook when she tried to settle her cup back in its delicate saucer.

Edward spoke up for the first time. His slender features were drawn down in concern. "Dearest... Are you all right? All this talk is upsetting you. Perhaps we should go." He made to stand, but hardly got out of his chair before Merl Gates cut in.

"Nonsense. Mrs. Tinsdale is not upset by a little conversation... are you?" It was more an order than a question. She dragged in a couple of breaths and willed her stomach to unclench.

The fear she felt was not so much from what had happened in that alley as from what had come after. She was made more uneasy by the shame and guilt of what had happened later. She had made love to Luke Scanlin. The one thing she'd vowed she'd never do again. He was like a drug in her system. The more she saw him, touched him, heard his voice, the more the addiction grew. And it was a sweet addiction, lush and sensual and carnal.

She had gone to his room, she had sought him out. Somewhere deep in her heart she had known what would happen, had wanted it to happen. And it had. Oh, Lord, it had been more wonderful, more sensual, more erotic, than she'd ever imagined.

Her body pulsed to life, nerves thrumming, and she quelled her rampant emotions. She straightened and squared her shoulders, suddenly afraid these men could sense the erotic path of her thoughts. When she spoke, her voice was shaky even to her own ears, but she toughed it out. "Of course, Mr. Gates. I have nothing to worry about."

Never mind that one word from Luke and her whole life would dissolve faster than snow in the summer. While she didn't think he'd be so cruel as to do it deliberately, he did have a temper, and a word spoken in anger was as destructive as any other.

"What about Brody?" Robert Lister's voice broke into her thoughts, and she glanced up, grateful for this distraction. "Where was he through all this, as if I didn't already know?" He shook his head.

"Captain Brody was..." She sipped her tea and composed her words carefully. After all, Edward was a friend and supporter of Brody's, and she didn't want to have a scene here. "At the marshal's request, he made his men available for a search."

"Ha!" Merl made no secret of his dislike for Brody. "I'll just bet he did. And I'll bet you were glad to see the marshal."

"I—"

"Yes, Becky," a male voice said from very close behind her, making her jump. "Were you glad?"

The sound of his voice went through her like a lightning bolt out of a clear sky. She whirled, her sleeve catching on the tablecloth and making her teacup clatter dangerously in its saucer. Luke stood there, dressed in black trousers and a midnight blue shirt closed at the neck with a string tie. His battered Stetson was in his hand, his black hair ruffled. His eyes were soft, and there was the barest hint of a smile on his lips.

All she could do was stare.

He tore his gaze away and greeted those gathered, then moved around the table, shaking hands.

All the while, he was thinking, *She's here.* Luke had spotted her the minute he walked into the dining room. She was dressed in the latest fashion—he knew that, even if he didn't know the name of the style or the fabric. It was dark green, all flat and fitted in the front. It had a high neck, long sleeves, and a bustle, and so much material in the back that he wondered that she could sit down. As it was, she was perched, sparrowlike, on the edge of the chair.

She wore a saucy little hat—pale silk, he recognized that, with tea roses and ribbons trailing down her back.

She was beautiful—regal, actually. She sure was something. Watching her sitting with these important men, well, it made him proud that Rebecca, his Rebecca, had made such a place for herself with the power men of this town.

And, as he looked at her, an ache welled up in him, from deep in the center of his chest. Had any man ever wanted a woman this much? Had any man ever had as much at stake?

After the introductions, he dragged out the only empty chair, which happened to be opposite her.

"Double bourbon," he told the waiter.

"Little early, isn't it?" she said, before she remembered where she was.

If her rebuke bothered him, he didn't show it. In fact, he smiled—a heart-stopping, lazy smile that made her fingers tremble.

"I'm celebrating," he returned.

Robert spoke up. "Celebrating what?"

Rebecca held her breath.

Luke didn't hesitate. "An addition to my family."

"Congratulations. Your wife have a baby?" Robert replied.

"No" was all he said, and Rebecca released the breath she'd been holding. Was it always going to be like this? Was she going to spend the rest of her life on pins and needles, wondering if he was going to show up, wondering if he was going to say the wrong thing, reveal her indiscretion all those years ago? Was she never to get past that? Was Andrew never to be safe? How long could she live like this?

"Hello there, Ed," Luke said as he accepted his drink from the waiter. He made a slight gesture of salute. "Didn't think I'd be seeing you again so soon."

The other men watched the exchange silently, curiosity apparent in their expressions.

Edward's response was less than friendly. "What are you doing here?"

"I was invited." He sipped his drink, his gaze openly focused on Rebecca. "Sorry to be late. Official business," he lied smoothly. He wasn't about to say he'd been staring out the window for the past several hours trying to figure out a plan to win over the lady sitting four feet away.

Edward's mouth drew into a hard line, and he leaned toward Rebecca in a way that left no doubt he was staking a claim.

Luke hesitated for a fraction of a second, not liking the man's possessiveness.

Merl Gates spoke up. "So you and Mr. Pollard know each other."

"We've met."

The waiter appeared and took their luncheon orders. Rebecca didn't have much of an appetite. She struggled to make small talk over her plate of poached salmon steak and boiled potatoes.

There was a great deal of talk about Luke's part in Andrew's safe return. All those present agreed that Luke was a hero, and quite the topic of conversation these days. There was even the suggestion that he might consider running for political office, that these men would be glad to discuss it further with him.

"I'm not a politician," Luke told them.

"That's exactly why we want you. We're tired of the same handful of men simply moving from one political office to another and back again. Nothing ever changes . . . except for the worst, of course."

Luke shook his head. "Gentlemen, I'm flattered, but—"

"Don't decide now. Think on it, and we'll talk again," Merl said in a no-nonsense tone.

Luke chuckled. "All right, if it'll make you happy, but I don't see any reason why I'll change my mind."

"We'll see," Merl muttered. "We'll see." He forked a bit of chocolate cake into his mouth. "What about it Rebecca? Would the *Times* support the marshal here, if we convinced him to run for some office . . . oh, say, like . . . mayor?" He glanced up, raising his eyebrows.

Before she could answer, Edward cut in. "I hardly think the marshal is interested in being mayor. He's made that quite clear, and I don't think we should force him."

"He's thinking it over," Merl returned, scraping his fork over fine china to get the last bit of frosting.

"You know that I'm running for mayor," Edward said flatly.

Merl feigned surprise. "That's right. I'd forgotten. Well, you haven't declared yet, have you?"

"No."

Merl nodded. "That's why I'd forgotten."

"I had thought I would have your support."

"You'll have the *Times*," Merl countered.

Rebecca spoke up. "Actually, he doesn't."

Everyone looked surprised. "That is he would, certainly, if...I still owned the *Times*. I don't. I sold it two days ago."

One could have heard a pin drop in the stunned silence.

"But—"

"How? When?"

"Tell 'em why, Becky," Luke said.

"I don't care to explain my reasons. Suffice it to say it's done. The sale is complete."

"Well," Merl muttered. "I had no idea."

Edward cut in. "It's all for the best, dear Rebecca. It's been too much for you for a long time, and you're better off out of it. Why, a woman of your delicate nature in such a harsh business...well, it's just not right."

"Edward, really, I—" she began, then stopped, unwilling to discuss her anger and regret at having to surrender the paper. She would certainly have given all she owned, indeed her very life, to save her son.

"Now, now, dear." He patted her hand. "It's not up to you to save this city. Let Frank Handley and that new syndicate handle things." He cast a smug glance around the table. "They've already promised to support me, and—" he focused his attention on her "—when I'm mayor, you can count on me to see that there are changes made. Of course, as my wife, I'll value your opinion.''

Rebecca's head snapped up. "Edward, I—"

"It's all right dear." He patted her hand again. "I know I shouldn't have said anything, but—" he grinned at the others present "—I'm certain I can trust these gentlemen to keep this confidential until we make a formal announcement at the party tomorrow night.''

She hadn't promised Edward, and yet, as she looked at Luke, she thought perhaps it was for the best. If she married Edward, quickly, then there would be no discussion. Perhaps Luke would be less inclined to press his paternal rights, perhaps he'd be less likely to come around, perhaps she'd be less likely to ache deep inside every time she saw him. If she gave in to Luke, if she allowed him to tell Andrew that he, not Nathan, was his father, then she would have to tell Ruth that her only grandson, her son's only son, wasn't.

What was to be gained? She would not put her own desire before her son and, yes, even her dear mother-in-law.

No. She would do without Luke. She would marry Edward and be done with it. It would solve a great many problems.

With the thoughts still fresh in her mind, she said, "Yes, it's true. Edward and I are to be married, though no date has been agreed to," she said, as much for Edward as the others, "and we would prefer to make a formal announcement."

"The hell you are," Luke said, his voice menacingly quiet.

The silence was absolute.

The men looked to Rebecca, a look of shock on every face.

Rebecca's head reeled and, before she could speak, Edward spoke up. "Scanlin, how dare you say such a thing! How dare you use such language in front of a lady! You have overstepped yourself, and *we*—" he emphasized the last word "—will not tolerate it." He surged to his feet. With his hand on her elbow, he pulled Rebecca up and grabbed her jacket.

They started away. Rebecca's step faltered ever so slightly. She couldn't help glancing back over her shoulder, willing him to understand, willing him to forgive her, perhaps. She wasn't certain. She only knew that this was the right thing for her to do.

If she hadn't looked back, if she hadn't hesitated, Luke might have believed her. He might have believed that she genuinely cared for the man. But she did look back, and that was enough to tell him that she wasn't certain, that she was remembering all that they had shared—including a son.

And as he watched her walk away, a plan formed in his mind. It was direct. It was forceful. It was seduction—just as lush and carnal and erotic as he could make it.

Because when they were together, when she let her guard down, the fire that flashed between them was hotter than summer lightning, and more dangerous.

"Well, that certainly is a surprise," Merl muttered, meaning more than the announcement. He sank back in his chair.

"Agreed," Robert said, as did John.

Luke sat down again, his gaze still focused on the empty doorway they had disappeared through.

John cleared his throat awkwardly. "I take it, then, Marshal, that you know Mrs. Tinsdale . . . and don't approve of her plans."

"I know Mrs. Tinsdale very well, and no, I don't approve of her plans."

"Why is that, Marshal? Edward Pollard—"

"Is an egg-sucking—" He broke off, then started again. "He's not the man for her, no matter what she thinks."

John chuckled, and Merl laughed.

"Well, Marshal, I think it's safe to say that we all agree. Mrs. Tinsdale is a fine lady, and Edward is . . . a royal jackass. He's got political ambitions, you know."

"Yeah, I know. I heard. Did he think Rebecca would use the *Times* to help him?"

"Probably," Robert supplied. "Now that she's sold it . . . You wouldn't happen to know why she sold it, would you, Marshal?"

"She sold it . . ." Because I didn't have the ten thousand dollars she needed to save her son, he almost said, but didn't. "Because it was the only way to raise the ransom money in cash in a couple of hours."

"Strange. Why didn't Edward arrange for the money from the bank?"

Luke studied him along the line of his shoulder. "I've been wondering the same thing myself. It's almost as if he wanted her to sell the paper," he mused.

"Well, that's obvious. You heard what he said. A lot of men feel a woman has no place running a business."

"Rebecca isn't just any woman."

"Agreed," John supplied. "She's proven herself to be a capable editor, and her sense of fair play has won her a great deal of respect in this town. When Nathan died, we all thought she'd retire to a quieter life, being a widow and all. We were startled when she took over the *Times*." He lounged back in his chair. "Truthfully, I gave her two months before she packed it in. Damned if she didn't prove me wrong," he added with admiration. "We're going to miss her at the helm of the *Times*. She was doing a lot to bring attention to the corruption in this town."

Robert leaned in. "Well, Edward said some syndicate had taken over. We should talk to them, see how they feel."

Merl shook his head. "Sounds to me like they've already talked to Edward and are prepared to support him."

Luke's brow drew down in a frown. "And you gentlemen aren't?"

"If we could find a better candidate, then, honestly..." Merl lowered his voice so that only those at the table could hear. "We would support someone else."

"Surely there must be someone else in this city to run for mayor," Luke said.

"You know how it is, Marshal. Everyone has an opinion of what's wrong and even what to do about it, but no one wants to give up their precious time to actually do anything about it."

"What about one of you?" Luke asked pointedly.

Merl chuckled. "We are as guilty as everyone else, I'm sorry to admit. We've all got businesses to run, and to be mayor would mean putting those businesses aside for years, if a person was serious about doing a good job. What we need is someone who doesn't have business obligations, someone who's honest, someone who has the best interests of San Francisco in mind." He turned fully toward Luke. "We need someone like you, Marshal."

"Whoa, now, wait a minute there." He held up one hand. "I've got a job, thank you."

"Marshal," Merl returned with a negligent wave of his hand. "You could quit."

Robert piped up. "Yes, why, half the town's talking about the way you saved that boy."

"True," John added eagerly. "Why, Marshal, you're a hero, and heroes make wonderful candidates."

"No thanks," Luke said firmly.

"But, Marshal, we need you. You'd have our full support and... guidance."

"You mean you'd want to tell me what to do," Luke returned bluntly. "When I do a job, gentlemen, I'm my own boss, and—"

Merl cut across his words. "Perfect. Then you'll do it!"

"No. No. And *no,*" Luke said emphatically.

"You said you'd think about it." Merl reminded him. "It would mean settling down. Steady work...for a few years, anyway." He chuckled. "Good salary, house to live in..."

Luke dragged in a long breath and let it out slowly. If he wanted Rebecca, if he wanted his son, he'd need a home and a steady job that didn't mean every time he went out he might not come back. Still, politics?

"Just think about it," John was saying. "Don't make a hasty decision you'll regret later."

Yeah, Luke thought, he knew about hasty decisions.

"Okay," he said. "I'll think on it a couple of days, but I'm not—repeat, not—making any promises."

"Fair enough. We want some serious help with this Barbary Coast situation."

"You're really serious about closing it down."

"Damned straight." Merl helped himself to another cup of coffee from the silver pot on the table. "The Coast is an abomination. We're not so naive as to think that men don't need someplace to let off a little steam. But the Coast is a mess. There's murder going on down there. Prostitution. Men being shanghaied. White slavery. No one's doing anything to stop it. If this city is going to grow and expect the nation to take us seriously, then we've got to clean our own house. We've tried to get the mayor and Brody to listen, but they turn a deaf ear to all our complaints. We're not alone in this. I can list close to thirty civic and community organizations that feel as we do."

"With so much support, why isn't anything happening?"

"Exactly what we're wondering. There's only two things that make any difference—power and money. We decided that with as much money as changes hands down there, money was the key. Short of calling out the vigilantes again like in '56, we decided instead to hire a man to investigate and see what he could come up with. After about two months, he noticed that every Friday night a man appeared and an envelope was exchanged. He followed the man, who seemed to be making rounds. He would go from one place to another, and each time, an envelope was exchanged."

"Who was the man?" Luke's interest was piqued.

"Don't know," John shook his head regretfully. "Our man, Collins, was following the messenger when he was waylaid in an alley and beaten pretty bad. After that, he refused to go back."

"Can't blame him for that," Luke told them.

"Oh, no, we were disappointed, but we understood."

"Did you hire someone else?"

"No. It's difficult to know who to trust. Besides, that was only a week ago, and we haven't had time."

"Collins," Luke repeated thoughtfully.

"Yes. You want his address?"

"Please. I think I'll pay Mr. Collins a visit, and then . . ." He stood, picking up his hat as he did. "I'll think about your suggestion, gentlemen." He took the piece of paper John handed him with Collins's address on it and slid it into his trousers pocket. "I'll be in touch."

With that, he left. Now he had two plans, and they both required some preparation.

Chapter Nineteen

After a jubilant Edward left, Rebecca went into the kitchen and made herself a steaming cup of tea.

"Are you really going to marry him?" Ruth's question was blunt. She joined Rebecca at the kitchen table and helped herself to a cup of tea from the pot.

"Yes, I am."

"Why? You've never seemed interested before. Not in him. Not in anyone."

Rebecca didn't answer for a moment. She looked down into the half-full cup, then up and beyond Ruth, through the kitchen window, to the bare branches of the oak tree outside. "It's time," she said into the cool air.

"One doesn't usually get married on a schedule, or is there a rush of some sort?" They were friends, more than relatives, and they'd shared almost everything since Nathan died. "Is there something you want to tell me?"

She shook her head. "There's nothing to tell. Edward asked, and I said yes."

"He's asked before."

"Yes, I know."

They sat in silence for a long moment before Ruth spoke again. "Of course, all the other times there was no Marshal Scanlin in the picture, so to speak."

"He's not in the picture now."

"Then why the rush? You've turned Edward down at least twice, and then the marshal shows up..." She let the implication hang between them.

"I want to settle down. I want a home for Andrew, with a mother and a...father."

Ruth sipped at her tea. "And you think Edward is the right man for the job?"

Rebecca didn't answer. The silence spoke volumes.

"Does Luke know?" Ruth said very softly.

"Yes. He was at the luncheon today when Edward made the announcement."

Ruth arched one brow. "Did he...say anything?"

"Like what?"

"Oh, I don't know. I thought he might have something to say, some opinion." She toyed with her cup. "He seems to care for you and for Andrew. And Andrew likes him a lot."

"I know."

"I like him, too. He's a good man, Rebecca."

"I thought so, too...once."

"Not now? Why?"

Rebecca pushed the cup and saucer away from her. "I don't know." She looked away. "I knew him a long time ago. We were both different. We were both young and impulsive and—"

"In love," Ruth supplied.

Rebecca's eyes came up slowly to meet Ruth's gaze. "It was a lifetime ago."

"He still loves you, you know. He didn't tell me that, of course, but I've seen the way he looks at you when he thinks no one is watching. He loves you, all right. Take my word for it."

"There've been a lot of mistakes made in the name of love. Promises made and believed, all in the name of love. People get hurt."

"Ah..." Ruth gave a knowing nod. "So you're looking to play it safe, are you?"

"Yes" came her emphatic answer.

"Well, it's up to you, but—" she stood and carried her cup and saucer over to the sink "—I can tell you that anything worth having has a risk attached. I've never seen it otherwise." She put the dishes in the sink and turned back to Rebecca. "I've also never known you to be afraid."

"Maybe you don't know me as well as you think."

"Maybe I know you *better* than you think. As a matter of fact, you'd be surprised at the things I know." She walked out of the kitchen.

Luke was angry when he left the luncheon. He knew exactly what she was trying to do. She was trying to put him off, to put up another barrier between them. She was trying to protect Andrew.

He knew all that, and he was still plain damned angry. No, he wasn't hurt or confused. He was angry—gut-twisting, fist-curling angry. She wasn't going to get away with this. Yes, he knew it would be awkward to tell Andrew the truth. Yes, he knew there were risks, knew there was scandal to be avoided. But this was his son they were talking about, and his woman.

Yes, she was his. He was in love with her, and he damned well wasn't walking away this time. And neither was she. They were going to be together. Luke

Scanlin and Rebecca Parker, the way it should have been.

He made two stops, at the tailor's and the mercantile, before heading for the investigator's office. It took only a few minutes conversation to learn that the pickup man made his rounds every Friday night, late, about one in the morning. The investigator had followed the man as far as Blood Alley, then lost him. That was when the lights had gone out.

Luke got the names of the saloons on the list and a wish for good luck from the man.

Luke sat at a corner table in Fat Daugherty's saloon. He'd been here before, and the bartender seemed to recognize him as a repeat visitor. No one seemed aware of his identity or why he was here.

He played a little poker, coming out only a little the worse for wear after a couple of hours. All the while, he kept his eye on the bar.

By midnight, he relinquished his chair at the poker table and moved to a secluded place in the corner. From there he could watch the doors and the bartender easily.

He was working on beer tonight. This was his fourth mug. It wasn't much better than the rotgut. This looked like horse piss and tasted about the same. But he was less likely to get sick from it or have a hangover tomorrow.

And tomorrow he needed a clear head. Tomorrow he was going to see Rebecca. Only she didn't know it, not yet.

Along about one-fifteen, Luke spotted a man in a black suit striding purposefully to the bar, pushing his

way through the crowd as he did. Judging by the bartender's expression, the man wasn't asking for a drink.

The man said something that was impossible to hear
over the noise. Grim-faced, the bartender nodded and
produced a brown envelope, which he forked over to
the man, who tucked it inside his jacket pocket, then
turned and left.

Luke got up slowly and made his way through the
crowd. By the time he got outside, the man had disappeared. Damn.

Luke scanned the area. Where the hell had he gone
so fast? Jesus, a whole night wasted. He was about to
step off the sidewalk when a man, the same man,
nearly knocked him down as he rode out of the alley
and headed north on Grant.

Luke swung up on his horse and took off after him,
trying to keep up in the dark streets without getting so
close as to be detected. The man zigzagged through
residential streets, and twice Luke thought he'd lost
him, only to spot him again.

When the man turned onto Broadway, Luke slowed.
He saw the man dismounting in front of the only
house on the block with lights on. Luke dismounted
and, tying his horse, closed the distance on foot.

He recognized the house immediately.

"Son of a bitch," he muttered as he positioned
himself in the shadow of a tree across the street.

He watched and waited. Twenty minutes later, the
man came out and rode away. Luke crossed the street.
The front door was unlocked, and he wasn't inclined
to ring the bell.

He let himself in. He knew the way to the office in
the back. He walked carefully, noiselessly, stopping in
the open doorway.

"Hello, Frank," he said, and the man surged out of his chair.

"What the—" His eyes widened. He took a half step to the right.

"No use, Frank," Luke said, coming into the room and closing the door behind him. "I've seen the money." He took another step closer. "And the man bringing it."

"I don't know what you're talking about. He just owed me some money. There's no law against that."

"Did I forget to mention—" he took another step "—that I know where the man came from, and why he was bringing you the money? I've been following him all night. Let's stop the lying—" he pushed Frank down in his chair "—shall we?" It was an order, not a request. "You and I have some talking to do."

Chapter Twenty

Luke arrived at Rebecca's house about ten Saturday night.

"Mrs. Wheeler," he said as he walked into the entryway. "Nice to see you again."

"And you, too, Marshal," the beaming housekeeper returned. Seeming to know what, or more precisely who, Luke wanted to see, she added, "*Everyone* is in the parlor."

Luke smiled politely.

He took a deep breath and raked his hands through his hair. It was his only outward show of nervousness. All the way over here tonight he'd cautioned himself about propriety, about the need for calm. She would not refuse to talk to him now, not in this crowd, not without making a scene. How would she explain her refusal to talk to the savior of her son?

All he had to do was go up to her and say, "Becky, come with me. We have a few things to discuss." Then they would slip away to another room. A bedroom came quickly to mind, causing the blood in his veins to heat noticeably.

He stood in the doorway a full ten seconds before the whispers started. A handful of the people present knew him, but most did not.

The beautiful women smiled and nodded in a provocative way that a man instinctively understood.

The men he had had lunch with greeted him, bringing with them their wives and others who were anxious to meet San Francisco's newest hero. He politely repeated their names, offered brief answers to their questions or courteous acknowledgment of their praise and compliments as he edged forward.

He scanned the room with interest. And those around him wondered who it was the marshal was searching for so intently.

He hadn't seen Rebecca yet, or Edward, or even Ruth.

The parlor was ablaze with lights, and the carpets had been rolled back, exposing the polished plank floor for those who wished to dance. Those in attendance were bedecked in jewels and satin and evening attire.

A small quartet—harp, cello and two violins—was ensconced near the hearth, playing a demure selection of waltzes. He still hadn't seen Rebecca.

Rebecca saw him, or more precisely sensed his presence, the instant he walked into the parlor. Her first excited thought was that he was wearing evening clothes. It was a major concession on his part.

Wearing all black, with only the white of his high starched collar peeking above his perfectly knotted black tie, he'd never been more handsome, more elegant, she thought. She didn't miss the fact that most of the other women present were noticing the same. Before the thread of jealousy could tighten, she reminded herself that she didn't care if he was the most handsome man in the room. She didn't care that his shoulders were wide and his smile dazzling enough to make her heart take on a shallow, rapid rhythm.

And she especially didn't care why he was here, tonight, now. But he was headed straight for her, and that rapid beating of her heart got faster with each closing step.

Luke's progress was impeded, but not deterred.

"Just part of the job," he said for about the tenth time to another person who offered congratulations on his rescue of Andrew. He spotted Rebecca then, over the heads of the others gathered around.

She was standing with a couple, a tall, dark man and a beautiful blonde. They were chatting, she was smiling up at the man in a way that sparked resentment in Luke, and he didn't even know the man.

If his possessive tenseness showed to those he spoke to, they didn't reveal it. Still, it was several more minutes before he could disengage himself from those wishing to know all the details of what was being referred to as "the great rescue of the decade."

It didn't take long for people to realize that he was a man on a mission and that the object of his quest was the beautiful Rebecca Tinsdale. Most were not surprised. After all, there had been rumors. She had let the man stay in her home—an odd thing for a total stranger, unless they were not strangers, unless they were something . . . more.

Yes, that had been the gossip for days and, judging by the way the marshal was closing in on his prey, it looked very much as if the rumors were correct.

The whispers gathered strength, like a storm cloud building before the first lightning strike. It seemed there was an almost breathless anticipation in the room.

Luke reached her in four more strides. He acknowledged the couple she was with.

The man offered his hand. "Logan McCloud."

"Mr. McCloud," Luke answered, his gaze fixed on Rebecca.

"And my wife, Katherine."

"Ma'am." He spared her a glance. "Rebecca, I want to talk to you." He forced a smile to those present. "Would you excuse us a moment?"

It was a rhetorical question, since he'd already taken her hand in his steely grip and was striding toward the French doors that opened onto the porch and the yard beyond.

Everyone watched them leave, everyone except the one man who might have objected. Edward was in the dining room conducting some campaign business, the old handshake-and-a-promise that was the mark of a politician.

So Luke was able to pull her from the room without confrontation, which was fortunate, some said, for Edward.

White lace curtains fluttered and lapped against his pant leg as he exited keeping her in his tight grip. Outside, he sought the shadows at the farthest end of the porch.

The evening was cool. The breeze off the bay was moist with the threat of fog by morning. Rebecca shivered against the damp chill as the air caressed her bare shoulders and arms.

She was prepared for some demand, some lecture, some order. She was not prepared for him to push her back against the rough cold stone of the house wall and kiss her.

It wasn't a gentle kiss, a sensual invitation to pleasure. No, this was a kiss of possession, one that was fierce and demanding and overpowering.

The fierce relentlessness of his kiss startled her, and she pushed at him, twisting her head as she did, tearing her mouth from his.

"Stop it! What's the matter with you?" she demanded hotly as she continued to shove at the wall of his chest. She expected him to comply, she expected him to realize that they were on her porch, in her home, and that at any moment someone could, and probably would, walk out here and catch them in this compromising position.

He didn't budge. "You, sweetheart. You're what's the matter with me." His voice was a growl, and he leaned into her, trapping her between him and the wall. The instant he saw her, all his caution vanished. He'd been up all night, thinking about her, about her with Edward, about her with any other man. Jealousy overpowered reason and ate at him. His mouth sought hers again.

"I want to go back inside, Luke." She tried to move, but he grabbed her hands and held them outspread against the wall.

His face was a breathless inch from hers. His body pressed hard against hers, so that she felt the stone against her back and the buttons of his vest through the silk bodice of her dress.

"What do you want, Luke?"

"You."

"No!" she snapped, ignoring the fact that she was trapped and powerless to stop him.

His head lifted abruptly, his own anger flashing fire-bright in his eyes. "Tell me, sweetheart, are you and Edward lovers . . . also?"

It was the "also" that got her, that sent her temper boiling over. She was not willing to give him the satisfaction of knowing that there had been only two men in her life, and only one who haunted her achingly lush dreams. So it was her temper that made her say, "Yes."

It wasn't the answer he wanted, needed. His eyes turned as cold and hard as flint. "You're lying."

"Am I?" she taunted.

"You and that weasel?" he returned in a mocking tone.

"Think what you will," she countered, and tried to twist free of him.

"I think," he started softly, "he doesn't make your heart beat faster. He doesn't caress your skin the way I do, touching all the soft, sensitive places that make you shudder. He doesn't know how to kiss the edge of your ear or the tips of your breasts. He doesn't make you moan in surrender when he's inside you."

"Why, you— How dare you say such vile, disgusting—"

"There's nothing vile or disgusting about it, except in your own frightened little mind. I'm in your blood and you're in mine, and the sooner you admit it the better off we'll both be."

She shook her head in denial. "No." Her voice was shaky. "It's not true."

"Isn't it?" he murmured, and slowly dipped his head and kissed her. Not on the lips, but on the delicate spot behind her ear. His lips were warm and teasing, making her shudder as delicious shivers skipped up the backs of her legs.

When he lifted his head this time, he smiled. It was a slow, lush smile, with a touch of smugness that was more roguish than enraging.

"You and I were meant to be together." His mouth covered hers in a passionate kiss, full of desire and the knowledge that comes from shared intimacy. Her body flared to life like a candle in a dark room. Her fingers trembled with the sudden need to touch him.

He leaned into her, letting her feel the weight of his body against hers while he looped her arms around his neck. Pulling her more fully into his embrace, he deepened the kiss, his mouth slanting one way, then the other, tasting, testing, promising. Willing her to know he loved her. Willing her to admit she loved him, too.

He kissed her cheek and her brow and the slender bridge of her nose. He laved at her ear with the tip of his tongue. It was seduction he was working and, fair or unfair, it was his only hope.

His hands splayed upward, his fingers caressing the smoothness of her bare flesh above the silk edge of her dress. Muscles tensed, and blood drummed hot and hurried in his body.

Rebecca's eyes drifted closed against the magic he was working on her. He slid the lace ruffles from her shoulders, kissing and licking the heated flesh there before his hand brushed, feather-light, over her breasts, where they strained against the confines of her dress.

She stood very still beneath his hands, telling herself that resistance was useless, and hating the fact that her body warmed and opened to him in ways so familiar yet so unnerving.

He cupped her breast through the fabric, his thumbs rubbing with aching gentleness, enticing her nipples to peak. His black eyes were bright with desire.

"Say it, Becky," he murmured as he nipped, then kissed, the exposed skin of her shoulder. "Say you feel the magic."

"No," she managed, her voice shaky.

"No?" he repeated in a gentle tone, then took her mouth in his again, his tongue dipping inside to tease the tender flesh there, to dance and flutter and ignite the ancient pulsing deep within her.

He swayed back and forth against her, letting her feel his arousal, letting her know what being with her did to him.

It was then that she felt the chill of the night air on her legs, and realized with stark terror that he'd hiked up the hem of her dress. She shoved at his chest. He didn't budge. She felt his hand on her thigh, the warmth of his touch penetrating the thin lawn of her pantalets. His hand glided around to cup her buttocks.

Restless, tense, he moved against her, his hand stroking her thigh. She was shamed to realize she was helpless against his sensual onslaught, and she felt his fingers slip between her legs.

Oh, Lord, this couldn't be happening, but it was. She was powerless to stop him, didn't want to stop him. The nearness of him, his touch, aroused her passion and drowned out all logic. Her body heated in eager anticipation of the familiar pleasure he offered. Moisture gathered at the juncture of her legs, and she stood motionless under his hands.

Logic demanded that she resist the building waves of sensation. But the flame of desire was already surging in her blood, skimming over her skin like a fast-moving prairie fire, engulfing all in its path.

He kissed and teased and touched her in all the heated, urgent places, all the places that set the languid need spiraling up in her. She steeled herself against his touch, refusing to acknowledge the rapture his gently stroking fingers caused as they found the opening in her pantalets and slid easily into her wet, aching core. Her breath caught as he touched her deep, deep inside. Pleasure, raw and carnal, uncoiled and shot upward, making her groan, making her dig her fingers into his shoulders for support, crushing the fine wool of his jacket as she did.

"I want you," he groaned against the delicate curve of her ear, his breath warm and wet.

He stilled and glanced at the open doorway nearby. Had he heard voices? Releasing her, he stepped around to protect her, to conceal them both in the shadows.

"Luke, please..." she begged. She had heard the voices also.

"I thought I was, Princess," he murmured, and moved her back a few steps, to the farthest corner of the porch.

She was terrified and aroused and horrified by this wanton desire that overcame all reason, that made her stay here with him in the rich darkness.

"Rebecca..." he groaned as his mouth ate at hers. His hands frantically traveled from shoulder to waist and lower, pulling up her dress again.

"You can't..."

"I am," he countered, already unbuttoning his trousers. Hooking his hands under her arms, he lifted her and, bending slightly, he entered her, his driving need peaking more rapidly than he'd expected. Back and shoulder muscles strained and knotted as he held her securely. He moved in a rhythm their bodies recognized. Desire drove him, drove each deep thrust, each heated stroke.

Voices reached her ears from somewhere nearby. The very real danger only added to the carnal pleasure that he was creating in her.

His mouth closed over hers, his tongue mimicking the rhythm of his body in hers, and suddenly thought was lost, her body craving the release that only he could offer. She clung to him, clawed at him, moved on him, demanding that he fill her completely, while her body melted lushly around the hard, pulsing length of him.

"That's it, Becky. Give in to it. Let it happen."

Encouraged by his words, and the thrusting motion of his body, she pressed in tighter. It seemed natural to wrap her legs around his waist.

Luke slid his hands under her bottom and turned so that he leaned against the wall and supported her full weight in his cupped hands. Their position more secure, he glided into her again, more slowly this time, feeling her pulse and constrict around him in a way that sent his heart rate soaring faster than a comet.

Rebecca whimpered as the pleasure washed over her, as he filled her completely, touching her deep inside and sending shock waves of passion washing over her.

Luke barely breathed, barely moved, his body focused on the luxury of this sensation. Her legs rode high on his hips, and he penetrated her more deeply than ever before.

Though it was sheer madness to cling to him, to give herself over to him, Rebecca was inundated by the extravagant enchantment, the urgent desire, that was melting her reason as fast as it was liquefying her body.

What was it about him that made her risk all for him? But as he kissed and laved at her mouth, as he moved with sure and certain strokes inside her, she knew the answer. She loved him, she realized as the first tiny tremblings of the ultimate bliss convulsed within her. Another heartbeat, another powerful stroke, and she cried out at the peaking desire. Luke quickly covered her mouth with his, absorbing the pleasure-driven cry, and continued the demanding rhythm.

"I love to hear you scream, Princess, but this is not the place. We wouldn't want anyone to come to see what the commotion was."

"There wouldn't be a—" He moved inside her, and she gasped as pulsing need surged through her and the incredible flutters started again. No, she thought, this couldn't be happening. The ache coiled tight inside her, and she knew, God help her, that it was happening.

She struggled against the impending climax, determined to restrain herself, to somehow deprive him of his control. But her body would not still, and tingling nerves and soul-searing passion would not relent.

Aching, tensing, she moved faster and harder, seeking release from this pleasurable pain. Her body reached for the rapture it knew was near. She climaxed in a heart-pounding liquid rush. Feeling her release, responding to her sensual delights, Luke gave in to his own need and slid into her once more. At the same instant, Rebecca kissed him, her mouth soft and inviting against his, and she absorbed his groan as she felt him pour his shuddering release into her throbbing channel.

It was a perfect union, one of pleasure given and taken, lush and erotic and equal.

Minutes later, he was buttoning his trousers and adjusting his shirt and coat. She was straightening the green silk of her dress, pushing at the errant curls that had come loose to drape down her back.

Rebecca stood in ecstatic shock and base anger. Furious at him, and angrier at herself for responding to him so easily, so wantonly.

As she looked at him, she wanted to strike out, to deny what had happened, to rant and scream in indignation, but how could she? There was no turning back this time, no pretense of denial. And so, more ashamed than she'd ever been, she turned away.

His voice stopped her. "Marry me."

She stood there, her back to him. She dragged in a lungful of cool night air. "Eight years ago I would have given anything to hear those words from you."

"And now?"

She refused to face him. "Now, it's too late."

"Why?" He came around to face her. "Why is it too late? We can be married. We can be a family."

She shook her head resolutely.

"I want you." He took her shoulders in his grip. "I want my son."

"How will I explain to Andrew that the man he thinks is his father, isn't?"

"I don't know. We'll find a way."

"How?"

"I don't know. I don't care. All I know is that I want you—both of you."

"But I do care. If I marry you, everyone will know what I did—what we did. They'll know that Andrew is illegitimate."

"He's not illegitimate."

"Only because Nathan married me when he knew I was pregnant."

"Dammit, I know that. I can't change it. I would if I could, God knows, but I can't. I'm grateful to the man. What do you want me to do?"

"I want you to leave me alone. I want you to leave Andrew alone."

"No. You're mine. Both of you belong to me."

"You gave up any claims when you left."

"The hell I did."

"We're not property. We're not some saddle gear you forgot and now have come back for. There are people involved here, scandal to be considered."

"We'll move."

"Oh, move. Just like that. Pack everything up and move. To where?"

"How do I know? Texas, Colorado—I don't much care."

"And that's the trouble, Luke. You don't care about anyone or anything but yourself and what you want. You were selfish enough to walk out eight years ago with never a backward glance, and now you're being just as selfish because you've decided that you want a family."

"Not 'a family.' I want *my* family."

"We don't belong to you, no matter what you think."

"I think I just proved you wrong."

"That was lust."

"The hell it was."

"It was. And I'm not risking my life and Andrew's and Ruth's to satisfy your selfishness *or* my lust.

"What's Ruth got to do with this?"

"She's his grandmother. The only grandmother he's ever had. You want me to tear them apart?"

"She'd understand."

"Would she? Do you want to tell her? Do you want to say, 'Pardon me, your only grandchild isn't your grandchild at all, and we're leaving to avoid the scandal? Hope you'll be fine all alone for the rest of your life?' "

"For chrissakes, Rebecca, I wouldn't be that cold."

"Maybe not, but any way you slice it, it's the same thing. I won't do it. I owe her more than I could ever repay. She was there for me when I had *no one else*, and I won't repay her like this."

"And what am I supposed to do? Pretend I don't have a son?"

"Why not? Until a few days ago, you weren't very interested."

"Until a few days ago, I didn't know."

"But you could have, Luke, if you'd cared about anyone but yourself." She took a step. "Goodbye Luke," she said quietly, and walked away.

He watched her go, and a pain swept over him, a longing, so intense that he had to steel himself or be crushed by it. He thought to call out to her. To tell her that she was right, that he had been selfish, then and now. That he loved her so damned much that he thought the rest of his life would be no more than a shell without her and Andrew to fill it. But at the last second, just before she turned the corner, he stopped and realized he'd said it all, and it wasn't enough.

Hands braced on the porch rail, fingers curled white-knuckle tight against the painted wood, he faced the night, a night as black and bleak as he felt.

It was then that he heard the unmistakable click of a gun hammer being pulled back. In the next second, a raspy male voice snarled, "I've been looking for you, Scanlin."

A soft breeze stirred the bushes beyond the porch. Luke didn't move. He strained to see into the darkness to find the source of the voice.

"Get the hell down here," the voice ordered rough and furious.

Luke straightened, all his senses tuned and focused on the man who stepped out of the bushes. He was dressed in rumpled black, his hair was slicked back, his face was pale.

"Riggs," Luke muttered. "I thought..."

"What? You killed me? Not hardly. But you did kill my brother, you son of a bitch, and I intend to even the score."

As discreetly as possible, Luke edged his hand toward the opening of his coat, and the gun tucked in his shoulder holster.

"Hold it," Riggs snarled, spotting the motion.

Luke froze.

"Don't even try. I'd hate to splatter your brains all over that nice porch. Now take it out and toss it over here. Come on." He gestured with the gun he held.

Reluctantly Luke obliged, all the while watching

the man, waiting for an opening, a chance to do...
something other than stand here and be gunned down.

"What now?"

"Now, you and me is gonna take a little walk away
from all these witnesses. Like I said, we got us some
unfinished business."

Luke glanced toward the open doorway. Rebecca
was in there. He hoped to hell she didn't walk out here
now.

"Come on. Come on," the gunman said, waving his
gun for emphasis again.

"All right, Riggs." Luke started toward the stairs
near the doorway.

"Don't try nothin'," the man warned. "I don't
wanna hurt nobody else, but I will if you make me."

Luke nodded. The odds were all in the man's favor.
If Luke went with him, he was a dead man. The man
was advancing, matching Luke step for step. At the
top of the porch stairs, Luke stopped still.

There was no way he was going with this guy, and
there was no way he could let him get away and possibly come back for Rebecca or Andrew.

A round of sudden laughter erupted from the house.
The gunman glanced away for a split second. It was all
the time Luke needed. He hurled himself at Riggs,
slamming into him, and they hit the ground with a
bone-jarring thud. The gun arched through the air and
landed a few feet away in the grass.

Luke scrambled to his feet. He started for the gun.
Riggs was up, and he grabbed Luke from behind.
Luke slammed his elbow into Riggs's ribs. The man
cried out, and Luke was able to break free and turn.

"You son of a bitch!" Riggs shouted, loud enough
that those inside the house heard and came outside.

"What's going on?" someone said.

Luke was a little too busy to answer. In complete silence, they faced each other. Luke was between Riggs and the gun. He knew that if he tried to turn, Riggs would be on top of him. He also knew that there was no way Riggs could get the gun, not without going through him.

"Give it up, Riggs," Luke told him as the two of them squared off against each other.

Riggs charged at Luke. Head down, he rammed into Luke's midsection. Air whooshed out of Luke's lungs, and he landed on his knees. He grabbed hold of Riggs's legs as he lunged for the gun.

The man sprawled facedown in the grass, his hand outstretched. When he rolled over, there was a gun in his hand.

Luke threw himself on top of Riggs, pinning his body down as he reached for his gun hand. They rolled back and forth, Riggs trying to free himself from Luke's weight, Luke determined to wrench the gun free.

Riggs groaned as he managed to work the gun closer and closer to their bodies, murderous intent in his eyes. Suddenly there was a shot, and then another.

More people rushed out from the party. Men scrambled down the stairs and rushed toward the two men lying still and lifeless on the lawn.

A steady trickle of blood formed a pool against the side of the men.

"Marshal, are you all right?"

Luke felt a hand on his shoulder, then another, felt ʳeone helping him up. His breathing was ragged, ˟e burning pain in his side hurt like hell.

"I—" He sagged to sit on the ground, and his hand instinctively sought the .45, lying nearby.

"Someone send for the doctor!" a man called. He pulled a handkerchief from his pocket and pushed it against the spreading red stain on Luke's white dress shirt.

It took only a glance to see that Riggs was dead, shot through the heart.

"What happened?" the man nearest was saying.

"One of the... kidnappers..." Luke managed. Every breath hurt, and talking hurt more. "Damn," he muttered as he looked down to check the flow of blood.

"The doctor's on his way," the man said. "Let's get you—"

"Luke!"

It was Rebecca's voice. Rebecca's scream. In an instant she was there, kneeling in the bloodstained dirt beside him.

"Oh, my God!" Frantically she touched his face, his shoulders. She spotted the blood. "Are you all right?"

He looked at her kneeling in the dirt beside him, her face a ghostly white, her hands clutching at him. "I'm all right."

"You're not all right. Oh, God, you could have been killed!" she ranted. Then, in front of everyone, she pulled him into her arms and kissed him.

He didn't move, didn't dare to.

"Becky, honey, you're, uh, getting your dress all messed up."

"I don't give a damn about the dress. Are you all right?"

"I'm okay."

She insisted on helping him to his feet.

"Just took a chunk outa my side, is all, and—"

He was struggling to his feet when suddenly a hand grasped Luke's shoulder and, taken unawares, he was jerked back, releasing Rebecca.

"Get away from her!"

Edward stood there, his face mottled with rage. "What the hell is going on?"

Luke had his arm draped around Rebecca's shoulders and was letting her pretend she was actually holding him up. God, it was pathetic. He was shot and bleeding, and all he could think about was keeping his arm around her, feeling her body next to his.

Edward grabbed Rebecca by the wrist, his grip surprisingly tight, and pulled her away. Rebecca winced as his fingers dug into the tender flesh of her wrist. She managed to twist free.

"Edward," she cried, "for heaven's sake, what's wrong with you? Luke's been hurt, can't you see that? This man was one of the kidnappers, and he tried to..." Tears threatened at the realization that it could be Luke lying there in a pool of blood. "Tried to kill Luke, and—"

"Luke," Edward snarled. "Luke this and Luke that. All I hear these days is Luke Scanlin's name. I'm sick of it, and I'm sick of you, Scanlin. You're interfering in my business."

Luke braced his feet. A couple of men stepped up, as though to help him, but he waved them away. "Well, Ed, you're right about that. I have been interfering in your business, but you see, I'm gonna marry Rebecca—"

"The hell you are!"

Luke smiled, a slow predatory smile. "Who's gonna stop me? You?"

"Edward! Please! He's hurt."

Ruth rushed to Rebecca's side, Andrew hot on her heels. "What going on?" Ruth asked, sizing up the situation in a glance. She held Andrew tightly against her side, trying to cover his face with her skirt to prevent him from seeing such a grisly sight.

Andrew was having none of it. "What happened? Who hurt the marshal? Is that man dead, Grandma?"

"Shh, Andrew," she said gently. "Go back in the house," she told him, but he didn't move.

Edward's eyes glittered with rage. "All right, Scanlin. I don't care if you're a marshal. I don't care if you're God Almighty. I've had enough of your insults."

Rebecca tried again. "Edward, this is hardly the time." Her voice was firm and low as she tried to defuse the situation before someone said the wrong thing.

But Edward wasn't listening. Unbelievably, he took a menacing half step toward Luke, who never moved, just stood there looking calm and relaxed, as though it were the most natural thing in the world for him to be bleeding.

"Don't even try it, Ed. Bad as this hurts, I can kill you and not even think twice about it." The .45 was still in his blood-soaked hand.

No one moved.

Rebecca's hand flew to her throat. "Luke!"

Edward's hand clenched into fists, and he took another step. "You don't scare me, Scanlin." His eyes locked with Luke's as he continued to advance.

Violence, like a strong electrical current, flashed between the two men. Rebecca had never seen Edward behave in such a manner.

Luke's voice was low, and deadly cold. "Well, I oughta scare you, Ed. I oughta scare the hell outa you. You see, I had a nice long chat with your lawyer, Frank Handley, this afternoon."

Edward froze.

Confused, and more than a little angry, Rebecca shouldered into the middle. Eyes blazing, she pushed at one, then the other. "Are you both out of your minds?" Her tone was incredulous. "Stop this at once, do you hear me? Luke, we've got to get you inside."

"Rebecca, stay out of this," Luke ordered hotly. His gaze riveted her. "It's between me and—"

"No!" she shouted.

"Becky, get the hell out of the way! Old Ed here has something in his craw, so let's have at it. Go on, Ed." Luke motioned with his arm, and was rewarded with a stabbing pain through the ribs. Clenching his jaw, he continued, "Tell everyone about what you and Frank have been up to."

Edward straightened. "Don't try to change the subject, Scanlin," he countered smoothly.

Luke didn't miss the furtive way Edward scanned the crowd. *There's no escape this time, Ed.* He kept his pose calm. "I'm not changing the subject, Ed. Go on and tell these folks how Frank's been fronting for you all these months."

"Fronting?" Rebecca questioned quietly.

The other men echoed her.

"Yeah," Luke continued, shifting his weight to his other leg. He could feel the blood oozing down his

7

side, along his leg under his trousers. He knew he was losing a lot of blood, but he'd be damned if he'd pack it in now. Not now!

Gritting his teeth, he said, "I had a nice long talk with Frank. Seems he wasn't ready to go to jail for kidnapping and bribery and falsifying government records, among other things. Seems Frank has been working for Ed here."

Edward took a carefully measured step backward, and several men closed in around him cutting, off any retreat.

"Go on, Marshal," Merl Gates said.

"Well, it seems that Ed here has been extorting money from the saloon and gambling-hall owners down on the Coast, in exchange for protection. He made sure that licenses were granted and renewed, and that new licenses were approved. He even made sure that the police weren't too interested in what happened down there."

Shock and disbelief colored Rebecca's face as she turned to face him. The night was deadly quiet.

"It's a lie," Edward shouted defiantly. "It's all a lie. Scanlin's trying to win you over, Rebecca. Surely you can see that!"

Rebecca didn't say a word.

Luke did. "Shall I have Frank brought around? He's over at the hotel. One of my deputies is keeping him company."

Never taking her eyes from Edward, Rebecca said, "There must be some mistake."

Luke shook his head. "Sorry, Becky. There's no mistake, and I'm afraid it gets worse."

Her eyes flew to Luke. "Worse?" She felt cold inside.

"Frank tells me that it was Edward who was behind Andrew's kidnapping. He did it to get control of the paper—and, I suspect, of you."

"Oh, no. It can't . . . be." She had to grip herself to stop the sudden trembling, to control the sickening feeling deep in the pit of her stomach.

Every man there was silent, watching, waiting.

"It's a lie!" Edward shouted. "There's no proof."

"Well, Ed, I think we'll let a jury decide that. We'll see if they believe you or Frank Handley. I think when we check on who really owns that syndicate that bought the *Times,* we'll find your name."

Edward tried to turn and push through the crowd, but they stopped him cold. The sudden sharp sound of a gun being cocked, stilled his struggle.

Luke's voice cut through the night like a knife. "Mister, you better hope those men hold on to you, 'cause if they don't, then I'll be real happy to blow you in half for what you've done to Rebecca."

The men pushed in. "We've got him, Marshal, don't you worry," someone said.

"And we'll see he gets locked up nice and tight, and not in the city jail, either," Merl added triumphantly as they dragged Edward away.

Luke watched Rebecca. Watched the emotions play over her face. "I'm sorry, Becky. I didn't mean for you to find out like this. I mean, there's no easy way . . . It's just that . . ." Damn.

"Marshal!" Andrew rushed in, his face pale, his chin quivering. "Are you dying?"

"No, Andrew," Luke assured him. His fist curled against the pain, and he dropped down on one knee to look the child in the eye. He wanted to reassure him.

"Are you hurt bad?" Andrew's voice was quiet.

"Not too bad," Luke told him.

"My mom can make a bandage." His face was solemn. "She's real good at fixing things."

"I don't think she can fix this, Andrew," he said, and Rebecca knew he meant more than his side.

Ruth stepped forward. "Rebecca," she said firmly. "For heaven's sake, you better haul off and marry the man before he up and bleeds to death."

Rebecca didn't move. "I . . ." Guilt and regret tore at her. She wanted to say something, to explain, but how? Even after all of this, nothing had changed.

Ruth looked at Rebecca, her gentle eyes searching her daughter-in-law's, and she said, "Andrew needs his father."

"Ruth, I . . ." She actually thought to deny it, her love for Ruth was so great, as was her respect for Nathan, and her gratitude for all he'd done for her.

As though sensing her thoughts, Ruth touched her hand and gave a knowing smile.

"How did you know?" Rebecca asked on a thready whisper, feeling all her defenses dissolve.

Ruth spoke quietly, so that Andrew would not hear. "I've always suspected. When I saw them together, playing baseball . . ." She cut them a glance. "Well, just look at them."

Rebecca did. The men she loved, together. Her heart slammed hard against her ribs. Joy bubbled up in her. Could this be happening? Could all her fears be so easily dissolved?

What are you waiting for?

She hugged Ruth and then rushed to Luke. He stood and opened his arms to her.

He kissed her. When he looked up, he said gently, "I love you, Becky. I'll never leave you. Marry me."

There. He'd said it all. It was all he had to offer. It was everything he was. He held his breath.

Andrew tugged on his pant leg, and Luke looked down. "Sir, are you gonna be my father?"

Luke glanced at Rebecca, then back to Andrew. "Would you like me to be your father, Andrew?"

"Oh, yes, sir." The boy beamed.

"Then, Andrew—" his tone was rough with emotion "—I am your father." It was enough, Luke realized.

Luke's questioning gaze flicked to Rebecca. "You haven't said yes," he pointed out.

She hesitated long enough to look at Ruth, standing close by. At her confirming nod, she grinned and swiped at the tears streaming down her cheeks. "Yes," she managed, though her voice cracked with the pure joy of loving him.

A wicked glint flashed in his eyes. "Yes, and..."

"I love you," she told him, knowing it was true. She'd always loved him. Luke was her destiny.

He came to her then and pulled her more tightly into his embrace. She loved him. He'd heard the words he'd longed for, prayed for. He wanted to hold her now, and tomorrow, and all the tomorrows that God would give him.

Still in his embrace, he smiled down at her and said, "I think I know where there's a newspaper for sale."

She grinned back. "And I think I know who it will endorse for mayor."

"I love you." He hugged her to him fiercely, then hoisted Andrew up in his arms. "I love you both."

*   *   *   *   *

◊ Harlequin® Historical

WOMEN OF THE WEST

Exciting stories of the old West and the women whose dreams
and passions shaped a new land!

Join Harlequin Historicals every month as we bring you
these unforgettable tales.

Don't miss any of our Women of the West!

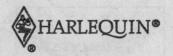

CHRISTMAS ROGUES

is giving you everything 🎄 you want on
your Christmas list this year:

✔ -great romance stories

✔ -award-winning authors

✔ -a FREE gift promotion

✔ -an abundance of Christmas cheer

This November, not only can you join ANITA MILLS,
PATRICIA POTTER and MIRANDA JARRETT
for exciting, heartwarming Christmas stories
about roguish men and the women who tame
them—but you can also receive a FREE gold-tone
necklace. (Details inside all copies of
Christmas Rogues.)

CHRISTMAS ROGUES—romance reading at its
best—only from HARLEQUIN BOOKS!

**Available in November wherever
Harlequin books are sold.**

OFFICIAL RULES
FLYAWAY VACATION SWEEPSTAKES 3449
NO PURCHASE OR OBLIGATION NECESSARY

Three Harlequin Reader Service 1995 shipments will contain respectively, coupons for entry into three different prize drawings, one for a trip for two to San Francisco, another for a trip for two to Las Vegas and the third for a trip for two to Orlando, Florida. To enter any drawing using an Entry Coupon, simply complete and mail according to directions.

There is no obligation to continue using the Reader Service to enter and be eligible for any prize drawing. You may also enter any drawing by hand printing the words "Flyaway Vacation," your name and address on a 3"x5" card and the destination of the prize you wish that entry to be considered for (i.e., San Francisco trip, Las Vegas trip or Orlando trip). Send your 3"x5" entries via first-class mail (limit: one entry per envelope) to: Flyaway Vacation Sweepstakes 3449, c/o Prize Destination you wish that entry to be considered for, P.O. Box 1315, Buffalo, NY 14269-1315, USA or P.O. Box 610, Fort Erie, Ontario L2A 5X3, Canada.

To be eligible for the San Francisco trip, entries must be received by 5/30/95; for the Las Vegas trip, 7/30/95; and for the Orlando trip, 9/30/95.

Winners will be determined in random drawings conducted under the supervision of D.L. Blair, Inc., an independent judging organization whose decisions are final, from among all eligible entries received for that drawing. San Francisco trip prize includes round-trip airfare for two, 4-day/3-night weekend accommodations at a first-class hotel, and $500 in cash (trip must be taken between 7/30/95—7/30/96, approximate prize value—$3,500); Las Vegas trip includes round-trip airfare for two, 4-day/3-night weekend accommodations at a first-class hotel, and $500 in cash (trip must be taken between 9/30/95—9/30/96, approximate prize value—$3,500); Orlando trip includes round-trip airfare for two, 4-day/3-night weekend accommodations at a first-class hotel, and $500 in cash (trip must be taken between 11/30/95—11/30/96, approximate prize value—$3,500). All travelers must sign and return a Release of Liability prior to travel. Hotel accommodations and flights are subject to accommodation and schedule availability. Sweepstakes open to residents of the U.S. (except Puerto Rico) and Canada, 18 years of age or older. Employees and immediate family members of Harlequin Enterprises, Ltd., D.L. Blair, Inc., their affiliates, subsidiaries and all other agencies, entities and persons connected with the use, marketing or conduct of this sweepstakes are not eligible. Odds of winning a prize are dependent upon the number of eligible entries received for that drawing. Prize drawing and winner notification for each drawing will occur no later than 15 days after deadline for entry eligibility for that drawing. Limit: one prize to an individual, family or organization. All applicable laws and regulations apply. Sweepstakes offer void wherever prohibited by law. Any litigation within the province of Quebec respecting the conduct and awarding of the prizes in this sweepstakes must be submitted to the Regies des loteries et Courses du Quebec. In order to win a prize, residents of Canada will be required to correctly answer a time-limited arithmetical skill-testing question. Value of prizes are in U.S. currency.

Winners will be obligated to sign and return an Affidavit of Eligibility within 30 days of notification. In the event of noncompliance within this time period, prize may not be awarded. If any prize or prize notification is returned as undeliverable, that prize will not be awarded. By acceptance of a prize, winner consents to use of his/her name, photograph or other likeness for purposes of advertising, trade and promotion on behalf of Harlequin Enterprises, Ltd., without further compensation, unless prohibited by law.

For the names of prizewinners (available after 12/31/95), send a self-addressed, stamped envelope to: Flyaway Vacation Sweepstakes 3449 Winners, P.O. Box 4200, Blair, NE 68009.

RVC KAL